Praise for *The Long and Far...*

"Multifaceted, layered, intens...
crime novel this year,...
—Sara J. Henry, Anthony Award...
A Cold and Lonely Place

"With sharp wit and prose that brings the 80s to life in all
its stone-washed glory, Lou Berney tells a complex story of
characters struggling to make sense of life in the aftermath of
massacre and abandonment. Affecting, funny, and unfailingly
honest, *The Long and Faraway Gone* is an extraordinary book."
—M. P. Cooley, author of *Ice Shear*

"Berney takes you places you're not sure you want to go and
brings you out again with a sure hand. *The Long and Faraway Gone*
is a satisfyingly complete deep-dive into a complicated history,
with not only suspense but also a compelling resolution."
—Carrie La Seur, author of *The Home Place*

"Slick, sleek, and wildly entertaining. These words sing,
managing to be at once lean and evocative, confident and wry.
Lou Berney makes everything look easy."
—Marcus Sakey, author of the Brilliance saga, host of
the Travel Channel's *Hidden City*

"Like Carl Hiaasen, Berney delights in the cartoonish. Like
Elmore Leonard, he can drive a plot. What sets him apart is how
well he evokes love, making the romance at the heart of this
cinematic book as compelling as the mystery."
—*Boston Globe*

"Witty and nimble comedic thriller . . . the exotic locales are
vibrant, the supporting cast larger than life, and the plot hums
along without a wasted page."
—*Publishers Weekly* (starred review)

"Every character is memorable. . . . The plot turns are constant,
and the dialogue is sharp."
—*Booklist* (starred review)

Also by Lou Berney

The Road to Bobby Joe and Other Stories
Gutshot Straight
Whiplash River

The Long and Faraway Gone

Lou Berney

wm

WILLIAM MORROW
An Imprint of HarperCollins*Publishers*

THE LONG AND FARAWAY GONE. Copyright © 2015 by Lou Berney. All rights reserved. Printed in the United States of America. No part of this book may be used or reproduced in any manner whatsoever without written permission except in the case of brief quotations embodied in critical articles and reviews. For information address HarperCollins Publishers, 195 Broadway, New York, NY 10007.

HarperCollins books may be purchased for educational, business, or sales promotional use. For information please e-mail the Special Markets Department at SPsales@harpercollins.com.

FIRST EDITION

Designed by Diahann Sturge

Library of Congress Cataloging-in-Publication Data has been applied for.

ISBN 978-0-06-229243-8

15 16 17 18 19   OV/RRD   10 9 8 7 6 5 4 3 2 1

For Rick

Bingham

August 1986

In summer, season of the Hollywood blockbuster, Bingham got to work at eight in the morning and didn't leave until long after midnight. His only break from the movie theater was dinner at six—thirty minutes of blissful, beautiful solitude he spent parked out by the lake, eating fast-food tacos and listening to the water slop against the red-clay bank.

Well, unless a crisis arose, which it usually did. Earlier today, for example, five minutes till six, an old lady rammed her Cadillac into the Dumpster out back. Bingham had hurried across the parking lot and found the lady scowling at the Dumpster and laying on her horn. The Cadillac's horn, instead of honking, played "Boomer Sooner," the University of Oklahoma football fight song.

"Ma'am!" Bingham said. "Are you injured? Should I call a doctor?"

She looked okay. The Cadillac, a tank, didn't have a scratch on it. The crushed flank of the Dumpster, on the other hand, looked like it was bent double with laughter.

"This is unacceptable!" She scowled at him. "This is intolerable!"

Of course it was. During the bargain matinee, the old lady had complained that Junior Mints were missing from the box of Junior Mints she'd purchased from the concession stand. She'd complained that the lobby ashtrays were dirty. She'd complained that the movie was too loud, the auditorium too chilly, the movie now not loud enough.

Bingham tried to look grave and pained and determined to right wrongs. But exactly what wrong here could the manager of the Pheasant Run Twin Theater be expected to right? He guessed the old lady had accidentally shifted into drive instead of reverse and then stomped the gas.

"This parking lot is a death trap!" the old lady said.

Bingham could feel the heat of the day radiating in waves up off the asphalt, radiating off the buckled Dumpster and the molten-glass sweep of the Cadillac's big windshield. He'd lived in Oklahoma City his entire life, thirty years, and couldn't remember an August this hot.

He tugged the collar of his shirt away from his neck, but that just let more heat in, not out. And the extra pressure on the knot of his tie made it feel as if someone had stepped on his throat.

"Ma'am, maybe you'd like to come inside where it's cool and—"

Bingham heard giggles and glanced over. His entire night-shift crew—his crack squad of lazy, lax, and disrespectful teenage doormen and concession girls—had crowded onto the exit stairs of auditorium number two. Bingham could practically feel the vibrating hum of their rapt attention. They were never so stoked as when they sniffed the possibility of someone's, preferably his, humiliation.

"Don't you have something better to be doing right now?" Bingham snapped at them. Like sweeping the lobby or wiping down the candy glass or restocking the nacho boats? Like maybe actually doing your jobs for once?

"Mr. Bingham," O'Malley said. O'Malley, the obnoxious dick, who despite repeated written warnings had the sleeves of his orange doorman's blazer pushed up to his elbows like he was in *Miami Vice*. Who had assumed his standard operating expression of angelic innocence (widened eyes) and sly amusement (an almost-smile). "You know, I don't believe there *is* anything better we could be doing right now, Mr. Bingham."

That triggered a new round of giggling.

The crabby old lady muttered something that Bingham couldn't make out. It sounded like, "You haven't furled the flag, mister."

You haven't furled the flag, mister?

And then she threw the Cadillac into reverse, missing Bingham's foot by an inch, and veered away.

Now, a quarter past midnight, Bingham still hadn't had dinner yet. And he wasn't close to being done for the night. The last of the late-show customers were gone, the doors locked behind them, but the hourly audits awaited him, along with the gross reports, next week's schedule, and a stack of purchase orders the size of a phone book.

It never ceased to amaze Bingham how much paperwork was required to run a movie theater that generated such little revenue. The Pheasant Run was a cramped twin adrift in a sea of massive new multi-multiplexes, situated at the far ass-end of a ghost mall that—too small, insufficient parking, no anchor tenants—had been half empty ever since the Oklahoma oil business went bust four years ago, in the summer of '82. Monarch Entertainment, which owned the Pheasant Run, was itself a struggling regional chain with a bleak economic outlook.

Like you're one to talk, Bingham reminded himself, *about bleak economic outlook.*

He'd been with Monarch since he was sixteen years old. He'd worked his way up from doorman to assistant manager to, now, manager. And yet his salary was still so low he couldn't afford a decent apartment, or a car with a consistently functional transmission, or an oral surgeon to extract a wisdom tooth that on bad days felt like a wood screw being screwed slowly into his jawbone.

He glanced at the security monitor on his desk. The monitor was pretty much worthless, with a fuzzed-out black-and-white picture the size of a wristwatch. Bingham couldn't even tell if that was O'Malley or his junior henchman lounging against the ticket box, yawning, when he should have been working. And the angle of the video camera was so narrow it captured just one small slice of the lobby, leaving the rest of theater entirely unmonitored. Where God only knew what violations of the Monarch Employee Handbook were currently afoot.

A few weeks ago, Bingham had found half a bottle of Evan Williams whiskey hidden behind the boxes in the storeroom. In the old days, in Bingham's day, you waited till your shift was over to get shitfaced, and you did it in the park behind the mall, not on the theater premises.

Bingham suspected that his teenage employees were also swiping one-sheets, and feeling each other up in the back row of the auditoriums during breaks, and using the lobby pay phone for personal calls, and letting half of Oklahoma City into movies for free. On top of that, they'd run off the one decent employee Bingham had landed that summer, a polite, obedient kid who went to Casady, the city's best private high school.

Bingham had grilled everyone, individually, about the bottle of Evan Williams. Nobody cracked, not even O'Malley's junior henchman. He was the baby of the bunch, sixteen years old according to his application but probably a year younger than that. Bingham had hoped he might be the weak link.

But O'Malley's junior henchman had just about perfected the sly angelic expression that his master was the master of.

"I don't know where it came from," he said.

An hour ago, though, a rare triumph, Bingham had been in the lobby when the pay phone rang. O'Malley's junior henchman had answered it, but Bingham moved quickly to snatch away the receiver.

"Give me that," he'd said.

O'Malley's junior henchman had shrugged. "It's your friend, Pet Shop Boy."

"Donald?" Bingham said. Donald was his loony friend who worked upstairs at the mall pet store. He trailed bits of cedar chips, the kind that filled the hamster cages, wherever he went. "What do you want, Donald?"

"Listen," Donald said. "There's this band playing the Land Run tonight. Blow off work and meet me there."

Bingham wondered sometimes how Donald could cross the street without getting hit by a bus.

"I can't blow off work, Donald," Bingham said. "I'm the manager of the theater."

"They're the next U2. Just this one time, trust me."

Every band that played the Land Run, according to Donald, was the next U2.

"Good-bye, Donald."

Bingham hung up. O'Malley had observed all this. Of course he had.

"I was under the impression," O'Malley said, "that personal calls were not allowed on the lobby pay phone."

Wow, it was amazing, how much Bingham couldn't stand O'Malley. The obnoxious dick. And he couldn't stand O'Malley's underage junior henchman, who followed O'Malley around like a dog, tail thumping. He couldn't stand the other doormen, Tate and Grubb, both of them lazy and dumb. He couldn't stand any of the cashiers or concession girls either, Melody and Janella and Theresa and Karlene.

Karlene was moving to Hawaii at the end of August. She'd saved her money all through high school. She was so stoked. She was so pumped. She was going to get a job at a resort and take classes in dolphin biology at the community college and learn to surf and and and.

Karlene! Shut up for two seconds about Hawaii!

August was always a staffing nightmare. Every August, the employees who'd graduated from high school the previous May left the theater and moved on with their lives.

And Bingham? Every August, Bingham stayed behind and scrambled to fill the schedule. With a new crop of teenagers who'd been put on earth for the sole purpose of making his life miserable.

He started filling out next week's schedule. What Bingham despised most about O'Malley, he decided—and he'd given the subject a lot of thought—was how *smug* O'Malley always was. Like O'Malley had already beaten the game. Like no turn of the cards could possibly surprise him.

Bingham, at age eighteen, had been the same way. It kind of boggled his mind now—all the surprises that life had up its sleeve. Just wait, you dick.

There was a knock. O'Malley, probably. To report that the doormen were done stocking the concession stand when probably they had not even begun. Bingham walked to the office door. He realized that O'Malley, or his junior henchman, had managed to reverse the peephole. Again. Hilarious.

He opened the door. A man stood there. Something was wrong with his face—his features were flattened and smooshed, like they'd been burned, like they'd melted together.

In the next instant Bingham realized the man had a pair of pantyhose pulled over his head. He had a shotgun in his hands.

Behind him stood another man. That man wore a rubber mask—Freddy Krueger from *Nightmare on Elm Street* but missing the fedora.

Bingham was surprised how long it had been since he'd felt true fear. Fear that cramped your bowels and ballooned your heart and made you feel five years old again, your older cousin dunking your head underwater at the YMCA pool as you kicked and thrashed.

"Stay quiet," the first man said. He placed the barrel of his shotgun against Bingham's chest and nudged him backward into the office. The design on his pale yellow T-shirt was cracked and faded—a dirt bike with flames coming from the exhaust pipe, above the words CUTT'N' LOOSE! "How many others working tonight?"

Bingham tried to think. He needed to sit down. The office was suffocating, sour with the smell of sweat. His? Theirs? He couldn't understand how the men had gotten into the theater. Bingham had locked the front doors himself. And the auditorium exits—

"How many?" the man in the Freddy Krueger mask yelled. He was all fired up, bouncing on the balls of his feet and jabbing his gun at Bingham. His gun was a pistol—like a toy cowboy six-shooter but much bigger, and not a toy.

"Five," Bingham said. O'Malley, O'Malley's junior henchman, Grubb, Melody, Karlene. And Theresa. "Wait. Six."

"What about the projectionist?" the first man said. Every time he moved his mouth, the fabric of the pantyhose sucked and stretched weirdly.

Bingham shook his head. "No. Harry's— He's already gone home."

The first man turned to the man in the rubber Freddy Krueger mask. "Round them all up."

Freddy Krueger used the pistol to give his partner a salute. He started to leave.

"Wait!" Bingham said. The man with the shotgun looked surprised. Or maybe that was just a trick of light and pantyhose.

"What?"

"You don't need them," Bingham said. "They won't even know you were here."

"Shut up."

"I'm the one you want. Okay? I'll give you the money and you can get out of here. I'll give you whatever you want."

The man with the shotgun turned to his partner. "You hear me? I said round them up."

Freddy Krueger started to leave again. Bingham took a step toward him. He reached for his arm.

"Come on. They're just kids. You don't have to—"

The man with the shotgun turned it sideways and used the butt end to punch Bingham hard in the chest. The pain was amazing, as if Bingham's sternum had been cracked in half. He stumbled backward.

"Open the safe," the man said. He pressed the barrel of the shotgun against Bingham's ribs. "Do it now."

Bingham lowered himself unsteadily to the floor and peeled back the corner of the office carpet. Sweat stung his eyes as he lifted the metal lid that covered the floor safe. The man with the shotgun stood right behind him, over him, breathing. Bingham dialed the combination. He handed up the night-deposit lock bag, heavy with the full weekend take.

"Let's go," the man said.

He marched Bingham across the lobby. For maybe two

seconds, three steps, someone out in the mall by the fountain might have spotted them through the glass front doors of the theater.

If the lobby lights hadn't been off, which they were. If the mall hadn't been deserted, which it was.

The one other place that stayed open late on weekends was the jazz bar upstairs, but even it closed at midnight. Bingham wondered what had happened to Otis, the after-hours mall security guard with the wild pimp Afro and the disco-purple Lincoln Continental. Tied up somewhere, maybe. Or maybe just taking a nap out in the purple Lincoln, as was his habit.

The man with the shotgun prodded Bingham up the narrow stairs to the projection booth. The doormen and concession girls were already there, lined up facedown on the floor between the projectors, their hands tied behind them with cord. The man in the Freddy Krueger mask prowled back and forth, jabbing his pistol at them and shouting "Bang! Bang!" And then laughing his ass off. He had the Freddy Krueger mask pushed up and off his face and was wearing it like a floppy hat.

A third robber sat on the workbench against the far wall, holding a strip of 35-millimeter film up to the light. He'd completely removed his mask—a bald rubber pirate head with a rubber eye patch. It sat next to him, drooping and deflated, staring into space with one empty eye.

The booth was weirdly quiet. Like they were in a submarine, the silence crushing in around them. Except for the robber going "Bang! Bang!" and a concession girl, Bingham couldn't tell which one, sobbing.

The robber with the shotgun stripped the pantyhose off

his head. "On the floor," he told Bingham. "Head down. Hands behind your back."

Bingham squeezed in at the end of the row, between Karlene and the projector for auditorium number two. He laid his cheek against the floor. The polished cement was unbelievably filthy, twenty years of machine grease and shoe scuffs and smeared ash from the two packs of Camels that Harry smoked every shift.

Karlene faced him, close enough to touch. Her eyes were glazed, her chin slimy with tears and snot. She wasn't the one Bingham could hear sobbing, though.

"It's going to be fine, Karlene," Bingham whispered as one of the robbers tied his hands tight behind his back. "You're going to love Hawaii."

"Bang!" the robber in the Freddy Krueger mask said, right behind Bingham.

Bingham closed his eyes and ignored the sticky liquid heat that spread beneath him. It wasn't as if the floor could get any filthier, could it?

He tried to picture his daughter's face. Tiffany was six, the result of a drunken, ten-minute fumble on one of his rare nights off. Her mother was one of the tough-looking girls who worked the door at the Land Run, checking IDs and occasionally introducing the bands. When Bingham found out she was pregnant, he'd offered to marry her. She'd just stared at him with an expression that said, *Are you out of your mind?*

Bingham hardly ever got to see his daughter. Tiffany's mother blew off his already meager visitation rights whenever she felt like it. If ever Bingham scraped together some money, he planned to hire a lawyer so he could see his daughter more often, so she wouldn't grow up wondering who was this stranger in a cheap suit who brought her a Cabbage Patch Kid every now and then, who always smelled like burned popcorn.

"No," Bingham heard O'Malley say down by the other projector. "No, wait a second, just listen."

"Shut up," the robber with the shotgun said. Bingham heard a thump.

The sobbing concession girl sobbed more loudly. Theresa or Melody. The workbench creaked as the third robber stood. He murmured something to the other robbers that Bingham couldn't make out. One of the other robbers murmured back. Murmur, murmur, murmur—back and forth, much like the bubbles that bubbled up from the bottom of the orange-drink tank.

Bingham realized what she'd said, the old lady who rammed her Cadillac into the Dumpster, before she drove off. Not, of course, "You haven't furled the flag, mister."

You haven't heard the last of this. That's what she'd said.

Well, that made more sense. Probably she was planning to call corporate and lodge a formal complaint against him.

Go right ahead, Bingham thought. *Go nuts with that.*

The robbers stopped murmuring. Bingham heard footsteps. He felt something cold and hard come to a rest, lightly, against the nape of his neck.

Tears were rolling down Karlene's cheek and off her nose and dropping to the grimy floor.

"Don't be scared, Karlene," Bingham whispered. "It's going to be fine. Close your eyes. You're in Hawaii. You're on a golden beach and the waves are rolling in and the breeze is perfect. You're living the life you've always wanted."

Wyatt

CHAPTER 1

October 2012

The Lexus, a block ahead, stopped at the Shell station. Wyatt played it safe and tucked into a gravel parking lot behind the Flamingo garage. He didn't want to spook Bledsoe. On the Strip, with all that traffic—a dozen lanes of stacked-up cabs and buses and rented Chevy Aveos buzzing around—you could practically sit in a guy's own backseat and he'd never notice you. Koval Lane, though, which ran behind the hotels, was deserted an hour before the afternoon shift change. If you wanted to stay invisible, you better keep your distance.

The overpass, just overhead, boomed and shuddered. Wyatt watched Bledsoe swipe his American Express black card at the pump. Wyatt had to smile. Bledsoe did everything with a flourish. Swiping his credit card, tucking into pan-roasted sea scallops, walking across a casino floor. With *panache*. Even when no one was watching. Even when he thought no one was watching.

The Lexus and the black AmEx were red flags. Or were they? Over the past eighteen months Bledsoe had been late three times on the Lexus lease. He'd been dinged two grand in fees on the card. That might mean something. Or anything. Or nothing.

Bledsoe, who worked at Caesars, was up for a big job at the Mirage—senior vice president of sales and marketing. The Mirage loved him. They loved the M.B.A. from Wharton, the three years at Caesars, the two years before that at Citibank. They loved Bledsoe's fresh vision and his functional Mandarin (junior year abroad) and his panache. But until Wyatt filed his report, the Mirage wasn't going to offer Bledsoe a job picking pubic lice off the Jacuzzi filters.

Wyatt had been on Bledsoe for the past two weeks and, so far, had nothing to report.

Bledsoe got up every morning at eight, the crack of dawn by Vegas standards. He hit the gym in his building and ran four miles on the treadmill. Curls, crunches, squats. Afterward he showered, gelled back his hair, and flirted with the girl—petite, blond, bangs—who taught a hot-yoga class at nine.

On the way to Caesars, Bledsoe stopped at Starbucks for a venti americano, room for cream, the first of three he'd knock back before noon. He worked clients all day and all night, laughing and slapping backs and just generally spreading around the Bledsoe panache. His only real meal of the day was around five, at the hotel steak house, where he caught up with e-mail and flirted with the girl—petite, blond, bangs—who brought him his sea scallops and heirloom-tomato salad, oil and vinegar on the side.

After lunch Bledsoe usually ran a few errands. He picked up his dry cleaning. He picked up hair gel. He filled up the Lexus. He returned a wonky Blu-ray player to Best Buy or browsed the

Pottery Barn at Rampart Commons. He flirted with the girl who sold sunglasses from a kiosk at Rampart Commons. How did you guess? She was petite. She was blond. She had bangs.

Oh, yes, Bledsoe knew what he liked. So why, then, was his girlfriend a tall, athletic redhead, no bangs? Why was his other girlfriend a full-figured brunette, no bangs?

A mystery. Or maybe not. People, in Wyatt's experience, often wanted what they didn't have. Or, if you preferred an even bleaker perspective, they often had what they didn't want.

Bledsoe, at age thirty, seemed to have it all. The job, the car, two very attractive girlfriends he managed to juggle without either girl finding out about the other, a closet full of Tom Ford suits. A huge glass-walled bachelor pad on the next to top floor of a luxury tower complex called Veer, right in the heart of the Strip.

Wyatt checked to see if any of that secretly annoyed him, that a kid eleven years younger than him drove an eighty-thousand-dollar Lexus and made three times the money he did.

No, Wyatt decided he was cool. He had what he wanted, wanted what he had. A four-year-old Honda Accord in good shape and paid off. Perfectly suitable suits from J.Crew. A three-bedroom house that was small but comfortable. The house was almost paid off, too. And Wyatt worked for himself, which meant he took the jobs he wanted, passed on the ones he didn't. He might never get rich, but neither would he ever find himself pacing around a Shell station, checking his email and voice mail and text messages yet again, sweating it out while some corporation decided his professional fate.

Wyatt yawned. How long did it take to gas up a Lexus? Well, yeah, by now he knew exactly how long it took to gas up a Lexus.

Wyatt would put Bledsoe's two girlfriends in his report, but

this was Vegas, and Bledsoe was single. The Mirage might be disappointed if a prospective vice president of sales and marketing at
a Vegas casino *didn't* have more than one girlfriend. They would
question his panache.

The companies that hired Wyatt to do deep background on
pending high-level hires cared about drugs, gambling, money
problems. They cared about sexual orientation, but only if the
candidate was trying to keep his or hers a secret.

There was a tap on Wyatt's window. A security guard glared
down at him. He was a beefy guy, late fifties, squeezed into a
brown-on-brown uniform. His glare seemed more perfunctory
than sincere.

Wyatt rolled down his window and smiled. "Good afternoon,
Officer," he said.

The security guard's lips pressed together and his glare turned
more sincere.

Wyatt had yet to figure it out, the central mystery of his life,
why so many people assumed, automatically, that he was being a
smart-ass. People he'd never met before, who didn't know him
from Adam, who unless they were clairvoyant couldn't possibly
have any clue that, yes, occasionally, Wyatt could be a smart-ass.

It had happened his whole life, for as long as Wyatt could remember. The teacher would call roll, and Wyatt would answer
"Present," and the rest of the class would giggle. The teacher
would shake her head and clench her jaw.

Wyatt wished someone would explain to him how you could
be a smart-ass by saying "Present." Or by telling a security guard,
"Good morning, Officer."

"This is a restricted lot, sir," the security guard said. "Employees of the Flamingo only. I need you to move your vehicle."

Wyatt stuck his hand out the window. "Wyatt Rivers," he said. "Nice to meet you."

The security guard continued to glare, but Wyatt's hand wasn't going anywhere, and in the end the security guard broke down and shook it.

Wyatt was a big believer in the civilizing power of the handshake, of genuine eye contact, of just basically acknowledging the fundamental existence of the person standing in front of you.

That didn't happen as often as you'd think. People lived in their heads. They walked in their sleep. They exchanged vague pleasantries and half glances and were rarely, when it came right down to it—when roll was called—truly *present*.

"I'm a private investigator," Wyatt said. "I'm doing background on Mr. Panache up there at the Shell station. With his hair gelled back? The Mirage wants to hire him, sales and marketing. He's come up pure as the driven snow so far. A couple of credit dings, but that's it. And two fairly serious girlfriends he's juggling, but the Mirage doesn't care about that."

The security guard shifted from one foot to the other, tilted his chin up, and scratched his neck. He was trying to figure out if Wyatt was telling the truth and, if so, why in the hell?

Wyatt took the stance that if you had nothing to lose by telling the truth, why not tell it? The truth was usually more interesting than a lie.

"Much money in it?" the security guard said finally. "Private investigating?"

"Not bad," Wyatt said. "But remember, it's not always as glamorous and exciting as watching a guy gas up his Lexus."

The security guard scratched his neck. Wyatt spotted a slight twinkle of amusement in his eye, like a fish darting and catching the light just for an instant. *You want to tell me about glamorous and exciting? I'm the guy watching a guy watching a guy fill up his Lexus.*

Bledsoe had finally finished. He racked the nozzle, and Wyatt dug out his wallet. "Here's my card," he told the security guard. "Give me a call if you're really interested. I'll tell you which certification classes aren't a waste of time."

The security guard took Wyatt's business card. "Appreciate it," he said uncertainly.

Wyatt rolled his window back up and eased onto Koval, thirty yards behind Bledsoe's Lexus. The Lexus drove two blocks down Koval, turned west on Sands Avenue, crossed the Strip, and jumped on I-15.

Wyatt had no problem keeping up. For a guy who did everything else in his life with panache, Bledsoe sure didn't drive that way. He obeyed the speed limit, he stopped for yellow lights, he signaled well in advance of turns and lane changes.

Did that mean something? Anything? Nothing?

Wyatt picked Bledsoe up at Rampart Commons, at the sunglass kiosk, where he was chatting up the petite blonde with bangs. When Bledsoe finished there, he crossed to Pottery Barn. Wyatt took the opportunity to find a bench and call Laurie. He got dumped straight to her voice mail.

"So I'm at Rampart Commons," he told her voice mail, "and I'm thinking, hey, maybe while I'm here, I'll buy my girl a little something. A little something we can both enjoy, if you get my meaning, you and me in the privacy of the boudoir. So I go into Victoria's Secret, right, and get this—they don't have a single thing that fits me. Can you believe it? At least nothing flattering. So I guess I'll end up getting you a lime juicer from Williams-Sonoma. Which actually, upon reflection, we might well find some creative use for in the . . ."

Bledsoe emerged from Pottery Barn and headed for the parking lot. Wyatt killed the call, but he didn't follow Bledsoe.

Pottery Barn. Pottery Barn? Twice in one week?

Wyatt himself had nothing against Pottery Barn. He liked the cheerful, sunny catalogs, the leather club chairs and Nantucket farmhouse tables. He had his eye on one of those farmhouse tables.

But Bledsoe? Wyatt had never been inside Bledsoe's bachelor pad high above the Strip, but everything he knew about the guy argued, emphatically, for the presence there of designer faucets, granite counters from a special quarry in Italy, and a sleek, low-slung sofa with cushions made of polished titanium.

Wyatt just couldn't square the corners, hard as he tried—a farmhouse table from Pottery Barn in a bachelor pad like that? In a high-end, high-rise apartment building called Veer?

Bledsoe got into his Lexus. Wyatt let him go. He took out his phone, set the timer for two minutes, and crossed to Pottery Barn.

"Hi there! Can I help you find something today?"

The female clerk who greeted Wyatt at the door was built like a beer keg and had dark hair. Wyatt glanced around. None of the other female clerks in the store were blond or petite either. No bangs in sight.

The correct explanation is often the simplest one—Occam's razor—but not always. What fun would that be? Wyatt would be out of a job.

"I'm just looking," Wyatt told the clerk. "But I'm not really sure what I'm looking for. I've got a feeling I won't know what I'm looking for until I see it. Does that ever happen to you?"

"That does sometimes," she said. "Sure. I know what you mean."

"And maybe I won't end up seeing anything at all. That's the frustrating part about this kind of approach."

He saw a guy, an employee, standing over by the bookcases.

Early twenties, short hair and clean-cut. The guy wore a long-sleeved dress shirt with the cuffs buttoned at his wrists.

Maybe he was wearing the long-sleeved shirt because it was chilly in here. Occam's razor. It *was* chilly in here. Or maybe he kept his arms covered because his arms were covered with tattoos.

Did it mean something that his arms might be covered with tattoos? Anything?

Probably nothing. But it was all Wyatt had, and he knew that Bledsoe didn't come in here twice a week to price farmhouse tables or flirt with dark-haired girls built like beer kegs.

The Mirage loved Bledsoe. They wanted Wyatt's report to come back clean. But only if Bledsoe was in fact clean.

"Will you excuse me, please?" Wyatt told the girl. He strolled across the store and reached the bookcases just as the timer on his iPhone chimed.

Wyatt pretended to check caller ID. He pretended to answer a call.

"Bledsoe!" he said. "My brother!"

The clerk who might or might not have been hiding tattoos glanced over at Wyatt and then glanced quickly away. And then glanced back again.

Wyatt almost wished it hadn't been that easy. It was not, in his defense, always that easy.

"Yeah, bro," Wyatt said into his phone. "I'm there now. I thought I was supposed to meet you here. Where are you?" He looked around and pretended to settle his gaze, for the first time, on the clerk with the long sleeves. "Yeah. I think so. . . . Okay."

Wyatt put his phone away and examined various bookcases until the clerk with long sleeves came over to him.

"Hey, bro," Wyatt said quietly. "You Bledsoe's guy? I'm Josh."

The clerk did a quick sweep to make sure no one else was around.

"Who?" the clerk said. "He didn't say anything to me."

"Look," Wyatt said. "I'm in a bind. Can you hook me up or what?"

"Let me call him," the clerk said.

"Whatever."

The clerk took out his phone, eyeing Wyatt the whole time, and then put his phone back away.

"How much you need?" the clerk said, and Wyatt knew—a spark of victory, a twinge of sympathy—that Bledsoe could kiss the Mirage good-bye.

Wyatt

CHAPTER 2

Wyatt brushed the salmon with olive oil while Laurie made gin and tonics.

"After all that?" she said when she brought the drinks out. "That whole long message and you didn't get me a lime juicer?"

"I was too busy closing a deal for a half an ounce of crystal meth."

"You didn't actually buy it, did you?"

Wyatt took a sip of his gin and tonic. It was perfect. And the light out here was perfect—a soft desert dusk that turned the mountains a soft gunmetal blue. Laurie, bare brown feet and hair down after a day at the office—she was perfect, too.

"No. Bledsoe's dealer didn't have the product on hand, and I said I didn't have the cash. So he and a few of his biker buddies are gonna stop by here later. We probably should leave your porch light on for them."

Laurie smiled. She didn't check to see if he was kidding. She'd stopped doing that a long time ago.

Wyatt had told Bledsoe's meth dealer that he'd be back in an hour with the cash. The guy was probably still waiting. Wyatt supposed he'd better steer clear of Rampart Commons for a while. He'd have to get his Pottery Barn farmhouse table online.

He pulled Laurie close and kissed her. She'd been popping garlic-dusted almonds, but she still tasted good. After a bucket of beer and a dozen hot wings, after a burp, even first thing in the morning—the girl always tasted good.

"How about you?" he said. "Busy day?"

"Don't get me started."

She was the executive director of a nonprofit that had a finger in everything from affordable housing to dog rescue. Laurie took a deep personal interest in all of it—each affordable house, each rottweiler mix.

"That's the problem with the world," he said. "You save it today, and tomorrow it's gone and gotten itself into trouble all over again. It's like a Kardashian."

He put the salmon on the grill. Laurie sat down and propped her bare brown feet on the picnic table. She sipped her gin and wiggled her toes at him.

"Ah," she said.

"Ah?"

"This is wicked nice."

She did that for him, the heavy Boston accent, because he always took the bait. He always took the bait because it made her giggle. It was like a drug, her giggle. He couldn't live without it.

"Give me a break," he said. He sat down across the table from her. "You're not from Dorchester, you know. You're from the mean streets of Cambridge."

"I'm from Brookline."

"Oh, sorry. The mean streets of Brookline."

"You're from San Diego," she said. "What do *you* know about it?"

"I know you'd be the first mixed-race daughter of Episcopalian college professors in the history of Dorchester."

She giggled and wiggled her toes at him again, insistently. He obeyed and massaged her foot. The warmth of her skin, the pulse of the vein beneath his thumb—Wyatt would have been happy to sit there forever, till his body turned to bone and leather and dust, just looking across the table at her, at the stars glittering along the ragged edge of the darkening mountains.

"This is what I'm thinking," he said. "India. India or Thailand, somewhere like that. We get married on the beach, under a full moon, with a shaman to perform the ceremony. Shaman? Is that what they're called in India? On the beach with lemurs chattering in the coconut palms."

She took another sip of gin, then set her glass down. She gazed at him across the table. Laurie was usually easy to read, her face guilelessly expressive, each thought and feeling like a bubble bursting to the surface. Except—like now—every once in a while.

Wyatt moved his hand to her other foot, started squeezing, and the moment passed.

"You're wicked good at that," she said, and burst out giggling again.

WYATT'S OFFICE WAS on Harmon, on the second floor of an open-air shopping and professional plaza. A strip mall, in other words, but at least at the upscale end of the spectrum, with freshly painted peach stucco, no check-cashing or massage joints, and a mom-and-pop restaurant that served the best Burmese noodles in town. Wyatt's office, between an optometrist and an H&R Block, was a former bakery that had gone bust a few years ago. It still smelled like cake frosting.

Wyatt could have worked from home—a lot of freelance investigators did—but rent in Vegas was cheap, and he liked having his own office. The space, the routine, the . . . what was the opposite of solitude? Whatever it was, he liked that, too. The front of Wyatt's office was glass. The H&R Block accountants always waved to him when they stepped outside to make personal calls on their cell phones.

When Wyatt first moved in, he'd scraped the popcorn finish off the ceiling, troweled on drywall compound for texture, and repainted. He'd torn up the cheap tile floor and replaced it with quality Berber carpet. He'd purchased good furniture, good fixtures for the bathroom. Every Wednesday a sweetly spacey ex-stripper in a van delivered fresh flowers—the name of her business was Flower Child—and carted the old ones off.

Some clients were surprised when they came by for the first time. They expected a PI to have a seedy office above a seedy bar, to wear a stained trench coat, to keep a .38 and a bottle of cheap booze in the bottom drawer of the desk.

Wyatt didn't own a gun. In the bottom drawer of his desk, he kept a spare cell phone charger and a box of memory cards for his Nikon DSLR.

His office, this morning, smelled like cake frosting and the fresh frangipani blossoms, floating in a bowl of water, that the Flower Child had dropped off yesterday. Wyatt popped his laptop open and finished writing up the Bledsoe report. He always felt a little edgy when he wrapped a case. Ants in the pants. The same feeling he'd had, back in his newspaper days, when he turned in a story. The great thing about daily journalism was that there had always been another story—you never had time to breathe. That was the great thing about private investigating, too.

Two potential new clients had called earlier in the week: A husband suspected that his wife was cheating on him, and a wife suspected that her husband was cheating on her. Wyatt wondered what the odds were, that the one wife was cheating with the other husband. Ten thousand to one? He made a mental note to run the proposition past his buddy at the Luxor sports book. In Vegas you could get odds on anything.

He'd just picked up the phone to call the suspicious husband back when the office door opened. Gavin stood there. Wyatt almost fell out of his chair.

"Whoa," he said.

Gavin ran security and surveillance for the Mirage. He was the one who'd given Wyatt the Bledsoe job, and a dozen other jobs over the past couple of years. But usually when Gavin had work for Wyatt—no, *always*—Wyatt came to Gavin, not the reverse.

Gavin looked around the office. "Not what I pictured."

"You pictured seedy," Wyatt said. "A bottle of cheap booze in the desk drawer."

"I pictured paintings." Gavin dropped his bulk into the chair across from Wyatt. "Pretentious fruity shit. French impressionists, parasols in the park."

"Says the guy wearing a tie with unicorns on it."

Gavin picked up the end of his tie and looked at it. "They're racehorses."

"Some fruity-looking racehorses."

Gavin considered. "Yeah." He dropped his tie. "My daughter gave it to me. I've got a favor to ask you."

"Let's hear it," Wyatt said.

"Don't be a smart-ass."

Don't be a smart-ass? Wyatt shook his head in disbelief. It was, truly, the central mystery of his life. "Tell me how 'Let's hear it' makes me a smart-ass?"

"The favor's a job," Gavin said. He glanced again at his tie. "Double your usual rate and my undying gratitude."

"For the Mirage?"

"For me." He grimaced.

"I like the look of that," Wyatt said.

"Smart-ass. It's a piece of cake. I'm doing you the favor."

Wyatt just smiled pleasantly at Gavin and waited until Gavin grimaced again.

"This girl—my wife's niece or cousin, I don't know—she's convinced she needs a PI. She has convinced my wife that she needs a PI. My wife has convinced me to get her a PI. You see where this is going? She's kind of a piece of work, the girl, I should tell you up front."

"Well, in that case how soon can I start?"

"And she lives in Omaha. My wife's niece does."

"You want me to go to Omaha?"

"Just for a day or two. Meet the girl. Listen sympathetically to her. Do . . . whatever. Make a few calls, poke around. If there's anything worth poking around in, which is doubtful. But, see, you're the good-faith gesture. You're the good-faith gesture that gets her off my wife's back and my wife off my back."

"They don't have private investigators in Omaha?"

"Have you been listening?"

"All right, all right." Wyatt said. Yes, he'd been listening. He just enjoyed watching Gavin squirm and shift and grunt with irritation. He'd never seen it before and doubted he'd see it again.

"The girl's name is Candace," Gavin said. "Candace Kilkenny.

She's from here in Vegas. A couple months ago, she's at work, running cocktails at the Wynn, and she gets a call. Out of the blue, some lawyer. He tells her she's inherited some live-music club in Omaha."

Wyatt, taking notes in the spiral-bound reporter's pad he always carried in his back pocket, lifted an eyebrow.

"Which part of that surprises you?" Gavin said.

"Every part of it."

Gavin nodded. "Yeah. The girl was surprised, too. An inheritance? A live music club? Omaha? She thought it had to be a scam, but no, turns out it's all legit. A regular of hers, an old guy that flew out a few times a year to play ten-dollar blackjack. You know the type. Turns out he put her in his will."

"At the top or the bottom of it?" Wyatt asked.

It was a more-or-less sincere question, but Gavin just glared at him and ignored it. "Now, you understand that Candace doesn't know a soul in Omaha," he went on. "She's got a five-year-old kid. She's never *worked* in a live-music club, let alone run one. So guess what she does? She moves to Omaha to run a live-music club."

"Why does she need an investigator?"

"She's got it in her head that some mysterious someone is mysteriously harassing her."

"Harassing her how?"

"I don't know. I don't care. My suspicion, the girl has an overactive imagination. You know what I care about?"

"It's coming to me. Just give me a second."

"I care about getting my wife off my back."

"That's it." Wyatt pretended to write it down, slowly and carefully, then flipped his notebook shut.

Omaha wasn't exactly on his bucket list, and he hated being

apart from Laurie, even if it was just for a couple of days. But Gavin sent a lot of business Wyatt's way, and he was a good guy. Maybe, Wyatt considered, he might be able to convince Laurie to come with him to Omaha. An exotic romantic getaway.

"Anything else?" Wyatt said.

"Her kid's a cutie-pie, according to my wife. Candace's kid is." Gavin took a folded sheet of paper out of his suit coat pocket and shook it open. He tucked in his chin and lifted his glasses off his nose. "I can't believe I need bifocals. I refuse to believe it. The kid's name is Lily. And wait. It's Oklahoma, not Omaha. Oklahoma City. I don't have the name of the club, but I have complete faith you'll be able to solve that mystery."

"Have you heard that old joke?" Wyatt said. "About steaks in Omaha?"

"I've got a feeling I'm going to."

"If you insist." Wyatt stood up. "Give me one sec, will you?"

He went into the office bathroom and shut the door behind him. He could feel the room spinning. But slowly, as if in the thirty seconds after that first carousel jolt of movement—*Oklahoma City, not Omaha*—everything around him had only moved a fraction of an inch to the left. Slow-motion motion sickness.

Wyatt had known a surfer once, right after he'd moved to San Diego, who after a few beers would go on and on about the crushing, elemental power of the ocean, about how you had to respect that, dude. Good advice, sure—but you know what was an even better idea? Respect the power of the ocean by staying out of the water in the first place.

That was Wyatt's philosophy when it came to the past: Stay out of it. By doing so he had lived a happy life. A life undrowned, unbroken on the rocks, unswept toward an empty horizon.

You caught a whiff of a certain perfume as you walked across the casino floor at the Bellagio and you kept walking. You caught a few bars of "If She Knew What She Wants" by the Bangles on the radio and you changed the station. You lived in the present tense, where the past has no power.

But Wyatt had already told Gavin that he'd do the favor for him. If he tried to back out now, Gavin would want to know why.

Wyatt ran through the lies he could tell. He knew that Gavin would buy none of them.

Wyatt's mouth tasted stale from the coffee he'd had with breakfast, so he scooped water from the faucet and rinsed his mouth. He returned to his desk and sat back down.

"So a guy from Omaha goes on a business trip to New York City," he said. "The guy he's meeting takes him out to dinner. They have a couple of steaks. Amazing steaks. Prime porterhouses, dry-aged. But expensive—this is New York City after all."

Gavin finished writing a check and tore it out of the book. "This is for a week, double your rate plus expenses. Don't say you never did nothing for me."

"The guy from Omaha says, 'You know, if we were in Omaha right now, these steaks would only cost ten bucks.' The guy from New York City just looks at him and says, 'Yeah, but we'd be in Omaha.'"

"That's why you're going, not me." Gavin stood. "Oklahoma. Shit. What's in Oklahoma? The wind sweeping down the plains. Have a nice trip."

Genevieve

September 1986

Genevieve stood, sweating, and watched the guy make Indian tacos. After every third or fourth taco, he'd pause, pop a zit, and then sniff his fingertips.

That pretty much captured it, Genevieve's definition of hell: stuck baby-sitting your little sister at the Oklahoma State Fair, a thousand degrees in the shade, the funk of cow shit fuming out from the livestock pens so thick you could taste it, and the Indian taco guy popping zits like they were going out of style.

Oh, and all that while totally straight. You know, just in case hell wasn't hellish enough.

No drugs. No drugs?

Genevieve was sweaty, her hair dead on her shoulders, her mascara melting. She watched Mr. Indian Taco pop another zit. Genevieve wished someone would remind her, please, why she had chosen today of all days to take Nancy Reagan's advice.

No, drugs!

Genevieve, hey, can't we talk about this?

No!

Genevieve's little sister, Julianna, had reached the front of the taco line. She glanced back at Genevieve and grinned. And waited. What was the little goofball waiting for? It took Genevieve a second to realize that her sister was wearing Genevieve's favorite shades, her wood-framed Vuarnets.

Brat!

Genevieve gave her the finger. Julianna lowered the Vuarnets and lifted one eyebrow like Tom Cruise in *Risky Business*. Genevieve refused to smile, but, God, the little goofball could crack her up. Even when Julianna was being a total pain in the ass. *Especially* when she was being a total pain in the ass.

That was kind of a genius gift, Genevieve supposed. An even more useful survival skill, probably, than being pretty or smart or whatever.

Genevieve studied Julianna as she paid for her Indian taco and tried to guess if her sister would ever be pretty. Right now, age twelve, five years younger than Genevieve, Julianna just looked like the goofball twelve-year-old she was. Sort of cute, Genevieve supposed, but—all those awkward angles and mismatched parts—like a cute ptero-dactyl. There were times when Genevieve would glance at Julianna and think, *You never know, maybe she'll grow into those legs someday and turn a few heads*. And then other times Genevieve would think, *No, get ready world, for a gawky, horse-faced girl who cracks everyone up and marries a sweet dull guy three inches shorter than she is*.

Genevieve had always been pretty, but she hadn't turned

pretty pretty until the summer before high school. Nick of time, and what a welcome relief that had been. Because Genevieve wasn't smart, and she didn't have a genius gift for cracking people up. At least nobody but her goofball little sister.

Who laughed like a spaz when Genevieve leaned over and studied the Indian taco and said, "Does Indian taste like chicken?"

"After this," Julianna said when she finished laughing, "I want to go see the freaks."

Yeah, Genevieve thought, like that was gonna happen when she wasn't on drugs. "You're the freak. Give me back my sunglasses."

"Oooh," Julianna said. "I'm so sexy. Everybody look at me. You can't take your eyes off me. I'm *Genevieve.*"

With a French accent and a flirty little cock of her hips. Genevieve refused to smile. She grabbed back her Vuarnets and put them on. With—a second later, just when Julianna was about to bite into her taco—a flirty little cock of her hips that made her sister laugh again like a spaz.

Two preppy college guys in Izods were scoping Genevieve out, from over by the freshwater taffy. She took off her Vuarnets again and held that thing between her teeth— the arm of the sunglasses or whatever it was called—while she pulled her hair back through a scrunchie. Just to watch the two college guys watching her. See? Genevieve had a genius gift, too.

College guys often had good drugs. Too bad that Genevieve was not, today, on speaking terms with drugs.

No! Can't hear you, drugs! Lalalalalala!

"Your mouth is too big for your head," Genevieve told

her sister. "You better hope your head grows, or you're gonna look like one of those snakes that can unhinge their jaws to eat an antelope or whatever."

"Then I can join the freak show. Do you remember Dad and Stan?"

Stan was the world's smallest man, barely three feet tall but perfectly proportioned, a perfect little doll man. He sat inside a tent, on a tiny chair, in the center of a roped-off sawdust ring. People stood at the rope and stared at him. Genevieve and Julianna's dad had taken them to see Stan once. Their dad shared his popcorn with Stan and asked him what he thought about Gerald Ford.

Their aunt used to say, about their dad, that he never met a stranger.

But no way did Julianna remember any of that. Genevieve had been barely nine when their dad was killed in a car wreck, which meant Julianna would have been barely four.

"You don't remember Stan. You were too little."

"I wasn't. I remember that Dad and Stan talked about politics."

"You just remember me telling you that."

"I don't! I remember Dad—"

"Shut up!" Genevieve said. She felt a slash of rage, white hot, blowing up out of nowhere. Here one second and then gone again so quickly that she was just a spectator, too close to a train that rushed past and sucked the breath out of her lungs.

She glanced at Julianna and felt bad. She wanted to explain: *It's not you. Well, mostly it's not you. It's you and it's not you. It's you, yes, because you're twelve years old and you shouldn't need a baby-sitter to take you to the fair.* Genevieve, when she was her sister's age, was running wild on the midway with her friends. Buying plastic barrels of root beer and spiking them with cheap rum. But Julianna was their mother's precious baby, and—especially after what had happened last month at that movie theater across town—she wouldn't let Julianna out of the house without a police escort. *My precious baby, Julianna, if anything like that ever happened to her, I would just et cetera, et cetera.*

And if anything like that ever happened to Genevieve? Genevieve noticed that their mother didn't get all melodramatic about that.

Their mother didn't want to let Julianna go to the fair at all. But Julianna begged and begged, and finally their mother caved.

"I trust you," she warned Genevieve, meaning of course that she didn't. She hadn't trusted Genevieve since the DUI last year. Since the time she'd caught Genevieve smoking pot when she was fourteen. Since ever, really.

"You're driving me out of my mind," Genevieve told Julianna. "It's like getting tortured. It's like getting tortured by a Nazi who smells like watermelon Jolly Ranchers."

Julianna giggled and bumped her head against Genevieve's shoulder like a puppy. She was so easy. She forgave and forgot, and rainbows filled the sky again. It made Genevieve furious. Julianna should tell Genevieve to go screw herself. She should tell Genevieve, *Screw yourself, you selfish, moody, mean bitch of a big sister.*

Genevieve just wanted to *bite* someone. God. It was the heat and the cow-shit funk. The funk of rancid egg-roll grease and generator exhaust as they walked up Food Alley toward the carnival games. It was—oh, yeah, by the way—*no drugs.*

What she would give right now for a single line of pure white snow. Genevieve shivered, just thinking about the ignition, the surge, the world filled suddenly with Tinker Bell sparkle.

Howard, alleged expert on these matters, had admitted to Genevieve that saying no to drugs and booze didn't get much easier with practice, not really. The craving never faded. Howard claimed he could still taste the first sip of scotch he'd ever taken.

"Not even a little easier?" Genevieve had asked.

"Maybe a little," he'd said. Howard, who was always so full of shit. That was the best he could do?

Julianna, excited, turned onto Carnival Row. Genevieve groaned. She wished now she'd picked up an extra weekend shift at Sonic. Carhopping for crotch change was preferable to this.

Well, maybe not. But half a dozen of six, or whatever the saying was.

C'mon, Genevieve. Be reasonable.

No, drugs! Shut your trap for two seconds, will you?

The minute Genevieve graduated from high school—seven months and counting, you better believe it—she planned to flee Oklahoma City, to fly, to get out of Dodge. She thought she might head to California. Or New York City. Thailand, maybe, where she'd heard that people lit paper lanterns that floated up into the night sky. Genevieve was up for anywhere, as long as it was far, far away.

"Oooh!" Julianna said.

"Oooh!" Genevieve said. "What?"

"Let's play the balloon game!"

The balloon game was a race. You used a pistol to squirt water into the mouth of a plastic clown. If your balloon popped first, you won a prize. Stuffed Pink Panthers hung like meat from the rafters of the booth.

"I know what!" Genevieve said.

"What?

"Let's not and say we did."

"Please! Please, please, please?"

"Give me a Jolly Rancher," Genevieve said.

A goat roper in a big cowboy hat won the first race. So Genevieve forked over two more bucks, and they tried again. Julianna won this time. She squealed and jumped around. The carny who ran the booth produced a Pac-Man key chain and told Julianna that if she won again, she could trade up to the next level of prize.

"Cheater, cheater, pumpkin eater," Genevieve told the carny. He was a lot older than she was, close to thirty, but sexy in a sort of dirty, long-haired, hippie way, with a dark, dirty tan and blue eyes and a diamond stud earring. A tattoo of a snake curled round and round one muscular forearm.

"You're rubber and I'm glue," he said, smiling and dangling the key chain from his index finger.

"I think you've got that bass-ackwards, Mr. Pumpkin Eater," Genevieve said.

"Says you."

"And the horse I rode in on."

She reached out and flicked the key chain so that it spun around his finger. He laughed, and Genevieve thought it might be the best feeling ever—to stop, if just for a second, thinking about drugs.

Although, God, just imagine the amazing drugs that a sexy, dirty, hippie carny probably had access to. Doy.

"Genni!" Julianna, meanwhile, was bouncing off the walls. "I want to play again!"

"Or you're gonna pee your pants, presumably?"

"Genni! C'mon! Please?"

Genevieve turned back to the carny. "If my little sister doesn't win a Pink Panther, she's gonna presumably pee her pants right here. You are officially warned."

The carny looked Genevieve over. He took his sweet time, very sexy, and then yawned, and then stretched, and then yanked down one of the stuffed Pink Panthers.

"What the hell?" the goat roper who had won the first race complained. "That ain't right!"

The carny snapped around—*snap!*—and gave the goat roper a stare so electric with menace that Genevieve expected the colored lightbulbs that trimmed the booth to buzz and dim.

The goat roper blinked. And he wasn't some small sissy guy either. He looked away, then slid from his stool and slunk off. Genevieve heard him mutter something under his breath, but only when he was at a safe distance.

The carny turned back to Genevieve and smiled. It was official: Julianna was no longer the only girl at the balloon race about to pee her pants with excitement.

"So, hey," the carny said. "Some of us are gonna party later. Just after dark, out back at the trailers. Why don't you come by?"

"Whatever," Genevieve said. She grabbed Julianna's

wrist and pulled her away from the booth. Julianna hugged her Pink Panther like she'd just given birth to the baby Jesus. Genevieve waited till they were almost to the end of Carnival Row before she glanced back. And sure enough there he was, the sexy carny, watching just like she knew he'd be.

GENEVIEVE HAD STARTED smoking pot when she was fourteen. Everyone smoked pot. Who didn't smoke pot at parties? Or on break from your shitty job at Baskin-Robbins, the only place in town where you didn't have to be sixteen to work. You could lie about your age to get a job at other places—a lot of people did that—but why bother? Those jobs were none the less shitty.

Pot was fine, but pot was boring. Ludes made Genevieve feel gross and sluggish. Cocaine, on the other hand—oh, my. Genevieve had been introduced at age sixteen, when she and her friend Lacey snuck into a college party. That first rush was like nothing Genevieve had ever experienced before.

Why, hello there!

Most normal humans, like her friend Lacey, could do drugs on the weekends or at parties and then go on with their normal human lives. Genevieve, apparently, was not a normal human.

God. The stupid shit that Genevieve had done when she was on drugs. And she had done it without a second thought.

But why blame the drugs for that? According to her mother, Genevieve had never given a second thought to anything. Her mother said Genevieve had never cared about anyone but herself.

So please explain why Genevieve, if she was so selfish and self-centered, had practically raised Julianna by herself those first few years after their dad died. Fixing her breakfast, fixing her dinner, giving her baths. Julianna permanently attached to her like she was a tumor or something, even after Julianna was way too big for Genevieve to carry around on her hip.

While their mother worked all day and ran around with her girlfriends all night and only managed to drag herself home so she could yell at Genevieve about the laundry not being done.

Typical Genevieve, their mother would say if she could hear her now. *It's always all about Genevieve, isn't it?*

"Genni?"

"What?"

It was dusk. They were sitting on the curb in front of the rodeo arena, watching the colors of the midway catch fire. Genevieve felt gritty and grimy and tired. But with the sun down, and the light mellow, and a cool breeze blowing, and those amazing midway colors—all the hard edges, both the world's and Genevieve's, seemed a tiny bit softer.

"I'm scared about high school," Julianna said.

"You don't start high school till year after next, you dork."

"I know."

Genevieve knew. She listened to the screams drifting over from the midway, the bad hair metal, the muted clank and hiss of the rides.

"Look," she told Julianna. "High school is like anything. It sucks. But you'll live."

Why that should cheer up her little sister was a total mystery to Genevieve, but it did. Julianna smiled and tore off a hunk of pink cotton candy. She was a bottomless pit.

Howard had told Genevieve once that she needed to listen to her better angels. Genevieve wasn't sure what that meant. Were some angels good and others even better? Or were some angels not good at all? Kind of an alarming notion when you stopped to think about it.

Speaking of bad angels, here came her friend Lacey, walking toward them. She was with a couple of girls Genevieve recognized in a vague sort of way. She thought they might be cocktail waitresses at the new Marriott on the expressway.

"Small world," Lacey said, smirking.

Genevieve corrected her. "Small town, actually."

"Hi, Lacey," Julianna said.

Probably, Genevieve admitted to herself, she was Lacey's bad angel, and not vice versa. From the age of ten on, starting with a pack of Kools she stole from her mom's boyfriend, Genevieve had done most of the leading-astray. Lacey's mother had warned Lacey to stay away from Genevieve soon after the two girls met in third grade. Lacey's mom wasn't fond of Mexicans or even white people, like Genevieve's mom, who had married a guy who was part Mexican. *Southside trash.* Genevieve had overheard Lacey's mom say that about Genevieve's mom one time. Which excuse me? Not only were there plenty of nice neighborhoods on the south side, but until last year Lacey had lived three blocks from Genevieve.

"Stuck with the brat?" Lacey said, smirking because Lacey would never be caught dead in such an embarrassing situation. With her little sister at the fair on a Saturday night. With *her* hair dead on *her* shoulders and *her* mascara a mess.

The pupils of Lacey's eyes were flared. The cocktail waitresses were high also, chewing gum way too fast and giggling for no reason. All three girls had on pristine slutty makeup, just like the robot girls in the "Addicted to Love" video.

Yeah, well, I'm still hotter than you, Genevieve wanted to tell Lacey, *and always will be.*

Instead she said, "Do you remember when we overheard your mom tell your aunt that my mom was Southside trash? And you guys used to live like three blocks away?"

That blew Lacey's mind. It was too much to follow when you were on drugs.

"Did I . . . what?"

"Never mind," Genevieve said.

"We're gonna cruise the midway," Lacey said. "You want to come? Plenty of room in Santa's sleigh."

Wink, wink. Santa's sleigh—snow—cocaine. Get it?

Julianna was oblivious. She had decided to ignore Lacey after Lacey had ignored her. She was eating pink cotton candy and throwing hunks of it toward a jabbing sparrow.

Lacey had good drugs. Genevieve could tell. Why had Genevieve decided, today of all days, to say no?

Genevieve shook her head.

"You're such a loser," Lacey said. She and the robot cocktail waitresses strutted off. Genevieve felt like bursting into tears.

"She's always so mean," Julianna said.

"I'm meaner than she is."

"But you're my sister."

"See? Life sucks."

"Why are you crying, Genni?"

"I'm not. It's all the stupid dust in the air. It makes my eyes water."

The stupid dust, that, too, but also a sensation like she was being turned inside out. Genevieve wanted to go running after Lacey and Lacey's drugs. Would one line of blow really be the end of the world? Genevieve had been straight all day. Surely that counted for something.

She had to do something. She had to do something right now or she *would* go sprinting after Lacey.

You couldn't just sit around and not do drugs. Howard had explained that. So you flew model airplanes or played golf or did needlepoint until your fingers cramped. Whatever kept your boat afloat.

"Listen, Juli."

"What?"

"I'm gonna check out that party. Just for a few minutes. That one that guy was talking about."

Julianna looking alarmed was like a cartoon character looking alarmed. *Da-doing!*

"That skeezy guy at the balloon race?"

"Shut up. Just for fifteen minutes. Okay? I really just need to get out of here for a minute."

Julianna was winding Pink Panther's tail around and around her finger. "It's getting dark, Genni."

"Don't be such a scaredy-cat. There's like a million people here."

"A million skeezy people."

True. As soon as the sun went down, the families abandoned the midway and packs of rowdy young guys started funneling in, packs of slutty girls. *Southside trash.*

"That's why I want you to stay right in this spot," Genevieve said. "Okay? Just for like fifteen minutes."

Julianna looked away. She shrugged and nodded.

Genevieve felt guilty, a little. But she'd be back in fifteen minutes, before it was even *dark* dark. The carny trailers were close by, just behind the midway. And Genevieve would make it up to Julianna. She'd take her to the mall tomorrow. Or to Fun Skate. Or both. And you'd think that a day at the fair and a stuffed Pink Panther would count for something, right?

Genevieve just wanted to forget about drugs and her mother and life for a minute. That's all. She just wanted to laugh and flirt and feel the heat coming off a dirty, sexy hippie when he looked at her. If he offered her drugs, she would say no. It was as simple as that.

She stood, dug around in the pocket of her jeans, found her last crumpled ten-dollar bill. She dropped it in Julianna's lap. "I don't know how you could possibly eat anything else, Miss Piggy, but have at it."

"Okay," Julianna said, but still wouldn't look at her. God.

Genevieve told herself that her sister was twelve years old, she wasn't a baby. It wasn't even *dark* dark yet, there were millions of people around, and Genevieve would only be gone fifteen minutes.

Everything was going to be fine.

She squatted down and gave Julianna a quick hug. "I'll be back in a flash," she said. "And we'll get out of Dodge."

Julianna

CHAPTER 3

October 2012

One of Julianna's only vivid memories, from that time so long ago, was the psychic. October of 1986, the living room of the little house on SW Twenty-seventh, just off Olie. The psychic wore a gauzy black dress that swirled around her when she walked and a silver ring on every finger, even her thumbs. This was before anyone wore rings on their thumbs, anyone in Oklahoma City at least, and the psychic had also dyed her long hair a shade of deep, unnatural black, so black it was almost purple. You could tell that the psychic thought she made a striking and dramatic impression, but she didn't, not really. Her upper arms were pimply, her gray roots showed. She owned a shop called Moon Breeze, on a run-down stretch of Classen Boulevard, that sold New Age crystals and feathered dream catchers.

"Yes, yes," the psychic had said. She sat on the sofa with her eyes closed, rocking back and forth. "I see, I see."

"What do you see?" Carol whispered, leaning closer. Carol lived next door and had arranged for the psychic. She'd always been friendly enough with their mother, but after what happened, Carol had made it her mission to be their mother's best friend. Carol had landed her dream job.

"I see her," the psychic said. "She's alive."

"Genevieve's alive!" Carol said.

"I smell the ocean. I see her. She's smiling."

Julianna remembered that their mother had remained expressionless, her face slack and heavy, like a drop of water trembling on the lip of a faucet. Carol reached over to squeeze her hand.

"Genevieve's smiling!" Carol said.

"I hear the waves, I see—" The psychic stopped. Carol made a big deal of holding her breath and waiting for the next revelation. The psychic sneezed. "Sorry," she said. "Darn allergies."

It probably wasn't allergies that made the psychic sneeze, but all the patchouli oil she was wearing.

Who else was there that morning? Their Aunt Nancy and the psychic's boyfriend, who had an enormous belly and needed a cane to walk. And Joe, Carol's husband. He stood apart from the others, leaning against the wall, his arms folded across his chest.

It was a chilly, rainy day. Every now and then, the wind flung a spray of rain hard against the living-room window and made Julianna jump. She was sitting cross-legged on the dusty wood floor, right beneath the window.

She had been skeptical when the psychic arrived. The pimply arms, the gray roots. Julianna and Genevieve had driven past the run-down shop on the run-down stretch of Classen Boulevard many times. Now, though, when the psychic said she could smell the ocean and hear the waves, her voice was clear and certain, like the chime of glass on glass.

The sofa was faded red velvet. It, and the house, had belonged to their grandmother. When she died, the summer of 1983, the three of them moved in, Julianna and Genevieve and their mother. The house smelled like mildew, and the wood floors were warped, the neighborhood was so-so, but both the house and the neighborhood were a step up from the place they'd been renting before.

Their grandmother's house had a finished basement with wood paneled walls and a linoleum-tile floor, separated from the rest of the house by two doors and a flight of steep, narrow steps. Genevieve had staked her claim right away. She dragged her mattress down to the basement, her boxes of records and clothes and makeup. For the first time in her life Julianna had a room to herself, though she still spent most of her time downstairs with Genevieve.

That red velvet sofa that used to be Grandma's. Remember it? Remember the linoleum floor in the basement? Remember how we went to the carpet store and begged them and they gave us some of the carpet squares they used for samples? Each square was a different color, a different kind of carpet. You made a joke about that, about used carpet, something dirty and hilarious, but I can't remember what it was.

When the psychic said that Genevieve would be home soon, Julianna saw Joe frown.

"Oh!" Carol said. "Did you hear that?"

Julianna's mother remained expressionless. Carol leaned across and squeezed her hand again.

Looking back, Julianna wondered if Carol truly believed what the psychic said or if she was just clueless. Maybe Carol believed that hope, no matter how faint or false it might be, was a necessary kind of nourishment, like the cookies and tamales and ham casseroles with cornflake crust that she'd brought over every day since Genevieve disappeared.

Her husband, Joe, was not clueless. Julianna understood that now. He could see the pain in her mother's eyes.

"It's Christmastime," the psychic said, rocking back and forth. "and Genevieve is walking up the—"

"That's enough," Joe said quietly, but with sufficient force to turn the psychic's head.

"Honey," Carol warned him.

The psychic's boyfriend stirred. He was in the easy chair, pinned beneath his huge belly.

Joe worked at a gas station, a mechanic. There was always grease in the grooves and swirls of his knuckles. He had seemed so old to Julianna at the time, but he was probably forty or so, only a couple of years older than Julianna was now.

"That's enough," Joe said again. And then, after thinking about it, "Thank you."

The psychic lifted a hand, five silver rings, and bowed her head. She rose from the sofa, paused to sneeze again, then exited in a dramatic swirl of gauzy black fabric. Her boyfriend hobbled out on his cane after her.

Another spray of rain cracked against the window. One of Julianna's legs, crossed beneath the other, had gone to sleep.

At the time, in that moment, Julianna hated Joe. She wanted to hear the psychic finish telling them how her sister would come walking up the driveway at Christmas.

The day after Carol brought the psychic to their house, or maybe it was a few days later, the two detectives stopped by. Carol and her husband were still there—or there again—Aunt Nancy, too, and the rain hadn't stopped. Julianna sat cross-legged on the dusty wood floor. The little house smelled like mildew and ham casserole.

It had been three weeks since the Saturday night that Genevieve had vanished from the state fair. The younger of the two detectives, the grimmer of the two, told their mother that the police were still working hard to find Genevieve. They continued to pursue every possible avenue of investigation.

Joe understood what they were saying. "Nothing?" he said. "You got nothing at all?"

The older detective, Fitch, cleared his throat but didn't answer. Their mother remained expressionless. Aunt Nancy said, "Hell."

"That's *good*, though, isn't it?" Carol said after a second, looking around from face to face to face. "If there's no evidence that someone— That's a *good* thing. It means Genevieve . . . it means maybe she wasn't . . . maybe she just . . . she could have just . . . jaunted off on her own! To California, the ocean."

"That's possible," the older detective said, carefully. "However, unfortunately, as we've explained before—"

"We're operating under the assumption that foul play was involved," his younger, grimmer partner said.

Because why, if Genevieve had jaunted off on her own, would she have left behind her car? Her purse? Her little sister?

The police had found the old Cutlass still parked right where Genevieve and Julianna had left it, in a grassy field used as an overflow lot, not far from the Made in Oklahoma Building. They'd found the purse, empty, in a ditch half a mile from the fairgrounds. A security guard had found Julianna sitting alone outside the rodeo arena, at nearly midnight, more than three hours after Genevieve told her she'd be right back.

"But you don't *know* that it was foul play," Carol tried again. "You don't know that for *certain*."

Just shut up! Julianna remembered thinking. *Shut up!* She supposed that was the exact moment she stopped hating Joe and started hating Carol.

"No, ma'am," the younger, grimmer detective said again. "We will continue to pursue every possible avenue of investigation."

Did the detectives already know, three weeks after Genevieve disappeared, that they would never find her, never find her body, that twenty-six years later no one would have any idea what had happened to her? Probably they did. Julianna understood now what those two detectives had understood then, that the State Fair of Oklahoma—thousands of visitors, armies of vendors and roadies, all those Future Farmers of America and itinerant carnival workers—was a bad place to go missing. The on-ramp to Interstate 40 was less than two hundred yards from the south gate of the fairgrounds. You could leave the fair at midnight and be in Albuquerque for breakfast. Or Memphis. Or anywhere.

And it was a bad time to go missing, too, 1986. Before cell phones, before ATMs and security cameras everywhere, when people still used cash, not credit cards, to buy gas and groceries and fast food.

"Just remember what Bronwyn saw," Carol told their mother. Bronwyn was the psychic's name. Carol reached over and squeezed their mother's hand. "Hold on to that, Eileen."

Their mother remained expressionless. The detectives left. Julianna remembered the rain, the rain, the rain. It seemed like it rained every day for weeks that autumn. In November they watched the Oklahoma-Nebraska football game on TV. The players slipped and slid all over the muddy field.

After Genevieve disappeared, Julianna's relationship with her mother changed. How could it not? They'd lost not only Genevieve but also an essential part of who they themselves were.

The simplest conversation at the dinner table was exhausting, too heavy to carry far.

How was school.

Okay.

Maybe they would have drifted apart anyway, as parents and children often did. Julianna turned thirteen and became a teenager. Her mother studied for her real-estate license. Julianna left for college. Her mother met a man who liked to fix things, who thought he could fix anything, and a year or so after Julianna started nursing school, her mother and the man moved to California. Julianna's mother called to tell her about the move, a polite courtesy. Julianna wished her the best. The conversation, thirty seconds, was exhausting.

Her mother passed away in 2004. Julianna had flown out for the funeral, a small service at a suburban cemetery on the fringes of the Inland Empire. She laid flowers on the gravestone and felt only what had already been missing for a long time.

JULIANNA WAS THINKING about the psychic today because the new anesthesiologist, the one from Russia, wore a silver ring on her thumb.

"I think we are all okay here, then," she told Julianna. She handed the chart back and noticed Julianna looking at her ring. "You like? It is antique. My grandmother."

"It's very nice," Julianna said. The anesthesiologist walked away, her sneakers squeaking, and Julianna thought how much she disliked that sound. She disliked the bright, cold lights overhead and the saline bags hanging like organs, fat and glistening, from the skeleton spines of IV stands. The greasy feel of hand-sanitizer foam and the boxes of latex gloves in different sizes. Small, medium, large, extra-large, 2XX.

Julianna, a nurse, basically disliked hospitals. How was that for irony?

She especially disliked the parts of the hospital that were designed to make you forget you were in a hospital. The blond wood, the framed prints of flowery meadows. As in, Isn't this a warm, cheerful place? A place where you have nothing to be afraid of?

Julianna supposed that in the old days hospitals didn't try so hard to disguise what they were: places where you suffered and died.

She worked downstairs in Recovery. That was another irony. For Julianna. And for a lot of the patients who ended up there.

Genevieve would have come up with something funny to say about all the different sizes of latex gloves. Julianna could hear her.

Poor fella, goes in for a prostate exam and the doctor snaps on a pair of those 2XX's.

"Oh, Nurse!" The elderly woman in number nine. She had summoned Julianna four times in the past thirty minutes.

"How are you feeling, Mrs. Bender?" Julianna said.

"I'm such a pest, aren't I? But it's so chilly in here."

"You're not a pest. I'm glad you buzzed me."

Julianna pulled another blanket from the cabinet and fanned it over Mrs. Bender. The surgeon had removed most of the rest of her colon, but her blue eyes were bright and fierce.

"Is my son back?"

"Not yet," Julianna said. The son: balding without grace, good suit worn poorly, an expression like he'd just swallowed a burp. He'd stepped out forty-five minutes ago to make a quick call. He'd treated Julianna like a waitress. She was no longer surprised that so many people did.

Julianna took Mrs. Bender's hand and gave it a gentle squeeze.

"You have the most beautiful eyes, Mrs. Bender."

"You're one to talk, sister." Mrs. Bender managed a faint, sly smile. "But yes. I was quite the beauty in my day."

"Hearts were broken?"

"Not enough, if you take my meaning." She gave Julianna a wink. "That's my advice to you."

Julianna smiled. "I'll keep it in mind."

"My son, you know, is newly single. Available, in other words." She watched for Julianna's reaction, with that faint, sly smile.

"I know, I know, you're much too lovely for him," Mrs. Bender said. "I can say that because he's my son and I love him. Because why should I lie? Life is short."

"I'm sure he'll be right back," Julianna said.

Mrs. Bender nodded. She closed her eyes as a wave of nausea washed over her.

"Make hay while the sun shines," she murmured. "Make hay while the sun shines. Make hay while the sun shines."

Julianna stepped out of the room and pulled the curtain shut. Donna, magenta scrubs, sneakers squeaking, bustled around the corner looking for her.

"You're off in ten, aren't you?" Beneath Donna's perfume was the tang of nicotine.

"I am," Julianna said.

"We're getting drinks. Gonna get our hooch on. What do you say?"

"As enticing as that sounds."

"You're no fun."

"I'm really not."

Donna spanked her on the ass with a clipboard and moved past, sneakers squeaking.

YOU SHOULD HAVE seen my big sister, Mrs. Bender.

After twenty-six years, that was still Julianna's first reaction whenever someone told her she was pretty. Whenever someone, every now and then, told her she looked hot or fine or beautiful, in a bar, on a beach, in the crew cab of a Dodge Ram, let's get those panties off you, babe.

You should have seen my big sister, you want to talk about beautiful.

Awkward. When your first boyfriend is stroking your cheek and leaning in for a kiss and you burst into tears.

Genevieve would have been mortified. She would have disowned Julianna on the spot. Genevieve would have said, *Juli, you dork, you make me feel like bursting into tears.*

You want to talk about beautiful? One time Genevieve had slipped off her sunglasses, just that, nothing more, and a guy passing by on a motorcycle had swerved and almost wiped out.

It was Genevieve. It was the way she slipped off her sunglasses. The way she did everything.

Genevieve said it blew her mind, how Julianna could be such a major dork.

"Does this make me a dork?" Julianna would ask. She'd do her version of Kevin Bacon's big dance in *Footloose,* and Genevieve would have to bury her face in a couch pillow, laughing.

Julianna's first boyfriend, junior year of high school, didn't have a clue why she'd burst into tears. All he'd done was stroke her cheek and lean in for a kiss, tell her she was the prettiest girl he'd ever known.

Julianna's ponytail always gave her a headache by the end of shift, so she snapped off the rubber band and shook out her hair as she walked to the parking garage. She drove the long way home, down Western instead of the Broadway Extension, and stopped to pick up dinner at Whole Foods. It was on Western, not far from where the old railroad bridge used to stand, the one that high-school kids covered with graffiti every football season. The city had torn the bridge down years ago to extend Classen Boulevard. Julianna couldn't remember what, if anything, had been torn down to make room for Whole Foods, even though the store was barely six months old. An apartment complex, maybe?

The landscape of memory was like that. Sometimes the near seemed far, far away and the faraway was right beneath your feet.

Julianna filled her biodegradable cardboard carton with chicken tikka masala, basmati rice, and some sad-looking broccoli. A guy with his own carton, and a nice smile, shook his head.

"That broccoli," he said. "You're braver than me."

She smiled back and moved on to the lentils.

"The masala looks good, though," the guy said.

"Excuse me," she said, and reached past him for a biodegradable cardboard lid.

He had ginger hair and smelled like soap. She guessed he was . . . thirty-two? Six years younger than her. He wore pressed khakis and a pale blue button-down shirt. Julianna guessed he worked at one of the big energy companies, Chesapeake or Devon.

Energy. When Julianna had been growing up, it was still called the oil and gas business. And there'd been an old brick mansion at the corner of Sixty-third and Western, where the Chesapeake campus was now. The mansion, their mother said, was a home for bad girls.

"*Dumb* girls," Genevieve told Julianna. "They don't know what a rubber is?"

Julianna giggled, but she was only ten or eleven at the time and wasn't entirely sure herself what a rubber was. Or what exactly qualified a girl as "bad." She had worried that Genevieve might be sent to the mansion on Western, since Genevieve drank beer and cut classes and snuck out at night to go see her friends. One time she'd come home from a party drunk and their mother had thrown a fit.

The guy stepped around Julianna and spooned rice into his carton.

"Doctor?" he said. Probably he guessed by her scrubs that she was a nurse but hoped the question might flatter her.

"Nurse."

"Cool."

"Sometimes it is."

"Right. Oh, right. I can imagine. It's not like on TV, is it? Like that one show."

"I don't know. I doubt it."

"It's not glamorous, in other words," he said.

"Glamour is rare."

"My name's Ryan, by the way."

She wondered how often Ryan from Chesapeake or Devon, with the ginger hair and the nice smile, the easy confidence, hit on women at Whole Foods. Should Julianna feel special? There were three other women at the food bar. One had a wedding ring, one was less attractive than Julianna, one more so.

"Julianna," she said.

"I'm bad at this," he said. It was meant to be disarming, and almost was.

Julianna assumed her best caregiver face, concerned and sympathetic. "You're bad at picking up dinner?"

Two of the three other women at the food bar, the married

woman and the one more attractive than Julianna, kept stealing glances, lingering over the soup tureens so they could watch this little scene unfold.

The guy smiled his nice smile again. He seemed earnest and sweet. On the weekends he played golf, in an OU visor, in a sweater vest with the logo of the Oak Tree Country Club embroidered just above his heart. "Listen. Were you planning to eat in? We could grab a table."

"Let's go to your place," Julianna said, and for a second all the soup ladles stopped clinking.

In the parking lot, next to his car, they kissed for a while. Julianna's mind wandered. Two teenage girls passing by giggled at them. Julianna hadn't had sex with a guy since her brief spring fling with one of the radiologists at the hospital six months ago. Six months! Genevieve would be horrified. *You dork!*

She guessed that Ryan with the ginger hair would be fine in bed, unimaginative but diligent. He was a nice kisser. Part of her wanted him, part of her didn't. It was a coin flip, really. She kissed him and waited to see where the coin landed.

"Wow," he said when they finally broke apart.

"You're a nice kisser," she said.

"You, too."

When she started to walk away, he said, "Wait, you should— I'll give you my address, or do you want to ride with me?"

She stopped and turned and watched his face. "Did you think I was serious?" She assumed her caregiver expression again, concerned and sympathetic. "You didn't, did you?"

When she got home, she heated up the chicken tikka masala and ate in front of her laptop. There was a Facebook page she'd discovered: "Remember When in OKC." It was unbelievably banal. Someone would post, "Remember Springlake Amusement Park over on Eastern Avenue?" And someone else would reply, "Yeah! With that big wooden roller coaster!"

Still, though, Julianna made a point to scroll through the new posts every day. You never knew what you might find, or where, so you had to keep looking. You could never, ever stop looking. That, at least, was her position on the matter.

Wyatt

CHAPTER 4

The flight to Oklahoma City landed ten minutes late. Wyatt stepped out of the Jetway and into a terminal that bore no resemblance to the airport he remembered. The old Will Rogers World Airport had been cramped and claustrophobic and dimly lit, with low ceilings and floors that seemed always to slope down, down, down, no matter what direction you were headed. The ceilings of the new terminal soared. The walls were glass and pale stone. The light of a clear blue October morning was almost bright enough to blind him.

Times change, Wyatt told himself. It wasn't as if Oklahoma City had been frozen in amber for twenty-six years, breathlessly awaiting his return. Life goes on. His life had gone on. So get over yourself.

He headed downstairs to the car-rental counter. The woman working for Avis stared at his driver's license. Wyatt had legally changed his last name when he turned twenty-one and dropped his first name. He knew that the photo of the man bore little resemblance to the boy he'd been. He couldn't help it, though—he tensed anyway. The woman was in her forties, old enough to maybe, just maybe, recognize him.

"You thought I was George Clooney, didn't you?" Wyatt said. "Tell the truth."

The woman smiled and set his driver's license on the edge of her keyboard so she could enter his information into the computer.

"I just haven't seen the new Nevada licenses yet," she said.

"I knew it. It's the rugged good looks and the . . . what?"

She laughed this time. Wyatt relaxed. You see? Twenty-six years. *Get over yourself.*

He crossed to the parking garage, tossed his bag into the front seat of a black Altima, and called the number that Gavin had given him.

No answer, no voice mail. Wyatt frowned and checked his watch. All morning he'd been fanning the flame of a tiny hope that he might be able to wrap Candace Kilkenny's case in a few hours and be home by dinnertime. A guy could dream, right? But less than fifteen minutes on the ground and already he'd hit his first snag. It was ten forty-five. He would need to be back at the airport by four, at the very latest, to catch the last flight back to Vegas.

He dug his laptop out of his bag and ran a reverse search on Candace Kilkenny's phone number. He got lucky. The number belonged to a landline, and, even luckier, the landline belonged to an address just south of downtown, five minutes from the airport. Wyatt retracted his original frown. The flame of hope flickered back to life.

Merging onto I-40, he caught his first glimpse of that familiar downtown skyline, squat and boxy, hunkered down on the prairie like it was riding out a storm. His stomach clenched. There was something so familiar as well about the great blue dome of sky overhead. Having lived most of his adult life in cities like San Diego and Pittsburgh, Oakland and Las Vegas, Wyatt had forgotten just how flat Oklahoma City was. The sunsets, he remembered—when the clouds racked up on the horizon and the colors turned lurid—could be epic.

The sunsets, the sunsets, the sunsets. His stomach clenched again, but Wyatt ignored it. There was one new skyscraper downtown, twice as high any other building, but it seemed to belong to another city, another world, a different future.

He turned south onto Walker, away from downtown, and started checking addresses. This part of town, unlike the airport, had not been given a makeover during Wyatt's absence. A few old brown-brick commercial buildings that were boarded up, a body shop in what looked like it used to be a church, a Spanish-language church in what looked like it used to be an A&W drive-in, vacant lots filled with sun-bleached weeds.

Wyatt realized the address he was trying to find was the Land Run, down at the very end of the block.

The Land Run? *That* was the place Candace Kilkenny had inherited?

The Land Run had been an Oklahoma City institution back in Wyatt's day, the best place in town, usually the only place in town, to see the indie rock bands the local radio stations never played. The Beat Farmers. The Replacements. Lone Justice. Bands stopped off on their way from Dallas to Kansas City, from Memphis to Phoenix. There was a rumor—Wyatt didn't know if it was true—that once you played the Land Run, you could drink there for free, in perpetuity.

Wyatt himself had managed to sneak into only a couple of shows. His fake ID, when he was fifteen, could not have been more woefully unconvincing, and the Land Run had the toughest door in town. Hot girls with hard eyes who just glared until finally you broke down, snatched back your shitty fake ID, and slunk away into the night.

Wyatt could picture that shitty fake ID of his like it was yesterday—a temporary Connecticut driver's license on green card stock, with a stranger's name, address, and date of birth written by hand in blue ink. It hadn't even been laminated.

He parked across the street. The Land Run occupied a two-story brown-brick building that had been beat to hell in 1986 and was beat to hell now. Back in the 1940s, the building had been a public library. When the library closed, some of the fixtures had been left behind. Wyatt remembered how card catalogs had lined one wall next to the Land Run's stage. The custom was, you used a car key to scratch your initials in the cherrywood finish.

The big sign out front was still there: *The Land Run!* in cursive neon set inside a cursive metal trough and beneath that an old-fashioned marquee with movable letters made of heavy molded plastic, translucent red, so that when the sign was illuminated at night, the letters would seem to glow.

LIVE MUSIC AND COLD BEER
FRIDAY: RED MEANS RUN
SATURDAY: DADDY'S SOUL DONUT

Plastic marquee letters like that weighed a ton, especially the capitals, the *M*'s and the *S*'s. Wyatt could almost feel the weight in his hands. He shook off the memory and climbed out of the car.

The Land Run's big black wooden door was locked, so he gave it a bang. He gave it another bang.

"Go away!" a voice called from inside, faint. "We don't open till five."

Wyatt banged the door again.

"Dipshit!" the faint voice called from inside.

Wyatt took out his phone and dialed. After a couple of rings, a woman picked up.

"If you're the dipshit at the door," she said, "I'm not gonna tell you again."

"Gavin told me you were a piece of work," Wyatt said, "but I can't imagine why."

She hung up. A few seconds later, Wyatt heard the scrape and clunk of a dead bolt, and the big black door swung open, breathing forty years of stale beer and perfume-scented sweat into his face.

"Hi!" said the woman who opened the door. "I thought you were just some dipshit."

"I like to think I'm more of a jerk-off," Wyatt said.

"You're the private investigator?" She eyed him skeptically. "You don't look like a private investigator."

"You don't look like a Candace Kilkenny."

Not even close. She had skin the color of fresh cinnamon, and dark hair pulled back in a ponytail that highlighted the exotic cant of even darker eyes. Wyatt put her at twenty-three, maybe twenty-four years old.

"I don't? Wow, really?" she said. She stood with her fists on her hips, legs wide, a colossus astride the world, all five feet, two inches of her.

Wyatt liked her already.

"Everyone always thinks I'm some mail-order bride from Thai-

land," she said, "and I'm like, 'Screw you! I grew up in Arizona!'
I'm all-American trailer trash! I've never even been to Thailand,
not since I was like six months old! Give me a break!"

"I'm glad we've cleared that up. I feel as if it was starting to
come between us."

"I thought you'd be some big tough guy. Like Gavin? Gavin
looks like he could kick somebody's ass."

"Hey," Wyatt said. "I'm six feet tall and reasonably fit. Almost
six-one. Who's to say I don't kick the occasional ass?"

"Doubt it." But she reached out and gave his bicep a squeeze.
A hard one. "Maybe."

"My name's Wyatt. Wyatt Rivers."

"Wyatt Rivers." She looked doubtful about that, too. "You
want a beer? Come on in."

She led him inside. Wyatt saw that the wooden cabinets that
once held the card catalogs were still there. The stage. The bat-
tered old bar. The Art Deco skylight that had probably never been
cleaned and the rickety balcony that twenty-six years later still
seemed on the verge of collapse. Posters for past shows covered
every available inch of wall space.

Wyatt sat on a lopsided stool at the far end of the bar while
Candace drew him a draft.

"I want to put in a kitchen," she said. "Just a little one, for
hamburgers or whatever, so we can open for lunch. Can you
imagine the lunch business we'd do, all the people who work
downtown?"

Wyatt reached for the beer and noticed on the wall behind
Candace a show bill for the Hüsker Dü show. May 1, 1986. He felt
his stomach clench again, not so gently this time. He checked his
watch. The last plane back to Vegas left at four. He flipped open
his reporter's notebook.

"Gavin says someone has been harassing you."

"Someone's been totally harassing me!"

"My mistake. Totally harassing you. Tell me."

"It started a couple of weeks ago. Three weeks ago? I get to work, and all the beer kegs out back, the empties, somebody had tipped them over and rolled them around, all over the parking lot. Two days later, totally same thing!"

She waited. Wyatt waited. If that was it, the Case of the Tipped-Over Empty Beer Kegs, his prospects for making that four-o'clock flight back to Vegas had just improved dramatically.

She reached across the bar and thwacked him in the sternum with the knuckles of her small, cinnamon-brown hand. The pain was surprisingly sharp. "Stop it!" she said.

"Stop what? I'm listening attentively."

"What you're doing with your eyebrow."

"Ms. Kilkenny," he said, keeping an eye on her hand in case she decided to thwack him again, "just because your beer kegs—"

"Shut up, I know," she said. "Call me Candace. It's not just the beer kegs. There's more. Okay? A couple of nights later, the sign—my big sign out front?—somebody climbed up there and rearranged all the letters one night. They took the letters and moved them around so they spelled things like, you know, 'Touch my cock' and 'Anal surprise.' People were driving by and honking all day the next day, until I went out there and looked. And 'Fur pie delight.' That was another one."

Wyatt tried to control his eyebrow. "I see."

"Do you know what a pain it was for me to get on the ladder and move all those letters back where they were supposed to be? It's already a pain, because I have to go up there and change the band names every Sunday night. But this happened every single night for a week! And the church down the street, the pastor, he called to complain. He thought I'd turned the place into a strip club or something."

"Did you call the police?"

"The police said it was probably just kids. They said there were gangs around here. The Southside somethings. The Southside Locos. They said I was lucky I didn't have gang graffiti coming out of my wazoo."

"I'll go out on a limb and assume that's a paraphrase."

But since when, he wondered, had there been Latino gangs in Oklahoma City? Or had there always been Latino gangs and he'd just been too much of a clueless Northside teenager to know it?

And while he was at it, since when did a lot of people work downtown, who might flock through the doors of the Land Run if Candace opened them for lunch? When Wyatt had left Oklahoma City for the last time, twenty-six years ago, downtown had been a ghost town. Tumbleweeds rolling along Main Street, all the businesses moving north to new office parks in the suburbs.

"So the police just blew me off when I called them about the bird poop," Candace said.

"The bird poop?"

"This was last week. I came out after work and my car was covered with bird poop. I mean totally! You couldn't even see in the windows! It looked like a big piece of candy, that white candy I hate."

"Divinity," Wyatt said. He didn't like it either. "But Ms. Kilkenny, Candace—"

She thwacked him again. He hadn't even seen her hand move. "No! I know what you're going to say. No! The car parked right next to mine didn't have any poop on it at all. Neither did the car on the other side. Explain that!"

Wyatt stalled by taking a sip of his beer. Probably Candace had parked beneath a tree filled with birds. Probably kids had rearranged the letters on the signboard. Probably it was just the wind, sweeping down the plains, that had scattered the empty beer kegs.

This was the kind of case that Wyatt had been forced to take when he first started out in the business. Missing toy schnauzers and nursing-home feuds and, once, an elderly defrocked priest who was convinced that the mob had put a contract out on him because of a confession he'd heard—in 1968.

Oh, and cases like that—nobody ever paid on time. Nobody ever paid in full. The toy schnauzer tried to bite you, and the elderly defrocked priest kept putting his hand on your leg.

Wyatt took another long pull of his beer. He was going to make *Gavin* pay in full for this.

"So who do you think would want to do something like this?" he said. Other than, of course, the wind, the birds, and the Southside Locos. "Why would somebody want to do it?"

She looked at Wyatt with curiosity, like she wondered how he managed to tie his shoelaces every morning. "If I knew that," she said, "I wouldn't need you."

Fair enough. Wyatt flipped the page in his notebook. "So you inherited this place?"

"From Mr. Eddy." Candace nodded. "He was such a sweet old dude. And he used to crack me up, all these funny stories he had."

She explained how Mr. Eddy had visited Vegas four or five times a year to play blackjack. He'd gone through a bad divorce a few years before and had no kids, he was a lonely old dude, he liked the company of the dealers and cocktail waitresses more than he liked actually playing blackjack. Whenever Candace had a break, he'd buy her dinner in the food court and tell her stories of his life.

"Did you know one time he had to kick Elvis Presley out of here?" Candace said. "Elvis played this big show in town, at the old arena downtown right before he died, and afterward he stopped by the Land Run because he'd heard that the music was so good. But then Elvis started talking shit about OU football, and there was almost a riot. Mr. Eddy said he just about crapped his pants. He was only like twenty years old or something, and his mom, who owned the place, was out of town."

Wyatt paused to do the math. Elvis had died in '77 or '78. "Mr. Eddy was in his early fifties when he died? That made him an old dude?"

"Sure," Candace said. And then she grinned at him, a big white flash of teeth against her cinnamon skin.

"I'm only forty."

"And six-feet tall. I remember."

"So you and Mr. Eddy—"

"There was no sex!" she said. But really it was more like four exclamation points crammed into one sentence. *There! Was! No! Sex!*

"Okay, okay," Wyatt said, "I'll stop insisting there was."

"I know your mind's in the gutter just like everybody else's. Mine would be, too, I guess. But we were just friends. No matter what Mr. Eddy's brother thinks. Mr. Eddy always made me order some kind of vegetable at the food court, because it was good for me. He! Was! A! Sweet! Old! Dude!"

"Can we stop referring to him as an old dude, please?" he said.

"I was so sad when I heard that he died. I'd been wondering where he'd been. It was an aneurysm. And then when I heard about his will and that he'd left me this place . . ."

She re-created the moment by parting her lips slightly and letting her eyes go glassy with shock, like she'd just witnessed a vision of the Virgin Mary shimmering near the card catalogs.

"I just about crapped my pants!"

"But in a good way."

"Yeah! Shut up. I mean, nothing good like that ever happens to me!"

"Tell me about Mr. Eddy's brother," Wyatt said.

Candace groaned. The groan turned into a sigh. The sigh turned into a hiss.

"Say no more," Wyatt said.

"He wants me to sell him the Land Run," Candace said. "I told him no. I told him no like a million times! He can't get it through his thick head why I won't sell."

"And why is that?"

"I don't know. I mean, I know this is kind of a grody place and all, but . . ." She paused to take a look around.

Wyatt swiveled on his stool and took another look, too. All in all, the Land Run was in pretty decent shape. It was a dive, but no worse a dive than it had been twenty-six years ago. More than could be said for most things.

"But it's yours," he said.

"Yeah!" She checked to be sure he wasn't making fun of her. "Yeah. It's mine. And business is good! It's hard. You wouldn't even believe how hard. I sleep like four hours a night. But I'm the boss!"

Mr. Eddy's brother. Wyatt jotted it in his pad. He circled it.

Candace glanced up at the balcony. "You can come down and say hi for a minute. He won't bite. If he tries to bite, just bite him back twice as hard."

Wyatt looked up. A little girl, the five-year-old cutie-pie that Gavin had told him about, stared gravely down at him from between the bars of the balcony railing. She had fair skin, blue eyes, a messy tangle of blond curls.

"Where'd you steal her?" Wyatt said.

Candace laughed. "I know, right? She took after her dad. Not his personality, though, thank God."

Gavin hadn't mentioned the father. Candace wasn't wearing a ring. "Is he in the picture?" Wyatt said. "Her dad?"

"Brandon? No! I dumped his butt. We got divorced two years ago. A couple of months ago, he moved to Hawaii. He sends— Wait." She found a box behind the bar and pawed through it. She handed a postcard to Wyatt. A golden beach, silky blue waves, hula dancers. "He sends Lily a new one every week."

"That's nice of him."

"No. Ha. He just wants me to know how great his life is since I dumped his butt."

Wyatt flipped the postcard over. *"Greetings from paradise! The new place is great, right on the beach!"*

"See? A new one every single week. How he just got a raise at work, or a better job, or a new condo, or his new girlfriend is an Instagram bikini model from Australia. Like, right."

Wyatt realized that the little girl, Lily, had suddenly materialized next to him. As if she'd teleported soundlessly down from the balcony, like a vampire. She climbed up onto the stool next to him.

"What's your name?" she said.

"Wyatt."

She considered that. "Okay."

"What were you doing up there, lurking in the balcony?" Wyatt said.

The little girl looked at her mother.

"Hiding," Candace said. "But like an animal does, getting ready to jump out and get you. *Rrraarrrr!*"

"I wasn't," the little girl told Wyatt, her face grave. "Lurking. I was reading a book."

"Okay," Wyatt said.

She slipped off her stool and headed back to the balcony stairs, taking what had to be the most tortuously circuitous route possible, around every single table and chair on the floor, some of them twice. It made Wyatt dizzy just to watch.

"So," Candace said. She stood with her fists on her hips again, legs apart, astride the world. "What's the plan?"

Wyatt

CHAPTER 5

Wyatt started by interviewing the Land Run's staff as each employee arrived for his or her shift. Candace claimed they all loved her, but Wyatt intended to verify that.

The bartender was a woman named Dallas—in her early thirties, wearing a tank top that showed off shoulders and arms covered with elaborate tattoos. She told Wyatt that the new owner had raised wages across the board when she took over.

"She can be a firecracker," Dallas said, "but she treats me right."

Farcracker. The woman's Oklahoma twang surprised Wyatt a little, at odds with the tattoos and the silver hoop in her nostril. But why should it be at odds? *Times change,* he told himself.

"What about customers?" Wyatt asked. "Any problems recently?"

She considered, then shook her head. "No. Not that I can think of."

Not that I can thank of.

Fudge, the giant black guy who worked the door, said Candace was the best thing that ever happened to the Land Run. And not just because she'd bumped him a dollar an hour.

"She one of the *people,*" he said. "You know what I'm saying? She understand what it like, to be on your feet all night."

"I know what you're saying," Wyatt agreed.

"Her swag is *legit,*" Fudge said, and then watched to make sure Wyatt wrote that down.

The sound engineer, Jonathan, smelled like the inside of a bong and was not a fan of the new policy on shorter and less frequent breaks. Candace had won him over, though, when she let him start programming the walk-in music that played over the Land Run's sound system before bands went on. The late Greg Eddy had reserved this power for himself, much to Jonathan's frustration.

"Greg was a very nice dude," Jonathan said. "No doubt. But you know what he considered the best Pearl Jam bootleg of 2003? Perth, not Mexico Three. Yeah! And Bonner Springs wasn't even on his list. He said he *admired* Bonner Springs. Yeah!"

Neither Fudge nor Jonathan could remember any recent incidents with angry customers either. They couldn't guess who might be harassing—*totally* harassing—Candace.

After he finished with the staff, Wyatt went outside. He circled behind the Land Run. There was a square of cracked asphalt between the back of the building and a stockade fence that marked the property boundary. A rusted metal sign nailed to the fence said EMPLOYEE PARKING ONLY!

There were four cars in the lot, but Wyatt could tell that the ten-year-old Ford Focus belonged to Candace. She'd washed it but not quickly enough, and the bird shit had done a number on the paint job, which had puckered and faded in places. Wyatt studied the asphalt around the car. He wasn't sure what he was looking for. Something, anything, nothing.

A few feet away, he saw a crushed empty Coke can that the wind had blown against the stockade fence. He crouched and lifted the empty can. Beneath it were what looked like a few grains of sand, or rice, or . . . what? Wyatt picked one up.

Birdseed. The empty can on top had kept the seeds from blowing away, from being gobbled up.

Something, anything, nothing.

He walked back to his rented Altima and called Gavin.

"I told you the girl was a piece of work," Gavin said by way of a greeting.

"I'll give it another day or two, because she intimidates me, and I like her, and I agreed to do this. In that order. But there's probably no case. You're the one who explains that to her when I'm safely back in Vegas."

The silence of a man calculating pot odds. "All right," Gavin said finally.

"Let me ask you a question."

"Can I stop you?"

"What would you do if you wanted birds to shit all over somebody's car? Just the one car, precision bombing."

Wyatt could picture Gavin shifting in his office chair, custom-built to comfortably accommodate his bulk.

"Bread crumbs," Gavin said after a second. "I'd put bread crumbs all over the car. Or birdseed."

Wyatt nodded. Probably the birdseed he'd found beneath the empty Coke can meant nothing. Or maybe, if it meant something, just that the kids who rearranged the marquee letters had pulled another prank.

He dialed Laurie next. She sounded out of breath.

"You're not having sex with another guy right now, are you?" he asked.

"Just one guy? No."

"Good. Because I was getting ready to go buy you a present."

"I had a meeting downstairs, and I took the stairs back up. I'm in such bad shape."

"I beg to differ," he said. "Your shape could not be more ideal."

"Speaking of presents, I'm still holding my breath on that lime juicer from Williams-Sonoma. Don't blame me if your gin and tonic tonight is less limy than ideal."

Wyatt shifted his phone to the other ear. "It looks like I'm gonna be stuck here a couple of days."

"What? Where?"

"Here. I didn't tell you? I had to go out of town this morning. A job for Gavin. A favor. He came to me, if you can believe that. You should have been there."

Wyatt thought for a second that the connection had gone dead. "No," Laurie said. "You didn't tell me. Where's there?"

"Oklahoma City. The Paris, France, of Oklahoma. I'll be back by Thursday or Friday at the latest. Or die trying, believe me."

"Wyatt," she said. And then there was another second of silence.

"What?"

"Nothing. Love you."

Why? he wanted to ask.

That thought startled him, flashing up out of nowhere, like it belonged in someone else's head.

"Love you, too," he said.

He drove north: Reno to Broadway, Broadway to NW Twenty-third. On Western Avenue he passed the First Presbyterian Church and Fairlawn Cemetery. He remembered how O'Malley had announced one night, out of the blue, that you haven't lived until you've played Frisbee in a cemetery after midnight. So after the late show ended, after they'd cleared the auditoriums and cleaned the concession stands, everyone had piled into cars and driven out to Fairlawn. They'd played Frisbee till one or two in the morning, when the cops chased them off.

The past had power. The past was a riptide. That's why, if you had a brain in your head, you didn't go in the water.

But what was Wyatt supposed to do? Buy Laurie a lime juicer? Eat dinner and check in to a hotel and watch ESPN until he fell asleep? Just pretend that he wasn't already in the water, being gently tugged farther and farther from shore?

Yeah, pretty much, Wyatt admitted, that's exactly what he should do.

But instead—just one quick, harmless stop before he bought a lime juicer and ate dinner and watched a few hours of ESPN—he drove over to the Pheasant Run.

It was still there, at the busy intersection of NW Sixty-third and May Avenue, and it was still a mall of sorts—the May Market Plaza, according to the sign. What had once been the entire main building of the mall, two levels of shops, was now a giant Burlington Coat Factory, and the single-story wings had been expanded and opened up to direct parking-lot access. A Staples, a Bed Bath & Beyond, a discount shoe store.

The movie theater had been at the back of the mall, on the ground floor of the main building. Wyatt didn't need to step inside the Burlington Coat Factory to know that no trace of the theater remained. He knew, if he went inside, he wouldn't feel a thing.

He drove around back, to the parking lot behind the main

building. The two auditorium exit doors had been sealed off and plastered over, but the concrete steps remained, the metal handrails. Wyatt remembered sitting on those steps, leaning back against those rails. On break, after hours, with O'Malley and Theresa, with just Theresa.

He parked across the street but didn't get out of the car. The light had begun to soften. It was that time of the day when they always clocked in for the night shift, half an hour before the bargain matinee.

Wyatt, for the longest time, had not been able to understand what the female detective kept trying to tell him. His ears were still ringing. He was shaking. He was embarrassed because he couldn't stop shaking.

He'd been sitting in the parking lot behind the theater auditoriums. On a strip of grass between the parking lot and the street, in a blaze of ambulance headlights and police strobes. The paramedics had already checked him out. They couldn't believe, with all that blood, that none of it was Wyatt's. They smeared salve on his wrists, where the cord had cut into the skin, and gave him a Valium.

The female detective crouched next to him. Wyatt remembered that she wore the kind of square-toed black shoes that a man would wear. He didn't remember her face at all.

Was she young? Old? Was it tough being a woman in a man's world? Was that why she wore those shoes? Or were they just part of the departmental dress code?

What the female detective kept trying to tell Wyatt, what he couldn't understand, was that everyone else in the projection booth was dead. O'Malley had been shot in the head. Theresa had been shot in the head. And Tate, and Melody, and Karlene.

Mr. Bingham, too. Everyone was dead but him. None of the blood was Wyatt's.

Wyatt had been positioned, facedown, between Theresa and Melody. The gunshots were so loud that his ears hadn't stopped ringing for days. Even now Wyatt's right ear was only about half strength.

Why?

But he was too dazed to ask that question. That question would come later. So Wyatt just stared at the female cop's square-toed black shoes and shook his head and said, over and over again, "What?"

Why? Once that question came, it would never go away.

"You're lucky," the female cop told him, patting him on the knee. "This is your lucky day."

Julianna

CHAPTER 6

Julianna planned to buy DeMars dinner—she owed him a dozen dinners. When she called to invite him out, though, he said he'd pick up some ribs and bring them over to her place. She knew why. He wanted to snoop around, check the fridge, peek into the bedroom and make sure her bed was made.

She opened the door and gave him a hug, a kiss on the cheek.

"Go ahead, Detective," she said. "Check the fridge. Fruits and vegetables. Fresh towels in the bathroom. I am one together girl."

He chuckled. "Let's eat these ribs."

It had been more than a year since she'd seen him, but he looked the same as always. The ramrod posture, the gleaming brown head, the goatee flecked with silver. He'd had the silver in his goatee—no more, no less—when Julianna first met him, fifteen years ago. He'd inherited Genevieve's cold case when the original lead detective retired. He'd inherited Julianna.

"I can't believe Mayla is almost fourteen," Julianna said. She

knew better than to talk business when Charlie DeMars was
eating.

"Birthday in a few days. Almost tall as me."

"And how's Angela? Is she counting the days?"

"Says she is."

"Wait till you're home all day, in her way. Underfoot. See what
she says then."

"You right, you right. But how about you? There any young
gentlemen in the picture I need to know about?"

He'd been trying for years to marry her off. Trying to set her
up with the straight-arrow sons of his friends, lawyers and land-
men and architects. But Julianna had been in a real relationship
once, a few years out of nursing school, and it had ended badly. It
had started badly, with Julianna losing interest almost before the
boxes were unpacked.

"Julianna," Eric had always pleaded, "I want to understand you."

He was a nice guy. Julianna felt bad for him. She'd tried her
best. She and Eric had lived together for almost a year before he
finally recognized he was trapped in a burning building.

"At the moment, no," she said to DeMars now.

DeMars finished his ribs and stole one of hers. "So you doing
all right, I see."

"I've been doing all right for a long time now, DeMars."

"I know."

He was probably the kindest man Julianna had ever known.
She wished she could spend the rest of the evening chatting
about his daughters, his golf game, Kevin Durant's newly developed jab-step move. Julianna knew that nothing would make
him happier.

"I think I might have something," she had to say instead.

He didn't sigh or frown or shake his head wearily. "All right."

"You remember Abigail Goad's statement." She was the rancher's wife from Okeene, the third of the three eyewitnesses who had seen Genevieve after she left Julianna. She was the last person who saw Genevieve before she vanished from the face of the earth.

Genevieve had left Julianna outside the rodeo arena at dusk, approximately 7:30 P.M. At approximately 7:40 P.M., the first eyewitness—Genevieve's friend Lacey, who they'd run into half an hour earlier—saw Genevieve again, on the midway. The second eyewitness was a corn-dog vendor. He told police who canvassed the fairgrounds that he'd seen a woman fitting Genevieve's description around 8:00 P.M., farther down the midway, hopping over a pile of hydraulic cables and cutting behind a ride called the Himalaya. Although, on second thought, maybe the woman had blond hair instead of brown. And, on third thought, maybe it was the Ferris wheel, not the Himalaya. Maybe it was closer to 7:30. When he'd been pressed—Julianna read the cop's notes from the original interview—the corn-dog vendor admitted that yes, he and the rest of the crew at the corn-dog stand had burned a doobie or two earlier in the evening, and yes, that might conceivably have compromised his recollections.

But the third and last eyewitness—Abigail Goad, a rancher's wife from a small town in western Oklahoma called Okeene—was precise and matter-of-fact. She'd seen Genevieve on the other side of the fairgrounds, in Food Alley, the area where most of the food concessions were concentrated. She gave police a detailed description of Genevieve and described exactly what she had been wearing: jeans, sneakers, and a white BORN IN THE USA T-shirt. Abigail Goad had noted the T-shirt in particular because that morning there had been a letter to the editor in the *Daily Oklahoman* about how rock and roll was the devil's music and how the state legislature should bar Bruce Springsteen if he ever tried to make a tour stop in Oklahoma.

Abigail Goad remembered the time exactly, too, a few minutes before 9:00 P.M. She had been on her way to meet her husband and sons beneath the Space Tower. They had gone to look at the antique cars while she browsed the Made in Oklahoma Building.

"You remember how Abigail Goad said Genevieve was talking to a man in a cowboy hat," Julianna said.

"*Might* have been talking to a man in a cowboy hat," DeMars said.

The rancher's wife from Okeene had been fastidious in the interview she gave police. If she wasn't absolutely certain about something, she made sure to say so.

"*Might* have been. Okay." Julianna set her laptop on the table. She scrolled down the "Remember When in OKC" Facebook page until she found the photo. She clicked to enlarge it. "Look."

DeMars leaned over. The photo had been taken at night. In the foreground, blown out by the flash, a woman in her thirties grinned as she bit into an egg roll. Behind her was a food trailer with a sign that read—in red letters that were supposed to look like Chinese characters—YUM YUM FOO!

The photo caption said *"Fair Food 9/20/86!"*

"That's where Abigail Goad saw Genni," Julianna said. "Food Alley. I remember that Chinese place."

She remembered the *smell* of the place. Hot grease, burned meat, ginger, and garlic. Julianna had wanted the fried sweet-and-sour pork for dinner, doused in an orangish sauce that looked excitingly radioactive, but then changed her mind at the last second and had an Indian taco instead.

"All right," DeMars said.

"Keep looking." She knew he'd already seen the man in the

cowboy hat. At the edge of the frame, his back to the camera, standing in line at the barbecue trailer next to the Chinese place.

"Juli," DeMars said. "Come on, now."

"Half the guys at the fair had cowboy hats. Right? And we don't know what time this photo was taken. We don't even know what night, really. The caption could be the wrong night." The State Fair of Oklahoma ran for eleven days in 1986, from Thursday, September 18, through Sunday, September 28. Genevieve had disappeared on the first Saturday night of the fair. The police had not begun to canvass until Tuesday. "But just listen to me. What if this photo really *was* taken on the night of the twentieth? What if the lady who took it has other photos, too? She must have, right? And what if in one of those photos we can see his face? The guy in the cowboy hat?"

Julianna didn't say it aloud, what else she was thinking: *What if in one of those photos we can see* her?

When Genevieve disappeared, cell-phone cameras were twenty years in the future. Otherwise Julianna would have had hundreds of online fair photos to pore over, thousands of them, each dated and time-stamped, each individual flash illuminating some dark corner of that night.

Julianna could close her eyes and see that BORN IN THE USA T-shirt like it was right in front of her. Genevieve had bought it at a concert in Dallas the year before. A lot of her friends were into metal and thought Bruce Springsteen was faggy. The headband he wore, the stupid dancing on MTV. But Genevieve had been a fan before he became so popular, when his music was muddy and brooding. On the album cover for *Darkness on the Edge of Town,* he looked scrawny and grimy and haunted, like someone who could have lived down the street from them.

"All right," DeMars said. "What if?"

He meant that it didn't help them—so what if they found a photo with the face of an anonymous man in a cowboy hat? They'd never be able to identify him. They'd never be able to find him. Abigail Goad had passed away in 1988, after a stroke, so they would never even know for sure if he was the man that Genevieve had been talking to. That she *might* have been talking to.

But Julianna refused to think that way. You had to open every door and see what was behind it. DeMars, as kind and smart as he was, didn't understand that. This was his job. It was just a job.

"Maybe I'd recognize him if I saw his face," Julianna said. "Maybe he was someone Genni knew, or someone we'd seen earlier. He could have been following us. Or maybe the lady who took the photo remembers something about him. Maybe she saw something."

DeMars slowly smoothed a hand over his silver-flecked goatee and waited. His hands were big, the color of some rich, dark wood.

"I sent her a message on Facebook," Julianna said. "The woman who posted the photo. But that was a week ago, and I haven't heard back. So I thought there might be something you could do."

"Juli."

"DeMars, just—"

"Listen to me now. You been talking."

"Fine."

"We do this, don't we? Every year or two."

"This?" There was more poison in her voice than Julianna intended. DeMars pretended not to notice.

"You want an answer," he said. "I understand that. But there's not an answer. There'll never be an answer. It's been twenty-six years. Your sister is gone, and you are here. That's the only answer there is. You are here."

They sat in silence. Julianna closed her laptop and timed her breathing to the slow green pulse of the sleep-indicator light.

"Oh, DeMars." She smiled. "You think I'm still that girl. I'm not."

"All right."

At certain points in her life, Julianna's obsession with what had happened to her sister—with finding an *answer*—had threatened to consume her. But now she had a life and a career. Friends. Fresh towels in the bathroom.

She felt so angry, suddenly, that she wanted to pick up her laptop and smash it against the wall. Because who was to say she *shouldn't* be consumed by what happened to Genevieve? Not Detective Charles DeMars, for whom this was just a job. Fuck him.

She smiled again. "All I wanted, De Mars, I just wanted a favor. I thought you might be able to do me a favor. If you can't, no problem. No hard feelings."

He was an excellent cop and could read her mind. She guessed he would try now to put her on the defensive, on her heels. *You don't think I care about all this, Juli? You don't think I care about you?*

Julianna didn't understand why he hesitated. "What?" she said.

He smoothed his hand over his goatee. "Crowley popped up."

For a moment she didn't register the name. And then, for an even longer moment, she didn't register what DeMars was saying.

"What?"

"State system flagged him, so they let me know. Because the investigation's still ongoing, officially. He applied for a job down near Chickasha, so they ran a background check. The Indian casino down there."

Julianna was so surprised she felt as if she were in a dream, the kind where you tried to run but couldn't move, where you tried to cry out but couldn't speak.

Crowley. Christopher Wayne Crowley. She hadn't thought about him in years. He was the carny who worked at the booth where Julianna won her stuffed Pink Panther. Early on, in the first few days after Genevieve disappeared, he'd been the primary suspect in the case—the only suspect, really, the only solid lead. Julianna told the detectives how he'd flirted with Genevieve and invited her to meet him later. Genevieve, at the time, probably thought Julianna had missed all that, too enraptured by her new Pink Panther to notice. Julianna, of course, missed nothing. It was Genevieve she had been enraptured by, and she monitored her big sister's every breath with fascination.

Crowley had been arrested twice before, once for possession and once for assault and battery. The police picked him up and questioned him for hours. He denied at first that he remembered Julianna, then denied that he'd ever invited her to come by his trailer. Finally he admitted that he'd invited her but swore she never showed up. He'd been disappointed when she hadn't.

The police couldn't find any physical evidence in the trailer or his car, but they were certain he was lying. Julianna had seen the official transcripts of the interview. She remembered a handwritten note about Crowley that some cop had jotted in the margin of the transcript: *"Lies like he breathes."*

Crowley stuck by his story. It was Abigail Goad, the rancher's wife from Okeene, who cleared him. She saw Genevieve alive and well at 9:00 P.M. in Food Alley. Ten minutes earlier, at a 7-Eleven store a block from the fairgrounds, Crowley had been arrested for trying to shoplift a six-pack of beer. He spent the night in Oklahoma County Jail.

So much for the one suspect, the one solid lead.

A year later Crowley was convicted on another drug charge, in Tennessee. Julianna, fourteen years old, a freshman in high school, found the address for the prison and wrote him a letter. Even though Crowley could not have murdered Genevieve, Julianna was convinced he knew more about what happened that night than he'd told police. *Lies like he breathes.*

He didn't reply to that first letter, or to any of the others she sent him. The last few, in the winter of 1991, were returned with a stamp on the envelope that said the addressee was no longer in custody. Fitch, the detective who had the case at the time, checked for Julianna. He found out that Crowley had served his full sentence and been released without condition: no parole officer, no forwarding address, no trace.

DeMars tried again to track Crowley down when he inherited the case—when . . . well, Julianna begged and bitched and bullied. But he came up empty, too, and so did Julianna every time she used the Internet to find Crowley on her own. DeMars told her that Crowley was probably dead. He told her to forget about him, and eventually she had.

But now.

"He's here?" she said. "In Oklahoma?"

"He doesn't have any answers, Juli. He never did."

"Let's make sure."

"We did. Long time ago."

We. Meaning the police, the original detectives in the case, all the people like DeMars for whom the case was just a job.

"When?" she said. "When did Crowley pop up?"

"Few months ago."

"A few months ago." She pressed her palms flat against the table. "And you just now . . ."

Julianna realized he hadn't been planning to tell her at all. Face-to-face, though, he'd had a pang of guilt, of pity, something. She nodded. "I see."

"I talked to him. Went down there, where he's staying at. Crowley said what he said before. He doesn't know anything."

"Why didn't you let me know?"

He didn't bother answering that.

"Where's he staying?" she said.

"I told you. I already talked to him."

"I want to talk to him myself."

"You don't."

"Where is he? He didn't get the casino job." Not with two felony convictions and prison time.

"No."

"You have to tell me."

He leaned back, ramrod straight, and lifted his chin—the move he used to show you that he wasn't playing. "Is that what you think?"

Her neighbor's kids were in the backyard, running around with their dog. Julianna could hear the laughter and panting and happy growling.

She went into the kitchen and cut two slices of the lemon meringue pie she'd bought at the German bakery DeMars liked.

"My favorite," he said when she set the plate in front of him. "Look at that."

"I'm sorry," she said. "I was out of line."

He ate the slice of pie in four big bites, then squared up the loose crumbs with his fork and ate those, too. "You don't want anything to do with him, Juli," he said. "He's bad news. You have to trust me on that."

"I do."

"All right."

"What about the other thing? The woman on Facebook?"

"Give it another week," he said. "You don't hear back from her about the photo, I'll see what I can do."

"Thank you, DeMars."

He reached across the table and took her small hand in his big one. He leaned in and let the lines on his forehead soften. This was another one of his moves, the gentle father. "Forget about Crowley. All right? He doesn't have the answer. You are here. That's the answer. Forget about him."

"I will," she said, and gave his hand a squeeze. "You're right. I promise."

Wyatt

CHAPTER 7

Wyatt's father was stern and humorless, a buzz-cut high-school basketball coach. One time the school principal made him phone a player on his team to apologize for an incident at practice. Wyatt's father had thrown a basketball and nailed the kid in the head with it. Wyatt's father called the kid and told him he was sorry—he'd been aiming for the kid standing next to him. Wyatt's mother laughed, but his father didn't understand why. He just looked at her like he always did, with vague and patient disgust.

It wasn't until Wyatt landed the job at the Pheasant Run—in September of 1985, the day after his fifteenth birthday—that he realized just how lonely and unhappy his life had been up until then.

His first day of work at the movie theater, O'Malley came over to Wyatt and asked him who his favorite band was. Wyatt panicked. He was fifteen years old. O'Malley was seventeen and a half. They inhabited different universes.

"I don't know," Wyatt said.

"I like that," O'Malley said, nodding. "An open mind. I'll bring you some tapes. Come here."

O'Malley straightened the knot of Wyatt's official Monarch Theaters tie. The tie was black polyester, to match the slacks. The blazer was orange.

"Thanks," Wyatt said.

"What's your name? You want some Junior Mints or Raisinets? Here's what we do. Just take a couple of pieces from every box, two or three max, then put the box back in the case. Ingenious, if I do say so myself."

It *was* pretty ingenious. This was back before boxes of candy were sealed or shrink-wrapped.

"Michael," Wyatt said. "My name's Michael Oliver."

"Michael?" O'Malley said. "Hmm. You look more like a Heinz to me."

So that first day O'Malley made Wyatt a name tag that said HEINZ. This was back when you used a special device to punch letters into an adhesive plastic strip.

"Heinz!" Melody said when she saw the name tag pinned to the lapel of Wyatt's blazer. She was a ferocious-looking black girl, cornrows and muscular forearms, who rarely ever stopped giggling. "What is that? Like the ketchup? What kind of name is that? I thought I heard every crazy white-boy name there is. Heinz!"

"He's Czechoslovakian," O'Malley explained gravely. "A refugee from political persecution. His family makes sausage."

"In the Sudetenland," Wyatt said, because his sophomore history class had been studying World War II. O'Malley grinned, and in that instant Wyatt felt—he could still feel it now, remembering the moment twenty-six years later—like he was home, like he'd come home.

Wyatt had never seen cornrows before, not up close. He'd never seen a girl with forearms like that. Melody smelled like Strawberry Splash Bubblicious and popcorn grease. Everyone who worked at the theater smelled like popcorn grease. It baked into your pores like pottery glaze.

The cashier, that first day, had been Karlene. Oh, Karlene. She was a talker. O'Malley would watch and wait until Mr. Bingham approached Karlene to check the box-office numbers, and then O'Malley would slide over and ask Karlene a question designed to set her off. *Hey, Karlene, how was your day off yesterday?* At which point he'd slide back away and leave Mr. Bingham trapped there for the duration of Karlene's never-ending answer.

Karlene was tall and tan and stacked, as they used to say back then, with a riot of frosted blond hair that made her look like a girl rushing the stage in a Whitesnake video. Rumor had it that O'Malley and Karlene had slept together a time or two before he started going out with Theresa. O'Malley refused to confirm or deny.

"Always respect the privacy of your paramours," he told Wyatt once.

O'Malley said shit like that all the time. Wyatt didn't know where he came up with it.

The girls at the theater, the cashiers and the concession girls, wore orange polyester uniforms that matched the doormen's blazers. The hem fell just above the knee, and a zipper ran all the way down the front of the dress, top to bottom.

Those zippers drove Mr. Bingham crazy. He tried occasionally to enforce the official Monarch Theaters policy of full zip, but the girls just laughed at that. It got hot in the concession stand during a rush, and the uniforms were already ugly enough—no way was a teenage girl with any self-respect going to compound the embarrassment by zipping all the way up to the neckline.

"A free society," O'Malley said, "cannot legislate cleavage."

"I couldn't do it even if I wanted to," Karlene said. "My boobs are too big."

She demonstrated: zip up, zip down, zip up, zip down.

O'Malley, Wyatt, and Grubb watched. After a minute, Janella behind the candy case grabbed the soda gun and hosed them down with water.

Once their shift ended, the girls changed out of their uniforms so fast you wouldn't believe it. They used the cramped little room at the bottom of the projection-booth stairs, across from the manager's office, where Mr. Bingham posted the week's schedule next to the clock and the metal rack of time cards.

Karlene always changed into tight, acid-washed jeans. She was a talker, a teaser, and a hugger. When Wyatt stocked the hot-dog rollers, she'd tell him to stop playing with his wiener, and then, as everybody laughed, she'd give him an apologetic hug.

Karlene was the second person shot in the head, after Mr. Bingham. Grubb was next, and then Theresa, and then Melody, and then O'Malley. Wyatt, lying between Theresa and Melody, should have been number five.

One week earlier Karlene had turned eighteen. They'd celebrated her birthday when they got off work, in the small neighborhood park across the street from the back of the theater. Most nights after the late shift, if the weather was good, the theater employees hung out in the playground there, drinking and talking and passing around the giant doobie that Grubb always had on hand. The night of Karlene's birthday, one of the other girls, Wyatt couldn't remember which, had brought a cake from IGA.

Heinz! Heinz from the Sudetenland! Wyatt hadn't thought about that in years. Melody, he remembered, had said one crazy white-boy name was good as another and refused to call Wyatt by his real name from that point on. Grubb, genial and permanently stoned, thought Heinz *was* Wyatt's real name. Karlene always called him "Sugar Pop" or "Pop Tart." O'Malley called him Michael, usually, but sometimes Heinz and sometimes "Little Buddy." Tate called everyone, male or female, "Man." Mr. Bingham rarely called Wyatt anything. *You. You there.*

When Mr. Bingham finally noticed the HEINZ name tag that Wyatt had been wearing for a couple of weeks by then, he assumed correctly that O'Malley had been behind this violation of the Monarch Employee Handbook and wrote O'Malley up. And then he took Wyatt aside for a heart-to-heart warning: Fair or not, Mr. Bingham said, Wyatt would always be judged in life by the people with whom he chose to associate himself.

Mr. Bingham had been such a dick, an officious and petty dictator, incapable of any genuine human emotion. O'Malley called him the Little Cheese.

The alarm on Wyatt's phone finally chimed. He'd barely had time to brush his teeth when Candace called.

"Wake up," she said. "Are you awake yet?"

"Who says I ever went to sleep?" Wyatt countered. "Maybe I don't plan to rest until justice is done."

"Shut it. I want an update."

"It's six o'clock in the morning, Candace."

"So?"

Wyatt stood by the window and watched dawn break, the line of the horizon smoldering like a fuse. His room was on the top floor of the hotel. Back in the eighties, the Marriott on Northwest Expressway had been the fanciest hotel in town, with the hottest nightclub and the best restaurant. Tate had plans, once he turned eighteen, to get a job as a barback at the nightclub. He said he'd heard the tips were outrageous, man, and so were the girls.

"Give me a day or two," Wyatt said. "You'll be the first to know when *I* know something."

Candace made the sound she made—groan to sigh to hiss.

"I have to make breakfast for Lily," she said.

"Sorry to keep you. I don't know what I was thinking."

"Get to work!" she said, and hung up.

WYATT SHOWERED, SHAVED, and got dressed. It was too early to eat breakfast—he was still on Vegas time—so he just made a cup of instant coffee in the room and drank it. He flipped through his notebook and found the number that Candace had given him for Jeff Eddy, the late Mr. Eddy's older brother.

When Wyatt called, Jeff Eddy's assistant told him that she might be able to squeeze him in that morning. But only, the assistant's tone made clear, if she moved heaven and earth to make it happen.

Wyatt drove downtown. Once there, he had a hard time getting his bearings. The buildings were the same, the old First National Bank and the courthouse and Leadership Square, but . . . the people. There were people everywhere! People and cars and buses and the morning hubbub of a real downtown, a real city. Men in suits, women in suits, a surge of pedestrians whenever a light changed. A line of people waiting outside a hip-looking coffee shop at the corner of Park and Robinson. A woman in yoga pants walking a yellow Lab. Trees in full autumn flourish along the median. Wyatt tried to think. Had there been trees down-town before?

And no, actually, not all the buildings were the same build-ings. There was the glittering glass skyscraper that Wyatt had seen coming in from the airport—fifty or sixty stories high. A huge new library, a new brick-faced arena. The old Colcord Hotel, a dead shell when Wyatt left town in 1986, had been renovated, as had the Skirvin, now a Hilton. Even the Myriad Gardens, he saw, now resembled actual gardens and not the surface of some barren and inhospitable moon.

Wyatt sat in his car at a red light, taking it all in.

Times change, he told himself again. *Life goes on.*

Get over yourself.

Jeff Eddy's office was in Leadership Square. Wyatt rode the elevator to the fifth floor and followed the engraved brass point-ers to a door marked EDDY COMMERCIAL REAL ESTATE APPRAISAL. He stepped inside. A woman behind the reception desk eyed him suspiciously. She was in her early sixties, with lots of makeup and a wine-colored silk scarf tied around her neck in the French fashion. At the corners of her mouth were the deep creases of a lifelong frowner.

"Yes?" she said, frowning.

"Wyatt Rivers. I have an appointment with Mr. Eddy. You must be his assistant. Emilia? Iago's wife in *Othello* and the most interesting character in that play, if you ask me. We spoke earlier."

She gave him more of the same frown. "Mr. Eddy is on a call," she said. "He'll be with you when he can."

When, in other words, the power dynamic had been clearly es-tablished. Wyatt had wondered, riding the elevator up, if Jeff Eddy would make him cool his heels or not. Now Wyatt knew something about the guy—just a little something, but something—he hadn't known before.

Wyatt took a seat on the sofa. The reception area was decorated with framed posters of former Oklahoma University running backs on two walls and current Oklahoma City Thunder basketball players on the third. Wyatt stood back up and crossed the room to examine a poster of Heisman Trophy winner Billy Sims. This put him side by side with Jeff Eddy's assistant, Emilia. It was always more effective to approach from the side if you wanted someone to lower her guard, rather than head-on.

Billy Sims, in his crimson-and-cream Sooner home uniform, leaped over two tacklers. The stands behind him were a sea of soft-focus crimson and cream.

"Cruise director," Wyatt said.

A moment went by. Jeff Eddy's assistant turned her head. "Pardon me?"

"I'm guessing you were a cruise director at one time in your life," Wyatt said. "Back in the eighties, when cruise ships were still kind of glamorous, a glamorous way to travel."

He finally looked over at her. She was still frowning at him, but in a different way now.

"Am I way off?" Wyatt said.

Another moment went by. "I was a stewardess," she said.

"No kidding."

"How did you know that?" She had turned all the way around in her chair to face him.

"I didn't," Wyatt pointed out. "Just a guess. The way you tie your scarf, like the French do? It's very cosmopolitan. And before you jump to any conclusions, I'm not being a smart-ass."

A smile—maybe, possibly—began to swim its way up to the surface of her face.

The door to the inside office opened, and a man stuck his head out. Jeff Eddy. He saw the empty sofa and looked surprised. Then he glanced around and saw Wyatt.

"Come on," he said. "I don't have all day."

"MY LITTLE BROTHER, I loved him dearly, but sometimes he didn't know his ass from a hole in the ground," Jeff Eddy said. "Pains me to say so."

It didn't seem to pain him, Wyatt noted. But he nodded politely. Jeff Eddy was jowly and sunburned. A golfer, Wyatt suspected. His body was pear-shaped, and so was his head. The shelves behind him were loaded with signed footballs, signed basketballs, a signed basketball shoe that looked big enough to fit a giant.

"So I take it you didn't think it was a wise decision," Wyatt said, "for him to leave the Land Run to Ms. Kilkenny?"

Now *that,* Wyatt noted, seemed to genuinely pain Jeff Eddy.

"A wise decision? A wise decision. Look. Greg was a child. He was gullible. He was gullible his whole life. I loved him dearly, like I said. He was my brother. But he was . . . okay, my complete dumb-ass of a brother."

Wyatt wondered if maybe the worst part of being dead was not being able to defend yourself against tools like Jeff Eddy. Though maybe when you were dead, you didn't give a shit what the tools said about you. Wyatt hoped, for the sake of the dead, so.

"That's one big-ass basketball shoe," Wyatt said, pointing to the shelf. "I apologize for stating the obvious."

Jeff Eddy shifted around to look, then shifted back again without comment.

"So she hired you?" he said. "The stripper? Why?"

"There have been a couple of incidents at the Land Run. Ms. Kilkenny thinks someone might be harassing her."

"Harassing her? And she thinks it's me?"

"She doesn't know who it is. That's where I come in."

"Well, it's not me." Jeff Eddy shook his jowly, pear-shaped head. "Unbelievable."

"She never said it was. And she's not a stripper."

"Excuse me. Former stripper."

"She's not that either," Wyatt said. "She's a former cocktail waitress."

Jeff Eddy shifted around again to glance at the big-ass shoe. "That's a signed Kevin Durant game-worn shoe from the first game he ever played in a Thunder uniform. Everybody in the city claims they were there for that game, but I was."

He lifted his chin, as if daring Wyatt to make such a claim.

"Not me," Wyatt said. "I live in Las Vegas."

"Look," Jeff Eddy said, "whatever she is, she's a gold digger. I know for a fact she took advantage of my brother. I know for a fact she manipulated him into leaving her the Land Run."

"But you didn't contest the will?"

Wyatt knew enough about probate to know that even if Greg Eddy's will was ironclad, his brother could have used lawyers to keep the estate tied up for months.

"I'll tell you the truth. I should have contested it. But at the time—what happened hit me hard, Greg going down like that. You know he was only fifty-two years old? My little brother."

"Who you loved."

"And I'll tell you the truth again. I really didn't want the damn place. It's a dump. It's not worth a damn thing, coming or going. I needed the hassle like I need a hole in the head."

Wyatt waited for Jeff Eddy to address the obvious question. When he didn't, and glanced with impatience at the big watch on his wrist, Wyatt had to ask it.

"So why are you trying to buy it now?" he said.

"Look," Jeff Eddy said. "The place is a dump. But it's been in my family for forty-six years. My brother worked there since he was fifteen years old. I don't know. The more I thought about it . . . maybe I'm sentimental."

"It's the principle of the thing," Wyatt suggested.

He wondered if anything Jeff Eddy had told him was true. He began even to doubt that Jeff Eddy had even been there for the first-ever game with Kevin Durant in a Thunder uniform.

"It is! It is the principle of the thing! You think the place is worth anything? Ask that client of yours what she pulls down on a good week. A good week. And here."

Jeff Eddy opened a drawer and lifted out a file folder. He found a sheet of paper and set it in front of Wyatt.

The county assessor's report. The Land Run was worth even less than Wyatt had expected. And he hadn't expected much.

Jeff Eddy took another sheet from the folder. "These are the comps. The commercial properties nearby that have sold over the past year."

Wyatt looked over the comps. Per square foot, they were even worse than the assessment.

"Can I take this?" Wyatt said. "And the assessment?"

"Be my guest. Have Emilia make copies for you."

Jeff Eddy checked his watch again. He made a production of it: a snap of the wrist, a lot of aggrieved staring and heavy throat-clearing.

"Are we done here?" he said. "This was a courtesy."

He stood up. Wyatt stood up.

"Just one more question," Wyatt said. "Two."

"Look. I have work to do."

"Fur pie?" Wyatt said. "Anal surprise?"

He checked Jeff Eddy's reaction but saw nothing there, one way or another.

"What the hell are you talking about?" Jeff Eddy said.

WYATT GOT INTO his car and drove up to NW Twenty-third, where he found free Wi-Fi at an indie coffee joint called Cuppies & Joe. It was in what used to be a 1920s bungalow. The new owners had preserved the original floor plan—living room with fireplace, dining room, bedrooms, all with the original, unrefinished wood floors. Lots of windows, vintage mismatched furniture, cupcakes made from scratch. The young, pretty cupcake maker came out of the kitchen, her apron dusted with flour, and poured Wyatt a mug of excellent coffee.

The old house next door had been turned into an art gallery. The old house next to that one was now a trendy-looking barbecue joint.

Across the street was a plasma clinic. Now, *that* was the NW Twenty-third that Wyatt remembered.

He spent an hour slogging across the Internet—such was the glamorous life of the modern-day gumshoe—but found no clues to Jeff Eddy's newfound interest in the Land Run. Wyatt didn't buy all that bullshit about principle, about sentimental value, and he didn't like how the most recent tax assessment Eddy had given him was from June. The latest comp was from August, and it was now October. Sometimes the best lie was just the truth left to ripen on the branch too long.

Wyatt stepped outside and called the city desk at the *Daily Oklahoman*.

In every city, at every newspaper Wyatt had ever worked, there was always one crotchety old lifer—a city-desk reporter or an editor with a bad comb-over and high-waisted slacks, an ink-

and nicotine-stained know-it-all who nursed ancient grudges and critiqued everyone else's copy, who ignored HR's pleas to please, please clean out his firetrap of a paper-crammed cubicle.

A woman answered the phone.

"I've got a question for you," Wyatt said. "At every newspaper, every city desk, there's always this one crotchety old-timer. You know the guy. He's always critiquing everyone else's copy and his cubicle is a firetrap."

The woman laughed. "Who is this?"

"But he knows the town. He's the guy who really knows his town, inside and out, past and present." Wyatt recognized the possibility, really the probability, that the species he was seeking had gone extinct when the newspaper industry tanked—layoffs, buyouts. "I'm a private investigator from out of town. I need to get the lay of the land."

There was a moment of silence. Wyatt thought the woman might have killed the call. But then she said, "You probably want Haskell. Bill Haskell. Hold on."

The line beeped a couple of times and then clicked.

"What?" a man's voice said. Strunk & White: Omit needless words.

Wyatt explained who he was and that he was working a case involving the Land Run. "You know it?"

Haskell grunted. "In the old Fenton Spry library building. What about it?"

"I've been shown evidence," Wyatt said, "that the property isn't worth much. While I trust the evidence, I don't trust the person who gave it to me."

"What's the evidence?"

"The tax assessment and some real-estate comps. But they're a few months old. I can't find anything online that might have

affected the value of the Land Run in the meantime." Wyatt
thought Bill Haskell might like that part, so he gave it an extra
nudge. "The Internet, as incredible as this might seem, has its
limits."

Haskell grunted again. "The almighty Internet."

"Do you know the inspiring story of John Henry versus the
steam shovel?"

"John Henry died at the end of the story."

"I don't want you to die, Bill. But I thought you might know
someone who might know someone who might know someone."

"Is that what private investigators do? Ask other people to investigate for them?"

"I'll buy you lunch," Wyatt said. "Or dinner. The best restaurant in town. And yes, that's how it works a lot of the time."

Haskell's third grunt was the charm. "I'll see what I can do,"
he said. Wyatt gave him his number, and Haskell hung up without saying good-bye.

Wyatt checked his watch. It was almost noon, and he was starv-
ing now. He got into his car again and drove over to Classen Boulevard. Back in Wyatt's day, everyone called Classen just north of
Twenty-third "Little Saigon." Now there were official street signs
that were more politically correct: THE ASIAN DISTRICT. Most of the
business names were still Vietnamese, though. Pho restaurants and
jewelers and law firms, travel agencies and pain-management clin-
ics. The bottom of one plastic sign had been sheared off in a storm.
All that was left was the top line, EXTENDED PAIN.

Wyatt picked a pho restaurant at random. Inside, the windows
were fogged from the steam rising off the bowls, and most of the
clientele hunched over the bowls were Vietnamese. Two good
signs. A third was the smell. That was the best sign.

The waitress brought Wyatt a bowl of broth and noodles and

skirt steak, rare, with a giant pile of fresh cilantro, sprouts, and greens on the side. Limes, hot sauce. Wyatt took a taste and left his body. He was sucked back through time and space to a pho restaurant just like this one. Maybe it *was* this one. Who knew? Back in '85 or '86, all the clientele had been Vietnamese, not just most. It was the first time he'd ever tasted food like this. O'Malley, who'd brought Wyatt here after a stop at Rainbow Records, seemed to know everybody in the place. He slapped backs and shook hands as he led Wyatt to a table.

Wyatt and O'Malley had made the trip to Rainbow Records almost every week, to barter free movie passes for cassettes. O'Malley had introduced Wyatt to the Replacements, the Pretenders, R.E.M. After the last show of the night, if Mr. Bingham went home before the doormen and the concession girls finished cleaning, O'Malley would go up to the projection booth and pop a cassette into the theater sound system. He'd crank the music so loud that the walls of the auditorium would vibrate. Sometimes the girls, Karlene and Janella, would climb up onto the narrow ledge in front of the screen and dance. Melody, too, once in a while. Never Theresa.

Karlene, who looked like a girl in a Whitesnake video, danced like one, all that frosted blond hair whipping around. Janella swayed to a secret inner groove. Melody—Melody could *dance*. Theresa would watch from the back of the auditorium and, if Wyatt was lucky, smile.

On the night of the robbery, they were all waiting for Mr. Bingham to go home so they could put in a cassette and crank the music in the auditoriums. O'Malley gathered them together in the storeroom to toast the end of the shift. It was a new tradition he'd started, the latest of many. Vodka in waxed-paper Dixie cups. O'Malley and Theresa and Karlene and Melody and Grubb and

Wyatt. Melody didn't drink but attended the ceremonies anyway. She sat on a stack of empty soda tanks, snapping her strawberry Bubblicious. O'Malley had them raise their Dixie cups and repeat after him: "Here's to dear old Boston, the home of the bean and the cod!"

Wyatt had no idea where O'Malley came up with the shit he came up with.

Wyatt's back was to the storeroom door when it banged open. In the time it took him to turn around, he was sure Mr. Bingham had busted them.

O'Malley said, "What the hell?" Grubb stood up too fast and lost his balance. Karlene screamed. Theresa grabbed Wyatt's wrist and squeezed hard. That's when Wyatt knew something bad was happening. Until then he didn't know if the rubber pirate mask was somebody's idea of a joke.

Of them all, O'Malley kept his head. He stayed cool. "Hey," he told the robber in the rubber pirate mask, "get out of here."

Wyatt, then and now, couldn't believe the balls on O'Malley. For a second it seemed the robber might actually back out of the storeroom and shut the door behind him. Was there, possibly, an alternate universe where the robber in the rubber pirate mask backed out of the storeroom and shut the door behind him?

But he didn't. "Everybody out," he said, waving his gun. "Let's go."

"Stay cool," O'Malley said. Talking to the robber, talking to the rest of them. "Okay. It's no biggie. We're all cool."

He led the way. Grubb next, then Melody. Wyatt saw the robber check out Karlene as she passed, his eye on her. Just one eye—the rubber pirate mask had a rubber eye patch. It was a terrible mask for a robbery. Who wore a one-eyed mask to a robbery?

In the projection booth, O'Malley tried once more to save them.

"Wait a second," he told the robbers, fighting against the cord that tied his hands behind his back. O'Malley tried to turn over and sit up. He had great faith in his ability to talk his way out of anything. "Just listen."

"Shut up," a robber said, the one who'd peeled the pantyhose off his head. Wyatt couldn't move. He was too scared, his hands were tied too tight. From the corner of his eye, he saw the robber lift his shotgun and bring it down on O'Malley's head.

Mr. Bingham did nothing, said nothing, absolutely useless as always. Theresa's face was turned toward Wyatt, but her eyes were closed. Wyatt closed his eyes, too. He could smell the perfume Theresa always wore. It sounded like Melody was sobbing, but really she was praying.

PleaseJesuspleaseJesuspleaseJesusplease.

The first gunshot, so unbelievably loud, was almost a relief. Wyatt knew that all this would be over soon.

The waitress had come back. She looked at Wyatt's bowl and then glowered at him.

"What's wrong?" she said. "You don't like?"

He took out his wallet and paid his check. "Just too much," he said.

It was too much. He shouldn't be here. He should never have come.

Julianna

CHAPTER 8

Julianna located Ben in the break room. His scrubs today: a deep, rich burgundy. Papal, almost, lacking only an ermine collar. He was talking to Donna, who listened with great interest. Who pretended to listen with great interest.

"Ben?"

He didn't love interruptions. He smiled, his beard parting—two rows of small, too-white teeth.

"Hi, Julianna. We were just discussing the schedule."

"Ben. I'm not feeling so great."

"Oh," Donna said, and clucked sympathetically.

Ben continued to smile at Julianna. Her shift had just started. He didn't love unexpected developments. He did not.

"I think I better go home," Julianna said.

Ben's management style owed much to the principles of non-violent resistance. He was Gandhi, prepared to smile and wait until the British surrendered to exhaustion and stopped beating him with their rifle butts.

"Diarrhea," Julianna said. "You know. *Whoosh.*"

Ben's beard finally closed back over his teeth.

"Oh, no!" Donna said. Cluck, cluck. Trying to help Julianna out but overdoing it.

"Did you take some Imodium?" Ben said.

"Ben," Julianna said. "I don't know if I want to talk about my diarrhea. Do you?"

He did not. He made a quick decision.

"Go home!" he said. His idea now. "Get well!"

Donna sent a text before Julianna was even out of the building: LIAR.

Julianna sent one back: WHO ME?

OUTLET MALL?

AND PEDI MAYBE. A lie on top of a lie.

The parking garage was deserted, her windows tinted, so Julianna changed out of her scrubs right there, in the front seat of her car. She pulled on a pair of jeans, a sweater. She caught a glimpse of herself in the rearview mirror. Would Genevieve even recognize her now? Julianna wondered. Likely not. When Julianna saw old photos of herself, age ten, eleven, twelve, she saw a girl who was still a girl: flushed cheeks, always smiling, honey-colored hair, honey-colored eyes that hid nothing from the camera.

Julianna knew, without a shadow of a doubt, that she'd recognize Genevieve now. Genevieve was already a woman when she disappeared, almost eighteen years old, the woman she was going to be. Time would have altered only her edges, her surfaces. Genevieve's skin, Julianna suspected, might show the years. All those hours she spent working on her tan, all that cocoa butter and baby oil. No one had warned her. And probably she would have softened in certain places, rounded out in others. But she'd still be a knockout. Even more of one. She'd still be Genevieve.

Julianna tried a smile for the rearview mirror, but that didn't help. It wasn't the same smile. Genevieve wouldn't recognize it in a million years.

She checked the location of the Indian casino on her phone. It was just south of Norman, I-35 the whole way. She made a left out of the parking garage in case Ben was spying on her. Not a far-fetched possibility, and he knew she lived north. *Okay, Ben, two can play at this game.* She circled the block and caught the highway off Fifth Street.

It was a warm October day, sunny and so blue. In fact, Julianna had warned Genevieve about laying out. In seventh grade Julianna learned about the ozone layer, about melanoma. But when did Genni ever heed a warning? Julianna remembered a quote Genevieve had found somewhere. It became her mantra:

When faced with two evils, choose the more interesting one.

Genevieve claimed it was from Aristotle. Or Shakespeare. Her story shifted. Years later Julianna searched for the quote and discovered that its source was the dissolute Scottish aristocrat who founded the Dewars whiskey empire.

Genevieve would still be a knockout. She would still be wicked and hilarious. When Julianna imagined her now—alive, age forty-three—this was how she imagined Genevieve: married to a rich, handsome guy ten years older than she was and sleeping around on the side with a rich, handsome guy ten years younger than she was. Having the time of her life, you better believe it.

It took Julianna about twenty minutes to reach Norman. She drove past the exit to the university—her alma mater, though so much of her undergrad years were now just a soft, tuneless blur. Julianna had started smoking pot her freshman year and thought it might save her life. It hadn't, but she'd given it every chance in the world. She'd given it the old college try.

The Indian casino was five minutes farther south, almost to the town of Chickasha. Julianna didn't know the name of the tribe who owned the casino. The Chickasaw? That seemed a reasonable guess. One of Oklahoma's Five Civilized Tribes. Which, a title like that, had taken all the fun out of studying them in junior high.

The casino was enormous, with an even more enormous parking lot. Ten-thirty on a Tuesday morning and it was packed with cars. Julianna pulled in to an empty space. She didn't have a plan, not really.

Inside, the casino was what she had expected. Smoke and clang, wolfish retirees bent over the slot machines, slapping away. A cocktail waitress passed by. Julianna stopped her and asked how to find HR. The waitress pointed to a door on the other side of the floor.

An unsmiling security guard. Two doors and a hallway. Finally Julianna found herself in a small, windowless office, across the desk from a chipper blonde in her early twenties. French nails, pearl earrings. The whole package. *GKODB!*

GKODB stood for "Go Kappa or die bitch!" It's what the Kappa sorority girls at OU always said to each other. Julianna's first roommate had pledged.

"So," the chipper blond sorority girl said. "You're interested in joining our family here?"

Julianna noted that none of the casino employees she'd encountered so far—the cocktail waitress, the security guards, this girl—looked Native American. Maybe the casino had made the tribe so rich that its members no longer had to work jobs like these.

"I'm very interested, actually," Julianna said. She remembered the note scrawled in the margin of Crowley's interview transcript: *Lies like he breathes.*

"Sweet!" the chipper blonde said. "You know you can do all this online now? It's super easy. But it's even better you're here in person!"

She rummaged around for an application. Julianna looked at the bank of file cabinets along one wall. Crowley's failed job application might be in one of those cabinets. And Julianna might be able to find it, if she could think of a way to get the sorority girl out of the office for a few minutes. The cabinets might be locked. If Crowley's application had been submitted online, Julianna was screwed. She hadn't even considered the possibility. There was a computer on the desk, but it was almost certainly password-protected.

Crowley was the missing piece. He had to know something—*something*—about what had happened to Genevieve. If Crowley didn't know, who did?

Julianna realized that the sorority girl had stopped rummaging around and was just staring at her now, smiling.

"You don't remember me, do you?" she said.

Julianna tried to place her. She was too young. She would have been way behind Julianna at OU, fifteen years or more. She looked as if she'd barely graduated.

There was something vaguely familiar about her, though. The brightness of her eyes. Her French nails.

"My name's Ariel Figg," the girl said. "Last May? I threw up everywhere from the anesthesia, and you were super sweet about it."

"Oh." The hospital, the recovery suite—not college. Julianna tried again to place her. Last May. She still couldn't do it. "Oh, of course."

"I had a D&C," the girl said. "I don't remember what that stands for? But Dr. Bazile, I remember he described it kind of like scooping out a cantaloupe. He was trying to make me feel not so scared beforehand, but I thought that was pretty gross."

Dilation and curettage, a minor surgical procedure that cleaned out the uterus after a miscarriage.

"Dr. Bazile is a good doctor," Julianna said, which was more or less true.

"I'm doing great now," the girl said. Ariel. "Good as new!"

"I'm glad."

"God has a plan. At least that's what I've always heard." She laughed. "Are you a Christian? Never mind. I have another question."

Julianna knew what it was going to be. She wondered what the chances were—that she'd run into a former patient here.

"Why do you want a job here when you're already a nurse?" the girl said.

The file cabinets along the wall appeared to be unlocked. One drawer was pulled partway out. Julianna could ask for a glass of water. That might give her a few minutes alone in the office. She could say that yes, she was a Christian, too, and she wanted to join the family here at the casino because she wanted a less stressful career, one in which the emotional toll— bonding with your patients, suffering as they suffered—was not so heavy. *And would it be too much trouble to get a glass of water, please? Ariel?*

Instead, though, Julianna said, "I don't. I don't want to work here."

The girl's expression remained bright and chipper. "Oh!" she said. "You don't?"

"I wanted to get an address. I wanted to find a way to get the address of a man who applied for a job here. It's the only way I know how to find him."

Julianna hesitated, then decided to see what the truth would do to that bright, chipper expression.

"He might know what happened to my sister," she said. "She disappeared twenty-six years ago and was never found. Her body was never found. She was kidnapped and murdered."

Nothing happened to the girl's expression. At least nothing that Julianna had expected—no shock or horror, no flush of embarrassment. The girl fingered one of her pearl earrings, and her bright eyes searched Julianna's face with interest, with curiosity.

"I'm just thinking about God's plan," she said after a long moment.

"Okay," Julianna said.

The girl reached across her desk and pulled the computer keyboard over.

"What's his name?" she said.

"Crowley," Julianna said, surprised. "Christopher Wayne Crowley."

"I shouldn't do this." The girl looked back up at Genevieve and laughed. "But fuck it, right?"

GENEVIEVE'S DISAPPEARANCE FROM the state fair had been news for about a day. Okay, maybe for a couple of weeks. She was beautiful—the *Daily Oklahoman* ran her picture with every story, a photo of her from the previous year's U. S. Grant High School yearbook. Genevieve had thought the photo made her look bucktoothed. She'd thought her ears, in general, were freakishly small. It didn't, they weren't.

"You don't think my ears are too small, do you?" Genni would say. "Do you think people notice my tiny ears?"

And then she'd turn to Julianna with her eyes so crossed you almost couldn't see the irises, just wet white jelly. It was demented. Julianna would shriek, mostly with laughter.

Genevieve who could keep a straight face forever, even when she was crossing her eyes like that, would say, "What is it? It's my tiny ears, isn't it?"

Oh, my God, do you remember that poster of Scott Baio you had? You thought I'd erased his eyes. You were so mad! You were twelve or thirteen. Genni loves Chachi, Genni loves Chachi. I thought you were going to kill me. I had to show you—it was just white construction paper that I'd cut out and Scotch-taped over Scott Baio's eyes. I'd had to cut out dozens of white construction-paper eyes before I got it just right. He looked so scary! You told me that if the real Scott Baio went blind, it would be my fault. I cried and cried. Do you remember?

Genevieve had a little black-and-white TV down in her basement room. After *Joanie Loves Chachi* was canceled, they watched *Charles in Charge*. They watched *The Facts of Life* and *One Day at a Time*. Julianna was crushed when *One Day at a Time* was canceled. She had loved the show because it was about two sisters. Julianna was Valerie Bertinelli, and Genevieve was Mackenzie Phillips.

Julianna had even suggested they start calling each other by the characters' names— Barbara for Julianna and Julie for Genevieve.

"I know!" Genevieve had said.

"Genni!"

"Let's not and say we did!"

One time, when Genevieve's disappearance was still news, Julianna had gone into the kitchen to make cinnamon toast for breakfast. The two detectives were there, drinking coffee at the table. They didn't see her. The older detective tapped the newspaper in front of him, the photo of Genevieve. Julianna heard him say Genevieve had a face that played.

It hadn't played for long, though. One problem, you see: Genevieve was almost eighteen years old when she disappeared. If she'd been younger, fourteen or fifteen, it would have made for a more compelling story, a *simpler* story. But because Genevieve was almost eighteen, her beauty—the directness of her gaze in that yearbook photo, the sly humor in her smile—had cut both ways. Julianna could imagine now what a lot of people back then must have thought when they saw that photo in the newspaper or on the flyers that their neighbor Carol helped staple to telephone poles all over town. Genevieve looked like a girl who was looking for trouble. Was it really such a big shock that she'd found it?

And she'd grown up on the Southside, near Capitol Hill. That didn't help. Genevieve was an indifferent student and not on the cheerleading squad. Her father: part Mexican, gone. Her mother: the kind of woman who married a part Mexican.

And, of course, new news kept crowding in, elbowing Genevieve aside. There was apartheid in South Africa and OU football and Patrick Duffy returning to the TV show *Dallas*. (The entire last season had been a dream!) In the middle of October, police tracked down the men responsible for the movie-theater massacre back in August and killed them in a shoot-out. That was all that Linda Cavanaugh on KTVY Channel Four talked about for days. In November there was Iran-Contra and a molester of the elderly who climbed through the windows of nursing homes. In December the molester was caught. A crash on the Broadway Extension killed an entire church choir. Genevieve disappeared again, from the news this time.

Crowley by then had disappeared as well. No new leads had

emerged. No old leads paid off. January, February. The detectives stopped coming over every few weeks to give Julianna's mother an update. The grim young one would just call now, to say that they continued to pursue every possible avenue of investigation.

Carol's husband, Joe, came home from work one evening that spring and saw Julianna sitting on the front steps of the house on Twenty-seventh. He parked at his house and then walked back over, across the lawn lush with purple henbit and dandelion. For a few weeks in the spring, the weeds in Oklahoma City were beautiful. Joe sat down next to her. He smelled like the garage where he worked—like grease and men.

"Sometimes," he said after they sat there in silence for a while, "life doesn't make sense. You understand that?"

Julianna had gone inside without a word and shut the door behind her. She thought that might have been the last time she spoke to Joe. He and Carol moved that summer, to Colorado. Julianna learned later that the detectives had looked at Joe as a possible suspect. They'd looked at just about every man and boy who'd ever crossed paths with Genevieve. All the guys at school she'd ever gone out with, all her co-workers at Sonic, all her neighbors, old and new. Everyone had an alibi. Everyone checked out. Joe and Carol had been in Dallas the first weekend of the fair. Denny, the boy who lived down the block had been in bed with a broken ankle, suffered the day before while scoring a touchdown against the Carl Albert Titans.

But Joe and Denny and the others were never real suspects. Crowley was the only real suspect, at least until he wasn't. He'd been there. Genevieve had been on her way to meet him. He had to know *something*. It was inconceivable he didn't, no matter what DeMars said.

Crowley, after all these years. Julianna had put him so far out of her mind that he'd ceased to exist for her. And now, suddenly, here he was.

She realized her hands were shaking. Her thinking, though, was steady. DeMars had warned her that she didn't want anything to do with Crowley. Julianna *didn't* want anything to do with him. She was just going to ask him a few questions. She just was going to find out, for herself, what he did or did not know about Genevieve.

She put her hands on the steering wheel and squeezed. She was parked down the block from the address the girl at the casino had given her. The address was a crappy little house in a neighborhood of crappy little houses, just off South Robinson, only a few miles from where Julianna and Genevieve had grown up. Every house on the block had an old car up on blocks, or a kiddie pool turned upside down in the weeds, or windows blocked off by bedsheets, or a scrawny dog up on its toes behind a rusty chain-link fence, panting and peering over. There was one beautiful old oak tree. Someone had hung a tire swing from the thickest branch.

Crowley's house was no better or worse than the others. The windows were blocked off by bedsheets and what Julianna guessed were black plastic lawn bags. She didn't see a dog.

She got out of her car and locked it. Noon on a school day, almost no one around. Two men wrestled what looked like a gravestone out of the bed of a pickup truck and carried it into the house with the beautiful old oak tree. They never even glanced at Julianna.

She climbed the cracked concrete steps to Crowley's porch. She took a breath, held it, and then knocked. She waited, knocked again. Her hands were really shaking now, so she stuck them in the back pockets of her jeans. She tried that, then took them out of her pockets and folded her arms across her chest.

The door opened. He looked down at her.

"Yeah?" he said.

He was so much older, so much heavier. Julianna had prepared herself for this moment driving here, but still it was a shock. The big sagging gut, the face seamed and creased and sagging, too. A wiry gray goatee. Tangled gray sideburns and eyebrows.

His eyes, though—still so blue. And his shoulder-length hair, greasy and dark and streaked with gray, was hooked behind his ears exactly like it had been hooked when he handed Julianna her Pink Panther. Handing it to Julianna but watching for Genevieve's reaction.

He'd been twenty-nine when Genevieve disappeared. That would make him, now, fifty-five years old.

"Christopher Crowley?" she said. A stupid question. Of course it was him.

"What do you want?" he said. Shifting with a wince from one foot to another. His blue eyes were alert, alive, moving over Julianna and then past her—to the yard, the street, up and down the street.

The tattoo of the snake on his forearm had not aged well. The lines were blurred and broken, the blue ink faded. He had a diamond stud in the lobe of his right ear. Julianna couldn't remember if he'd had it in 1986.

"My name is Julianna Rosales," she said.

"Who?"

"My sister was Genevieve Rosales."

His eyes moved back to her. He winced again and started to shut the door.

"I just want to talk to you."

"I got nothing to say."

"I just want to talk to you," Julianna said.

"I told that black cop."

She put her hand on the door to keep him from closing it. He looked at her hand.

"I wrote you letters when you were in prison," she said. "A long time ago. You never answered them."

"Move your hand. I'll tell you the one time."

She moved her hand. "I just want to talk to you," she said. "Five minutes."

His eyes had moved back to the yard, the street, the houses across the street.

"Leave me alone," he said, and shut the door without looking at her again.

Wyatt

CHAPTER 9

At a stoplight Wyatt flipped through his notes. If somebody was screwing with Candace, he concluded, there was a strong possibility that Jeff Eddy was the one doing the screwing. He had motive—he wanted her to sell him the Land Run—and he was definitely a tool.

But. Wyatt just wasn't feeling it. Not yet at least. Jeff Eddy felt wrong. Or maybe he felt too right, too on-the-nose.

On the other hand, though, in Wyatt's experience as both a newspaper reporter and then a private investigator, he'd found that real life was often much simpler than the twisty-turny plots you saw on television. A lot of times, the bad guy was exactly who you thought the bad guy was.

If there even *was* a bad guy, Wyatt reminded himself. If somebody really *was* screwing with Candace.

Wyatt's phone rang. Laurie. He started to answer it but then realized that the light had changed from red to green. The drivers behind him, polite Oklahomans, refrained from honking. Wyatt waved and pulled in to the intersection.

His uncle lived in an old neighborhood along the edge of Memorial Park, on a tree-lined street of two-story Prairie-style houses with sweeping eaves and deep porches. At one time this had been among the most desirable places in the city to live, right off the old Classen Boulevard streetcar line. By Wyatt's day, though, mandatory school busing had done a number on neighborhoods like this, driving out everyone but the old, the poor, the old and poor.

Now, he saw, the area had perked back up. For every junker with a quarter panel duct-taped in place, there were a couple of late-model Subarus. For every slump-shouldered house on a broken foundation, there were two others with fresh paint and new walkways.

His uncle, Wyatt's last living relative in Oklahoma City, still lived in the house where he and Wyatt's father had grown up. It was in decent shape. The paint on the shutters was peeling, but the flower beds brimmed.

Pete was sitting on his porch, in a wedge of sunlight that had managed to sneak beneath the overhanging eaves and between the columns. He peered out when Wyatt got out of his car.

"Who's that?" he said.

"Uncle Pete," Wyatt said. "How are you?"

"Mikey! Why, my favorite nephew!"

His one and only nephew. Wyatt smiled. His uncle had been cracking the same joke, in the same deadpan baritone, since Wyatt was in diapers. Wyatt realized this was the only part of his trip back to Oklahoma City that he hadn't been dreading.

"Come here, Mikey," Pete said. "Let me get a look at you."

Wyatt had prepared himself for a shock—it had been twenty

years since he'd seen his uncle in person—but Pete looked just the same. The hedgehog head of gray hair, a face like an old baseball glove you found in the attic. "Lived-in" was probably the polite way to describe it. Pete had looked seventy-five years old when he was fifty. Now, closing in on eighty, he still looked seventy-five. Shoulders back, chin up, and a smile, as always, tugging at the corner of his mouth.

Only his hand gave him away. It weighed nothing when Wyatt shook it—bone and vein and crumpled onionskin paper.

"I'm back in town," Wyatt said. "I thought I'd drop by and say hello."

"Well, come on in."

Wyatt followed him inside. It wasn't too bad—just a hundred years' or so worth of old newspapers and magazines and junk mail piled everywhere. Pete settled himself on the sofa. Wyatt took a seat next to him. The house smelled like Old Spice and feet, which made Wyatt want to open a window. His father had worn Old Spice, too. Wyatt didn't hold that against Pete.

"Mikey," Pete said. "Son of a gun. I remember when you were just a twinkle in your father's eye."

"I find that hard to believe," Wyatt said.

His uncle knew what he meant—Wyatt's father was not the twinkly sort. That smile tugged at the corner of Pete's mouth.

"How have you been, Uncle Pete?" Wyatt said. He called his uncle once a year or so to say hello. The last time had been . . . last year at Christmas? Or maybe the year before? Wyatt wasn't sure.

"Just fine, just fine. How do you like my flowers out front?"

"An impressive display."

"The gay fella who lives next door, he helped me with those." His uncle lowered his voice, conspiratorial. "You'd never guess it."

Wyatt lowered his voice, too. "That he lives next door?"

His uncle's rumbling baritone chuckle filled a room better than most laughs. "Son of a gun," he said. "Mikey!"

Pete had always been the opposite, in every possible way, of Wyatt's father. He was generous and kind and funny and, when Wyatt was growing up, pretty much constantly drunk. In 1995 he stopped drinking—joined AA and stopped cold—the day after Timothy McVeigh blew up the Murrah Federal Building in downtown Oklahoma City. Pete's wife, Beverly, had worked in the Social Security office, on the side of the building that took the main force of the blast. Beverly needed an emergency root canal the morning of April 19 and had called in sick. She was on the other side of town when the bomb went off.

Beverly passed away in 1999. Pete remained sober. He told Wyatt once that he'd stay sober through all eternity to pay off the extra four years he got with her.

"I remember," Pete said, "you were a worker. You were the worker in the family. When you set your mind to something. Oh, my."

Wyatt was surprised. "Me?"

"Nose to the grindstone. Remember what Daddy always said?" Pete's eyes floated for a second, lost. It was like watching a car hit a patch of ice and fishtail. "No. Your father, I mean to say. He was the worker. You're Michael. I know that."

"I know you do," Wyatt said.

His uncle rubbed the rolled arm of the sofa, back and forth.

"I haven't lost my marbles yet," he said. "Not all of them. You're the detective. The private eyeball."

"That's right."

"Florida. Tampa, Florida."

"That's right. Vegas now, though. The last couple of years."

"And before that—Minnesota. You worked for a newspaper. And somewhere back east before that. Massachusetts."

"Now you're just showing off," Wyatt said.

"I remember one time we went downtown to see the Harlem Globetrotters."

Wyatt had been eight or nine years old. A bleak, gray Sunday in February. Inside, though, it was all color and heat. The laughter had leaped around the arena like a living thing.

"I only had enough money for a Coke or a pack of Globetrotter cards," Wyatt said. "You said—I don't remember what you said. But you told me to buy the Coke. When I got home, maybe it wasn't even until the next day, I put my hand in my coat pocket."

And there were three packs of Harlem Globetrotter trading cards his uncle had purchased on the sly, had slipped into Wyatt's pocket while he wasn't looking.

"I remember another time," his uncle said. "You called me from school. No, I think the school nurse did. I picked you up, and we went for a drive. Just the two of us driving around and shooting the breeze. You were almost old enough to drive. I told you I'd give you a lesson, just as soon as you were—"

He stopped himself as the memory sharpened and he realized the circumstances of the drive.

September, or early October. Wyatt had returned to school after missing the first two weeks of his junior year—a month after what happened at the movie theater. Going back to school wasn't awful. Nobody stared, nobody whispered. The locker doors banged like they always did, the chalk tap-tapped on the blackboard, the warm narcotic breeze drifted through the classrooms in the afternoon and put everyone to sleep. For an entire class period, sometimes, Wyatt could do it—he could imagine that nothing in him or the world had changed.

But how, all the other times, was he supposed to sit in geometry class and not go out of his mind? He probably did go out of his mind. One day, when he was very, very sure he could not stand another minute in his own skin, he lied and told the school nurse he had a stomachache. He lied and told her his parents were in Chicago. So she called his uncle to come get him. And Wyatt lived to fight another day.

"We drove around the lake," Wyatt said, "and then we stopped for a root beer at Coit's. At Coit's? I think so. Or was it the A&W on Wilshire? I think the A&W was already gone. Both places had the frosted mugs, I remember."

His uncle rubbed the arm of the sofa. He found a thread and picked at it. A crumpled Kleenex was tucked into the wrist of his cardigan.

"That was a hard time for you, Mikey," he said. "I know it was."

When Pete dropped him off at home that day, he'd turned to Wyatt. He'd been drinking, probably, but his eyes were always clear, his baritone always steady, no matter how drunk he might be. He'd put his hand on Wyatt's shoulder and told him . . . what, exactly? Wyatt couldn't remember. He remembered the root beer in a frosted mug, the hand on his shoulder.

A week or two later, Wyatt's father found a job coaching basketball at a high school just outside San Diego. An old navy buddy of his was the principal there. They'd moved in early November.

Wyatt's phone rang. Bill Haskell, the reporter he'd asked to find out about the Land Run's true value. Wyatt excused himself and moved to the porch.

"It's a new map," Haskell said.

"A new map?"

"No. A new *MAPS*. Capital *M*. Capital *A*. Capital *P*. Metropolitan Area Projects. A series of sales-tax initiatives to fund civic improvements. The most recent one, a few years ago, paid to upgrade the arena to NBA standards. There was another one before that for the public schools, one for Bricktown. The last measure passed with sixty percent of the vote."

"You know, I enjoy a buried lede as much as the next man, Bill."

Haskell grunted. "The drums have begun to beat for a new MAPS. So I'm told. Softly at this point—only a few people are in the know thus far. I talked to my man in the mayor's office, and he refused to confirm nor deny."

"Which means he confirms."

"Yes."

"What's the new project?"

"A convention center, a central park, a residential and retail district."

"Let me guess," Wyatt said.

"South of Reno," Haskell said. "Out to the eastern edge of Keeler Park."

Wyatt pulled up Google Maps on his phone. The Land Run, at Walker and SW Sixth, was located two blocks from Keeler Park.

"Bill," he said, "I owe you one."

Wyatt clicked off. So that explained why Jeff Eddy had changed his mind so abruptly and now wanted to get his hands on a so-called dump like the Land Run. If city development money came pumping into the neighborhood and made the desert bloom, the land beneath the Land Run would bloom right along with it.

Double the value? Triple? Wyatt didn't know. He didn't really care. The exact lushness of the bloom was beside the point.

He pulled up the numbers on the most recent MAPS ballot measure. He confirmed that it had passed with 60 percent of the vote.

He thought for a second and then called Jeff Eddy's office. His assistant, Emilia, answered.

"Emilia," Wyatt said, "I feel like we've been drifting apart."

"Mr. Rivers," she said, in such a way that Wyatt thought there might be a 30 percent chance she was not 100 percent unhappy to hear from him. "How may I help you?"

"The boss man, please. Tell him it's important. Tell him I've got some earthshaking news."

"Hmmm," she said. Or maybe it was "Hummph."

After a second, Jeff Eddy came on the line. "What do you want?"

"I've got some earthshaking news," Wyatt said. "You're not gonna believe this, but the Land Run might be worth more than we thought. I found out about this tax initiative that's in the works, the very early works. I'm quoting my source. Big development money for the neighborhood. Can you believe it? I hope you're sitting down. I wanted to be the first to tell you."

Wyatt could hear Jeff Eddy breathing.

"Wait," Wyatt said. "You didn't already know about all this, did you? I feel stupid now."

Wyatt heard a pop and a buzz as Eddy hung up on him.

A few seconds later, Wyatt's phone rang. Eddy again. Wyatt wondered if he was calling back just so he could hang up on him again.

"Look," Eddy said. "I think what's happened here, I think we've got off on the wrong foot."

His voice was friendly and folksy now, a big hearty slap on the back.

"Did we?" Wyatt said.

"Let's get together again. I'd like to fill you in on a couple of important facts about the situation. Before . . . you know, this gets more complicated than it has to."

Wyatt was pretty sure he knew what that meant. "Before I tell my client, in other words, that the Land Run is worth a lot more money than she thinks it is?"

Was it possible to hear someone grimace? Wyatt discovered that it was.

"No, no," Eddy said. "That's not it at all. I just want you to have all the facts when you talk to her about this. The big picture. That sounds reasonable, doesn't it?"

"It sounds reasonable," Wyatt agreed.

"Hey, now, I got an idea," Eddy said. "You like football? Why don't you come on out to the OU game with me tomorrow night? I've got club seats on the forty-yard line."

"I generally prefer to sit in the stands," Wyatt said.

Jeff Eddy laughed the fakest laugh of all time—the three-dollar bill of laughs.

"We'll grill some steaks beforehand," he said, "drink a few beers, get to know each other a little bit. What do you say? And in the meantime we put all this other business on hold."

"Sure," Wyatt said, "why not?"

AFTER THE GUNSHOTS Wyatt remembered nothing. He was deaf. He was blind. He didn't open his eyes until he felt fingers press against his neck and he heard someone yell, as if from a great distance away, "This one's alive!"

Wyatt's left eyelid wouldn't open at first. It was like a window that had been painted shut. His eyelid was painted shut with blood. He heard someone say, as if from an even greater distance away, "Oh, shit. Oh, shit. Oh, shit."

The janitor had arrived at seven to clean the theater restrooms. Mr. Bingham hadn't been there to let him in, so the janitor tracked down Disco Otis, the security guard. Disco Otis had peered through the glass doors and noticed the bloody footprints leading away from the projection-booth stairs. He called the police. The first cops arrived at 7:37 A.M., which meant Wyatt had been lying there in the darkness for almost six hours.

Wyatt learned all that later. To him, there in the projection booth, it was as if no time had passed at all. He heard the last gunshot and felt the cop's or paramedic's fingers press against his neck, one beat right after the other. Wyatt had thought at first that the fingers and the voice belonged to one of the robbers. He waited for another, final gunshot. He prayed for it.

He remembered very little of what happened next. Someone must have cut the cord that bound his wrists behind his back. Someone must have led him back down the narrow projection-booth stairs and across the lobby and out of the mall. The female detective in the black, square-toed shoes? Maybe her. Wyatt remembered her shoes but not her face. He remembered her voice, gentle but urgent, as they sat on the strip of grass behind the auditoriums and police lights strobed across them.

"Is there anything else you remember, Michael?" she'd said. "About what happened? Try hard, hon. Anything at all?"

Wyatt had told her everything he remembered. He told her everything again. And then the two male homicide detectives took over. The one Wyatt remembered, the one who was obviously in charge, was an older guy with acne scars. Detective Siddell. His voice was less gentle than the female detective's.

"Look at me, Michael," he said. "Look me in the eye. Are you telling us the truth?"

Wyatt didn't understand. Why did the detective with acne scars think he wasn't telling them the truth? Wyatt, at that point, didn't understand anything.

He described the robbers, as best he could, over and over and over again. *Big nose, I think? A mustache. Red hair. Reddish hair. I think. In their twenties. Or thirties. Darker hair. Big eyebrows. Like a skeleton's face, sort of, bony. The other one was taller.*

Wyatt had caught barely a glimpse of the two robbers without their masks on. He'd been too scared to look at them. He hadn't seen the other robber's face at all. Wyatt had been facedown on the floor of the projection booth. All he could see, really, was Theresa's face next to him. Their shoulders touched. Her eyes were closed.

The next thing he remembered, he was in a room in a hospital. And then he was in a different room of the hospital with his father and two different detectives. Or maybe these detectives were Oklahoma State Bureau of Investigation agents. Wyatt remembered realizing that he'd lost his black clip-on bow tie. Mr. Bingham took five dollars out of your paycheck if you lost your bow tie.

The police, Wyatt learned later, considered him a suspect at first. He supposed they had to. Five people dead and Wyatt, miraculously, unharmed. The scene in the projection booth made sense only if Wyatt had been working with the killers. But it made no sense that Wyatt had been working with the killers. He was a fifteen-year-old kid with no criminal history. And he was telling the truth. He was telling the police everything he knew. They must have realized that pretty quickly.

But *why?* There had to be some reason the robbers had killed everyone else but left Wyatt alive.

"Do you have any idea, Michael," Detective Siddell had asked, in his ungentle way, "why you're still here and the others are . . . gone?"

Wyatt had no idea.

Why?

Did he think one of the killers knew him? Did he think that a gun jammed before the killers could . . . finish? Did he think something—some noise from downstairs, maybe?—caused them to flee? Did he think they lost track of their victims and mistakenly believed that Wyatt, covered in the blood of the others, was dead? What did the killers say before they left the booth?

Wyatt had no idea. He hadn't heard them say anything before they left the booth. He was deaf and blind. He didn't even know that the three men had left.

In October, all the way across the country in Kingman, Arizona, a woman called police to complain about the loud music coming from the apartment below hers. A county sheriff's deputy responded. He knocked on the door of the apartment and identified himself. A shotgun blast tore through the door. The deputy, before he died from his wounds, managed to crawl to his car and radio for backup.

An Arizona state trooper by chance was less than a minute away. He reached the apartment complex as three men were attempting to flee the scene. A bullet shattered the trooper's right elbow, but he switched his weapon to his left hand and managed to keep the three men pinned down until two more county deputies arrived. In the gunfight that followed, two of the men were killed. The third man shot himself in the head when more cops showed up and he realized he was surrounded.

Investigators found—discarded on the floor of the apartment in Kingman, beneath the couch—a key to a motel room in Oklahoma City. The manager of the motel confirmed that three men had rented room number 7 at the Sooner Be Here Inn on the 39th Expressway from June 29 to August 16. When police in Oklahoma City searched the weed-choked vacant lot next to the motel, they found an empty night-deposit bag, flecked with dried blood.

Detective Siddell, the one with acne scars, showed Wyatt photos of the three men who had died in Kingman. Mug shots. All three men had done time. They had done time early and often.

"Are these the guys?" Siddell asked. He'd become, after that first night and day, Wyatt's primary law-enforcement contact. Everything Wyatt said went through him. Everything Wyatt learned came from him.

"Yes," Wyatt said. He stared at the photos of the faces spread out on the table. He tried to understand.

"Do you know them? Do you know one of them from somewhere? Do you recognize their names?"

Wyatt stared and stared. He felt deaf again, blind. He didn't understand.

"I don't," he said.

Siddell didn't ask Wyatt if he was sure. Siddell knew it. He gathered up the photos and slid them into a manila file folder.

"I don't understand," Wyatt said.

Why am I still here and all the others gone?

That was the only question that remained, but now there was no one left alive who could answer it.

"Who knows?" Siddell said.

Ballistics had matched two of the guns in Kingman with the two guns that had been used in the projection booth. The case was closed. Justice had been served.

Why am I still here and all the others gone?

Wyatt sat at the bar in the Marriott, his laptop open. The bartender came back over, and Wyatt ordered a plate of pasta. He glanced at his empty glass of scotch and did a double take, shock and horror.

The bartender, a young guy, laughed. He poured Wyatt another three fingers and tried to sneak a peek at the screen of Wyatt's laptop. Wyatt turned it toward him so he could see.

"I just created a dummy Facebook account," Wyatt said. "What you have to do, though, you friend your target's friends first, before you friend your target. That way he'll confirm without even thinking twice about it. But will I be able to gather anything useful from Jeff Eddy's Facebook page? I can't say for sure, Andrew. Probably not. But there's an improvisational quality to all this. Like playing jazz."

The bartender's smile was uncertain.

"I'm a private investigator," Wyatt said.

"No shit?" the bartender said.

"No shit."

The bartender had more questions, but a couple of businessmen at the other end of the bar were flagging him down. "Sorry," he said, and headed off.

He did seem sorry to go. Or maybe Wyatt just wanted to think that. Or maybe it was Wyatt who didn't want him to leave, not before his pasta arrived and he could focus his attention on that.

On the way back to the hotel, Wyatt had taken May Avenue instead of the highway, so he could drive past the Pheasant Run again. The Burlington Coat Factory that used to be the Pheasant Run Mall. Wyatt remembered how the interior of the mall had been designed to look like you were outside in Paris or New Orleans, with brick floors and lantern-top streetlamps and wrought-iron railings along the second-floor balcony. Directly across from the movie theater was a brick fountain that never worked.

On her break sometimes Theresa would sit on the edge of the broken fountain and lean her head against the streetlamp and smoke a cigarette. Wyatt would stand at the ticket box and make funny faces at her through the plate-glass front of the theater. The lobby camera connected to the monitor in Mr. Bingham's office could see only his back. If Wyatt worked hard enough at it, if he made enough funny faces, Theresa might give him the finger and half a smile.

Wyatt thought about his uncle. Was memory like a river that slowed over time to a trickle? Or was it like a house with many rooms that became a house with fewer rooms and then finally just a single room you could never leave?

Was that the worst fate in the world? It depended, Wyatt supposed, on what room you ended up in.

Wyatt's first week at the theater, his first several weeks, Theresa had ignored him completely. O'Malley told him not to take it personally. Theresa took but mild interest in the petty affairs of doormen.

O'Malley and Theresa were a couple at the time. They'd been together for almost a year, on and off. Or, as O'Malley put it, waxing and waning, waning and waxing. Wyatt remembered the way during the Saturday-night rush that Theresa would rest her fingers on O'Malley's shoulder when she reached across him for ice or a popcorn bucket. Wyatt remembered the first time she did that to him.

Why would they kill Theresa and not Wyatt? Why would they kill O'Malley and not Wyatt? Why would they kill Melody and Karlene and Grubb and Mr. Bingham? And not Wyatt? Why, after killing everyone else, would they leave a witness—an *eyewitness*—alive?

It made no sense. Wyatt didn't know the killers. He'd never seen them before in his life.

It was a question that could never be answered, so Wyatt had stopped, long ago, asking it. He had tried his best to stop asking it.

Why am I still here and all the others gone?

The bartender returned with his pasta. Wyatt gave his glass, empty again, a nudge with his elbow.

"Please, Andrew," he said, "don't let this ever happen again."

THE NEXT MORNING the chirp of Wyatt's phone woke him. He checked the time—later than he'd thought, almost eight—and the caller. Candace, of course. Calling for an update.

"I was going to call you first thing," he said, before she could get a word in. "I have been devoting my life to your cause."

"Shut up, shut up, shut up!" she said, her voice shaking with anger. "Shut! Up!"

"What is it?"

"What do you think? Where are you? Get over here!"

Julianna

CHAPTER 10

J ulianna spent the afternoon at the Nichols Hills Starbucks. Around two, Ben called to see how she was feeling. Julianna thought he might. What was he expecting? To catch her with the sound of a party in the background? The squeals and dance beats of bacchanalia that would allow him to bust her?

"How's the diarrhea?"

"It's still diarrhea, Ben."

"Electrolytes are your friend."

"My best friends right now."

"Okay. Well. Feel better."

Feel better. Julianna hated when people said it like that, like it was an order. Fuck you. What if I don't want to feel better?

"I will," she told Ben. "Thanks so much for checking on me, Ben."

She hung up and logged back onto Facebook. Still no reply to her message. She'd sent it eight days ago now. Julianna tried to think of reasons that the woman who posted the state-fair photos had not responded. Julianna's message had been deliberately innocuous and lighthearted. She hadn't wanted the woman—her name was Mary Hilger Hall—to think Julianna was some obsessive weirdo.

"Hi! Loved your fair photos from 86. Memories! Do you have more? Please let me know!"

Maybe Mary Hilger Hall checked her Facebook messages only infrequently. She could be away on vacation. She could be in the process of scanning more fair photos for Julianna's viewing pleasure.

Julianna clicked over to the woman's Facebook page, to see if she'd been active in the past few days. But Mary Hilger Hall had her privacy settings set to Friends Only. Julianna debated the wisdom of sending a friend request. Why not? What was there to lose? She clicked and sent it.

She logged off Facebook and opened the photo that Mary Hilger Hall had posted. Julianna studied the woman biting into her egg roll, blown out by the flash. The woman had big hair and bigger earrings: oh, the eighties. Was the eater of egg roll Mary Hilger Hall? Was she just, at the time, Mary Hilger? Behind the woman was the Chinese place in Food Alley that Julianna remembered so vividly. At the edge of the frame, standing in line for barbecue and his back to the camera, was the man in the cowboy hat.

"Fair Food 9/20/86!"

Julianna zoomed in on the man in the cowboy hat. The pixels ballooned and ruptured. The man's head was turned slightly to the left, just the rumor of a nose beneath the brim of the caramel-colored hat. His head was turned slightly *away* from the window of the barbecue place where he was waiting in line. As if, maybe, he were talking to someone standing next to him, someone standing just outside the frame of the photo.

When Julianna won her Pink Panther—when Genevieve had helped her win the Pink Panther—there'd been another man at the booth, playing the game with them. Julianna didn't remember if that man had left before or after she won her Pink Panther. She did remember he wore a cowboy hat. Brown. Or black. A brown or black cowboy hat. Genevieve had made a remark about him later, as they strolled toward the midway. Julianna couldn't remember what it was. Genevieve had laughed unkindly.

Julianna's coffee had gone cold. She went to the counter for a refill and then realized she'd cut the line. Lost in her own fog. She apologized to the woman waiting to be served, an attractive, glum blonde. The diamond on the woman's wedding ring was spectacular. Nichols Hills was the wealthiest neighborhood in Oklahoma City.

The woman smiled. It made her look even glummer. "You're fine," she said.

You're fine. Julianna hated when people said that, too. Fuck you twice. Who are you to say so?

"Sorry," Julianna said again. "I'm out of it."

"You're fine."

Julianna sat back down and opened a Word file. The timeline. Abigail Goad, the rancher's wife from Okeene, had positively identified Genevieve at 9:00 P.M. in Food Alley. The last time Genevieve had been seen on earth. She'd been talking to a man in a cowboy hat. Genevieve *might* have been talking to a man in a cowboy hat.

Julianna needed to know when, precisely, Mary Hilger Hall's photo had been taken. She needed to know if there were other photos. She needed to know if there was a photo that showed the man in the cowboy hat talking to a beautiful brown-eyed girl wearing her favorite BORN IN THE USA T-shirt. If there was a photo that showed the man's face.

The sun had set on September 20 in 1986 at 7:30 P.M. It would have been completely dark by 8:00. The fair closed at 11:00. Food Alley emptied out well before then.

It all came down to Crowley. Julianna was sure of it. At 8:50 P.M., ten minutes before the rancher's wife saw Genevieve in Food Alley, Christopher Wayne Crowley had been arrested at a 7-Eleven store a block from the fairgrounds. But Genevieve had headed toward the midway an hour earlier. It had been around 7:45 P.M. that Genevieve gave Julianna a ten-dollar bill and told her she'd be back in a flash.

The walk from the south parking lot at the fairgrounds, where the carnies parked their trucks and their trailers, to the 7-Eleven on May Avenue took approximately ten minutes. The 7-Eleven was gone now, but Julianna had walked the route when she was in high school. She'd timed it. So that left almost an hour that Genevieve might have been with Crowley in his trailer.

There was no question that Genevieve had been on her way to see Crowley. Genevieve's friend Lacey had seen her. The corn-dog vendor had seen her. And Julianna, at the time, had known exactly where Genevieve was going, and why. Of course she'd known it. Genevieve was going to get high with the skeezy carny dude.

If she'd made it to Crowley's trailer, if Crowley had lied to the police about that, he had to know something. Maybe he knew the name of the man in the cowboy hat.

Maybe, maybe, maybe. If, if, if.

Julianna could hear DeMars's voice. *Juli. You squeezing it too hard, trying to make the pieces fit when they don't.*

And she could hear Genevieve's voice. She could really hear Genevieve's voice as if her sister were right there behind her, looking over Julianna's shoulder at her laptop and making that face she made. Genevieve could roll her eyes without rolling her eyes. Julianna had watched that face drop guys dead in their tracks when they tried to hit on Genevieve without what Genevieve considered sufficient creativity.

You dork! I'm gone! I'm dead! Don't you have anything better to do with your life?

Guess not, Julianna thought.

Don't be mad at me, Juli.

Why in the world would I be mad at you, Genni? Except for . . . you know, everything?

Julianna closed her laptop. Outside Starbucks dusk was falling. She looked at her watch. Where did the time go?

Julianna had pretended to be oblivious, but she'd known about the coke for a long time. There were days and nights when Genevieve came home so high, so flying, so manic and glittering, that Julianna didn't even recognize her.

"Let's dance!" Genevieve said one time. She put a cassette in her boom box and turned the volume up. Sheila E. She dragged Julianna up onto the bed with her. Julianna wrenched her wrists free and turned the music off so their mother wouldn't come down to the basement and see Genevieve like this. It was after midnight.

Genevieve danced and bounced without the music and then flopped onto her back, cracking up. She flung an arm out toward Julianna, a hand, fingers wriggling, searching for Julianna in the space between them.

"I love you," she said. "I love you, I love you, I love you."

Julianna went upstairs to her room and shut her door.

When Genevieve was high, the part of her that made her Genevieve—mean and funny and curious and generous and stubborn and selfish and ferociously loyal—disappeared. Cocaine was magical, but it was like the worst kind of magic trick.

For a long time, Julianna had known that Genevieve liked coke better than she liked her. But she hadn't realized that Genevieve *loved* coke more than she loved Julianna. Not until that day at the fair, that dusk, when Genevieve—without thinking twice about it, without a single glance backward—left Julianna alone and terrified so she could go get high.

Genevieve knew how dangerous the fair could be. Everyone knew it. How could she leave her little sister behind on that curb, the sky turning from blood orange to black? Genevieve knew what could have happened to her. What happened to Genevieve could have happened to Julianna.

Julianna had selected pink cotton candy, not blue, because pink matched her new Pink Panther. Genevieve should have realized this and gone for the kill. She should have made fun of Julianna until Julianna could stand no more. Genevieve should have helped herself to a giant handful of cotton candy without asking and warned Julianna that if she got her grubby paws all over the upholstery of her Cutlass on the way home, there would be hell to pay.

Instead, though, she left Julianna behind and went off to find the carny. Because she thought he was sexy, because she thought he would have drugs.

Don't be mad, Juli. Don't stay mad.

Julianna's phone rang. DeMars. She sent the call to voice mail and tucked her phone back into her purse. She took out her car keys.

CROWLEY'S HOUSE WAS dark. Julianna, parked down at the other end of the block, couldn't be sure if the lights were off inside or if the light inside was just blocked by the bedsheets covering the windows. She thought about pulling closer or getting out of her car and strolling past. But she'd made up her mind—if she was going to be here, if she was going to do this, she had to be careful.

If she was going to do *what,* exactly? Julianna wasn't sure, not really. Now, before she could decide, the door to the house opened: a wink of bluish light as Crowley stepped out and onto the porch.

She watched him. He moved heavily as he walked to the pickup truck in the driveway—each step an effort, like a man climbing a hill. But also heavily in the way a boulder rumbles down a hill. Out of my way or else.

He heaved himself up into the cab of the pickup. His old Ford was a total piece of shit. The driver's door was just primer, no paint, and the tailgate was missing completely. The truck shuddered when Crowley started it up. Julianna could hear the near-death rattle from a block away.

She ducked beneath her dash. The truck rattled and roared past. Julianna dug for her keys. Stupidly, she'd put them back in her purse. Finally she found them and started her car and made a hard U in the middle of the street. She managed to spot the flare of Crowley's taillights just before they disappeared. Left on Robinson.

Julianna followed, staying as far back as she could without losing him. Crowley drove fast, cutting between lanes, shooting through intersections when the yellow light turned red. Julianna got trapped behind one red light, but Crowley stayed on Robinson, flat and straight, so she was able to catch up.

They passed blocks of run-down buildings, taquerias and liquor stores and pawnshops. Crowley turned onto Reno, and Julianna followed. After a few miles, he stopped at a bar, a big wooden barn of a place, lots of cars and motorcycles in the parking lot. THE DOUBLE R RANCH. Julianna circled the block twice, to give Crowley time, and then parked.

She waited. She wanted to go inside and sit invisibly in a dark corner and observe Crowley. See what he ordered, how he ordered it. Did he sit at the bar or at a table? If he sat at the bar, he would be watching the door in the mirror behind it. He would see her the instant she stepped inside.

Maybe that was fine. Slide onto the stool next to him and say, again, *I just want to talk to you.* Say to him, *I'm going to talk to you if it kills me.*

Julianna could hear DeMars's voice. She ignored it.

She waited until the next group of people entered the bar, three bearded biker dudes and a woman too old for the tight leather miniskirt she was wearing. Julianna slipped in behind them.

Inside, the place was dim and crowded and the smoke hung heavy, struggling to rise all the way to the wooden rafters. Music pounded: Led Zeppelin, maybe? Julianna looked for Crowley. He was sitting at the end of the bar. Not watching the mirror behind the bar but instead the shot glass in front of him. He turned it, lifted it, tipped back his head, let the booze roll down his throat. Not rushing anything, a committed drinker. He tapped the glass on the bar. The bartender brought the bottle over and poured Crowley another shot. Crowley watched the glass fill.

Julianna moved away from the bar. A few tables were empty, but she'd be too conspicuous by herself. Toward the back was a table with two women in their forties or fifties. Or maybe just their hard late thirties. Their faces were leathery and collapsed, like they were dragging deep on Marlboro Reds even though they weren't smoking.

One of the women, the redhead, glanced up. Julianna was wearing jeans and a V-neck sweater. She looked out of place in this place, but not too terribly.

"Let me sit here a minute and I'll buy you a round," she said.

One of the women, the redhead, swept a hand at the empty chair. The other woman just stared at Julianna, drunk, her eyes glassy. Julianna motioned for the waitress.

"Another round here," she said. "And a beer for me."

"What kind?"

"I don't care."

The waitress left.

"You got a cigarette?" the drunk woman asked Julianna.

"No."

Julianna watched Crowley pour down another shot. He was too far away, too many tables and people and smoke between her and him, for Julianna to make out his reflection in the mirror behind the bar. She couldn't make out the blurred blue tattoo of a snake on his forearm or the diamond stud in his ear.

The barstool next to Crowley was empty. Julianna watched him lean over, heavily, and say something to the woman sitting on the other side of it.

The waitress brought the drinks. Julianna gave her a twenty and told her to bring another round of drinks when these were finished.

The drunk woman lifted her drink. It looked like a mojito. "Whooo!" she said. And then, "Whooo."

Julianna took a sip of her beer. Bud Light? It tasted like something you'd wring out of a dirty rag.

The redhead was smirking. "Boyfriend or husband?" she asked Julianna.

"Boyfriend," Julianna said. "If he's meeting that bitch here again, I'm going to kill 'em both."

The redhead smirked. "Which one is he?"

"None of your damn business."

"Do you have a cigarette?" the drunk woman asked again.

The redhead lifted her big purse off the floor. Turquoise leather, trimmed with rhinestones. She opened it and showed Julianna its contents: a small black gun in a turquoise leather holster that matched the purse.

"But I'd use me a knife," the redhead said. She set the purse back on the floor and laughed. Her laugh was sandpaper and ground glass. "A big old butcher's knife."

The woman that Crowley was talking to had moved over onto the empty barstool between them. She had one thick brown braid that fell almost to her waist and wore a denim vest, nothing on beneath it.

She leaned into Crowley now, to hear what he was saying. When she turned her head, or shook it, or bobbed it to the music, her heavy braid barely moved. Crowley watched the woman like he'd watched the shot glass fill. Julianna felt a shiver move through her.

"He's the one at the table by the door," she told the redhead, picking a table at random.

"Hmm," the redhead said. "The squirrelly one or the— No. Girl like you, bet you go for the big boys, don't you? The strong, silent type."

"That's him."

"He's a cutie. How's he measure up in the cock department?"

"Why?" Julianna said. "You the last slut in Oklahoma City hasn't gone down on him yet?"

The redhead laughed.

A biker dude with a giant walrus mustache had made his way over. His buddies at another table observed.

"Ladies. Buy y'all a drank?"

His mustache moved, but you couldn't see his mouth underneath. It was like watching a sock puppet talk.

"Can't you see we're having a weighty discussion here?" the redhead said. "I mean."

Walrus Man chuckled, "I can get weighty."

"I bet you can," the redhead said. "Now, go away. I'll let you know if you're needed."

He chuckled again, hesitated, and then returned to his table. Julianna thought the redhead could do better tonight than Walrus Man. She was hard-looking, but more attractive than Julianna had noticed at first glance. Probably the redhead agreed she could do better than Walrus Man but wasn't yet positive about it.

"I need a *fucking* cigarette."

"*Damn,*" the redhead said. She lifted her purse back up, pawed around, came up with a single broken cigarette. She handed it to her friend and lit it for her with a turquoise Bic. The flame wavered. The tip of the cigarette wavered. "Hold still, Carla May."

Crowley paid his tab, cash, without taking his eyes off the woman on the barstool next to him.

Where had he been for those fifteen years since he was released from prison? What had he been doing? Julianna didn't really care. She wanted to know what he'd been doing for fifty-five minutes in September of 1986. Did he see Genevieve? What did he say to her? What did she say to him? Was there someone else in the trailer with them? The man with the cowboy hat?

"That guy at the end of the bar," Julianna asked the redhead. "With the long hair and the goatee. Have you ever seen him in here before?"

"You do go for the big boys," the redhead said. She squinted. "No. Never have."

"Mr. Blue Eyes," the drunk friend said.

Julianna and the redhead looked at her. She grinned.

"Carla May," the redhead said. "Did that man *romance* you and I didn't hear the juicy details?"

"He wanted to romance me, all right. He bought me a drink is all, the other day."

"Did he say anything?" Julianna asked.

The drunk friend frowned at Julianna. "Like what?"

"Like anything."

"I don't recall." She looked at the cigarette between her fingers and mourned the spreading ash. "Mr. Blue Eyes. I had to go pee, then I don't know where he went."

Julianna watched Crowley stand. He held out a hand, the gentleman, and helped the woman with the braid off the barstool. He followed her toward the door, close behind and towering over her, his big hand on her shoulder now. Julianna felt another shiver.

If she hurried, she could head them off at the door. Maybe Crowley would talk to her for five minutes, just to get rid of her. And he wouldn't want Julianna to tell the woman with the braid that he was an ex-con, that he'd been the primary suspect in the kidnapping and murder of a teenage girl. Or would he care? Would the woman? This wasn't the Starbucks in Nichols Hills.

Julianna stayed seated. When Crowley and the woman reached the door, he stopped and glanced back across the big room, a quick scan. For an instant, Julianna was certain he'd seen her. But his eyes skimmed past, no drag or hesitation.

He put both hands on the woman's shoulders and steered her out the door.

The waitress brought two more mojitos. The two guys at the closest table were getting ready to make their move. Julianna could see it. The redhead could see it.

"Have fun tonight," Julianna told her. She stood up.

The redhead shook her head and laughed. "Well, hell if I know what you're up to."

"Hell if I know either," Julianna said.

The drunk friend lifted her fresh mojito, "Whooo."

Julianna

CHAPTER 11

Julianna followed Crowley's truck back to his house. She parked down the block again, closer this time. There were a lot of other cars parked on the street, both sides, and the streetlight on the corner was out. Julianna didn't think Crowley would notice her even if he was looking.

He wasn't looking. He unlocked the front door of his house and opened it but then wheeled around and pushed the woman with the braid up against the doorframe. He closed a fist around her braid and yanked it, like a bellpull. The woman's head tilted up and back. Julianna could see the white of her throat, the white of her smile.

Julianna watched them make out: Crowley's fist tight on the braid, the woman pinned against the doorframe, her body pushing and moving against his. He was so much bigger than she was, taller and heavier. She was probably five-five or five-six, Julianna's height. Julianna couldn't see Crowley's other hand until the woman suddenly bucked, buckled, and Julianna realized that he had his other hand between her legs.

The woman had lost one of her spike-heeled shoes. Her bare foot stroked his calf.

Crowley knew what he was doing, apparently. After a minute or two, they moved inside. The door banged shut behind them.

Julianna pictured the groping stumble to the bed. Or the sofa? The mother-of-pearl snaps on the woman's denim vest popping open, Crowley's hands on her breasts, his mouth, the weight of him pressing down on her.

Julianna remembered one time, at almost the very beginning of the investigation, when the two detectives had been standing around in the driveway eating a late lunch or an early dinner. One of the detectives, the older one, shared his fries with Julianna— crinkle-cut fries from a white Braum's bag. He was asking Julianna how she liked school, what her favorite classes were, when a cop in a uniform interrupted to report that Schmidt and the others were on it—*Schmidt and all them*—checking the Cutlass for blood and semen.

Julianna had felt the detectives go rigid. The young, grim one grabbed the patrol cop by the elbow and marched him off. The older detective asked Julianna, quickly, which one she would pick, french fries or Tater Tots, if she had to eat one and only one for the rest of her life.

"Now, give it some thought," he said. "Only fools rush in."

The thought of blood in Genevieve's car didn't freak Julianna out. No, yes, of course it did, but Julianna had seen blood. She was familiar with blood. When she was nine, she'd opened a peel-top can of chocolate pudding and sliced her finger on the sharp edge of the lid. Another time, in kindergarten, Julianna had seen a little boy fall off the top of a slide. His teeth were red when he cried.

Blood was everywhere, part of life. But: semen. *Semen.* Julianna, at twelve years old, was young for her age. The baby of the family, sheltered by her mother and, yes, to some degree even by Genevieve. So Julianna had only the vaguest notion of what semen was. She just knew it was gross and filthy and scary and it happened during sex, which was gross and filthy and scary.

Blood *and* semen. The combination created a new, exponential horror. Julianna had nightmares for weeks, months. Some nights she would wake up in the middle of the night and just wish she were dead.

Crowley and the woman with the braid had been inside the house for forty minutes. Still going at it? Going at it again? Julianna wondered what would happen if she knocked on Crowley's door now. He'd be pissed, standing there with his dick swinging in the wind, but he might also be . . . *spent.* Julianna, if she were lucky, would catch him in that brief moment when a man can do nothing but surrender.

I just want to talk to you.

Julianna told herself she'd wait five more minutes and then drive home. After those five minutes ticked by, she told herself she'd wait five more. After an hour the door to the house opened. The woman with the braid picked up the spike-heeled shoe she'd abandoned and slipped it back on. Crowley was already halfway to his truck. The woman had to hurry to catch up and climb in. Her braid, Julianna could see in the glare of Crowley's headlights, had begun to fray.

Crowley dropped the woman off at her car, in the parking lot of the Double R Ranch. The lot was still almost full. Julianna guessed Crowley would park and go inside again for a drink. Instead he pulled back onto Reno and then caught I-44 at Tenth Street. He took it north, away from his house. Julianna followed. She had come this far, had she not?

Crowley broke off I-44 and onto the Lake Hefner Parkway. North. The shittier parts of northwest Oklahoma City fell away. The nicer parts rose up to meet them. Nichols Hills was just to the east. Quail Creek was farther north. Julianna lived in between, in the Village, not as ritzy as the other two neighborhoods but nice enough and well situated. There were parts of the Village that were nicer than others: Julianna's house was on the border between two such parts. She felt a moment of irrational alarm when Crowley took the Britton Road exit—her exit—but then he turned left instead of right and headed toward the lake.

The lake. Why? Julianna had to be very careful now. It was almost midnight, and once they passed the cluster of restaurants at East Wharf, there were only a few cars on the dark lake road. She stayed far back, occasionally losing the truck's lights and then picking them up again when the trees thinned. The landscape around the lake, a reservoir, had been flat and featureless when Julianna was a girl. But in recent years money had been spent, improvements had been made. There was a boathouse now, walking and jogging trails, lots of trees. At the right time of year, at the right time of day—sunset, when the water reflected back an even deeper, richer version of the sky—the lake could be beautiful. But the trees, at the moment, were a pain in Julianna's ass.

Crowley stayed right at the fork and curled around the southern fringe of the lake. Julianna really didn't know where he was going now. And then he was gone. She lost his lights and couldn't find them again. She braked in the middle of the road—there were no cars behind her—and looked back. The only place Crowley could have turned off was Stars and Stripes Park. But the park entrance was gated after dark. Wasn't it?

The road was too narrow to make a clean U-turn, and there wasn't much of a shoulder to work with here. Julianna had to ease her car carefully up onto an incline bordered by heavy brush. She nosed against the brush, testing the give, then shifted into reverse when she'd created enough space.

Headlights snapped on—brights—right behind her. Crowley pulled his truck tight against the back bumper of her car, pinning her in. Julianna thought her heart was going to punch its way out of her chest. She opened her door and got out. Gnats churned in the blaze of Crowley's brights. Julianna had to shield her eyes.

"Turn those off, please," she called.

After a few seconds, Crowley killed his lights. The night went black again. There were no streetlamps out here, and the nearest house was a quarter of a mile away. Crowley had picked the perfect spot. The only light was the moon—half full or half empty, Julianna didn't know which. The lake road here was so quiet, just the crickets and the wind, that she could hear the whistle of a train crossing Britton, miles away to the east.

Crowley climbed out of his truck and walked over, heavily, a boulder rolling slowly toward her. All night Julianna had been a spectator—now she was part of the scene. She had to keep herself from taking a step backward. Crowley stopped a few feet away and folded his arms over his chest.

"You been following me for how long?" he said. "Since at the bar?"

He moved to his left. She turned to keep him in front of her.

"I told you to leave me alone," he said.

"I just want to talk to you."

"Didn't I?"

"You did."

He moved to his left again and took a step closer.

"What you got there?" he said. He smiled a little. "Behind your back there. Pepper spray."

She was holding her cell phone behind her back. She'd already dialed 911. All she had to do, if she needed to do it, was hit the SEND button.

"Yes," she said.

"Bullshit."

Another step to his left, another step toward her. He looked down at her. He smelled like the bar. Julianna supposed she did, too. Stale smoke and beer. But Crowley smelled of something else as well, sharp but faint, musky. Or maybe that was just Julianna's imagination, since she knew what he'd been doing half an hour ago.

He saw the phone she was holding.

"They can't track with a cell phone," he said. "You gotta tell 'em where you're at. Is that what you was gonna say? 'Hurry, please, I'm out by the lake somewhere.'"

He was so close now that Julianna could feel the heat coming off him. She realized, too late, that he'd been shading left and turning her on purpose, so he could back her up against her car. She had nowhere to go now.

"I'm not scared of you," Julianna said.

"I didn't ask if you were."

"I just want to talk to you."

"Listen to me," he said. "Listen to me good, now. Your sister?"

"Yes."

"I don't know what happened to her. I was in jail that night. How would I know what happened to her?"

"Before you were arrested," Julianna said.

"That was . . . shit, almost thirty years ago. I told the police everything."

"Everything?"

He studied her and then lifted a hand. Julianna flinched. Crowley smiled again. He brought his index finger close to her lips, as close as he could get without touching them.

"Shush, now," he said.

Julianna saw the headlights before he did. The car came up behind him and then slowed to a stop. The passenger-side window slid down, and the driver, a man with glasses, leaned over.

"Y'all all right?" he said.

"Just fine," Crowley said.

Julianna could see the driver peering at her, waiting for her to answer.

"Fine," she said. "Thank you."

The window slid up, the car pulled away. Crowley took a step backward. Realizing, maybe, that he hadn't picked the perfect spot after all.

"I just want to talk to you," she said. "Let me buy you a drink. Talk to me for five minutes and tell me anything you remember. Anything."

"Leave me the fuck alone," Crowley said. "You understand?"

Julianna shook her head. "No. I won't."

He turned and started walking back to his truck. "You're a crazy bitch."

"Please," she said. She didn't know what else to say. "Please. I know."

He'd been about to swing himself up into the cab of the truck. After a second he reached into the cab and popped the brights back on. Julianna closed her eyes. She could feel the gnats churning around her.

"I can buy myself a drink," Crowley said. He turned the head-lights off.

"What do you want?" Julianna said.

"I told the police everything. So we're clear on that. I told 'em way back when."

"What do you want?"

"Can you cook?"

"Cook?" Julianna said, surprised.

"Turkey and stuffing. Cornbread stuffing. Mashed potatoes and gravy. I know it ain't Thanksgiving yet."

"You want me to make you dinner?"

"Way to a man's heart," he said. "I ain't had a home-cooked meal since I don't know when."

Julianna tried to read him. A glimmer of pity? Weary resig-nation? Or had she just been turned again without realizing it, positioned right where he wanted her? It was laughable, how im-possible it was to read Crowley. Julianna felt bad for the people over the years who'd tried to read her.

Another pair of headlights crawled up the lake road toward them. The driver slowed. Julianna waved him on.

"Tomorrow night," Crowley said. "Tell me your address."

Julianna knew that an evening of small bad decisions had led to the precipice of this monumentally terrible one. She no longer heard DeMars's voice in her head. That voice had given up long ago.

"And pie," Crowley said. He was watching to see which way she would break, enjoying the moment. "Whatever kind, so long as it's sweet."

Wyatt

CHAPTER 12

C andace had told Wyatt on the phone that someone broke into the Land Run during the night and turned it upside down. Wyatt realized, when he stepped inside and looked around, that she'd meant it literally.

Everything in the Land Run really *had* been turned upside down. Everything: the tables, the chairs and the barstools, the amps on the stage, the cash register, and the flat-screen TV. Each and every one of the framed show bills—there must have been fifty of them covering the walls—had been flipped. The pour spouts had been removed from the bottles behind the bar and the bottles balanced on their necks. Jars of olives and cocktail cherries, napkin holders. Even the cutout metal silhouettes on the restroom doors, a cowboy and a cowgirl, were now heels over head.

Candace came out from behind the bar with a mop. Wyatt saw that the floor back there beneath the rubber-tread mat was wet with spilled liquor. He could smell it now.

"Don't step there!" she said.

"I'm standing still," Wyatt pointed out.

"I don't care. I just mopped there. You were getting ready to step."

"You know me so well."

The Land Run's overhead lights and wall sconces hadn't been turned on yet. The primary source of illumination was the skylight above—a shaft of early-morning peach and gold and dust that slanted down like a toppled Roman column. It fell on Candace and made the scene look like something from a Rembrandt. Well, if Rembrandt had ever painted a furious Thai-American woman with a pair of plastic butterflies holding her hair back.

"Do you believe me now?" she said. "Do you?"

"Did you call the police yet?" Wyatt said.

"Ha," she said, just as a cop emerged from the back.

"Looks like somebody used a pry bar to jimmy your back door," the cop said. "Between the door and the frame? Popped that sucker right open."

"Really?" Candace said. "You sure?"

The cop either missed the sarcasm or chose to ignore it. He had the tranquil expression of a man *this* close to retirement.

"Anything stolen?" Wyatt asked Candace. "Damaged?"

Candace shook her head. "I told him already. I don't keep cash here overnight. Nothing damaged unless you mean like three or four hundred bucks' worth of booze spilled all over the floor. Unless you mean my time, which I don't have enough of to start with, when I have to spend all day today turning those stupid posters right side up."

The spilled booze, Wyatt considered, hadn't been the point. The bottles wouldn't balance unless the pour spouts were removed. The spilled booze was just a secondary consequence.

So what, Wyatt wondered, *was* the point? Steal nothing, destroy nothing. Just turn the place upside down.

The cop had walked over to the nearest wall and was looking up at the upside-down show bills.

"Might've been a buncha kids," he said. "Fooling around? Who else'd do something like this? I never seen anything like it."

Wyatt considered how long it must have taken somebody to turn all those show bills upside down. To flip all the barstools and chairs. To yank the pour spouts from two dozen bottles of booze. To unbolt the flat-screen TV from its brackets and then find a way to bolt it back in. To do a grid search afterward and make sure nothing that could be flipped had not been flipped.

Unless there had been more than one somebody. But even then.

"Seems like an awful lot of effort," Wyatt said. "For a bunch of kids. When I was kid, Officer, and maybe your experience was the same, effort was the least of all possible temptations."

"I'll tell you what I think." The cop turned back to them. "Get you a security system. Or a big old dog."

"Ms. Kilkenny told you about the other incidents?" Wyatt said.

"Yes, of course I told him," Candace said. "And stop calling me that."

"She did," the cop said. "About the birds and such."

He kept a straight face, but the way people do when they want to make clear they're keeping a straight face. Wyatt could feel Candace vibrating next to him at a frequency that was about to blow out the glass in the Art Deco skylight above them.

Wyatt didn't think the cop was dumb. The cop, like everyone, was just keeping a finger on the pulse of his own self-interest. He had real crimes to solve, real criminals to catch, so he saw the evidence in front of him the way he wanted to see it. Humans, by nature, did this all the time. They wanted something, so they found reasons to support that desire. And then they convinced themselves that the reasons came first, that the reasons led to the desire and not the other way around.

Wyatt tried not to do that. He always tried to listen to the evidence, no matter how much he didn't like what it was saying.

"I'm gonna go out to the car and write up the report, ma'am," the cop told Candace. "You can send a copy to your insurance, and they'll pay for any damages, after the deductible and all."

"Wait," Candace said. "What? Wait! Aren't you going to check for, like . . . DNA or whatever?"

The cop did the thing with his face again, straight but not straight. He glanced at Wyatt to see if Wyatt was in on the joke.

"No, ma'am," the cop said. "Not in this instance."

Candace was about to have a stroke. "So that's all?" she said. "A report?"

Wyatt set a hand lightly on her shoulder before she could say anything else. One way or another, the cop was walking out the door of the Land Run in the next thirty seconds. Wyatt figured he might as well walk out friendly, not pissed.

"Thanks very much, Officer," Wyatt said. "We appreciate all your help."

"You betcha," the cop said. He appreciated being appreciated. Who didn't?

After the cop left, Candace turned and punched Wyatt in the ribs with a small brown fist.

"All his help?" she said. "All his *help*?"

"DNA?" he said.

"I know. That was stupid." She went back behind the bar and started mopping again. "You didn't have to, like, grab me. I wasn't going to go all batshit on him."

"That wasn't blindingly obvious to me."

"So do you have any ideas yet? About who's doing this to me?"

Wyatt told her what he'd found out about the new tax initiative.

"There's a good chance the Land Run is going to be worth a lot more than it is now," he said.

"I don't care! I'm not selling!"

"I'm not asking you to. I'm just letting you know why Jeff Eddy wants to get his hands on it now."

Candace wiped sweat off her forehead with the back of her hand. She flung the sweat away. "So that's all?" she said. "All day yesterday, and that's all you've found out?"

Wyatt really wished he didn't like her as much as he did. If he didn't like her as much as he did, he was pretty sure he'd already be back in Las Vegas by now.

He realized that Candace's daughter, Lily, was up in the balcony again, pale and luminous in the shadows, watching him. He waved at her. After much deliberation she waved back. One finger only, though, the absolute bare-minimum requirement for a wave. And then she melted away.

"I'm going to check the door," Wyatt said. He walked past the restrooms, down the short corridor to the back exit. He stepped outside and took a look at the door. Definitely jimmied. Wyatt saw where the wood of the frame had been gouged and splintered. He used his thumb to measure. Maybe a pry bar, but maybe a tire iron. The distinction might matter. It might not.

He took a photo of the door with his phone and then looked out across the back parking lot. The eight-foot stockade fence ran the full length of the property line, from the street to the east all the way to Land Run's next-door neighbor on the west, a boarded-up body shop. Wyatt doubted that whoever wanted to turn Candace's life upside down had entered the back lot from the street side—it was too exposed, even late at night, with a street-light only a few yards away.

One of Wyatt's favorite quotes from college was from Flannery O'Connor. She said, or at least this is how Wyatt remembered it, that the writer should never be ashamed of staring—that there is nothing that does not require the writer's attention.

Or the detective's. So he stared. After a minute he noticed that one of the flat six-inch cedar planks in the stockade fence—the plank farthest to the west, flush against the wall of the body shop, seemed to be very slightly lower than the others.

Wyatt walked over. He reached up and gave the plank a shake. It came free. So did the one next to it. The nails that connected the planks to the horizontal rails, Wyatt saw, had been pried out, and the lower rail itself had been sawed away—the planks had been leaning against the upper rail.

Crouching, sucking in his breath, Wyatt squeezed through the opening that someone had made in the fence. On the other side, a narrow alley—not even an alley, really, just a dirt track—cut past the old warehouse directly behind the Land Run. The dirt track appeared to be freshly scuffed.

Wyatt thought about how the Land Run had been turned upside down. There was an element of humor to the delivery, but he suspected that the message itself was earnest. Whoever broke into the bar last night wanted to show Candace, literally and figuratively, how easy it was to turn her life upside down.

Wyatt squeezed back through the fence and went inside. Candace had climbed on top of a card catalog. She was turning the show bills on the wall next to the stage right side up.

"Do you want some help with that?" Wyatt said.

She didn't dignify the question with a glance. "I'm not paying you to turn the stupid posters back around."

"You're not paying me at all," Wyatt reminded her.

Candace lifted a show bill off the nail. *"U2, February 17, 1982, 8 P.M."*

"Dallas and Jonathan are coming in early to help," she said. "You need to find out Who! Is! Screwing! With! Me!"

"He came through the fence in back. Past the warehouse behind you. He or she or it."

"Why not 'they'?"

Maybe. Wyatt just had a feeling. This—the attention to detail—didn't feel like a team effort to him.

Candace turned another show bill. *"Tool, December 4, 1992."*

"It's not like this is some gigantic breakthrough," she said. "That whoever did this came through the fence in back."

It wasn't. It was a single pinprick in the dark fabric of the night. But put together enough pinpricks and eventually the dawn bled through.

"Come on, baby," Candace said. "I'm going to take you to mother's day out."

Wyatt realized that Lily was sitting cross-legged on the stage. She had teleported down from the balcony.

"Bye, Wyatt," she said.

"Bye, Lily," he said.

ON THE WAY to his car, Wyatt's phone rang. Laurie. He'd meant to call her back last night. But he'd had a few drinks, he was tired, he didn't like to talk to her unless he could give her his full attention. In Wyatt's opinion that was the secret to a successful relationship. One of the secrets. In love as in life, you had to be *present*.

"Tell me what you had for breakfast," he said. "Tell me what you're wearing. Read me the minutes of the most boring meeting you had yesterday."

"What time is it there?" Laurie said. "Are you one hour ahead or two?"

"One. Do you have any idea how much I miss you? It's apocalyptic."

Wyatt checked the bars on his phone.

"Hello?" he said.

"Wyatt," she said finally. "Are you coming back?"

The question took him by surprise.

"What?" he said. "Am I coming back? What are you talking about?"

"I don't know."

"Of course I'm coming back. I'll be back in a few days. At most."

She didn't say anything. Wyatt could picture her expression, her eyes. The one moment out of every million when the surface obscured the depths, when he was blind to whatever the hell was down below.

"Laurie," he said. "Why would you ask something like that?"

"I don't know." He heard her sigh. "Since almost the beginning, really, that's how I thought we'd end. I can't explain it. Just this weird sense. That one day you'd just leave and I wouldn't even realize it."

"What? Laurie. What?"

"What's the longest, Wyatt, you've ever lived anywhere? In one place? Before you had to . . . I don't know."

Another question that so baffled Wyatt he didn't know how to answer it.

"I love you," he said. "I want to marry you. I've told you that. I tell you that all the time."

"You do," she said, and Wyatt knew the tone, the point. Laurie had said before that he never talked in a real way about making what they had permanent. Whenever they began to talk about it in a real way, according to Laurie, Wyatt turned slippery—a rubbery, muscular eel, able to flatten and elongate and squeeze away through the most impossibly tiny gap in the conversation.

Well, that was bullshit.

Wyatt took his time. He knew he had to be careful.

"I've told you this, babe," he said. "The reason I've never had anything last with a woman before—I've never met the girl of my dreams before. Until I met you. You. And I've moved around a lot because— C'mon, Laurie. Who doesn't move around a lot anymore? It's America in the twenty-first century."

"I don't care about getting married," she said. "You know I don't care about that. It's about— I want to feel like when we're together, we *are* together. I want to feel like you're *there*."

"I'm not?"

"Have you ever had a conversation with someone at a party?" she said. "It's a wonderful conversation, but then you realize the other person has been edging toward the door the entire time."

"Laurie," Wyatt said. "Listen to me. That's ridiculous."

"You really don't understand?" she said. "You really don't see it?"

Wyatt didn't want to have this conversation right now.

"We can talk about this when I get back," he said. "We can talk as much as you want."

"I just want . . . I want you to *think* about this," she said. "Really think about it. About us."

How could she know him so well but not know him at all? Wyatt didn't understand.

"I don't need to think about us," he said. And then, before the silence could stretch too thin, "But I will. Okay? I will."

After Wyatt said good-bye to Laurie, he sat on the hood of the rented Altima for a minute. There were only a couple of clouds in the sky. He'd heard, when he was a kid, that Oklahoma City had more sunny days than almost any other city in the country. He didn't know if that was true or not, but he thought it might be. Even in the winter. January and February could get cold down on the southern plains, but there were also long periods of bright, blazing blue, the temperature in the sixties and seventies.

It was O'Malley, Wyatt remembered now, who'd told him that Oklahoma City had more sunny days than anywhere else in the country. They'd been loitering in the lobby, waiting for Mr. Bingham to emerge from his office so they could then quickly look busy. The new doorman had been there, too, the snobby rich kid who only lasted a month that summer before he quit. He'd sneered and said O'Malley was full of shit.

"What's your point?" O'Malley had asked pleasantly, and the new guy didn't know what to do with that.

Wyatt walked back around to the Land Run's employee parking lot. He set the loose planks aside and squeezed through the stockade fence again.

The warehouse behind the Land Run appeared to be abandoned. The loading bays were empty, and there was gang graffiti everywhere, balloon letters and demented squiggles. On the other side of the building, though, several cars were parked out front. Wyatt found a door and pressed the buzzer next to it. He waited. Just as he was about to give up, a lock clanked and the door swung open.

He stepped into an empty stairwell. He heard music above, so he climbed the set of shaky metal stairs to another door. This one opened onto the top floor of the warehouse, a huge airy space flooded with sunlight. At the far end of the room, a band was rehearsing—a drummer, guitarist, and bass player noodling without a lot of enthusiasm through what sounded like an acid-rock version of "Folsom Prison Blues." Closer to Wyatt, at his end of the warehouse, a cluster of kids in their teens and twenties, hippies and white rastas, sat cross-legged on the floor. They were dipping strips of newspaper into buckets of white goo and then placing the strips on a wire-mesh armature the size and shape of a giant head.

The kids weren't paying much attention to the job at hand and none at all to the music. They were focused, rapt, on the action in the very center of the room—a shirtless guy in a tartan kilt who squatted and then slowly lifted himself off the floor with his hands.

"Yeah!" a kid with fingerless gloves and a Shriner's fez called out.

"Hey, Lyle!" the guitar player called from the other side of the warehouse. "We need to work on the vocals at some point, man."

The guy in the kilt ignored them both. He extended one leg, then the other, still balanced on just his hands. He flexed his bare toes.

Lyle. The kilt, the vocals. Wyatt put the pieces together. The guy doing yoga was Lyle Finn, lead singer for the Barking Johnsons, the most well-known rock band from Oklahoma City. Well, maybe the only well-known rock band from Oklahoma City. The Barking Johnsons had started out in the late eighties and were best known for psychedelic rock, trippy stage spectaculars, and Lyle Finn's general eccentricity—not necessarily in that order.

A guy came out of an office and walked over to Wyatt.

"Hey," he said. "I'm Dixon. The band's manager."

He was in his forties, wearing creased khakis and a polo shirt with a smear of what looked like blueberry yogurt on the collar.

His face was friendly but slightly bewildered. He looked like a suburban dad who had awakened one morning and discovered, to his surprise, that he was now the manager of a rock band.

"Wyatt Rivers," Wyatt said. He shook the guy's hand. "I'm a private detective."

"Oh. I thought you were the balloon dealer."

"That's a job?"

"Lyle wants me to buy him a hot-air balloon. Like, a full-size hot-air balloon? I have no idea what he plans to do with it. Private detective?"

"The new owner of the Land Run has been having some problems at her place lately. She asked me to look into it."

"Candace?"

"You know her?"

"Sure. She's cool. She booked a couple of the baby bands I manage. What kind of problems?"

Wyatt told him about the marquee letters, the bird poop, the break-in.

The manager frowned. "Huh," he said.

Wyatt had noted that the bank of windows along the south wall of the warehouse provided a good view down into the alley and the Land Run's back parking lot.

"Last night," he said, "did you happen to notice anyone or anything suspicious? It would have been late, after the Land Run closed."

"No. I took off early yesterday. Five or six o'clock. Lyle was the only one still around last night."

"Can I talk to him?"

"You can try."

Wyatt didn't know what that meant, but he followed the manager to the center of the floor, where Lyle Finn's yoga poses were becoming increasingly spirited. Wyatt hoped the guy was wearing boxers or briefs beneath his trademark kilt, because Wyatt had no desire to see his johnson, barking or otherwise.

"Mr. Finn," he said, "I'd like to ask you a couple of questions."

Finn glanced at Wyatt and then scissored his legs around, ending up balanced on his hands again.

"They say I have a way with words," he announced. "'They,' whatever that means. A way with words. But check it out. I say *away* with words. Away! Or *aweigh*. Like anchors aweigh? Because words are anchors. They anchor us, man. Because what is a sentence? What is a lyric? I want to make a record, man, where it's just, like, drums and a guitar and the beautiful wrenching cry of me giving birth. You know? I would love to be pregnant, man."

He balanced on his hands and waited for Wyatt's reaction. Wyatt checked to see if he had one. He didn't.

"Great," he said.

"Lyle," the manager said, "just talk to the guy like you're a normal human being for a second, will you?"

Finn lowered himself to the floor and then sprang to his feet. Wyatt would never have guessed that Finn was almost fifty years old. He was tan and lithe, with long, golden, luxuriously cascading hair. On album covers and in music-video close-ups, his eyes were always filled with childlike wonder.

Finn pulled on a T-shirt and gave Wyatt a hug.

"*Like* a normal human being," he said. "Did you hear how Dixon said that? Dixon doesn't think I'm capable of *being* a normal human being."

The manager nodded. "That is correct."

"You're not that blogger from yesterday," Finn informed Wyatt. "I mistakenly thought you were that blogger from yesterday."

"He's a private investigator, Lyle."

The band had given up on their lead singer and ended the song they were playing. The guitar player cracked open a bottle of beer. The drummer climbed on a Segway and rolled over to watch the groupies building the giant papier-mâché head.

Finn put his hands on Wyatt's shoulders and stared deep into his eyes. His hair smelled fantastic.

"You have my full and undivided attention," he said.

"Thank you," Wyatt said. "How late were you up here last night?"

"Byron!" Finn waved at the drummer. "Can I ride your Segway, Byron?"

The drummer rolled over and helped Finn onto the Segway.

"So I just, like, lean forward to go?" Finn said. He turned to Wyatt. "I concentrate better when my brain is in a dynamic state."

He shot off, spun around, shot back over. The groupies whooped and clapped. Finn beamed.

Wyatt could see he needed to get Finn offstage, away from an audience, if he wanted to have anything that resembled a real conversation with him.

"Lyle," he said, "can we go outside and talk in private?"

"Why?" Finn shot off again. "Privacy is piracy! Anything I say to you I can say to the whole beautiful universe!"

The groupies whooped and clapped.

"If you're thinking we might trade jobs," Wyatt told Dixon as they watched Finn zip past, "you can forget about that."

"I've been doing this for twenty-three years," Dixon said. He shook his head, bewildered. "Lyle! Please surrender the Segway!"

Finn did a few more figure eights, then looped back over. He followed Wyatt downstairs and out to one of the loading docks. Finn looked around—for an audience, presumably. When he found one lacking, he sat down with his back against the wall and turned his face up to the warm October sun.

"So you're a private investigator?" Finn said. "Right on."

"Is the kilt comfortable," Wyatt said, "or is it just the thing you do?"

"My shtick?" Finn said. "It's both. Now it is. It started out because I was tired of getting my ass kicked in high school."

"You figured wearing a kilt in high school would stop you from getting your ass kicked?"

Finn looked more his actual age in this light. Wyatt could see the wrinkles, the fine crosshatching.

"I figured if I was gonna get my ass kicked every day in high school anyway, because the jocks thought I was some weirdo, this weird arty weirdo, I might as well go full-on, full-out weirdo, you know?"

"How did that go?"

Finn cupped his hands in front of him. "According to the Vedas, if one sows goodness, one reaps goodness."

"So here's the deal," Wyatt said. "Somebody broke into the Land Run and turned it upside down. Literally. Did you happen to notice anything suspicious last night, late?"

"No way! The Land Run?" Finn sprang to his feet. "I love that place, man. I love playing there. The energy is phenomenal. We played our very first show there. You know, the first show that wasn't in, like, somebody's basement. No way, man! The Land Run?"

Wyatt tried again. "Last night. Did you see anything at all? The windows in your warehouse look right down on the back of the Land Run."

"I was in back most of the night, at the kiln. Clay is the one truly honest artistic medium. Earth, hands, fire. What I'm into now, I use clay to create functional erotic art."

"Say no more," Wyatt said. Please.

"They're *not* dildos. I find it deeply offensive when people call them that."

"Lyle."

"Do you know what Filipino sailors do for the pleasure of their female sexual partners? They're called *bolitas*. They make incisions in their penis and insert tiny metal ball bearings."

"Lyle."

"What?"

Wyatt put his hands on Finn's shoulders. "Did you see or hear anything last night?"

"I don't think so. No. Wait." He put his hands on Wyatt's shoulders. "You don't think it's me, do you?"

"What?"

"The Land Run is just on the other side of the fence. What if whoever broke in there really meant to break in *here* and they just got the building wrong? It's starting to freak me out, man. What if, you know, this is all about me?"

Wyatt suspected that when you were a rock star, it was always all about you.

He eased out from beneath Finn's hands. "I think you're good," he said.

Wyatt made his way back up the alley between the Land Run and the warehouse. Candace's nearest neighbor to the east, on the other side of the vacant lot, was a place that sold discount cigarettes. Wyatt walked over and went inside. The guy behind the counter, an older Latino man packing cartons of Parliaments into a box, nodded to him.

"Hello, my friend," he said. "What can I do for you?"

The guy's smile was friendly but guarded. Wyatt guessed that the discount-cigarette business was not exactly as pure as the driven snow. Wyatt explained what had happened last night at the Land Run. He asked the guy if he'd heard or seen anything.

The guy pondered and then shook his head. "I am afraid not, my friend."

Wyatt wasn't shocked. He thanked the guy and walked out to his car. In the parking lot behind the Land Run, he heard two voices he couldn't quite make out—one quietly angry, one quietly angrier. Wyatt squeezed back through the hole in the fence, made his way up the dirt path, and peeked around the corner. Lyle Finn was now standing on the loading dock of the warehouse with Dixon, his manager.

"You better believe me, Lyle!" the manager said. He went inside, slamming the door behind him.

Finn closed his eyes and pressed his hands together as if he were praying. After a few seconds, he opened his eyes and kicked the door. He kicked it again.

"You better believe *me*!" he said.

Interesting, Wyatt thought.

Julianna

CHAPTER 13

Julianna got to work late. She planned to leave early. While shuttling between the hip replacement behind curtain number four and the hysterectomy behind curtain number nine, she schemed. Diarrhea again? Ben, knowing Ben, would demand to see a stool sample. The funeral of a loved one? No. Ben, under the guise of sympathy, would be certain to pry. He would question the last-minute notice. He would ask her when she'd return. He might chat up Donna and discover that Julianna no longer had any loved ones.

"How are you feeling, Mr. Bell?" she asked the hip replacement. An old man whose new body part would survive far longer than the rest of him.

"It hurts a little," he said. Julianna was unsure if he was smiling or grimacing.

"I know it must," she said.

He seemed warmed by the glow of her concern. "Thank you," he said.

For what, exactly? People said the strangest things when they first stumbled from the mists of anesthesia.

Julianna had gone to nursing school because she thought caring for others might give her the kind of peace that getting high every afternoon did not. And the state had paid her way, room and board included. Julianna's test scores in college had been excellent, either despite or because of all the pot-smoking.

Her biggest surprise, once she became a nurse, was how talented she was. How talented in certain ways. She recognized connections that others did not, and her intuitive leaps were generally correct. And without even trying she was able to make her patients feel as if she really cared for them. Wasn't that, at the end of the day, just as good as the real thing?

Ben ambushed her in the break room. He wore special sneakers that never squeaked—Julianna was convinced of it.

"Julianna," he said. "We need to talk."

"Sure."

He tapped his iPad and frowned. Tapped and frowned. She knew she was in deep shit.

"I'm sorry I was late, Ben," she said. "I had a rocky night."

"The diarrhea."

"Yes."

"Julianna."

"Yes."

"I'm concerned. May I be perfectly candid? I feel as if certain patterns are emerging again."

"Can we talk about this later, Ben? I just got a call from my neighbor. Apparently ONG was doing work on the block, digging up a gas line to repair it or something, and they accidentally let my dog out of the yard."

Ben looked up from his iPad. He was a dog person. Julianna knew this about him.

"You have a dog?" he said.

"A Lab mix. Candy. She's a rescue."

"You shouldn't keep her in the yard," Ben said. "Dogs are den dwellers. They like to be indoors, surrounded by the scents of their pack. They're much safer and happier indoors."

Julianna was already exhausted by this conversation.

"I don't have a fucking dog, Ben," she said. "But I have to go. It's only an hour early."

He pursed his lips with deep disapproval. He stood between her and the door. Julianna weighed her options. She could threaten to knee him in the balls, or she could really put the fear of God in him.

"Let me get this straight, Ben," she said. "You want to have this conversation without a representative from HR present? Because I have to say I feel very uncomfortable about that."

His eyes widened. Then narrowed. But what could he say? Those who were sticklers for rules had to submit when the rules stickled them back.

He stepped aside. "Of course."

"Thank you."

"Julianna?" She was almost out the door. "I'm going to schedule you in ER the rest of the month."

She turned back. "ER? I haven't worked ER in two years."

"Phil is on paternity leave. They need a floater for the overnight."

Ben's beard parted: two rows of tiny white teeth, a smile, victorious. Overnights in the emergency room were often hellish, the worst punishment he had the authority to unilaterally inflict upon her. Julianna didn't care. She had to go.

"Sure," she said.

She made it home a little after six and took the turkey out of the oven. Just in time. The skin was beginning to blacken. She set the pan on the counter. A second later the smoke detector shrieked. Julianna had to open windows and wave a dish towel until it stopped.

She peeled and boiled the potatoes. She knew how to make mashed potatoes, but the gravy came from Whole Foods, and the apple pie, too. Would Crowley notice? Care? Julianna doubted it. She suspected that despite what he claimed, the very least of Crowley's objectives for this evening was a home-cooked meal. What he really wanted: to test her, to play with her, to bat at her with a finger until she either showed her claws or scampered away in fright.

Maybe he thought, if he played his cards right, she would have sex with him. Maybe he imagined a dinner that ended with her pressed up against the wall like the woman with the long braid, her head tilted back and throat bared, Crowley's hand between her legs.

Julianna poured the store-bought gravy into a saucepan and turned the heat to simmer. In the bedroom she changed from her scrubs into jeans and a fitted tee, a blouse over the tee, black leather boots with two-inch heels. Not enough height to make up the difference between her and Crowley, but better than nothing. She tried the blouse buttoned, unbuttoned. She left it unbuttoned.

She felt safe enough. Julianna hadn't told anyone about this dinner, but Crowley would have to assume she had. There was no way she'd invite an ex-con into her home without taking at least minimal precautions. She couldn't be *that* crazy a bitch.

How many times while she was growing up, Julianna wondered, had she sprawled on Genevieve's bed and watched her sister get ready for a date? Genevieve: fresh from the shower, nose to nose with her own reflection in the mirror above her dresser as she squeezed the eyelash curler tight. A turban made from a towel, her bare shoulders still jeweled with moisture, the Talking Heads or Maria McKee on the boom box.

Genevieve never spent hours and hours primping like some of the girls Julianna knew later in college. Genevieve was lazy, always running late, and—most important—she had no need to primp. Her natural beauty could be adjusted but not improved. The eyelash curler, mascara, a swipe of lipstick—that was it. Julianna had inherited this same minimalist approach, even though, especially now, nearing forty, a little foundation would not have killed her. As Donna at work had pointed out to her a few times. As in, *You've got nice skin, girl, but.*

She put on mascara. Lipstick only a half shade darker than her own lips. The doorbell dinged. Julianna checked the time. She was not expecting Crowley for another ten minutes. She supposed she shouldn't be surprised. The games had begun.

At the door she took two breaths, steady, and then put her eye to the peephole. She froze.

DeMars.

Every light in her house was on. Her car was in the driveway. The doorbell dinged again. She opened the door.

"Detective," she said, and smiled. "What a surprise."

"Look at you."

"At me?"

He smiled back at her. His mind kept working. Julianna had never known it to stop.

"Be careful, Detective," she said. "You're on thin ice."

"You look nice. You always look nice. This evening you look a different kind of nice."

"Well played."

"I been married a long time, Juli." He smoothed his silver-flecked goatee, striking a pose, and then chuckled.

Her heart raced, each beat stumbling up against the one ahead. If Crowley arrived while DeMars was still here, Julianna would never see either one of them again. That, and she didn't know what else would happen.

"Come on in," she said.

"You sure?"

"I'm sure."

"But you've got plans for the evening."

"Do I? DeMars. Ask if you're going to ask."

"You have a date," he said, palms up, "then that's none of my business."

He could tell that her heart was racing. Her cheeks were probably flushed. The fresh mascara, the boots. Did a part of DeMars suspect that all this had something to do with Crowley? Probably so. To be a detective, to see all the things he saw on a daily basis, he had to suspect the very worst in people.

Julianna didn't want to lie to him. Not in the state she was in. You had to be at the top of your game to get a lie past DeMars.

"You are correct," she said. "That's none of your business."

He chuckled again and handed her a slip of paper. "You need to answer your phone," he said. "I called you a couple of times."

Julianna took the slip of paper and unfolded it. On it, in De-Mars's steady hand, was written a phone number and a name: "Mary Hilger Hall." At first the name meant nothing to Julianna, and then she realized who it was: the woman on Facebook who'd posted the Food Alley photo from the '86 state fair.

"Oh," she said.

"I talked to her," DeMars said. "Just for a minute. Didn't tell her much. Didn't think you'd want me to. She said go ahead and give her a call. She's not sure she can help, but she said she'll try."

Julianna's love for DeMars at that instant almost broke her into pieces. But she didn't have time for that. She stole a glance at his watch. Crowley would be there any minute, any second.

"Come on in," she said again. "Do you have time for a beer?"

Such a transparent bluff. She was ashamed of herself. Her only hope was that DeMars really did think she had a date tonight and that was why she wanted him gone.

"You be good, now," he said.

He dipped his head so she could give him a peck on the cheek and then walked to his car. Julianna watched him drive away. DeMars had just turned the corner when she heard the rattle of Crowley's truck—from up the block, the opposite direction.

It was too late for her to go back inside. Crowley parked on the street and lumbered across the lawn toward her.

He had his hair in a ponytail instead of down. His plaid shirt was pressed. As he climbed the two steps to her porch, his blue eyes moved over her—from her boots to her face, then all the way back down to her boots again.

"Waiting out front for me," he said. "Eager beaver."

Yes, she felt safe enough. Julianna told herself that if Crowley planned to do her harm, he wouldn't have driven his own truck. The neighbors would take note. Someone might jot down the license plate. Crowley could see it was that kind of neighborhood.

"You're late," she said. And thank God he was.

"I'm whatever the hell I want to be," he said amiably. He tipped his chin up. The wiry gray goatee, a strong jaw. Julianna glimpsed, beneath all the sag and crease, the young man he'd once been—the ruins of an ancient civilization half buried in the jungle. Crowley's nostrils flared. "I smell something tasty."

But *was* it his own truck? Julianna realized she didn't know.

"Let's go inside and eat," she said.

She followed him in. She shut the door behind her but didn't lock it. Crowley glanced at the dining-room table, set for two, and moved past into the living room. He dropped heavily onto the sofa. Letting Julianna know, again, that all this was on his terms, not hers.

"You got any whiskey?" he said. "Beer if you don't."

She took a tumbler from the cupboard and filled it with Maker's Mark. Crowley took a sip.

"That'll do," he said.

Julianna felt surprisingly calm as she carved the turkey. Her heart had run itself ragged during the conversation with DeMars. It took a breather now, coasting.

The kitchen opened onto the living room. Crowley sat and watched her carve.

"You know what that reminds me of?" he said. "One time in the yard down at McAlester. This old boy took a shank to his little buddy and just split him up. I mean it. But did it calm as can be. Just another day at the office."

He smiled at her. Julianna knew what he was doing. She scooped potatoes onto his plate and ladled gravy. Green beans. A roll.

"White or dark meat?"

"As long as it's juicy."

"How do you know I won't poison you?" she said.

Crowley's gaze, moving around her living room, came back around to her fast. Julianna smiled at him.

She carried their plates into the dining room and sat down.

After a minute she heard the sofa springs creak. After another minute Crowley entered the dining room, carrying the bottle of Maker's Mark, his glass, an extra glass. He sat down across from her. Without a word he snapped his cloth napkin open and started eating.

"Tell me what you remember about my sister," Julianna said.

He shook his head, mystified. "Turkey with no stuffing."

"I forgot."

"You make this gravy yourself?"

"No."

He was a surprisingly well-mannered diner. Small bites, mouth closed when he chewed, elbows off the table. An occasional dab of the napkin to his lips. Julianna ate a little of the mashed potatoes and then put her fork down.

"Will you tell me what you remember about my sister?"

"Slow down, now." He reached for the bourbon and refilled his glass. He filled half of the glass Julianna supposed was meant for her. "Let's get to know each other."

His eyes were so blue. Piercing? Not exactly. The effect was more subtle than that. Like he was leaning in toward her when in fact he was sitting still.

"I don't want to know you," she said.

"Tell me a secret 'bout you that nobody else in the world knows. Nobody but you and me."

"No."

He nodded at the glass he'd filled for her. She hesitated, then lifted the glass and drank the bourbon down in one swallow. She held Crowley's blue-eyed gaze and waited for the booze to land. When it did, heat spread out to her farthest edges. A massive splash. A fat kid doing cannonballs in a pool. She laughed.

"I didn't know what semen was," she said. "I mean, I knew.

But I'd just turned thirteen. I was young for my age. There was a boy who lived down the street. He was older than me, a junior or senior in high school. I waited until I knew that his parents weren't home, and then I went over. I asked him if I could see his penis. I just came right out and asked him. I was curious. I wanted to see his penis make semen. I knew that the penis was involved. He said no, at first—no way! I was just this little pest of a little neighbor girl he'd never even noticed unless my sister was around. But he gave in. It was fascinating. I was fascinated. Afterward he was so embarrassed. He couldn't even look at me. Which was funny, because he was this big athlete at his high school, this cocky guy all the girls were in love with. But really he was a sweet kid."

Crowley had started to take a sip of bourbon but then forgotten to finish. Julianna saw the surprise in his eyes, the fresh wariness. He'd planned to keep her on edge. Now he was on the edge with her. Maybe he was wondering how the hell that had happened. Julianna stood.

"More?"

"Everything but the gravy."

When she returned from the kitchen, Crowley had the tumbler of bourbon in his hand, contemplating it, the way Julianna had seen him do in the bar. She put the plate in front of him and sat back down.

"Corn-bread stuffing," he said. "That's what my mama made. But my daddy's mama, she'd always made it from white bread. That was a war, let me tell you. Every Thanksgiving and Christmas. Long as they was together, at least."

Julianna remembered Denny, the boy who lived down the block from them. He went to U. S. Grant High School, and his letter jacket had an embroidered patch, the word GENERALS, sewn on the leather sleeve. He was good-looking, but Genevieve never had any interest in him. Bohunks bored her.

He didn't mind showing Julianna his cock. He thought it was kind of a hoot—innocent, educational. But when she told him she wanted to see *everything,* she wanted to see him do *everything*—that was why she was there, after all—he shook his head hard and pulled his jeans back up.

"You're just a kid," he'd said.

"You're chicken," Julianna said. "You're a big chicken."

"No I'm not. This isn't right."

"Chicken," she said. "I'm going to tell everyone you're a big chicken."

He stopped buttoning his jeans and stared at her. "You can't tell anyone about this."

That might have been the moment, Julianna thought, when she realized that power could be taken, not just bestowed. All you had to do was recognize the opportunity when you saw it.

"Hey!" he'd said. "I mean you can't tell anyone about this!"

Julianna just sat there cross-legged on the floor of his bedroom, her chin in her hand, and said nothing. She waited.

As he neared the end of the process, Denny let Julianna put her hand on his hand as he moved it up and down, up and down, faster and faster. In retrospect Julianna thought he might not even have noticed her hand on his. His eyes were closed, his face crumpled. He looked like he was in pain, like he'd banged his toe on the curb.

"Tell me what you remember about my sister," she told Crowley.

"What do you remember 'bout me?"

"About you?"

"I was a handsome young man, wasn't I?"

She noticed that he'd filled her glass again. She reached for it and had a sip. Just a sip this time. Her head felt light but clear.

"I remember you never took your eyes off my sister."

"You don't look nothing like her."

"Not really."

He finished the last bite on his plate and then studied her.

"Maybe a little," he said. "That was a long time ago."

"So you do remember her, then."

"Never said I didn't."

"You told her to come to your trailer later. When she left me, she was on her way to your trailer."

"Says you."

He pushed back from the table and stood. Shifted from one foot to the other and winced. He picked up the bottle of Maker's Mark and his glass.

"My damn back," he said.

She followed him into the living room. He lowered himself to the sofa, wincing again. For effect? Julianna thought maybe so. She took a seat in the chair across from him.

"Dumbest thing I ever did," he said.

"What?"

"Steal that beer from the 7-Eleven. I had the cash to pay for it. Hell, I had plenty of cash, but I left my billfold at the trailer. I thought, well, hell, ain't no sense walking another mile back and forth just for a six-pack of Budweiser. What'd a six-pack go for in those days? Five dollars? The clerk in the store wasn't paying no attention. Cop out in the parking lot was, though. Pulled in to get himself a doughnut, probably. But turned out lucky for me, didn't it?"

"You were in jail when my sister was last seen," Julianna said. "I know that."

"Whatever happened to your sister, I ain't the one caused it to happen."

"I want to know about before you stole the beer."

"Have another drink," he said.

"No."

He filled his glass again. His smile caught her off guard. It was a young man's smile, the same smile he'd smiled at Genevieve when he handed Julianna the Pink Panther plush toy.

"Aww," he said. "You ain't no fun."

If Crowley didn't give her what she wanted, Julianna decided, she'd call the police when he left and report a drunk driver in the neighborhood. She'd provide them with a detailed description of his truck. Crowley's blood-alcohol level had to be over the limit already.

"When you handed me that Pink Panther," Julianna said, "I was so happy. But it wasn't the Pink Panther that made me happy. I can't explain it. What made me happy was that my sister knew just how happy that stupid Pink Panther would make me."

That was the moment Julianna wanted to remember. Not the moment, later, when Genevieve looked past her toward the midway—looked *through* her, Julianna just an inconvenient apparition—and promised without meaning it that she'd be back in a flash.

Crowley was silent. He shifted on the couch and propped the toe of one boot against the edge of the coffee table. Alligator cowboy boots, polished. He'd dressed up for Julianna.

"She had a way about her," he said finally.

"Did my sister come to your trailer?"

"Yeah."

The heat from the bourbon, Julianna's pleasant buzz, vanished. The world sharpened around her. When she took a breath, she felt the silky mesh of her lungs expand.

"You're lying," she said.

Crowley smiled. "Minute ago I was lying when I said she never did. You gotta pick one and stick to it, darlin'."

Julianna stayed calm. Somehow she managed it. She knew she had one chance, this chance, at the truth.

"When?" she said.

"I don't know. A little after dark, must have been. I didn't know she'd turn up or not. I thought she might. I hoped she might. There were plenty of girls on the road, but your sister had a way about her. Like I said."

He was a big man—he took up almost half of Julianna's sofa. One boot up on the coffee table, having a sip of his bourbon, his blue eyes steady on her.

Was he lying? Why? Was he telling the truth? Why?

"And?" Julianna said.

"And nothing," he said. "She turned up, we talked for a minute or two, and then she left. I asked her did she want to come inside. Can't blame me—I thought that was why she was there."

"What did she say?" she said.

"I don't recall. But she didn't come inside. She left."

Julianna waited. For something more, anything more. She could feel the faint breeze of hope fading, dying. Crowley was just taunting her. Genevieve had never come to his trailer.

He saw he'd lost Julianna. "Believe me or not."

"I don't," she said. "What did you talk about?"

"This and that. The usual pleasantries." He tipped back the rest of the bourbon in his glass. "I had a guitar back then. Old acoustic guitar. I told her I could play her a song if she wanted. Every other girl, they all wanted me to play them a song. I was a hand-some young man, you remember. I said, Let's make some music together. Your sister, though, she said—I don't recall exactly what she said. She laughed and gave me a wink. She said, 'Let's not.' That was it."

The jolt of recognition caught Julianna off guard. She could hear that laugh, she could see the wink. Genevieve's most common response, whenever Julianna suggested how much fun it would be for the two of them to build a tree fort in the backyard, or dress up like the Bangles, or stay up all night playing board games.

I know what! Genevieve would say, as if she'd just been struck by the most brilliant idea ever.

"Let's not and say we did," Julianna told Crowley.

Crowley nodded. "That's it. Let's not and say we did. Made me feel two feet tall, but I had to laugh, too. Your sister had a way about her."

Julianna got up and went into the kitchen. She didn't want Crowley to see that her hands were shaking. She cut a slice of apple pie and slid it onto a plate. When she returned to the living room, he'd filled his glass again. She set the pie on the coffee table in front of him.

Genevieve *had* gone to Crowley's trailer. She *had* talked to him there.

It was as if Julianna had spent most of her adult life staring at a blank brick wall. And now, suddenly, a door had appeared in that wall.

Behind the door: the possibility that her sister, who had vanished from the face of the earth, had maybe not, after all, vanished without a trace.

Julianna had so many questions she felt dizzy. Why would Genevieve go to Crowley's trailer only to leave again? Why hadn't she returned to the spot in front of the rodeo arena where she'd left Julianna? How and why did Genevieve end up half an hour later on Food Alley, on the other side of the fairgrounds?

"Please tell me everything you remember about that night," Julianna said.

"I told you, the long and short of it," Crowley said. He took a bite of the pie, then put his fork down and pushed the plate away. "That ain't no home-baked."

"Why did she leave?"

"Don't have no idea. I tried not take it personal. Went to go got me some beer. You know what happened at the end of that story."

"Where was she going when she left?"

"Didn't say."

"Was there someone else there?"

"Someone else where?"

"Your trailer."

Crowley gave Julianna a look. "You think I planned to share her? No, I didn't."

"Or nearby. Someone who might have followed her when she left."

Julianna was thinking of the man in the cowboy hat, but she didn't want to lead Crowley.

"Don't have no idea," he said. "Not that I saw."

Genevieve *had* gone to Crowley's trailer. She *had* talked to him there.

That was all she could be certain was true, Julianna reminded herself, out of everything Crowley had told her.

"Why didn't you tell the police any of this?"

"Why do you think? They was looking for any reason to get further up my ass. And I didn't have nothing to do with nothing."

He patted the sofa cushion next to him. "Come on over here a minute, why don't you?"

Julianna stayed where she was, in the chair, two steps from the carving knife she'd left on the kitchen counter. Even if his bad back was a fiction, she thought she'd be able to get to the knife before Crowley got to her.

He held out his hand. "That pinkie finger there? See how it's crooked? That's from a cop picked me up one time for disorderly conduct. Murray, Kentucky. Broke my finger in two just for the fun of it."

"Are you sure that's all you remember?" Julianna said. "Do you remember anything else at all?"

Crowley pulled his boot off the coffee table. He got to his feet slowly, heavily.

"Where are you going?" Julianna said. She stood, too.

"Dinner's over, ain't it?" he said, his blue eyes innocent. "Unless you got something else in mind, of course."

"Just . . . wait," she said.

"I'm sorry, darlin'," he said. "I gave you everything I got."

He moved to the door. Julianna followed. She felt a panic rising in her. She had to fight to stay above it.

"Anything else," she said. "The smallest detail. Anything at all."

He opened the door but then stopped. "I do recall now she said one thing. Your sister did. Was the last thing she said to me, right before she took off."

"What did she say?" Julianna said.

"Didn't mean nothing to me at the time. Now I think about it, though, after what happened and all . . . well. Might be it means something after all."

Julianna reached for Crowley's arm. She gripped it tight.

"What did she say?" she demanded, and then in the next breath—when he turned back to her, when he smiled—she realized just how perfectly he'd played her.

He stepped even closer and put a finger beneath her chin. Julianna let him. He tilted her head back, gently, so that he was looking right down at her.

"Bet you'd like to know," he said. "Wouldn't you?"

Wyatt

CHAPTER 14

W yatt stopped back by the Land Run to ask Candace about Lyle Finn and then remembered she'd already left to take Lily to day care.

He got out his phone. He put it away. He wanted to call Laurie back but knew he needed to give her time. He couldn't understand what she wanted him to think about. He loved her. He wanted to spend his life with her. He'd never been as sure of anything *in* his life. What else was there?

He'd never told Laurie what happened to him at the movie theater twenty-six years earlier. She didn't know the name he'd been born with. But that was Wyatt's choice to make, wasn't it? He didn't want that night in the projection booth to be part of their life together. He didn't want it to be part of his life. It *wasn't* part of his life, at least not when he was anywhere but *here*, this city, where the past was a riptide.

Theresa, Wyatt thought, would understand. She'd had no interest in the sharing of feelings, no patience with the baring of souls. If you tried to tell Theresa the story of your life, your hopes and dreams—if, even more foolishly, you ever tried to ask about *her* life, *her* hopes and dreams—she would yawn, she would blow smoke at you, she'd bend close and run a finger along the shiny ridge of her shin, checking for any patches she missed when she shaved her legs that morning.

Theresa wasn't especially beautiful. She was just an ordinary seventeen-year-old girl with dark hair and a long neck and a slight overbite. So what made her so attractive? Her eyes were a strange metallic green, like the sky in Oklahoma when suddenly the wind died and you knew a tornado was near.

O'Malley and Theresa broke up for good at the beginning of the summer. The decision to split, he told Wyatt the day after it happened, was mutual and amicable. O'Malley never mentioned it again. Theresa, of course, never mentioned it all. Wyatt waited a couple of months to make sure they didn't get back together. And it took him that long, really, to work up the courage to tell Theresa how he felt about her. The first time Wyatt started to tell Theresa he loved her, the first and only time, she touched two fingers to his lips and said, "Shhhh," stopping him. She twisted the handle of the popcorn kettle with her other hand and watched the popcorn pour golden into the bin. She went on with her shift as if Wyatt had never said anything.

Melody, nosy Melody, was the only other employee around at the time, working the box office during Karlene's break. The box office was at the opposite end of the concession stand, and Melody was facing away from the popcorn machine. But Wyatt should have known better. Melody had eyes in the back of her head, she had supernatural hearing. Later that night she cut Wyatt a look—

sympathy, amusement, warning. Wyatt cut her a look back. Like, what? Like, I have no idea why you're looking at me that way! Melody just grinned. Wyatt was a terrible liar at age fifteen.

Why am I still here and all the others gone?

Wyatt didn't know any of the killers. He didn't recognize their names. Richard William Purdy. Dale Earl Barrett. Clifton Holly Needs. Their names meant nothing to Wyatt. Their faces, no matter how long Wyatt studied them, meant nothing to him. He'd never seen any of the three men before in his life.

Or had he?

For years after the murders, the possibility that maybe Wyatt *had* crossed paths with one of the killers, without realizing it, almost drove him out of his mind. His memories of the theater that summer were razor sharp, at work and after work, but he didn't remember in much detail the time he spent away from O'Malley and Theresa and the others.

Mornings in front of the TV. Mowing the lawn. Walking up to Roy Rogers for lunch or to Penn Square Mall for the used-book store. Was there some critical moment in there that he'd forgotten about? Some brief, chance encounter he had with a stranger that ended up, down the line, saving his life?

Or what about all the customers at the theater? Thousands of them over the course of a summer, a blur of faces. Two auditoriums, six shows a day each. During the rush you had to bust your ass. Wyatt didn't have time for more than a glance at any but the hottest of hot girls.

The police were sure that one or more of the killers had cased the theater before the robbery. But maybe *that* was the other way around. Maybe one of the killers happened to see a movie at the Pheasant Run and realized what a sweet score it would make.

Wyatt stopped at Whole Foods to pick up some of the apples he remembered his uncle liked, Honeycrisps, and drove to his house. His uncle was sitting on the porch.

"Mikey!" Wyatt's uncle said.

"How are you, Uncle Pete?"

The old man reached up to give Wyatt's hand a solemn, formal shake.

"As well as can be expected given the circumstances," he said in his deadpan baritone. It was another one of his favorite lines. "Sit down, Mikey. Take a load off."

He patted the cushion next to him. Wyatt had a seat on the rusted old porch slider—the place, in nice weather, where his grandmother would always sit and rock away the hours.

Wyatt handed the bag of apples to his uncle. His uncle peered inside.

"Honeycrisps! My word."

"The apple of kings, the king of apples," Wyatt said.

"That's just what Daddy always said."

"Uncle Pete," Wyatt said, "you took me to a ball game out at the fairgrounds one Fourth of July. It was the summer before my junior year in high school."

"Was it?"

"You remember the fireworks? After the game. We stayed for the fireworks."

"I sure do," Pete said.

Wyatt could still see how the fireworks came swimming up from behind the scoreboard in left field, fast at first and then slower, struggling until they lost all momentum, drooping and bursting apart. But he couldn't remember anything else—that was it.

"Do you remember anything else about that night?" Wyatt said. "Who we talked to? Anything out of the ordinary?"

His uncle stroked his chin. "Well, sure," he said. "We sat next to that fella with the trombone."

"With the trombone?"

"Sure. Out at Holland Park. When the Indians hit a home run, you remember, he'd blow his trombone. A big, fat fella who always wore a bow tie. Rudy or Ruby. Ruby, I think. Ruby Roberts. I know you remember him. Old Ruby with the trombone."

The Oklahoma City Indians had been the name of the minor-league team long before Wyatt was born, and Holland Park was where they played before the stadium at the fairgrounds was ever built.

Pete was lost again in the past. He couldn't help Wyatt. No one could.

Why am I still here and all the others gone?

There was no answer. The question was a loop without beginning or end, a tunnel that corkscrewed deeper, deeper into the bedrock and never found light. Wyatt knew this. And yet here, once again, he was.

"You remember old Ruby with the trombone, don't you?" his uncle said.

"Sure I do," Wyatt said.

WYATT HEADED BACK to the hotel to change his shirt before the football game. In the lobby someone called out for him to hold the elevator. Wyatt complied. A kid in his twenties—coat and tie, khaki slacks—hurried in.

"Mr. Rivers?" he said.

"That's me," Wyatt said.

The kid had broad shoulders and rosy cheeks and a bashful, aw-shucks smile. Probably, Wyatt guessed, a former power-hitting high-school first baseman from a small town in eastern Oklahoma.

On the lapel of his blazer was a hotel name tag: CHIP.

"My name's Chip," the guy said.

"I wish you would've let me guess," Wyatt said.

He punched in his floor. The doors slid shut, and the elevator began to rise.

"I'm not supposed to be here," Chip said.

"In a metaphysical sense?" Wyatt said. "Or in the sense that you just remembered you have a meeting in the banquet room?"

The guy smiled bashfully and shook his head. "No, I mean I work at the front desk. We're not supposed to approach the guests for personal reasons."

It was news to Wyatt, that he was being approached for personal reasons. He noticed now that the guy seemed nervous—opening his hands, closing his hands. Wyatt checked the display. Four floors to go.

"Fire away," he said.

"You're a private detective, right?"

"I am."

"My friend in food and beverage told me you were. I hope you don't mind. I don't want to get him in trouble."

"Don't worry. I blame my own big mouth."

"I need your help, Mr. Rivers."

"You don't," Wyatt said. "You may need *help*. That's entirely possible. But you don't necessarily need *my* help."

The kid, Chip, worked his way through that one. The elevator continued to shudder upward. Slowly, slowly.

"I can pay you. I'll pay you whatever you want." Chip hesitated. His hands opened, his hands closed. He bit his lower lip. "How much would that be, do you think?"

Finally the bell dinged, and the elevator doors slid open.

"Chip," Wyatt said, "I'm afraid my dance card is full."

"Oh."

It didn't appear that Chip knew what a dance card was. Wyatt wasn't entirely sure he knew either.

"I'm booked," he explained. "Busy. Unavailable."

"It's my wife," Chip said. "I think she . . . I think she's having an affair. It's eating me up, not knowing for sure. I feel like I can't even breathe sometimes."

He looked too young to be married. But how young was too young? He was probably twenty-three or twenty-four. Maybe he was already an old hand at marriage.

"Ask her," Wyatt said. "That's my best advice. A healthy relationship is best served by trust and candor, not the services of a private detective."

"I did ask her. She said I was being stupid. And maybe I am. But how do I know that? When do you know if you're being stupid or not?"

Wyatt didn't have an answer for that. He wished, selfishly, he did. "I'm sorry."

He stepped out of the elevator. His room was four doors down. When he got there and turned to swipe his key card, he saw that the kid was still standing there—forlorn, halfway in the corridor and halfway out—the jaws of the elevator trying to snap closed on him.

"All I need, Mr. Rivers," he said, "one way or another I just need to *know*."

Wyatt swiped his key card but didn't enter his room. Shit. He felt a certain amount of bad for the kid, but mostly he felt motivated by caution. Yesterday he'd asked a favor from the cranky reporter at the *Daily Oklahoman*. So how wise would it be for Wyatt to refuse now when the universe asked a favor in return?

If one sows goodness, one reaps goodness. According to the Vedas.

"I'll try to look into it, but no promises." Wyatt took out his notebook. "I'll need some information about your wife."

"Mr. Rivers. Thank you. Oh, man. Thank you so much."

"Don't thank me yet."

Wyatt's point sailed right by the kid, a passed ball the catcher never even saw. When Chip shook Wyatt's hand, he shook Wyatt's entire arm.

"Oh, man," he said. "I will. I won't."

THE DRIVE DOWN to Norman took Wyatt twice as long as it should have—game-night traffic, bumper to bumper, big-ass SUVs with crimson flags flapping from plastic arms wedged between window and roof. Some SUVs had four Sooner flags, one for each window. Wyatt felt naked without one.

When the crawl finally reached Norman, he had to park blocks from campus, in the patchy front yard of two college students who charged him twenty bucks for the privilege.

Wyatt scored the last spot in the yard. He squeezed his rented Altima between an Escalade (two flags, a vanity OU plate) and the porch of the house. The porch was crowded with more college students, the guys with tribal tattoos on their calves and struggling chinstrap beards, the girls in cut-off jeans and bikini tops. One shirtless guy was attempting to do a keg stand while another guy slapped at him with a wet towel.

Wyatt thought that looked like more fun than spending the evening with Jeff Eddy, but duty called.

The massive redbrick football stadium was in the center of campus. It dominated the campus, like a medieval cathedral surrounded by mud-and-wattle huts. Wyatt could feel the throb of religious excitement, of ecstatic near hysteria, as the crowd he'd become enfolded in funneled closer and closer to the stadium. Every thirty seconds or so, someone would shout "Boomer!" and then the rest of the crowd would roar back "Sooner!"

Wyatt knew that OU was now a very good public university, well regarded nationally. Back when he was a kid, though, people had joked that they wanted to build a school that the football team could be proud of.

Wyatt's father had lived and breathed sports—he'd loved, literally and without exaggeration, nothing and nobody else in his life but sports. O'Malley hadn't given a shit about sports. He gave a shit about books and movies and music. From the first day they met, he'd made Wyatt feel good about himself, not bad, for giving a shit about the same things. O'Malley understood that there was a world outside Oklahoma City, which in the 1980s could feel—for someone like Wyatt, from a family like Wyatt's—like a closed fist.

O'Malley had planned to move to California, or maybe Rome. Wyatt, after he graduated high school a couple of years later, or maybe even before if he saved enough money, would follow. He would take the spare bedroom in O'Malley's beach house or Renaissance villa.

One hot summer Sunday—it must have been late June or early July—they all drove down to Lake Thunderbird to drink beer and water ski. "Lake Dirtybird," everyone called it, because the water was a deep reddish brown. Janella's sister's boyfriend had loaned them his boat, under what false pretenses Wyatt couldn't imagine. O'Malley took control of the wheel and opened up the throttle. He blasted around the lake, ignoring the "No Wake" zones and seeing how closely he could cut past the shoreline. The girls in the back of the boat, Janella and Karlene and Theresa, laughed and gripped the gunwales and yelled at O'Malley to *"Slow down!"*

Like he would ever do that.

"Never fear!" O'Malley had hollered to Wyatt over the roar of the engine, the pummeling of the wind. "These walls can't hold us!"

Wyatt located Jeff Eddy, as instructed, in the choicest of choice tailgating spots. Eddy was wearing a crimson sweater vest with a white OU insignia above his heart. He forked sausages on a grill almost as big as Wyatt's rented Altima and held court, surrounded by four guys dressed in similar fashion, of similar age and jowliness, with similar tipsy, shit-eating grins.

The ladyfolk had hauled their high-end canvas folding chairs, margaritas in the cup holders, upwind from the billowing grill smoke. They wriggled their toes, comparing pedicures.

"Even better," Eddy was telling the others, "you 'member how Chunks here got his name? Night of that party we threw with the Deltas."

"Oh, hell no," one of the guys groaned. Chunks, presumably. The other guys grinned and snickered.

Eddy spotted Wyatt before Wyatt could make a break for it. "Wyatt, buddy!"

Eddy passed off the tongs so he could head over and give Wyatt's hand an overly hearty pump. And then another pump, a slap on the back. Wyatt couldn't tell you the last time someone had slapped him on the back.

"What are you drinking?" Eddy said. "We got anything you can think of."

"A pisco sour if it's not too much trouble," Wyatt said, just so he could appreciate the effort it took Eddy to maintain his totally bogus bonhomie. "No. How about a caipirinha?"

Eddy forced a laugh. "A beer all right?"

"You bet."

Eddy found him a Sierra Nevada and introduced Wyatt to the other guys as his business associate from Las Vegas. In addition to Chunks, there was Otter, Goose, and Big Boy. Wyatt didn't bother trying to keep them straight.

"Where'd you go to school?" one of the guys asked Wyatt. "Just don't say Texas."

"Or OSU!" another guy said.

Big Boy, clearly the drunkest of the bunch, was eyeing Wyatt, who had on a lightweight light gray suit, white shirt, no tie.

"So," Big Boy said. "You just come from the prom?"

The other guys held their snickers and waited to see if Wyatt could take a little good-natured shit or confirm their suspicion that he was some humorless, bed-wetting liberal.

"Funeral," Wyatt said. He looked down at his wing tips. "My mother."

You could hear the condensation beading on the neck of Wyatt's beer bottle. The four guys stared at him, then looked away, then lifted their glasses and bottles, in perfect synchrony, to take a long, uncomfortable drink.

Big Boy and Goose were drinking whiskey, Otter beer, Chunks a margarita.

Wyatt guessed that Big Boy and Otter were in the energy business—they were talkers, deal makers, hustlers. Chunks—watcher, lurker—was probably a lawyer. Taxes. Big Boy was the drunkest, but Wyatt thought it was probably Goose who had a problem with the bottle. His wife was the alpha blonde who kept glancing over at him, her mouth a tight seam. She was counting how many drinks her husband had, tapping her wedding ring against the side of her margarita glass.

One of the toughest things about being a detective, Wyatt supposed, was that you never really stopped detecting. You didn't get a coffee break.

Jeff Eddy put his hand on Wyatt's shoulder and forced another smile. This smile submitted even less willingly than the first one, like the driver after a high-speed chase getting wrestled to the ground by cops.

"He's kidding," Eddy said.

"I'm kidding," Wyatt said. "It was just a cremation ceremony."

From the stadium came a blast of brass as the OU marching band struck up the university fight song.

"Let's go watch some football," Eddy said.

"Boomer!" Big Boy yelled.

WYATT WOULD HAVE preferred for Jeff Eddy to just cut to the chase, but he supposed there were worse ways to kill an evening. It was beautiful out, cool and crisp, and Eddy was buying the beer and bringing it to him. Wyatt was pretty sure Candace would kill him if she knew he was here, if he were ever brazen enough to call this "investigating."

The third or fourth time Eddy went for beer, late in the second quarter, his wife scooted over to sit next to Wyatt. Her name was Karen. She was thin, expensively perfumed, with one eyebrow hiked in such a way that suggested either a natural haughty skepticism or recent facial work that had been done neither too well nor too wisely.

Wyatt tried to imagine what this fifty-something woman had

looked like when she was seventeen years old, what she'd been like, what future she'd dreamed of. He couldn't do it. She could have been anyone back then. Whoever she'd been back then could have become anyone.

"So," Eddy's wife said, "you're the private investigator has my husband's panties all in a bunch."

"I don't think I'm supposed to know that, Karen," Wyatt said.

"Well."

"Tell me more."

"Not me."

They watched the game for a few downs. Wyatt watched one of the Sooner defensive linemen at work against his opposite number—probing, faking, charging, spinning, hammering, curling. Each play was a ballet, each attack a chess move designed with the next three or four in mind.

Wyatt thought it was probably the only useful advice his father had ever given him: Don't just watch the ball. The real game happens on the edges.

"I've been coming to these games for forty years," Eddy's wife said. Her tone was neutral.

On a third-and-long, the Sooner lineman who Wyatt was tracking juked a blocker out of his shoes and broke through. The quarterback had to hurry his pass. It sailed high and wide.

"There are some parts of my life that feel now like they never happened," Wyatt said. He thought of the two years he'd spent in Minneapolis, the year before that in Charlotte. "Do you know what I mean? It's not that I don't remember them. It's that I don't even remember to remember them."

She nodded.

"How long have you and Jeff been married?" Wyatt said.

"Thirty-one years."

"Congratulations."

Eddy's wife turned to him. She put her hand on his forearm. "I want to know why Greg didn't leave the Land Run to Jeff."

"Ms. Kilkenny isn't a prostitute," Wyatt said. "She's not a stripper or a gold digger. I don't know what your husband told you. There was no sexual or romantic component to her relationship with your late brother-in-law."

"You're not listening to me," Eddy's wife said.

Wyatt was surprised. He thought of himself as an excellent listener. His livelihood often depended upon it.

"I don't want to know why Greg left the Land Run to that girl," she said. "I want to know why he didn't leave it to his own brother."

Jeff Eddy had returned with the beer. His wife scooted back over to her seat, and he sat down next to Wyatt.

"Now then," Eddy said. He lowered his voice, even though he didn't have to. The crowd was roaring, the band playing. "Let's talk some turkey."

"Let's talk."

"So you haven't mentioned it to Candace?" Eddy said. "This alleged new MAPS initiative?"

Alleged. "Not yet," Wyatt lied. "I wanted to hear what you had to say."

Eddy nodded. He was studying Wyatt, eyes narrowed, trying to get a read on him.

"I'd like to employ your services," he said finally. "With regard to the Land Run."

"With regard to the Land Run?" Wyatt laughed. "I foresee a potential conflict of interest."

"That's where you're wrong. And that's what you need to understand. Our interests, mine and Miss Kilkenny's, they're exactly aligned."

Wyatt couldn't wait to hear this. "Go on."

"Look. You think that girl is gonna be happy running that dump? You think she's gonna be happy a year from now when that dump goes bust and she loses everything?"

"Is that your plan? To keep screwing with her until she goes out of business?"

"What? No. I told you, I don't have anything to do with any of that. What I'm talking about, I'm talking about the reality of the situation. What does she know about running a place like that? Can I tell you a secret?"

"It won't leave this stadium."

"My brother never made a dime. He worked there seven days a week since he was fifteen years old. He knew the business inside and out. And it was all he could do to break even two years out of three."

Wyatt didn't know if that was true or not. It didn't really matter to him one way or the other.

"So what do you want from me?" he said.

"I want you to help Miss Kilkenny understand the wisdom of selling the Land Run. Find out how much she's willing to take. She'll end up with a nice little nest egg, and I'll be able to honor my brother's memory."

An OU receiver shook the coverage and caught a bomb in the corner of the end zone. The band played the fight song for— Wyatt's conservative estimate—the one-millionth time.

"Ms. Kilkenny will want a much bigger egg if she knows about the tax initiative," Wyatt said. "Sorry. The *alleged* tax initiative."

The groove between Eddy's eyebrows deepened. His lips disappeared. And then he recovered with a chuckle.

"We're still sitting here talking about this," he said. "You know what that tells me? That tells me you're a businessman."

Sitting there talking to Jeff Eddy—Wyatt was going to need a hot shower with lots of soap. On the other hand, he knew that Candace would really, truly kill him if he spent all evening drinking beer at a football game and came back with nothing to show for it. Wyatt decided to play along.

"Do you know that old joke?" he said. "A man goes up to a lady, a very prim and proper lady, and he says, 'Would you have sex with me for a million dollars?' I don't know what that would be nowadays, adjusted for inflation, but you get the idea. And the lady thinks about it and blushes, and finally she says, 'Yes, I suppose I would.' And then the man says, 'Okay, would you have sex with me for five dollars?' And the lady is just, like, terribly affronted. She says, 'How dare you! What do you think I am?' And the man says, 'Oh, we've already established what you are. Now we're just haggling over your price.'"

Eddy grinned. "I'm sure we can come to an agreement."

Wyatt

CHAPTER 15

Wyatt fled the game at halftime, after promising—for a figure to be determined later—to help bring the interests of Jeff Eddy and Candace into their natural alignment. On the way back up I-35, Wyatt had plenty of time to weigh the probabilities. Did Jeff Eddy's attempt to buy him off—and shut him up about the new MAPS—make it more likely that Eddy was behind what had happened to Candace so far? Or less?

Wyatt couldn't decide. He made it back to the city at about nine and drove around Bricktown. The area consisted of several square blocks of old warehouses east of downtown that had been renovated and converted into restaurants, clubs, shops. It was hopping tonight—there was a Thunder game at the arena on the other side of Broadway—and Wyatt knew that whoever had been in on the ground floor of the Bricktown MAPS development had made a killing.

Jeff Eddy wanted to get in on the ground floor of the new

MAPS development. Wyatt didn't blame him for that. He blamed him for being such a sneaky, sleazy tool about it.

Wyatt ate dinner on Automobile Alley, a stretch of Broadway that long ago had been lined with car dealerships. Abandoned for decades, the historic old Art Deco showrooms had been converted to upscale restaurants and shops. The grass-fed rib eye that Wyatt ordered was as good as anything he'd ever eaten in Vegas or L.A.

After dinner he headed over to the Land Run. There was a long line out front, but Fudge, the giant guy who worked the door, spotted Wyatt and waved him up.

"Yo!" he said. "What up, Mr. PI? Mr. *PI*. Mr. *VIPI*."

"How's your swag, Fudge?" Wyatt said. "Are we talking legit or not?"

"Oh, *legit*. No *question*." He bumped fists with Wyatt. "You see what happen last night?"

"I saw it."

"Somebody turn all this shit upside *down*. I'm talking *upside* down. Took us *all* day get it all turned right side *up* again. I'm talking all *day*."

"I'm on it," Wyatt said. "Is the boss around?"

"Yeah. But let me ax you a question first, Mr. VIPI. You know why they call me Fudge?"

Wyatt suspected he did know. But he noticed a couple of girls at the front of the line who were listening in. Fudge had noticed them, too. Wyatt was happy to oblige.

"You know, I don't," Wyatt said. "Why do they call you Fudge?"

"Because," Fudge said for the benefit of the honeys, "I am dark and sweet and *no* woman can't get enough of me."

The honeys giggled. Wyatt bumped fists again with Fudge as he stepped past.

Inside, the Land Run was packed and happily raucous as every-one waited for the next band of the night to take the stage. The crowd skewed white and youngish, with a lot of college-age kids, but other and older demographics were represented to a surpris-ing degree. There were hippies and bearded hipsters and barflies and yuppies and rednecks and a pair of elderly lesbians, holding hands. A white Sikh and a black cowboy.

The mix was probably different from what it had been in Wyatt's day. Hipsters, for example, had not yet been invented in 1986, and he spotted no girls now with 'Til Tuesday hair and eye shadow. But he was glad to see it was still a mix: Oklahomans from all walks of life brought together by a shared love of off the beaten-path music played loud in a scruffy, intimate venue—and adventurous enough to park their cars at night in a neighborhood like this one.

Wyatt remembered what O'Malley had called the Land Run: the Church of All Sorts.

He squeezed his way to the bar and caught the eye of the bar-tender. Dallas, with her elaborate, colorful tattoos and silver nose hoop. Tonight she had epic hair, a pompadour with a ponytail. Dark red lipstick, Cleopatra eyes.

"Hey there, you," she said.

"Dallas. You're looking very rockabilly tonight."

"That's the idea. You want a drink?" Her Oklahoma twang made it sound like *drank*. "Wyatt. Like the sheriff."

"No thank you."

"Your loss."

"Don't be that way," Wyatt said. "I feel like we can still make this relationship work."

"Too late. I'm fixin' to move on with my life."

She headed off with a toss of her ponytail. She pulled a couple of drafts and delivered them to the end of the bar. Banged four glasses down and hit them with ice, tonic, vodka, and lime wheels. Broke a twenty with one hand while with the other she hit two more glasses with ice and Jack Daniel's.

A minute later she worked her way back down the bar to where Wyatt was standing.

"I knew you'd be back," he said.

"Guess I can't stay away." *Cain't.* "You crack the case yet?"

"This close," Wyatt said. "Here. Let me see that one."

She let him have her forearm. Wyatt held it, he turned it this way and that.

"That's a tattoo of a phoenix, Dallas," he said. "Rising from the ashes."

"I know what it is. I designed it."

"Did you?"

"I apprentice over at Ink & Roses in the Plaza District. Three more months and out I go, on my own."

Wyatt traced the tail of the phoenix with his thumb. The tattoo had great color and detail. Every individual feather in the plumage was a different shade of red or yellow or green.

"A woman of many talents," Wyatt said.

"Get a room, you two," the grizzled old guy next to Wyatt growled. He had dyed black hair and a matching soul patch. He lifted his empty glass and rattled the ice cubes.

Wyatt gave Dallas her arm back, and she started making the old guy a fresh drink.

"You know where Candace is?" Wyatt said.

"Don't look now."

Candace was up in the balcony, at the rail, glaring down at Wyatt. He made his way up the creaking wooden stairs.

"Stop flirting with my bartender," Candace said. "Do that on your own time."

"I'm not. And I have my own time?"

"No. Not until you figure out who's trying to screw up my life."

He followed her to a booth at the far end of the balcony. The table was piled with stacks of invoices, inventory sheets, receipts. Half a dozen Red Bull empties and a plastic clamshell with the remains of a Caesar salad. A Disney Princesses coloring book.

Wyatt slid into the booth across from her. "Your office?"

"Mr. Eddy's, too," Candace said. "He told me. He said this way he could keep an eye on everything. He said what fun was it owning a place like this if you couldn't listen to the music? He was such a sweet old dude. That's him."

She pointed to the framed black-and-white photo that hung on the wall of the booth. It showed a kid barely out of his teens with a friendly, open face. Next to him stood a guy with an acoustic guitar who looked like a young Johnny Cash. Wyatt realized it *was* the young Johnny Cash.

"I left you like four messages," Candace said. "Where were you all day? What if it was an emergency?"

"You would have said so. I was at the OU game with Jeff Eddy. Drinking beer in the crisp autumn breeze."

Candace ignored the provocation and checked the incoming number that was making her phone buzz. She growled.

"What now?" she said into the phone. She listened. "No! It's not cool if they all come over! I said you could have just your boyfriend over." She listened. "No! I said she should be in bed by *eight*-thirty! She's five years old! Let me talk to Lily, please."

Wyatt picked up a postcard with a picture of a sea turtle soaring past a coral garden. The most recent rub-it-in greeting from Lily's father, Candace's ex. The postmark was from Paia, Hawaii, stamped Tuesday, the day Wyatt had arrived in Oklahoma City.

"Maui is better then ever. It's always nice weather. Sabrina and I have a house on the beach now. One wall is all glass. My new job pays two times what the old one did. Life is good!—Brandon."

Wyatt put the postcard back on the table. Karlene had been so excited about moving to Hawaii. She was scheduled to leave on the Wednesday after the Friday she was murdered. Her airline ticket had been purchased back in June, and she carried it around in her purse. Whenever a customer or Mr. Bingham really pissed her off, she'd take the ticket out of her purse, give it a big wet smack of a kiss, and then put it back away.

"Hi, baby," Candace said into the phone. "What's shaking? Did you brush your teeth yet? It's time for bed."

Wyatt remembered how Grubb one time, teasing, had asked Karlene if she'd let *him* kiss her ticket to Hawaii, too. Karlene had laughed and said he could kiss *this*. Grubb had said, "Yeah, I wish!" Everyone hanging out around the concession stand, Wyatt and Tate and Janella and O'Malley, had thought that was the funniest exchange in the history of comedy.

The lights went down, and the crowd downstairs roared as the band took the stage. Wyatt remembered the Hüsker Dü show in the spring of 1986, the crowd in front of the stage so packed you could barely breathe, Wyatt giddy because his terrible fake ID had finally worked. Theresa stood on his left, Karlene on his right.

What shape would Karlene's life have taken, Wyatt wondered, if she'd been allowed to live it? Would she have settled forever in Hawaii or spent six months there before she returned to Oklahoma, homesick and broke? Would she have ended up marrying a tool like Jeff Eddy? Would she have a kid and an ex-husband like Candace's who sent taunting postcards about his great life far away in paradise? Or would she be down on the dance floor of the Land Run right now, whipping her hair around like there was no tomorrow?

And Grubb, Theresa, Melody, O'Malley. Who would they be now, if they'd survived that night in the projection booth? What would they be? Where? Wyatt had tried hard over the years to resist this sort of speculation. He tried to remember the line from *Lear*. "That way madness lies." Or more madness. A different kind.

The band downstairs was playing an old-fashioned country-roadhouse stomp. A guy with a stand-up bass, a drummer with just a kick, a snare, and a cymbal, a female lead singer in red cowboy boots and a black net funeral veil.

Candace kissed Lily good night over the phone and hung up. She picked up the postcard Wyatt had been looking at.

"No way is Brandon's life that awesome," she said. "Jerk. He's probably sleeping in his car on the beach. He's probably working at Burger King."

"How long were you married?"

"Not long. I don't want to talk about that."

"Does he pay child support?"

"I don't want his money. I don't want to ever think about him again."

"It was that rocky?"

She sighed. "I picked the wrong dude. Okay?"

"You wouldn't be the first woman."

"I thought he was a nice dude. He could be, when he wanted something."

"When did you split up?"

"A couple of years ago."

"Does Lily ask about him?"

"No. Not really. I don't know. I don't want to talk about him. That's the past. Now, shut up about it, I'm serious."

She did look serious, in a way Wyatt had never seen her look before.

The woman onstage downstairs could sing. She was doing justice to a cover of Springsteen's "I'm on Fire." She was setting the song on fire.

"So what's *your* story?" Candace said. "Do you have kids? I don't know anything about you."

"I'm a mile wide and an inch deep. That's all you need to know."

"Why don't you have a girlfriend?"

That surprised him. "Who says I don't have a girlfriend?"

Candace leaned across the table and thwacked Wyatt in the sternum with her knuckle. "You were watching football and drinking beer?" she said.

"I was gathering intelligence." Wyatt told her about Jeff Eddy's proposal. "So all I need to do now is convince you to sell and find out what lowball offer you're willing to take."

"I! Am! Not! Selling!"

"Really? You never mentioned."

Candace glanced down at the woman onstage, then back at Wyatt. "Does all this mean Mr. Eddy's brother probably is or isn't the one screwing with me?" she said. "I can't decide."

"Neither can I," Wyatt said. "Now, tell me about Lyle Finn."

"Who?"

"Lyle Finn, your neighbor, lead singer of the Barking Johnsons."

"Oh! The goof in the kilt."

"That's the one." Wyatt doubted it was connected to his case—the little argument he'd happened to witness between Finn and his manager on the loading dock—but it was always best to leave no stone unturned. Especially when you had so few stones to turn over in the first place. "Are you aware he creates functional erotic art?"

"Functional erotic art? How does that work?"

"Gradually, I guess," Wyatt said, "and then all at once."

"That goof! I had to deal with him, like, my first week here. He was totally screwing Mr. Eddy over! He'd play a show here and make Mr. Eddy give him all the door and half the bar on top of that. Because, I don't know, he's this supposedly famous rock star and he was doing Mr. Eddy a big favor? But he's not that famous a rock star!"

"You told him that?" Wyatt didn't have to guess how Lyle Finn would have taken that news.

"Sure. And none of his fans drink! Not the hard-core hippie ones. They just get baked out in the parking lot before the show. So the bar take is, like, almost nothing to start with. I told him he could have half the door and none of the bar. Take it or leave it."

Wyatt picked up an empty Red Bull can and tossed it at Candace. She ducked out of the way.

"Hey!"

"You're right, Candace. I don't see how any of this information could possibly have been useful to me two days ago."

"Screw you!" she said. But she sounded almost more contrite than defiant. Almost. "I forgot about it. It was way back when I first took over. Do you have any idea how busy I am?"

"You've mentioned. So what happened after you punctured his ego and played hardball with him?"

"I didn't! It was a fair deal." She sold it for a beat, and then her big white smile flashed. "Nothing happened. He got pissed off. He said, I don't remember, something about how I was a thug and I was stepping on art with my boots."

"A jackbooted thug."

"Whatever. Do you think he's the one?"

"I don't know," Wyatt said.

An minor altercation seemed to be developing down at the

corner of the stage—an overenthusiastic young mosher and the
pair of elderly lesbians. Candace had already spotted it. She stood.

"Well," she said. "Find out!"

WYATT COULD SEE from the back lot of the Land Run that the
windows of Lyle Finn's warehouse were dark. He decided to call
it a day—it had been a long one—and track down the supposedly
famous rock star in the morning. The supposedly famous rock star
who had failed to mention his feud with Candace.

On the way back to the hotel, Wyatt drifted. Out to the lake,
around the lake. Back across town and past the Cowboy Hall of
Fame, home to the famous statue of an American Indian slumped
on his horse. Oklahoma was where the Trail of Tears ended.

He drifted through the neighborhood where Theresa had
lived—small old houses with weathered stone facing and peaked,
witch's-hat roofs. He rolled slowly along and tried to remember
which block Theresa had lived on.

He drifted over to May Avenue, up May Avenue. He stopped
at Homeland for a six-pack of beer and then, once again, found
himself back at the Burlington Coat Factory that used to be the
Pheasant Run Mall. He drove around back and parked.

The little playground, where the theater crew had often gathered late at night after work, was deserted. Wyatt was sad to see
that the rusty old merry-go-round was gone. Liability issues,
probably. And the swings and slide and jungle gym had been
updated. Only the playground's source of light was vintage—a
single fatigued streetlamp with a drooping gooseneck, barely
enough wattage to attract bugs.

Wyatt took a seat on a swing and cracked open a bottle of beer.
The playground faced, across the street, what used to be the back
of the theater. The OSBI investigators theorized that the killers

had entered the theater there, through one of the auditorium exit doors that were now plastered over.

Every night, after the last show ended and the last customer left, one of the doormen went through the auditoriums row by row—picking up empty popcorn buckets and nacho boats. After he bagged all the trash, he lugged it out to the Dumpster in the rear parking lot. You were supposed to pull the auditorium exit door shut and locked behind you, then come back in through the main mall entrance. But the doormen always just propped it open with a rock, so they could get back in that way and not have to trek around to the far side of the building.

According to the OSBI, the killers must have watched the theater and learned the routine. They waited until Grubb—on trash duty that night—turned his back to wrestle with the lid of the Dumpster, and then they slipped in through the door that had been left propped open. It was the only explanation. There were no signs of forced entry, and the double dead bolt on the glass front doors of the theater had been locked when the janitors arrived the morning after. The robbers could not have hidden in the theater after the last show. The doormen, going row by row through the auditoriums, stocking the bathrooms, would have discovered them.

Wyatt, rocking in the playground swing, wondered if the killers had lurked here, watching and waiting for Grubb to bring out the trash. Right here, on the spot where a week earlier Karlene had blown out the eighteen candles on her birthday cake.

It was just the luck of the draw that Wyatt hadn't been on trash duty that night. Would it have made a difference? Would he be dead now and Grubb alive?

The killers had timed it perfectly. Mall management was always trying to save money, so from midnight till eight there

was only a single guard on duty. Disco Otis, who positioned himself in the mall, outside the theater, until the crowds cleared and
Mr. Bingham locked the front doors. At that point Otis rotated
through the mall to the main parking lot, then around to the back
lot. The killers would have been inside the auditorium before he
made it there.

Wyatt stood and walked over to the new slide. It seemed shorter
than the old one. The old slide, he could climb to the top and see
the roof of his house in the distance.

The day after Wyatt tried to tell Theresa he loved her and she
shushed him by pressing two fingers to his lips, he worked the
matinee shift with her. Just the two of them—Theresa selling and
tearing tickets, Wyatt in the concession stand.

It was the longest seven hours of his life. Theresa acted like
nothing had happened between them. For her, Wyatt remembered thinking, nothing *had* happened between them. She told
him to get a new bucket of pickles from storage. She knocked
twice on the counter when she saw Mr. Bingham's office door
open, so Wyatt could pretend to be sweeping the lobby. She sat
on the edge of the fountain, smoking and yawning. Wyatt knew
he was going to die, of heartbreak or humiliation—he just wasn't
sure which would kill him first.

"You there," Mr. Bingham said at one point in the afternoon,
scowling. "What's wrong with you? Are you sick?"

In the parking lot behind the theater, after their shift ended,
Theresa paused by her car and asked Wyatt if he wanted a ride. He
didn't understand. He never needed a ride home. He lived only
six blocks from the Pheasant Run, just off Villa Avenue. Theresa
knew that.

"I always just walk home," he told her. "It's not far."

She shook her head and pressed two salty fingers to his lips. *Shush*.

Her mother worked evenings. Theresa had led him by the hand into her bedroom. When she'd unhooked his bow tie and dropped it to the floor, when she'd tugged his belt free and it curled to the floor, when she'd taken him in her hand and squeezed, Wyatt had felt like he was going to break apart into individual atoms.

Now, so far away from that night, so far away and so near, Wyatt just needed a drink. He returned to the playground swing and opened another beer. He was halfway through the first long drink when he heard a scuff behind him. Footsteps, moving quickly. Before he could turn, something hard hammered him between the shoulder blades. He dropped the beer bottle and staggered, the breath knocked out of him. Another blow caught him flush in the ribs. He dropped to his hands and knees, holding on for dear life as the earth tried to spin away from beneath him.

He turned and caught just a glimpse of his attacker—sunglasses, a hoodie drawn tight to hide the rest of the face. And then a club of some kind was whistling at him, a baseball bat or a two-by-four, and Wyatt rolled to his right. Wood cracked against the as-phalt, as sharp as a gunshot. He still couldn't breathe. Each breath made him feel like he was being yanked inside out.

He tried to get his bearings. His empty beer bottle had broken when he dropped it. Wyatt grabbed the biggest, sharpest shard he could reach and lurched to his feet, slashing wildly out. He hit nothing, lost his balance, and stumbled into his attacker. The hoodie, the sunglasses—it was too dark for him to see more than that—everything was moving too fast. The attacker kneed him in the groin. Wyatt dropped the shard and stumbled away.

He saw that the attacker's weapon was a wooden board, long

and wide and flat. It whipped around again and nailed Wyatt's knee. He fell again.

He knew that his most dangerous enemy was panic. He found the ballpoint pen in his pocket. When he heard the attacker move toward him again, he pivoted and made a backhand stab.

His attacker grunted with pain. Wyatt didn't know what part of the body he'd hit. The attacker's leg, he thought. Wyatt was curled on his side. His kneecap felt like it had been snapped in half.

He heard more scuffs. His attacker moving toward him. Or away?

Wyatt was out of ballpoint pens. Out of ideas. When in doubt, O'Malley had told him once, bluff. Wyatt managed to lift his head.

"Bring it on!" he yelled, and then threw up.

He waited. The scuffs became fainter. The attacker was running across the street, through the parking lot behind the Burlington Coat Factory. Was he limping? Wyatt couldn't be sure. The attacker disappeared around the corner of the building.

He'd dropped his weapon a few feet away. Wyatt realized that the board looked familiar—a six-inch cedar plank from a stockade fence—but for an instant he couldn't figure out why.

He heard an engine growl. Tires squealed. And then the squeal died, the growl faded. The night once more was as peaceful as it could possibly be, just the wind humming, just the chirr of cicadas in the park's trees.

Wyatt relaxed and threw up again.

Julianna

CHAPTER 16

Julianna woke early, the birds in her backyard silent and just a smudge of gray light between the trees. She'd not slept well. The few times she managed to go under, harrowing dreams had jolted her back awake. This morning she remembered none of the dreams, not a single detail.

She felt both exhausted and wired: about to collapse, about to come out of her own skin. She took a long, scalding shower. Crowley was gone, but she could still smell him on her, even after the shower.

He'd put a finger beneath her chin and tipped her head back.

"Bet you'd like to know," he'd said. "Wouldn't you?"

Julianna had stared up at him and refused to back down. Come what may. His finger against her skin was rough, callused, warm. She knew he could feel her heart racing.

"You're lying," she said.

"Your sister was fixing to leave, already walking away. But

then I asked her where she was headed to, and she stopped. I thought maybe she'd changed her mind. You know, 'bout wanting to come inside and hear me play my guitar. Hopeful young man that I was. But no. No, she didn't even turn all the way back round. Just looked over her shoulder at me and said what she did."

Crowley was lying. Julianna knew it. He'd planned all this. He'd been manipulating her since the night began. Genevieve had said nothing to Crowley that would shed light on her disappearance. There was only one chance in a thousand that he was telling the truth.

In other words: There was one chance in a thousand he was telling the truth.

Julianna could see Genevieve pausing, glancing back over her shoulder at Crowley. Her lips moved, but Julianna couldn't hear what she was saying.

"What do you want?" Julianna had asked Crowley.

He'd lifted her chin higher. He leaned down, his face so close that Julianna could almost feel the wiry prickle of his goatee. She waited, every muscle tensed, for his other hand to settle on her hip, to lock around her wrist.

Instead, though, he straightened back up and laughed. He pulled his finger from beneath her chin. A soft stroke, a flick.

He turned. Julianna, surprised, realized he was leaving. She grabbed for his arm again, and this time Crowley shot an elbow up and out, quick and sharp, knocking her hand away. He gave her one last innocent, blue-eyed smile.

"Don't worry, darlin'," he'd said. "I'll be in touch. I ain't done with you yet."

Over breakfast this morning, Julianna tried to clear her mind. She had no appetite but forced herself to eat a few spoonfuls of vanilla yogurt, a slice of wheat toast. She made tea. Clearing the mind, however, was easier said than done. If she didn't know what Genevieve had said outside Crowley's trailer on that night so long ago, she knew exactly what Genevieve would be saying now.

Juli! You are such a dumb-ass!

Because of course Crowley was lying. This—last night, now—was precisely why DeMars had warned Julianna to stay away from him.

So. Yes. She resolved to have nothing more to do with him whatsoever. As she stared at her phone. After half an hour of that, she grabbed her keys and got into her car. She needed to know what Crowley knew. She needed to know what he wanted in exchange for that information.

Oh, Juli. You're breaking my heart, what a dumb-ass you are!

Crowley's truck wasn't in the driveway. Julianna parked anyhow, on the street, and climbed the cracked concrete stairs to the porch. She knocked on the door, waited, knocked again. An old bedsheet covered the front window, so she couldn't peek inside.

She was so pissed at herself. Of course Crowley was lying, and of course he wasn't home. He'd stayed two steps ahead of her since the beginning, so why not now? Crowley knew she knew where he lived. The last place he'd be, if he didn't want her to find him, was here. And he didn't want her to find him. What fun would that be?

She tested the knob. Unlocked. She opened the door and stepped inside. It was, just as people said, like being outside her own body, like watching herself from a distance. All the while wondering, with mild curiosity, *What the hell are you doing?*

The light from the open door cut through the gloom and fell across a sofa, a coffee table, an old-fashioned big-screen TV, as big as a refrigerator. On the coffee table, there was an empty pizza

box and an empty bottle of Jack Daniel's. A knitted afghan—
alternating bands of pale spring colors, blue and green and pink—
was folded neatly over the back of the sofa.

Julianna shut the door behind her. The smell, musty but floral,
surprised her. On the wall closest to her hung a painted tin re-
table: a sinking boat, a drowning swimmer, a school of fish. The
Virgin Mary gazed down from the sky above, but you could tell
from her expression that her mind was elsewhere.

A light burned weakly in the hallway. Julianna moved toward
it, past the kitchen. The gloom was oppressive, the temperature
ten degrees warmer inside than out. It was like being in a cave,
or a coffin.

There were three closed doors. One on the left, one on the
right, and one directly ahead, at the far end of the hallway. Julianna picked the door at the far end of the hallway and opened it.
Inside was an unmade bed. Another empty bottle of whiskey sat
on the table next to the bed, next to a bunch of dusty glass grapes
and a box of matches.

She pulled open the drawer in the bedside table. Empty. She
was looking for . . . what, exactly? She didn't know.

She still felt both exhausted and wired. But more exhausted
than wired now, the equilibrium upset by the gloom, by the heat
so thick it was an effort just to breathe. The unmade bed looked
alarmingly inviting. She tried to remember which fairy tale it was
where the little girl snuck into a house, curled up in the bed, and
then fell asleep. Goldilocks?

The wind outside blew. The little house creaked and groaned.
It sounded like footsteps. Julianna waited. When the wind stopped
blowing, the creaking stopped, too. She stepped back out into the
hallway.

A ghost hovered at the other end of the hall, staring at Julianna with pale, empty eyes.

An old woman in a shapeless housedress, the lenses of her glasses catching the light from the one overhead bulb.

"¿*Quién es usted?*" the old woman said.

"Hello," Julianna said. Her high-school Spanish was gone, long forgotten. Their mother, who had married a half-Mexican man, had not wanted Julianna or Genevieve to even learn it in the first place. "I'm looking for a friend."

The ghost shook her head. "He is gone. Christopher. He just rent."

Christopher. Christopher Wayne Crowley.

"Do you know when he'll be back?" Julianna said.

The ghost shook her head again. The lenses of her glasses flashed. She mimed something—picking up something from the floor. A suitcase.

"He is gone. Yesterday."

Of course. He wasn't two steps ahead of her, he was three.

In her car, driving home, Julianna wondered how long Crowley would keep her waiting, suffering. It depended, she supposed, on how much pleasure he took from this part of the game. And how much pleasure he anticipated taking from the next part.

It was only ten o'clock in the morning when she got back to her house. That left her a full twelve hours before her overnight shift at the ER started to stare at her phone and go slowly out of her mind. And then she remembered the phone number DeMars had given her last night, just before Crowley showed up. Julianna had forgotten all about it.

She called the number. A woman with a breathless, Betty Boop voice answered. Julianna introduced herself. She wasn't sure how much DeMars had told Mary Hilger Hall about her. Enough, apparently.

"Oh, hon," Mary Hilger Hall said, "I'm so, so sorry about your sister."

"Thank you," Julianna said.

"It's just so, so sad."

Mary Hilger Hall explained she hadn't seen the message that Julianna sent her because it had gone to a certain kind of mailbox on Facebook versus the regular kind of mailbox, one that she'd never even known to check. Her outrage was lengthy and detailed. Julianna waited for her to take a breath.

"Do you think it would be possible for me to see the other photos you took?"

"Oh, of course!"

They made plans to meet at noon, at the Nichols Hills Starbucks. Julianna arrived a few minutes early. A woman at a table near the door waved to her.

"Julianna?" she said.

Julianna sat down across from her. Mary Hilger Hall was a large woman—not fat but broad-shouldered, thick-necked. Her chiffon flutter-sleeve top, pink, was assertively feminine. And the Betty Boop voice: a lifetime spent trying to convince people she really was a girl.

She had a yellow Kodak envelope in front of her, one hand laid protectively over it, as if she thought Julianna might make a sudden snatch for it.

"Thank you for meeting me," Julianna said.

"Do you want something to drink?" Mary Hilger Hall said. "I love their iced caramel macchiato, but I've already had too much caffeine today. And it's only noon!"

"No," Julianna said. And then, in case a stronger hint was necessary, "I can't wait to see the photos."

The hand on top of the envelope didn't move.

"So you think— Oh, my gosh. So you think your sister might be in one of my pictures?"

"I don't know."

"I remember we ate dinner at the Chinese place. The one you saw in the one picture I put on Facebook? My friend Sandy and I. It was around eight-thirty, I think. I'm almost positive we ate dinner around eight-thirty or so. A little later, maybe."

The hand on top of the envelope didn't move. Julianna took a slow breath and tried not to lose her shit. This woman, she realized, was really no different from Crowley. If Julianna wanted what Mary Hilger Hall had, Julianna would have to pay the price. She would have to get it over with.

"The last time I saw my sister was at seven-thirty P.M. A couple of people saw her on the midway a little bit after that. A girlfriend of hers and a kid working the corn-dog stand. At nine o'clock a woman from Okeene positively identified her on Food Alley. That was the last time anyone ever saw her."

"Oh, my gosh," Mary Hilger Hall said. "So maybe . . . oh, my gosh."

"May I see the photos now, please?"

The woman gave a start. Like *of course* Julianna could see them. Like she'd been *begging* Julianna this entire time to let her open the Kodak envelope. She did so now, slowly, with great drama.

"This is the first one," she said, taking the first photo out of the envelope and handing it across the table to Julianna. "I took a whole roll. Twenty-four pictures. I've been meaning to put them all online, but I just love that one of Sandy so much, with the egg roll. I think they're still in order, mostly. Cameras back then, you know, they didn't tell you the time of day. Mine didn't, at least. It was just an old Instamatic my mother gave me. With the little cube flashbulbs?"

Julianna looked at the photo. It was a daytime shot of the International Building at the fairgrounds, with the dirty white bubble on top that had been replaced several years ago by a conventional roof. Julianna remembered the suck and whoosh when you opened the doors to the building. Special doors. The pressure inside had to be kept high or the bubble would collapse. Once in a while, the bubble did collapse, and it was big local news.

The International Building had the best free stuff at the fair: tiny plastic flags from Ghana, little jars of jelly from Wales. As a little girl, Julianna had loved when the person staffing a booth wore the costume of his or her exotic native land.

"I know what!" Genevieve had said that day when Julianna begged to go inside. "Let's not and say we did."

"We got to the fair around five in the afternoon," Mary Hilger Hall said, leaning across the table to study the photo, too. "I know this is the first one because we—"

Julianna set the photo down and stood. Mary Hilger Hall looked up at her, surprised.

"Do you mind if I go over there and look at these in private?" Julianna said.

The woman frowned, befuddled, and then wounded, and then aggrieved. Julianna just smiled pleasantly, smiled pleasantly, smiled pleasantly—a skill she had learned at the feet of the master, Ben, at work. If Mary Hilger Hall thought Julianna was going to let her surrender only a single photo at a time, with commentary, she was out of her mind.

"Well," Mary Hilger Hall said finally, "I suppose . . ."

Julianna carried the envelope to a table on the other side of the room. She went through the photos slowly. In several of them, the people in the crowd were so tiny and so blurred it was impossible to make out any detail—wide-angle shots of the International Building and the Space Tower and the B-52 bomber that used to be on display not far from the livestock barns. Other photos were close-ups—a lamb wearing a knit hat, a box of saltwater taffy, a much younger Mary Hilger Hall mugging for the camera—with no one in the background at all.

Nothing, nothing, nothing. Julianna had almost reached the very bottom of the stack. In the photos, day turned to dusk and dusk turned to night. And then Julianna's heart stopped. It was a shot of the illuminated fountains outside the Made in Oklahoma Building. In the crowd stood a girl in her late teens, with stormy waves of chestnut brown hair. Blue jeans, a white T-shirt with an American flag, a pensive expression on her face as she watched the water leap and shimmer. She was hugging herself. In jeans and only a T-shirt, she looked like she was freezing.

Genevieve.

But almost before Julianna could finish that thought, she realized:

No. The girl in the photo was *not* Genevieve.

The resemblance was only superficial: the age, the hair, the clothes. This girl had a round face with small eyes, close together, light not dark, and she wore a pair of tacky dyed-feather earrings that Genevieve would never have worn. And the way this girl hugged herself against the chill, the way she slouched—Genevieve took great pride in her posture. She could set a book flat on her head and walk casually down the basement stairs. She could pivot at the bottom without missing a beat and walk casually back up again.

And when Julianna looked closer, she saw that the slouchy, round-faced girl in the photo was not wearing a BORN IN THE USA shirt—it was just a shirt with an American flag on it.

Mary Hilger Hall had left her table and crept closer. She hovered by a display of instant coffees, watching Julianna. Julianna ignored her and focused again on the photo of the illuminated fountains. She studied the rest of the crowd. Nothing. No Genevieve, no mysterious man in a cowboy hat. The faces were blurred and indistinct.

The next photo was the last photo in the stack, the one from Food Alley that Mary Hilger Hall had posted online.

Julianna stuffed the photos back into the envelope. She felt fine. Disappointed. A week ago this outcome might have destroyed her. Now, though, waiting for Crowley to contact her, she had more pressing devastations to worry about.

Mary Hilger Hall pounced. Eyes wide, hopeful, hungry. "Did you find anything?" she said.

Julianna handed back the photos. She pressed a hand to her heart and closed her eyes and took a deep, shaky breath.

"I did," she said, and then left.

HOW COULD YOU do that, Genni? How could you walk away and leave me there and never come back? All I had was you. All I've ever had was you.

Julianna spent the afternoon failing to nap. What had really happened between Genevieve and Crowley? What did she say when he asked her where she was going?

Would Crowley tell Julianna the truth? What would that cost her?

When she got to the hospital for her shift, she checked in with the supervising nurse. Julianna had worked in the ER for three years before transferring to recovery, but she knew this woman only vaguely. A tyrant, a Ben with ovaries.

The supervising nurse eyed Julianna suspiciously. "So. You're our floater?"

"I'm being punished," Julianna said.

"I assume your credentials are up to date?"

The supervising nurse knew they were. She was exactly like Ben.

Julianna's first patient was a homeless man with an upper-respiratory infection and severe dehydration. The aide worried that the man would be a difficult stick—he was in his seventies, with tiny, spidery veins—but Julianna had always been good at inserting an IV, ever since nursing school. She warmed the man's arm and eased in the catheter. No problem.

The ER was slow for a weekend night. But then again it was still early, only a little after one. The bars were still open. Julianna kept her phone with her, in the pocket of her scrubs, against regulations. If it vibrated, if Crowley called, she planned to answer it. She didn't care what, or who, she was in the middle of.

The photo bothered her. The girl by the illuminated fountains looked almost nothing like Genevieve, but only at second glance. At first glance the girl looked enough like Genevieve that even Julianna—Genevieve's own sister—had felt her heart stop for an instant.

The illuminated fountains and the Made in Oklahoma Building were very close to the north end of Food Alley. It was conceivable, Julianna recognized, that after the photo was taken, the girl who looked a little like Genevieve had walked over to Food Alley. It was conceivable *she* was the girl the rancher's wife from Okeene had seen, not Genevieve.

But no. Abigail Goad was the one absolutely reliable eyewitness. She'd examined a dozen family photos and been absolutely certain it was Genevieve she saw that night. She specifically identified the BORN IN THE USA T-shirt that Genevieve had been wearing.

Julianna's next patient was a man who had been mugged: bruised ribs, bruised knee, a laceration on his palm, a possible concussion, various facial abrasions. A police officer was taking his statement when Julianna entered the room.

The man looked up at her and smiled. "Wait till you see the other guy," he said.

Julianna smiled back and examined the laceration as the police officer finished taking the man's statement. The laceration was straight and not too deep, but it would need stitches. The police officer left. Julianna buffered lidocaine with sodium bicarbonate and prepped a ten-milliliter syringe. The man watched her.

"Will I feel a sting?" he said. "No. A slight pinch. What's the current euphemism?"

He was nice-looking, even in his damaged state. A nice smile. Julianna found his eyes interesting. They were in some agreement with the smile, but only some.

"You'll survive," she said. She injected the anesthetic slowly, starting inside the cut margin of the wound.

"What's your name? My name's Wyatt."

"Julianna."

She cleaned the wound with saline and examined it again. She realigned the skin and began to suture.

"Julianna," the man said, "have I ever told you that you have a gentle but knowing touch?"

She smiled again. She couldn't tell if he wanted to have sex with her or not. That was an uncertainty most men never thought to cultivate.

"Not recently," she said. "No."

"When I was a kid, seven or eight years old, I was trying to climb a fence at school. A chain-link fence that went around the playground. Do you remember— I don't know if this is still the case, but chain-link fences back in the day had these really sharp points all along the top. Where the wires sort of twisted together?"

Julianna remembered. The grade school she and Genevieve attended had just such a fence.

"Before lawsuits," she said.

"Exactly. Anyway, I think someone kicked a kickball over the fence or something, and I was racing to get it, and I got my palm caught on one of those twisty things and fell off. Twelve stitches. You always remember your first time."

She tied off the last suture. He wasn't wearing a wedding ring. Maybe it had been stolen when he was mugged.

"We're done," she said, and reached for the antibiotic ointment.

Her shift ended at eight. Crowley still hadn't called. Julianna had to cut across one of the visitor lots on her way to the employee garage. The wind had turned around during the night and blew now from the north, knifing through her. Oklahoma. Just when you though the Indian summer would never end, it did.

"Hi!" A woman getting out of her car called to Julianna and waved. Julianna didn't know why. She waved back and kept walking. "Julianna!"

Julianna turned. The woman hurried over, beaming. A girl in her early twenties, blond hair and big sunglasses, a sundress and three-inch cork wedges. She looked like she was headed to a spring-break pool party in Padre.

"Don't tell me you don't remember me *again,*" the girl said. She laughed happily. "You slut!"

She took off her sunglasses. Julianna recognized the French

nails, the bright eyes—the girl who worked in HR at the Indian casino, who had given her Crowley's address.

"Oh," Julianna said. "Hi."

"Ariel," the girl said. "You know how you can remember it from now on? Picture one of those old planes with the double wings doing a loop-the-loop. That's what my dad used to always say. Aerial tricks. Ariel."

Julianna took her car keys out of her purse. She displayed them as proof of her impending departure. "I'm just leaving."

"I'm just arriving. I'm going to find some cute dude nurse and let him stick it to me."

Julianna blinked, and the girl, Ariel, laughed.

Chemo. Julianna remembered now. The D&C that had landed the girl in Julianna's recovery hadn't been used to clean up a miscarriage. It had been used to diagnose uterine cancer.

"No, it's fine," Ariel said. "I'm totally okay. It's just like a precaution. And I didn't even lose my hair! They're using some groovy new drug, apparently."

She put her sunglasses back on. Too quickly, Julianna noticed. She looked over at Ariel's car. There was no one else in it: no father or mother, no sister, best friend, or boyfriend.

"I'm sorry about what happened to your sister," Ariel said. "I never told you that."

"You're here alone?" Julianna said.

"No! I mean, today. Today I am. I have a minute before I start, if you want to get, like, coffee or whatever."

The girl was only twenty-one or twenty-two years old. And she seemed, shivering there in the gusting north wind, even younger. Julianna felt an ache of something deep inside her—pity, perhaps. It took her by surprise.

"I have to go," she said. She started to move away. The girl moved with her.

"I wish I had some perfume. I didn't have time for a shower this morning, and I probably smell like a tweaker."

"I don't have any perfume with me."

"Give me your phone."

Julianna stopped. "My phone?"

"Your phone. Just for a sec. Gimme, gimme."

Julianna found herself, without really knowing why, handing her phone to the girl. The girl started punching keys.

"I'm putting my info in your phone," Ariel said. "And now I'm calling my phone with your phone. That way I'll have your number and you'll have mine. It's what we call a win–win situation."

A frantic, tinny hip-hop ringtone came from somewhere deep inside Ariel's bag. She gave Julianna her phone back.

"Bye!" she said.

Julianna watched her cross the lot, unsteady on the high cork wedges, and enter the building. A few seconds later, Julianna's phone rang. The pushy girl again.

"Listen," Julianna said, not bothering to glance at the caller ID. "Stop it. Leave me alone."

Silence, and then a rough, hoarse laugh.

"If you say so," Crowley said, and hung up on her.

Wyatt

CHAPTER 17

Wyatt drove himself to the emergency room. Every time he turned the steering wheel more than an inch or two, he felt like he was being impaled by one of his own ribs. His right knee hurt so much he had to work the gas and brake pedals with his left foot. And his hand—during the attack, Wyatt hadn't even registered that he'd sliced open his own palm with the shard of broken beer bottle. Gavin would love that.

In the emergency room, a cop took his statement and frowned when Wyatt provided his best description of the assailant. Male. White, probably. Around six feet tall, give or take. Medium to heavy build.

"That narrows it down, doesn't it?" Wyatt said.

The cop said they'd tried to pull prints off the board he'd been attacked with, but both the cop and Wyatt knew that the attacker had probably worn gloves. Wyatt told the cop about the case he was working for Candace, and how someone had broken into the Land Run two nights ago, and how Wyatt had discovered the boards in the stockade fence that had been pried loose for easy access.

"Huh," the cop said. "Same board used on you?"

"Presumably."

"Sounds like someone is telling you to drop it and go home."

Wyatt nodded. He'd come to the same conclusion.

The attacker hadn't been trying to kill Wyatt—he'd gone after Wyatt's back, ribs, knee—and the weapon had been chosen, and left behind, to send a message. Wyatt wondered how long his attacker had been on him—since his first visit with Candace, maybe. He hadn't noticed a tail, but then again he hadn't been looking. Probably he'd been tailed from the Land Run after he stopped by to see Candace. The dark, deserted playground was a good place to make a point.

All that was easy. The tough question was *who*. Jeff Eddy or one of his football buddies? Maybe Jeff Eddy was smarter than Wyatt gave him credit for and had realized at the football game that his attempt to buy Wyatt off was a bust. Maybe *he* was the one playing along with Wyatt, not the other way around.

Lyle Finn was the other most likely possibility. Lyle Finn or one of *his* buddies, one of the hippie groupies hanging out at the warehouse when Wyatt came to visit. Weren't hippies supposed to believe in the principle of nonviolence? Peace and love? Finn's manager, Dixon, didn't look like the kind of guy who would go after you with a board, but Wyatt knew that meant exactly nothing.

Maybe there was a wild card on the table that Wyatt hadn't even turned over yet. Was he getting close to finding out who was harassing Candace? If so, it was news to him.

The cop promised that a patrol unit from the Will Rogers Division would keep an eye on the Land Run, driving by at staggered intervals over the next several days and nights.

Wyatt thanked him. The painkillers a doctor had given him were starting to lose their kick. And now that the adrenaline had ebbed, the shakes rolled in. He couldn't remember the last time he'd been in a fight. Third grade?

"No fun, is it?" the cop said when he was about to leave.

"Not even a little," Wyatt said.

The nurse who took care of the slash on the palm of his right hand had skin with a faint olive tint and long, graceful fingers. Her name was Julianna. Wyatt had to work to get a real smile out of her, and even then he couldn't be sure if it was real.

"Julianna," he said as she stitched him up, "have I ever told you that you have a gentle but knowing touch?"

"Not recently. No."

He needed more painkillers. His knee ached, his ribs. His head hurt, too, now. What didn't hurt? Wyatt didn't want to think about the pain, so he told the nurse about the time he split his other palm open on the top of chain-link fence.

"Twelve stitches," he said. "You always remember your first time."

The nurse's smile came and went, like breath fogging a window.

There had been a time in Wyatt's life when every girl he met who looked vaguely like Theresa looked just like Theresa. Not now, though. And this nurse looked only vaguely, vaguely like Theresa. But she had the same dense weave to her—layers and layers. He suspected she was the kind of woman you stayed away from if you knew what was good for you.

Around five in the morning, Wyatt was finally discharged. His knee wasn't broken, only badly bruised, as were his ribs. The doctor told him that if the attacker had used the edge of the board instead of the flat side, he would have ended up in traction. A CT scan of Wyatt's head revealed no excessive bleeding or damage. The doctor wrote him a prescription for painkillers and advised him to avoid alcohol until the headache faded, as well as any activity that required a great deal of concentration.

Yeah, right. There was someone out there, after all, who'd just beaten him silly. Wyatt needed to figure out who, preferably before the guy took another crack at it.

Now, though, he was so tired he could barely keep his eyes open. He pulled in to the parking lot of the Marriott and shut off his engine. A tap on his window made him jump. A woman peered in, looking concerned. One of the breakfast waitresses at the hotel. Wyatt tried to remember her name.

"Mr. Rivers?" she said.

Wyatt opened his door and got out of the car. "I'm fine, Marisol," he said.

"You were just sitting there and like staring off into space."

"I was?"

She saw the bandage on his hand, the scrapes on his cheek. "Mr. Rivers! What happened?"

"You should see him," Wyatt said.

"Who?"

Wyatt calculated he had approximately sixty seconds to make it to the hotel lobby, up to his room, and into bed or he'd fall asleep where he stood. He started walking.

"The other guy," he called back to her.

HE SLEPT HARD, without dreaming. He woke only because his bladder was about to blow—he'd been too tired to take a leak before he went down the night before. No, not the night before, just earlier this morning. Was it still morning? Was it still today? He left the bathroom and pulled open the curtains of his room. Sunlight blasted him. His phone told him it was a little before nine on Friday morning. He'd been asleep for a grand total of about five hours.

He felt surprisingly all right, though, everything considered. He could flex his knee, a little, and his ribs were more sore than excruciating. Wyatt was afraid that if he went back to sleep, there was a good chance he'd wake up feeling worse than he did now, so he took a shower—tricky when you have to keep the bandage on your right hand dry—and got dressed. He tried calling Candace, but she didn't answer, so he went down to the hotel restaurant and drank more coffee than was probably wise.

A rush-hour fender bender had backed up the Northwest Expressway, so Wyatt looped around on May. He looked for the pizza place, Shotgun Sam's, where he and O'Malley had often swapped free movie passes for pizza. Shotgun Sam's appeared to be gone, unless Wyatt had his memories mixed up and it had been south of Thirty-sixth, not north.

The movie passes could be used at any Monarch theater in the chain. They came in books of twenty, and Mr. Bingham guarded them with his life. He counted them, he recounted them, he kept them locked in a drawer in his locked office. But O'Malley had his ways. He had a dozen ways. Once or twice a month, for example, he'd knock on Mr. Bingham's door and report that an unhappy customer in the lobby had a complaint. The complaint was always specific and plausible—how the butter-flavored topping on the popcorn tasted weird, for example. Mr. Bingham, who dreaded confrontation with anyone but his teenage employees, would unlock his drawer and hand O'Malley two passes to give the fictitious customer.

"For the widows and orphans," O'Malley would say to Wyatt when he tucked the passes into the inside pocket of O'Malley's orange blazer.

Among the crew the passes were community property—to each according to his or her need. One pass was good for a new-release cassette at Rainbow Records, a large pepperoni pizza from Shotgun Sam's, or a couple of Sonic burgers with Tater Tots. Three or four passes could usually be traded for a ticket to a concert at the Myriad or the Lloyd Noble Center in Norman.

At the mall, directly above the movie theater, was a small, dark bar where local jazz bands sometimes played. Ten Monarch passes got you a bottle of bottom-shelf vodka or bourbon, if one of the bartenders was in the mood to cut a deal with O'Malley.

One time O'Malley negotiated a deal with Donald, Mr. Bingham's friend who worked at the pet store upstairs: twenty movie passes for a giant iguana. The deal fell through when Pet Shop Boy couldn't deliver the iguana. No shock, since he had zero credibility to start with. He was always coming up with the dumbest moneymaking ideas possible, like a stagecoach taxi service for downtown.

Melody told O'Malley he should be grateful about the lost iguana. Her cousin, she said, had been bitten while on a mission trip to Belize, and a doctor had removed part of his foot.

"That's no lie," she said, nodding so emphatically that the beads attached to her cornrows rattled.

Wyatt drove up Sixty-third. He kept one eye on his rearview mirror. A dark blue sedan had stayed with him when he turned off Portland, but now it peeled away and pulled in to the PetSmart on the corner. Wyatt relaxed—a little.

He parked next to the playground and then walked the escape route he'd seen his attacker take. Through the park, across the street, into the lot behind the Burlington Coat Factory. The lot looked more or less the way Wyatt remembered it from his days at the movie theater. A little smaller, maybe. The asphalt had been recently resurfaced, and a new Dumpster—green, not blue, with a sleeker design and a lid that was curved, futuristic, plastic—had replaced the original monster.

Wyatt had hated that Dumpster. The lid was solid, heavy, rusted metal, like something salvaged from a torpedoed Japanese freighter. Every edge and corner was bent and sharp. And the permanent sludge in the bottom stank like you wouldn't believe, sour and poisonous, a smell that followed you around the rest of the night. You just hoped to find enough dropped change in the auditorium trash sweep to make the trip to the Dumpster at the end of the night worth it.

The rocks that doormen used to prop open the exit doors, Wyatt remembered, were actually chunks of concrete—all that was left of a broken parking block, yellow paint flaking, from the mall's front lot.

The new Dumpster was in a new location, at the far end of the lot, beneath what would have been, in 1986, the pet store. Wyatt flipped open the plastic lid and peered inside. He'd hoped his attacker might have tossed gloves, hoodie, or sunglasses as he was fleeing, but no such luck—the Dumpster was empty. He worked his way back across the lot, back and forth across an imaginary grid, one square yard at a time. Nothing. Wyatt supposed he wasn't surprised. His attacker was someone who'd meticulously turned every object in the Land Run upside down, who'd managed to tail Wyatt without getting made. If the gloves and hoodie and sunglasses had been ditched, they were probably somewhere he would never know to look.

He walked over to one of the auditorium exit doors that had

been plastered over, the one closest to the street. The four concrete steps. The imitation wrought-iron handrail, with a round
knuckled claw at the end of it—the last remaining evidence of the
building's original French Quarter theme.

It was strange to be back here, this parking lot, after so long.
Wyatt remembered standing on these steps with everyone else
that afternoon in August. The old bat in the Cadillac had bashed
the Dumpster with the force of an explosion—the crew heard the
boom and crunch all the way in the lobby and came running. Mr.
Bingham, when he got there, ordered everyone back inside the
theater, but no way—this was too good to miss. Wyatt remembered Mr. Bingham, slouched and sweaty, standing at the old bat's
window and melting down. He kept taking off his glasses and
wiping them with his tie.

O'Malley had said something that made everyone laugh.
What? Wyatt couldn't remember. Theresa, in front of Wyatt on
the steps, had leaned her head back and rested it on his chest.
Karlene had gathered her riot of frosted blond hair together and
lifted it up, to cool her neck. Grubb had asked Melody for a piece
of gum.

And here, now, a lifetime later, Wyatt still stood, all the others
gone.

He drove to the Land Run and parked in the employee lot
behind the building, empty at two o'clock in the afternoon. He
walked over and confirmed—the telltale gap at the far end of the
stockade fence, a plank missing—that the attack last night had
definitely been a message.

He looked around. The street to his right, the boarded-up body
shop to his left. On the other side of the fence, the windows of
Lyle Finn's warehouse mirrored back a flawless blue sky. Yester-

day morning someone, lurking somewhere close by, had watched Wyatt examine the fence and find the loose boards. Who?

Wyatt squeezed through the hole in the fence and followed the alley to the warehouse. A couple of Lyle Finn's groupies were on the loading dock—a girl wearing a leopard-fur fedora and a bearded dude in a pink inflatable-pig costume. The bearded dude was watching the girl wobble around the loading dock on a pair of short aluminum stilts, about two feet high, the kind that construction workers used when they drywalled a ceiling. She stopped when she saw Wyatt.

"Hi," Wyatt said. "Is Lyle around?"

The two groupies stared sullenly at Wyatt. The girl was having a hard time keeping her balance. The bearded pig reached out to steady her.

"Hello?" Wyatt tried again. "Lyle Finn? Oink once if you understand."

Dixon, the band's manager, came around the corner of the warehouse. He gave Wyatt a wave and walked over.

"Was it something I said?" Wyatt asked him. The girl began to wobble around again on the stilts. The bearded pig turned away to watch her. "They refuse to acknowledge my existence."

"Tell me about it," Dixon said. "Lyle has great fans, most of them, but the ones in the inner circle can get very protective. No. What's the word? Very *possessive*." He noticed Wyatt's face. And then Wyatt's bandaged hand. "What happened to you?"

"Just your typical weekday evening. Is Lyle around?"

"No. He always goes into seclusion somewhere beforehand. I don't ever know where. It has something to do with the creative potency of his seed point. Or something like that. I try not to really ever ask him follow-up questions if I can help it."

"Beforehand?" Wyatt said.

"Tonight's the parade." Without a change in his friendly, suburban-dad face, Dixon mimed stabbing himself in the stomach and committing ritual Japanese suicide. "I look forward to it all year."

Wyatt caught the two groupies on the loading dock glancing at him. He gave them his best, biggest smile, but it had no effect. They turned away. He wondered if he was losing his touch. Or if, on the other hand, maybe it was the bearded pig who had beaten the shit out of him last night. Gavin would love that, too, if he ever found out. Wyatt would have to make sure he never did.

"Oh," he said. "That's a shame. Because I was going to ask Lyle about his feud with Candace that neither of you happened to mention to me yesterday."

Dixon gazed off into the distance and stood very still, as if maybe Wyatt would forget he was there and eventually walk away.

"Yeah," he said finally. "Sorry about that."

"I caught the end of your argument with Lyle after I left. My guess, you suspected that Lyle is the one harassing Candace and you called him on it."

"No. Yes. Yes and no. Yes, he was mad at Candace about the new deal. I thought the new deal was fine, by the way. Who cares, you know? The Barking Johnsons would have to play the Land Run twenty times to clear what we clear one night at a festival or some arena in Japan. The Land Run's never been about the money."

"Is it the principle of the thing?"

"The thing is, Lyle's never thrilled when you tell him no. That's why he was mad at Candace. But he told me he didn't have anything to do with what's going on over there. He told me I was a dick for thinking that. And I believe him, the more I think about it. You said everything in the Land Run was turned upside down. Every single thing, right?"

Wyatt saw where he was going. He nodded. "It took a lot of focus, a lot of work."

"Lyle can focus. When he needs to. He's actually a very smart guy. But yeah."

"Maybe he had help."

"And it was *anonymous*. You know? Lyle doesn't really do anonymous."

"Says the longtime manager, outwardly exasperated with his rock-star client but willing to go to any lengths to protect him."

"Oh, believe me, I've buried a few bodies over the years. Figuratively speaking. But if Lyle was doing something like that, he'd want to show it off. That's my theory. I love the guy like a brother, but he doesn't clip his toenails without Instagramming it."

The manager had a point. But—just like the cop who'd convinced himself that the Land Run had been turned upside down by kids—Dixon had skin in the game. He wanted Lyle Finn to be innocent. He *needed* him to be innocent. You could talk yourself into believing anything if you needed it enough.

"What parade tonight?" Wyatt said.

"The Halloween parade downtown. Lyle always leads the March of a Thousand Barking Johnsons. This year it's zombies, and an insurance premium thirty percent higher than last year because Lyle thinks that mixing tiki torches and big papier-mâché zombie heads is an awesome idea."

The girl on the stilts stumbled and almost fell. The bearded pig caught her.

"I need to be stoned," Wyatt could hear the girl tell the pig. "I think it'll be easier when I'm stoned."

The bearded pig nodded in agreement. Finn's manager nodded.

"And everyone on stilts," he said. "I forgot the stilts. Awesome."

Wyatt laughed. He liked the manager of the Barking Johnsons. In different circumstances he'd enjoy having a drink with the guy and listening to what Wyatt knew had to be some entertaining war stories. But he had not neglected to note that Dixon—like Finn, like Jeff Eddy, like the bearded pig—was roughly the same size as the guy who'd attacked him. Dixon hadn't been limping when he came over to greet Wyatt, but Wyatt couldn't say for sure that his attacker had been limping when he took off either, or if Wyatt had even hit his leg when he stabbed him with the ballpoint pen.

"Thanks," Wyatt said.

He headed back up the alley and squeezed through the hole in the fence just as a paint-blistered Ford Focus pulled in. Candace got out and looked at him.

"What happened to you?" she said, in a tone implying that Wyatt had been at fault.

Wyatt held up his bandaged hand. "Doctor, will I be able to play the violin when this comes off?"

"Shut up. What happened?"

He told her about getting jumped. Her eyes went wide.

"What?"

"It's okay," Wyatt said. "I think someone just wants me to back off your case. I don't think he wanted to really hurt me."

Her eyes went even wider. "Is that supposed to make me feel better?"

"It's supposed to make *me* feel better, Candace."

"Crap!"

"Your concern for my well-being is touching."

"Shut up." She reached up and touched her knuckles to the big bruise on his cheekbone—not tenderly but more tenderly than Wyatt would have expected. And then she used her knuckles to whack him hard on the sternum. "Are you?"

"Am I what?"

"Are you gonna bail on me now?"

"Shut up. No. But I have a proposal for you."

"And wait," Candace said. "What were you doing in the parking lot at the Burlington Coat Factory at one in the morning?"

"I'd like to propose that you close up shop for a few nights. Lie low until I can figure out who's behind all this."

She started walking toward the Land Run. "Sure," she said.

"Candace," Wyatt said, keeping pace with her. "Just consider it."

They reached the back door. Wyatt saw that the door and frame had been repaired, a new, heavy-duty lock installed. Candace sorted through the keys on her ring. Attached to the ring, he noticed, was a rubber rabbit with only three feet.

Candace found the key she was looking for, unlocked the door, and then wheeled around. She pointed the key at a spot right between Wyatt's eyes.

"Screw!" she said. "You!"

"Just for a few nights."

"No! That's what he wants me to do, isn't it? He wants me to give up!"

Wyatt knew she wasn't wrong. But that didn't make her right.

"You're not giving up," Wyatt said. "You're just being careful."

"I *am* careful! I spent like two hundred bucks on this stupid lock!"

"You're just being more careful."

"I don't have two hundred bucks! Seriously! I can't afford to close for *one* night. I'm not going to! Screw him!"

She went inside and shut the door behind her. A second later the door opened back up.

"I knew you'd change your mind," Wyatt said.

"Come over for lunch tomorrow. You look like crap. One o'clock sharp. I'll text you my address."

She shut the door again. Wyatt heard the lock snap.

IT WAS ALMOST noon. Wyatt was still curious about the conversation he'd had with Jeff Eddy's wife at the game—why *did* Greg Eddy choose not to leave the Land Run to his brother?—so he drove downtown. He found an open meter on Park Avenue and walked across to Leadership Square. The lobby elevators were opposite a shop that sold Oklahoma City Thunder merchandise. Glass walls, a detective's best friend. Wyatt found a spot with a nice angle and browsed a rack of Russell Westbrook official authentic replica jerseys.

Ten minutes later he saw Jeff Eddy exit one of the elevators and make his way toward a sandwich shop on the far side of the lobby. Wyatt waited. Another elevator door slid open. Out stepped Emilia, Jeff Eddy's assistant. She pushed through the revolving doors, out of the building. Wyatt followed.

The sidewalks were packed, so he didn't need to give Emilia much of a cushion. Looking ahead, he saw that most of the lunch crowd was hooking left on Harvey—everyone seemed to be headed toward the new skyscraper. Wyatt decided to roll the dice. He crossed the street, picked up his pace, and made it to the corner half a block before Emilia did.

The lobby of the new skyscraper was much nicer and brighter than the lobby of Leadership Square, the food court more upscale. Wyatt grabbed a plastic tray. Sushi, soup, or salad? He guessed soup. If he guessed wrong, he knew he could always cut over to the cold-drink case.

He took his time selecting a bowl, a spoon. He took his time studying the selections. French onion. Split pea with smoked ham. Tomato basil cream. Lentil vegetable. He was about to move to the salad bar when he saw Emilia approach.

When you pretended to be surprised, Wyatt had learned over the years, you had to use a soft touch. A half blink, a quick recovery.

"Emilia," he said. "We have to stop meeting like this."

"Mr. Rivers," she said.

He thought he caught the beginning of a smile before she remembered to frown.

"Are you tailing me?" Wyatt said. "Did Jeff tell you to tail me? I'm not sure how I feel about that."

She touched the knot of her elegant scarf, scandalized, then realized he was kidding.

"I'm sure I have better things to do," she said.

"I would certainly hope so, Emilia. And I'm sure you have better things to do than have lunch with me, but I'm going to ask anyway."

"Oh, no. I don't think that would be a good idea."

"Just lunch, no business," Wyatt said. This was what behavioral scientists, and pickup artists, called building a permission structure. Start small and make it as easy as possible for your subject to say yes. "I just hate to eat alone. I feel like I'm back in high school, at a new school where I don't know a soul."

She hesitated and touched the knot of her elegant scarf again. A good sign.

"Well," she said finally.

They found a table for two on the edge of the dining area. Wyatt didn't push, he didn't rush. He found Emilia a delightful lunch companion. Her stories about flying for Pan Am in the seventies—about an oil sheik in the first-class cabin who got drunk on Dom Perignon and tried to play Russian roulette with a starter's pistol, about a pied-à-terre she shared for a time in the Latin Quarter with two other stewardesses—were great stories.

That, Wyatt supposed, was his secret. He liked people, he liked stories. The world was a fascinating place if you didn't hurry through it.

"Oh, my goodness," she said. "It's already one-fifteen."

"Back to the salt mines," Wyatt said. "What's it like to work with Jeff, by the way?"

She gave him a look. "By the way?"

Emilia was no fool. But Wyatt could tell she'd had a pleasant lunch. She appreciated his effort.

"Tell the truth," he said. "Your boss is kind of a tool, isn't he? Between you and me."

She hid her smile with a dab of her napkin. "Working for Mr. Eddy can occasionally be . . . *trying*."

"A tool, in other words. But even so, I don't understand it."

"Understand what?"

"Why Greg didn't leave him the Land Run. Jeff might be a tool, but he was Greg's only family in the world, right?"

Emilia set her napkin on the table. Wyatt watched her make the rapid, complex calculations that people make. The moment of truth.

"Mr. Rivers," she said, "I'm a person who values loyalty."

Wyatt nodded. While thinking, *Well, shit.* This was why, as a detective, you'd better enjoy the journey as much as you could.

Because sometimes you got all the way to your destination only to discover you weren't welcome there.

"Well," he said. "I understand. Begrudgingly. I really did enjoy lunch, though. Thank you."

He stood. She didn't. She was giving Wyatt a curious look. He sat back down. He realized he hadn't understood her at all.

"You're not talking about *your* loyalty," he said. "You're talking about Jeff's."

Her eyes blazed. "He had an affair with Greg's wife. He ruined Greg's marriage and destroyed his life. His own brother. *That's* why Greg didn't leave him the Land Run."

Wyatt

CHAPTER 18

Wyatt had checked for a tail when he left the Land Run. He checked again when he left downtown. He was clean as far as he could tell, but traffic was heavy and every other car on the road seemed to be a silver Honda CRV. On Hudson he bounced lanes at the last second and hooked onto Twelfth Street. The silver CRV he'd had his eye on continued up Hudson without him.

Emilia had given him the name of Greg Eddy's ex-wife, who'd moved to Florida after the divorce. Wyatt thought about calling to confirm she'd had a brief affair with Jeff Eddy and that Greg had been devastated when he found out. What was the point of calling, though? Wyatt believed Emilia. And, regardless, he already had all the evidence he needed that Jeff Eddy was a sleazy, duplicitous tool. In terms of the Candace case, the affair didn't really move the ball up the field. What Wyatt needed was concrete evidence that linked Jeff Eddy to the harassment.

Wyatt's phone rang. Gavin, calling from Vegas.

"Did you put up a fight at least?" Gavin said. "Or did you just let the guy knock you around until he got bored?"

"That was quick."

"Candace has developed a certain affection for you. I tried to explain her error in judgment."

"Thank you. You'll be getting the hospital bill, by the way."

"Are you all right?"

"You can rest easy."

"I *am* resting easy," Gavin said. "I'm just gathering facts."

"I'm all right."

"Do you have any leads?"

"Lots of them," Wyatt said. "Unless you mean something that actually leads somewhere."

"I told you to spend a day on this. A day or two, max. You're just my goodwill gesture. If you're trying to make me feel guilty by staying out there, it won't work."

"I believe you."

Wyatt listened to the staticky purr of cell-phone silence. The sound of Gavin trying to figure him out. Good luck with that.

"Send me the hospital bill," Gavin said, and hung up.

Wyatt checked his rearview mirror again. Once tailed, twice shy. Once tailed, jumped, and beaten senseless with a board, twice really, really shy.

He saw nothing suspicious behind him, so he pulled off Sixty-third and parked on the street next to the playground. He crossed to the lot behind the Burlington Coat Factory.

A thought had been nagging at him ever since he'd been here earlier that morning. Maybe the thought had been nagging at him ever since last night's football game, when he'd sat there listening to the University of Oklahoma fight song and remembering the old bat in the Cadillac, the car horn that played "Boomer Sooner."

The original Dumpster had been positioned near the back of the parking lot, centered between the two auditorium exit doors and parallel to the building, sixty feet away. Wyatt found the spot. Lifting the lid of the Dumpster with one hand, wrestling the bag of garbage up and over the side with your other hand—the doorman's back was turned to the auditorium. It would have been easy for the killers to slip through the propped-open exit door without Grubb spotting them.

But.

Wyatt stood with his back to the building. On the night of the massacre, the Dumpster had *not* been in its usual spot. The old bat's Cadillac had rammed the corner of the Dumpster—at an angle, hard. The force of the impact had turned the Dumpster sideways.

Right after the murders, Wyatt had forgotten all about the old bat in the Cadillac. Could you blame him? But then Detective Siddell walked him through the events of the day, over and over, a dozen times or more, and Wyatt remembered. Siddell took notes on the details and sent uniforms out to track the old bat down. That lead, as expected, led exactly nowhere.

Now, though, standing here again in the parking lot, Wyatt started to wonder. How much had the Dumpster been turned? He rotated forty-five degrees to his left. That seemed pretty close. Maybe it had been less than that, but even so . . .

He lifted the lid of the imaginary Dumpster with his left hand. He wrestled the invisible trash bag with his right. With the Dumpster turned forty-five degrees, or even, say, thirty degrees, Wyatt had a clear view of both exit doors. Grubb, when he dumped the trash on the night of the massacre, would've had that same clear view of both exit doors. There was no way one person could have snuck past him and into the auditorium, let alone three. Grubb would have seen them.

So how, then, did the killers get into the auditorium?

The question, Wyatt supposed, was academic.

His knee had started to ache. He was walking back to his car when his phone buzzed. A text from a number Wyatt didn't recognize: Are you busy?

Wyatt sent a text back: DEPENDS. WHO IS THIS?

His phone buzzed again.

SORRY THIS IS CHIP.

Who? For a second, Wyatt came up empty. And then he remembered: *Chip.* Who had begged Wyatt to find out if his wife was cheating on him. Shit. Wyatt decided to ignore the text.

CHIP FROM THE FRONT DESK SORRY.

Wyatt sighed and hit the CALL button on his phone.

"I haven't had a chance to look into anything yet, Chip," he said.

"Oh."

"It's only been a day." Had it? Wyatt couldn't remember now. "Or two. Okay, Chip?"

"So you're still going to help me, Mr. Rivers? You haven't changed your mind or anything? Because I know you said how busy you are, and—"

"It's been one day, Chip. I haven't changed my mind. You need to be patient."

"It's really hard."

"I'll call you when I know something."

Wyatt ended the call. It was a little after three, which gave him a few hours until the Halloween parade began downtown. He could go back to the hotel and take the nap he badly needed, or he could start looking into Chip's case. The choice was clear, unfortunately. Wyatt knew that the texts and calls would keep coming until he could give Chip some news, good or bad.

He took out his notebook and skimmed the information Chip had given him yesterday. Chip's wife, Megan, was a stylist who worked at a salon in Nichols Hills Plaza called A Snip in Time. According to Chip, she worked Tuesday through Saturday, nine to six. Most days she took a quick break at noon, for lunch, and another around four, for coffee.

Wyatt drove up Wilshire, through the heart of Nichols Hills. Rolling green-velvet lawns and big mansions—Spanish Colonials and antebellum plantation houses built in the twenties and thirties, a couple of sprawling bomb bunkers from the swinging sixties.

Nichols Hills Plaza was on Western, just north of Sixty-third. The parking lot was, helpfully, large and crowded with cars. Wyatt found a spot near the back that gave him a good angle on A Snip in Time. He rolled down his window and settled in.

Twenty minutes later a young woman stepped out of the salon and headed toward the Starbucks at the other end of the shopping plaza. Wyatt checked the photo that Chip had texted him. A match. Megan, Chip's wife, was a petite, fresh-faced pixie in her mid-twenties, with a sort of cubist hairstyle, lots of slants and streaks, chunky layers and wedges. In the photo, a candid close-up of her that it looked as if Chip had taken on a beach, she was smiling, her enormous brown eyes alive with mischief. In real life, this afternoon, hurrying to Starbucks, Chip's wife looked a little preoccupied, a little tired.

Wyatt tried to read her body language, her walk. Was this a girl having an affair? Was she feeling guilty, nervous, amped? Was she worn down by all the effort it was taking, the sneaking around and the lies and the need, at every turn, to rationalize her sins to herself? Was she worn out by all the excellent illicit sex she was having?

Or, on the other hand, was this a girl who worked way too many hours a week and just wanted to collapse on the sofa in front of *The Millionaire Matchmaker* when she got home from work, who was being driven up a wall by her needy and needlessly paranoid husband?

Wyatt waited for Megan to emerge from the Starbucks. When she did, carrying a big cup of coffee, she wasn't alone. A male barista in a green apron held the door for her and then followed her out onto the patio. He was small, lean, and black, with thick-framed hipster glasses and a carefully tended fauxhawk—the opposite in almost every way of big, bashful, apple-cheeked Chip. Wyatt remembered poor doomed Bledsoe back in Vegas and how the girls he chased looked nothing like the girls he caught.

The two of them stood for a minute on the patio, Megan and the barista, chatting. Just that, it seemed to Wyatt: chatting. But when Chip's wife turned to go, she paused and reached back to give the barista's hand a quick squeeze.

An innocent, friendly squeeze? Or not? Wyatt got out of his car and strolled down to Starbucks. Inside, the barista with the hipster glasses and fauxhawk was back behind the counter, pouring beans into a grinder.

Wyatt saw that he was wearing a wedding ring. Which didn't necessarily rule out the possibility that the barista was gay, but—this was Oklahoma after all—reduced the odds significantly. Still, though, Wyatt thought he'd better find out for sure.

He pointed at the kid. "I know you from somewhere, don't I?" Wyatt said.

The kid pointed back at him. "Do you ever go to the Starbucks at Nichols Hills Plaza?"

Wyatt laughed. A fellow smart-ass, a brother-in-arms. "C'mon. Help me out here."

"Okay." The kid studied Wyatt. "Nope. Sorry. Don't take it personally."

"Does your wife maybe work at that place on Twenty-third? The cupcake place?"

"Not that I know of," the kid said. "I wish she did. Those cupcakes rock."

That answered one question—he was married to a she. As for the larger question, Wyatt couldn't think of an offhand way to ask the barista if he happened to be banging a pixie hairstylist on the side.

Wyatt bought coffee, left a five-dollar tip, and returned to his car. An hour passed. Clouds came, clouds went. The coffee kept Wyatt awake. Around five-thirty the barista with the fauxhawk emerged from Starbucks. He made his way up to the hair salon and went inside. Five minutes later he came back out. A spring in his step? Maybe. He got into an old Jeep Cherokee and turned north on Western.

Was Chip's wife cheating on him? Wyatt wasn't prepared to call it yet. Gun to his head, he'd probably guess probably. But only probably. The evidence was far from conclusive. Wyatt waited. Six o'clock came and went—Megan was working late. At six-twenty still no sign of her, Wyatt started his car and headed downtown. He'd have to pick this thread up again later—or hope he could talk Chip into letting it go.

BROADWAY WAS SHUT down from Thirteenth Street on. Wyatt finally found a parking space a few blocks away and walked over to what appeared to be a staging area. He hit the skeletons first, a dozen people in full makeup and black bodysuits. The bodysuits were fitted with anatomically correct vinyl bones—arms and legs, rib cage and spinal cord, pelvis. When Wyatt passed, heads turned, skulls grinned. It was a little unnerving.

After the skeletons came floats. One flatbed trailer was deco-rated to look like a graveyard, with ghostly ballerinas practicing twirls between the headstones and snapping cell-phone photos of one another. The bed of another pickup was crowded with half a dozen somber, panting German shepherds dressed like tarantulas. Each dog had four extra jointed and furry legs, surprisingly real-istic, attached with elastic bands.

A woman painted green, head to toe, moved from dog to dog with a bag of treats. She paused to study Wyatt.

"What are you supposed to be?" she said. The whites of her eyes gleamed against her green skin. "Hold on. Let me try to guess."

The woman was kind of attractive. Because of all the green paint or despite it? Wyatt couldn't decide.

"Have you seen Lyle Finn?" he said. He stroked the head of the nearest German shepherd. The dog seemed to recognize the indignity of its situation but be determined to rise above it.

"I know," the green-skinned woman said. "Are you supposed to be like a white Obama?"

A white Obama? Wyatt supposed it was the suit he was wearing.

"Exactly," he said. "Have you seen Lyle Finn? And zombies, I think."

She shook her head. "Lyle's not here yet. He's always the very last part. He's the grand finale."

Wyatt borrowed a map of the parade route from a pair of bored teenage vampires, checked the time, and started walking. The sun dropped beneath the horizon and then detonated, torching the racks of clouds stacked up above the downtown skyline. Wyatt had forgotten how quickly, in the vast empty sky of the southern plains, the ordinary could turn so flamboyant.

Night fell. The crowds along Broadway built. Wyatt had to squeeze his way through the park across from the old newspaper building. By the time he reached Bricktown and the bleachers set up in the parking lot across from the baseball stadium, the marching band at the head of the parade—their plumed shakos splattered with fake blood, of course—had caught and passed him. They played a slow, gloomy version of "Oh, What a Beautiful Mornin'" from the Broadway musical *Oklahoma!* A nice touch.

Wyatt found a seat in the bleachers and watched the rest of the parade from there. The ballerinas in the graveyard twirled and scissor-kicked. A squadron of drag queens buzzed by on roller skates. The German shepherds, released from their truck, trotted somberly past in tight formation, their tarantula legs jiggling. A dozen demonic clowns piled out of a slow-moving hearse. And then back in. And then back out.

Some of the floats were charmingly half-assed. One was just a beat-up old Chevy with a pair of beach balls glued to the hood and painted to look like eyeballs.

The crowd applauded everyone and everything. After an hour or so, flames began to flicker in the dark distance, beneath the Bricktown bridge. Wyatt heard the hollow boom and shiver of a gong. A current of anticipation ran through the spectators on the sidewalks, up through the bleachers. The people around Wyatt stood, so he stood, too.

Here came the Marching Zombies. Until now Wyatt had seen only the unpainted papier-mâché heads. Now he got the full effect—crazed eyes, convincingly rotted and bloodstained teeth, missing chunks of cheek and jowl. The oversize heads were three

or four times the size of a normal head, so when you added in the
stilts, each zombie was nine or ten feet tall. And there had to be
at least a hundred of them, tiki torches ablaze, lurching forward
with every beat of the gong. Wyatt had to admit it was pretty
damn impressive.

Behind the zombies was an Aztec temple that had been con-
structed on a flatbed trailer. Lyle Finn—in his kilt and a white
tuxedo jacket with tails—stood at the top of the pyramid. With
one hand he bashed a gong. With the other hand he fired a confetti cannon out over the crowd.

"Obey!" a voice boomed over a PA system at the base of the
pyramid. Wyatt realized Finn was wearing one of those wireless
microphone headsets. "Obey!"

And that was it. The Marching Zombies lurched past and headed
toward the breakdown area, a block farther along, where the long
snake of the parade had stopped to curl up. Finn and the Aztec
temple rolled past, followed a few minutes later by a lone golf cart.
In the back of the golf cart rode a dazed-looking guy, still wearing
stilts, who was hugging half a cracked zombie head to his chest.

A guy in an EMT's uniform was driving the golf cart. Finn's
manager sat in the seat next to him. He saw Wyatt and gave him
two thumbs-ups. A hundred papier-mâché zombie heads hadn't
erupted in flames—a good night for all concerned.

Wyatt waited until the crowd of spectators thinned, and then
he walked over to the breakdown area. Marchers milled around
without their zombie heads, their real hair plastered with sweat.
Most of them were still on stilts. There was a lot of hugging and
high-fiving and spontaneous whooping, a lot of chugging from
the water bottles that parade volunteers in reflective vests were
handing out. Other volunteers were busy snuffing out the flames
of the tiki torches.

The Aztec temple was on the far side of the parking lot. Wyatt dodged a developing conga line and headed over. Finn stood on the bottom step of the pyramid, surrounded by a throng of adoring fans as he ate a candy apple. He beamed and waved to the sea of iPads held aloft that recorded the moment for posterity. His bare chest under the tuxedo jacket glittered—bits of metallic confetti that had blown back onto him during the parade and stuck.

Two zombies stood below Finn, flanking him. When a woman with a baby tried to hand the baby up to him—for his blessing? as an offering?—one of the bodyguard zombies waved her off. Finn waved her on. He gave the candy apple to a zombie, wiped his hands on his kilt, and lifted the baby above his head. The fans cheered. The baby's mother just about lost her shit, she was so excited, shrieking and snapping photos. After a few seconds, Finn gave the baby back and retrieved his candy apple.

Wyatt worked his way to the edge of the flatbed.

"Lyle!" he shouted over the song blasting from the PA. It was the Barking Johnsons song that everyone knew, a catchy, crunchy piece of hard guitar pop about time passing, horses, and the psychedelic robot jockeys who rode them.

"Can we talk?" Wyatt shouted.

Finn saw him and waved. "What?"

"Can we talk?"

Finn gave Wyatt the okay sign. "Right on," he said, and then added something Wyatt couldn't make out because the excited woman turned and stuck her baby in Wyatt's face. The baby took one look at him, turned red, and started squalling. The crashing downgrade from Lyle Finn to Wyatt was apparently too much to bear.

Wyatt edged politely away from the woman and the baby. He saw that Finn had left the pyramid. Wyatt looked around but didn't see him. He started to move around to the back of the float, but one of the bodyguard zombies blocked his path. The zombie held up a hand: *Stop.*

"It's okay," Wyatt told him. "Lyle said he'd talk to me for a minute."

The zombie crossed his arms over his chest and didn't move.

"Come on," Wyatt said. "Don't be an asshole."

The zombie peered imperiously down. Through the decomposing nostrils, Wyatt could see the eyes of the person inside the giant papier-mâché head. Wyatt thought it might be the bearded pig.

"Asshole," Wyatt said, and gave one of the zombie's stilts a little kick, a tap with the toe of his shoe. The zombie wobbled, listed, and then overcorrected. He pitched forward and fell into the crowd, which caught him before he hit the asphalt. Wyatt slipped past.

But Finn wasn't behind the Aztec pyramid either. Wyatt scanned the parking lot. He caught one quick glimpse of a white tuxedo jacket, tails flapping, as Finn turned down an alley between two brick warehouses.

Wyatt gave chase, hobbling after him. His knee felt like broken pottery, every step a hammer. He caught up to Finn where the alley hit a dead end: the Bricktown Canal. Finn stood on the edge of the water, staring glumly down at it.

"Hey, Lyle," Wyatt said.

Finn turned. He was still holding his candy apple. "Oh," he said, trying to act casual. "Hey."

"Great parade."

"Thanks for coming."

"Why the high-speed escape attempt, Lyle? I just wanted to talk to you."

"I wasn't!" Finn said. He assumed his standard album-cover

expression, eyes filled with childlike wonder. "I just . . . I thought you meant, like, let's talk tomorrow."

Wyatt waited to see how long he'd stick with that story.

"Okay," Finn said finally. "Yeah. I would prefer not to talk to you."

"Because you know that I know you lied about your feud with Candace? Because it's starting to look like you're one who broke into the Land Run?"

"I didn't *lie* about it."

"A sin of omission is still a sin," Wyatt said. So insisted his former client, the defrocked priest who was convinced that the mob had put a contract out on him.

"I don't believe in the concept of sin," Finn said. "Not how it's commonly understood."

"That explains a lot. Keep talking."

Finn didn't know what to do with his candy apple. He looked around for a trash bin. Finding none, he carefully set it on the brick sill of a boarded-up window.

He took off his white tuxedo jacket and tossed it to Wyatt. His bare chest glittered.

"What are you doing?" Wyatt said.

"Candace refuses to acknowledge the fundamental value of art. I understand the intrinsic tension between art and commerce. But Candace, man. She wants to profit from my art without a mutually beneficial exchange."

Finn took off the necklace he was wearing, a big wooden fang on a leather cord, and tossed it to Wyatt.

"Take that, too. Take everything."

"Okay," Wyatt said. "I get it."

Finn started to unbutton his kilt.

"Stop," Wyatt said. "I get it."

"People like you, like Candace—you're locusts. You're not sat-isfied until you've devoured the entire harvest."

"Is that why you've been harassing her?"

"I'm motivated by an artistic curiosity. People like Candace are motivated by a need to *devour*."

"I don't blame you for being mad at her. I know she told you that you're not a real rock star. That would make me mad, too."

Finn finally managed to unbutton the kilt. Underneath he wore boxer shorts decorated with the Communist Party hammer-and-sickle symbol turned into a happy face.

He looked up at Wyatt with disbelief. "You think I care about that?"

"I do."

"I'm not a rock star, man. I'm just this weirdo in a band. I care about making music. I care about being part of what, like, hap-pens when music gets made. I still live in Oklahoma City, man! I still live in my old *neighborhood*."

He had a point. And Wyatt still couldn't imagine, or maybe he just didn't want to admit, that *this* was the guy who'd jumped him in the playground and beaten him almost senseless.

At the same time, though, Wyatt noticed that Finn had deftly managed to avoid his question.

"Lyle," he said. "Just tell me the truth, okay? Are you respon-sible for what's been happening to Candace and the Land Run?"

Finn picked up his candy apple. He contemplated it for a long moment, Hamlet with Yorick's skull, and then tossed it to Wyatt. Wyatt wanted nothing to do with a half-eaten candy apple, so he stepped aside and let it sail past. Finn turned, too, at the same instant, and leaped into the canal.

Wyatt had thought the evening could hold no more surprises. He watched Finn frog-kick to the other side and pull himself out.

No. *Try* to pull himself out. The edge of the canal was three or four feet above the water, and Finn found his upper-body strength lacking. After several tries, he had to give up and frog-kick back to Wyatt's side of the canal.

Wyatt squatted down. "You were saying."

Finn held a hand out. "Can you help me up, please?"

"No. Answer my question."

"It's cold in here, man."

"Really?"

Finn shivered. His teeth clicked. "What was the question again?"

"Have a nice night." Wyatt stood and started to walk away.

"Wait! Fuck, man. Okay."

Wyatt squatted back down and gave Finn his arm. He heaved him out of the water and onto the pavement. Finn picked up his tuxedo jacket and used it to towel off his luxurious mane of hair.

"No," he said. "I didn't break into the Land Run or— What was it Dixon said? I didn't poop on Candace's car."

"Then why didn't you want to talk to me? Why did you just jump into a freezing canal to get away from me?"

"Because you're kind of scary, man. You've got a very darkish energy."

"No I don't."

"Can you hand me my necklace, please?"

"Answer the fucking question."

"See?"

Wyatt took a step toward him. Finn recoiled and almost fell back into the canal. Wyatt was fine with that. It would save Wyatt the trouble of pushing him.

"What aren't you telling me, Lyle?"

Finn looked old and pale, cold and miserable.

"I was mad at Candace, okay?" he said. "Yes. Not for the rock-star thing but because the Land Run is like my home, man. When Greg died, that was tough, man. He wasn't much older than me, you know. And just gone, just like that."

Wyatt tried to keep him on track. "So you were mad at her. And then what?"

"And then maybe after I got back to the warehouse, I said some things. About how I was mad at her. Maybe I went off on her a little. I go off on everything! That's what I do, man! But I don't mean it. I don't mean half the shit I say. I don't know if I mean it till I say it. Do you know what the definition of art is?"

Wyatt ignored the question. "So you think one of your group-ies knew you were mad at Candace and then decided to take mat-ters into his own hands."

"They're not groupies, man. They're as much part of the music as I am."

"Which one?" Wyatt said.

"I don't know, man," Finn said. "I really don't." He was look-ing even older and colder, even more miserable. "I wish I did."

Julianna

CHAPTER 19

On Monday morning Crowley called again. Julianna had thought he would. She couldn't be certain, though, and so the past twenty-four hours had been excruciating. Every time she'd tried to call Crowley back—twenty times, fifty—there had been a single ring, a click, dead air.

"So you still want me to leave you alone?" he said when she answered. Julianna could picture his smile. He was calling from a different number this time, probably using a prepaid cell phone. Untraceable. "I won't lie to you, that hurt my feelings. But I figured, I ain't proud. I figured, let's give this one more try and hope for the best."

Julianna had just arrived home after her overnight shift in the ER. She sat in her car, in her driveway, one hand gripped so tight on the steering wheel that her entire arm burned. A chubby black neighborhood dog on the loose trotted across her yard, head low, smiling sheepishly.

"I didn't know it was you," she told Crowley. "You know that."

"I want fifty thousand dollars."

"What?"

She hadn't expected him to want money. She didn't really know what she'd expected him to want.

"In cash," he said. "Hope I don't have to explain that. Tomorrow night."

"I don't have that much money."

"Get it."

"I don't have nearly that much money."

"Suppose we're both out of luck, then, ain't we?"

She waited. Crowley didn't hang up. "You're enjoying this," she said.

"Sure," Crowley said. "You would, too, don't lie."

"I don't have fifty thousand dollars."

"How much you got? I'm a reasonable man."

Julianna tried to think. She had around fifteen thousand dollars in her checking account. The equity in her house was nothing, really—she'd bought the house a year and a half ago, with only five thousand down, and her payments were still mostly interest. She wouldn't be able to get to that anyway, not in just a day or two. It would take time as well to cash out her 401(k) at work, if that was even possible. She had two credit cards she could use for cash advances. Two or three thousand? Each? She might be able to borrow money from Donna at work. She would never be able to ask DeMars, of course, for a loan.

What was she doing? Why was she even considering this?

Juli! You're such a spaz! You're embarrassing me!

"Hurry up," Crowley said.

If she told him the truth, Julianna suspected he would double or triple the number. But if she lied and came in too low, he might lose interest and walk away for real this time. She couldn't risk that.

"Twenty thousand," Julianna said. The truth. "That's all I can get with short notice."

The chubby neighborhood dog had circled back to her driveway. He looked up at Julianna and sneezed.

"Tomorrow night," Crowley said finally. "Midnight. You know that park out by the lake, out by that road where you and me had our first date?"

Stars and Stripes Park, on the shores of Lake Hefner. Julianna had been invited to a birthday party there when she was in second grade. Stars and Stripes had the best playground slide in the city, a metal rocket ship about to blast off, painted red, white, and blue.

After dark the park had been a hangout for druggies and dealers. Julianna had heard that later, in the eighties, gay men gathered there to have sex. Now, for a long time, Stars and Stripes closed at dusk. It would be deserted at midnight.

"No," Julianna said, "not there. We have to meet somewhere public."

"Don't be late. I'm heading to California straight from there. Show up late, you won't never see me again."

"Wait."

"What?"

"So it's enough?" Julianna said. "Twenty thousand?"

He laughed. "We'll see."

IT WAS STILL early, a little after eight. The Chase bank branch near her didn't open until nine. Julianna went online and logged into her Bank of America checking account. Only thirteen thousand dollars, and payday not until Friday. The cash-advance limits on her credit cards, though, were higher than she expected: five thousand dollars on the Sapphire MasterCard, three thousand on the Freedom Visa. She never used the Visa and didn't even remember why she'd signed up for it. She was glad now she had.

Twenty thousand dollars. Julianna tried not to think about what she was doing. Because what was twenty thousand dollars? It was nothing. And she saw no value in trying to pretend she was in a position to make a choice about any of this. She knew, and probably Crowley did, too, that she'd give anything, everything, to find out what had happened to Genevieve. So what, then, was she willing to give for the hope of that, no matter how faint it might be?

Anything. Everything.

At eight-thirty she drove to the Chase branch. She waited outside the building, watching the skinny man across the street thrust his sign at cars that passed. The sign advertised a special on oil changes. Julianna often passed the man on her way to and from work. He was always out there, rain or shine, cold or hot. A former patient of hers who worked in marketing had told her that people like the skinny man on the corner were called, in the business, "human directionals." She couldn't think of a more terrible existence.

She was waiting when a woman unlocked the doors. The woman couldn't stop yawning. She led Julianna to a teller window and swiped Julianna's MasterCard, punched in her PIN. While they waited for approval, the woman made small talk between yawns. Julianna thought the woman might be wearing last night's outfit—a wine-colored silk blouse, wrinkled, with a gigantic bow in front.

"Looks like it'll be," the woman said. She paused to yawn. "Just a gorgeous day."

"Yes," Julianna said.

The first advance was approved. The woman counted fifty one-hundred-dollar bills onto the counter. When Julianna nodded, the woman slipped the bills into a Chase envelope and handed it to her.

"You know you don't have to go," she said.

Julianna looked up, startled. "What?"

The woman yawned. "To a Chase branch. You can go to any bank or credit union that displays the Visa logo."

She swiped Julianna's second card and punched in the PIN. They waited.

"I'm here now," Julianna said.

The woman yawned and nodded. When the approval came through, she counted out another thirty one-hundred dollar bills. She put them in another envelope.

"Have a nice," she said. "Day."

Julianna's Bank of America branch was just up the street. She left a thousand dollars in her checking account and withdrew everything else.

When she got home, she placed the three envelopes on the kitchen counter and considered them. They were surprisingly slender. Her first thought had been to get home as quickly as possibly and stash the money somewhere safe. But was her house safe? Maybe this was Crowley's plan—to have her gather the money so he could rob her if she left at some point during the day. She remembered the way he'd looked around when she let him inside her house for dinner. He'd noted every detail.

Crowley knew she'd go immediately to the bank this morning and not wait until the last minute. This meant too much to her. She would never risk a five-o'clock glitch at the bank, or with one of the credit cards.

Julianna almost laughed. Crowley knew her so well. Better, really, than anyone else.

She wondered if he'd followed her from her house to the banks. She'd been so intent on getting the money that she hadn't thought to check.

Was she being too paranoid? Or not paranoid enough? Take your pick.

In the drawer by the refrigerator, she found a plastic bag from Target. She put the envelopes with the cash inside the bag, then wrapped it with packing tape. She opened the fireplace damper and taped the bundle to the metal wall of the firebox, as high up as she could reach. She closed the damper and moved the screen back into place. Crowley might think to look there. Probably he would. But Julianna didn't have any better ideas. She'd have to take her chances.

No shit, Sherlock.

Screw you, Watson.

Genevieve had taught her that exchange. It always cracked them up.

She ate a bowl of oatmeal, then tried to nap. She hadn't slept since the night before last, and her brain had started to feel wet and heavy, like a towel dropped on a bathroom floor. She needed, she knew, to be at her sharpest, her very clearest, when she met Crowley later that night. She needed a few hours of real sleep.

But real sleep: no. She drifted in and out of the shallow end. Her bedroom was too warm, too quiet. Around four, Julianna gave up, got up.

Now what? She had eight hours to tread water. Her specialty.

She thought of a movie she'd seen a few years ago. A woman moved into a spooky house. She saw ghosts. At the end of the movie, the woman realized that the ghosts were actually living people. The woman, the star of the movie, was the ghost. She'd been the one doing the haunting all along.

Julianna's date had fumed afterward that the premise of the movie was derivative and that Nicole Kidman's performance was mannered. He was not in a position, Julianna discovered later that night, to bag on anyone else's performance.

She went back online and checked the Facebook page— "Remember When in OKC." She scrolled down. Mary Hilger Hall had posted the rest of the roll she'd shot that night at the State fair. The photo of the teenage girl with the stormy waves of chestnut brown hair, Genevieve's look-not-quite-alike, had been poorly scanned. The focus was softer, the tint greenish. Julianna downloaded the photo anyway. She opened it and zoomed in. The digital girl resembled Genevieve no more or no less than the analog one had.

The illuminated fountains were just a stone's toss from the north end of Food Alley. After the show at the fountains ended, the girl in the white American-flag T-shirt had three choices: She could walk west toward the livestock barns, or head east past the big white arch and exit the fairgrounds, or turn south and enter Food Alley. On the other side of Food Alley were the carnival games, the midway.

The photo, according to Mary Hilger Hall, had been taken around eight-thirty on a Saturday night. So the livestock barns were closed. And what girl, sixteen or seventeen years old, would even consider leaving the fair so early on a Saturday night? The girl in the photo, with her feathered earrings and tight, acid-washed jeans, didn't look like the kind of girl who would go home just as the fun was getting started. In that respect she was exactly like Genevieve.

But there were so many reasons that the girl in the photo might have left the fairgrounds early and *not* gone to Food Alley. She was freezing, after all. Even if the girl *had* gone to Food Alley, that didn't mean that Abigail Goad—the one absolutely reliable eyewitness—had mistakenly identified her as Genevieve.

Julianna clicked around until she found a site called White-Pages.com. She tried to remember Lacey's married name. Her husband was a big-deal oil executive with family money on top of that. Higgins? Gibbons? She searched both. Nothing. Maybe Lacey was divorced. If she'd remarried and taken a new husband's last name, Julianna would never find her.

Diggins? A phone number popped up. Julianna didn't know if the number was either accurate or current. She dialed.

"Diggins residence," a girl said. Julianna guessed she was in her early teens.

"I'm trying to reach Lacey Diggins," Julianna said.

"She's not here."

"Do you have her cell-phone number?"

"Why?"

"My name's Julianna. I'm . . . I'm a friend of your mother's."

Of all the lies Julianna had told over the years, and there were oh, so many of them, this one was probably the most outrageously bald-faced.

"If you're her *friend*," the girl said, "then why don't you *have* her number?"

Lacey's daughter sounded just like her mother had when she was a teenager, bored and annoyed, the same acid sneer.

"I'm an old friend. From years ago."

"If you were a Pi Phi, I'm pretty *sure* you'd *have* her number."

"Before college. My sister was her best friend growing up."

In the background Julianna could hear the beeps and squeaks of the video game that the girl was playing on her iPad.

"Whatever," she said, losing interest in the conversation. She gave Julianna a number. "But she turns her phone off when she has *drinks* with the *girls*."

"Can you tell me where she is right now?"

"Why should I tell you that?"

"Why shouldn't you?"

The video game beeped. "Fine," the girl said. "Whatever."

Julianna drove downtown. The Devon Tower was the new glass skyscraper, beveled like the head of a chisel, almost twice as tall as the next-tallest building in the city. Julianna had been inside a few times, to eat lunch in the lobby food court, but she'd never been to the restaurant on the top floor: Vast. The name of the restaurant made Julianna want to groan. It would have made Genevieve groan. Someone had been paid a lot of money to come up with that name. *We'll call it Vast, for the view. Get it?*

She took the elevator up and told the hostess she was meeting friends for drinks. The hostess seemed dubious. Julianna supposed she should have worn something more stylish than Gap jeans and a faded OU School of Medicine sweatshirt.

She pointed across the dining room. "Lacey Diggins?"

The hostess relented and stood down. Julianna crossed to the table of six women by the windows. The windows! Floor to ceiling, wraparound. The view was disorienting. Julianna had never seen her hometown from this perspective. It seemed smaller, weirdly tilted, slightly exotic, like a toy town instead of a real city.

Lacey had always been skinny. Now she was so gaunt she looked like a dead leaf, golden and brittle. Genevieve said once that Lacey looked like the caged capuchin monkey in the play area at Tammy-Linn's, a children's-clothing shop that used to be in Northpark Mall. Not to be cruel, just as an observation. Lacey's best feature, Genevieve always said, was her blow job.

But Lacey wasn't, at age forty-four, unattractive. Her big eyes were the dark, pretty brown of old glass. She wore a gorgeous linen jacket.

Julianna was glad she'd never known what Genevieve said behind *her* back. Genevieve had said plenty to her face. She said Julianna, awkward at age twelve, was built like something the stoners in metal shop had welded together as a joke.

Oh, my God, Genevieve was so hilarious.

Julianna had last seen Lacey almost fifteen years ago, during the wilderness between college and nursing school. That had been Julianna's first systematic attempt to make sense of her sister's case. She begged, and finally Lacey agreed to get together for a drink. Lacey stayed for exactly five minutes, told Julianna nothing she hadn't already told the police in 1986, and was a total bitch, as usual, from beginning to end. She'd ordered a champagne cocktail, the most expensive drink on the menu, and left Julianna with the check.

"Because it needs to be a good cause *and* a fun night out, you know?" one of the women at the table was saying.

"We could do, like, a step-and-repeat wall, with photographers, when people arrive," Lacey said. "Like at a movie premiere?"

"Lacey?" Julianna said.

Lacey glanced up at her without recognition. A smile with that familiar curl to her lip. *Who the fuck are you?*

"Yes?" she said.

"Julianna. Genevieve's sister."

Lacey stood up and opened her arms. Julianna had no choice but to hug her. It was like hugging a bag of golf clubs.

"Julianna! It's so nice to see you." She turned to the other women. "Girls, this is a friend of mine from way back."

"I need to talk to you," Julianna said.

Ah. There they were: the startled eyes of a caged capuchin

monkey. Lacey strained to maintain her expression of delighted surprise. The other women at the table sipped wine and appraised Julianna, appraised her Gap jeans.

"I'm in the middle of something right now, Juli," Lacey said. "Why don't we make a date for later?"

A date for never, in other words. And, *How the fuck, by the way, did you find me?*

Julianna turned to the other women and smiled back at them.

"Lacey and my sister were best friends. They used to party like crazy. How much coke did you guys do, Lace? It's amazing you're not dead."

A nervous titter or two. This being Oklahoma City, odds were that at least a couple of the women at the table were married to megachurch pastors. Julianna locked eyes with Lacey.

"Did you ever know," Julianna said, "what Genni used to say your best feature was?"

Lacey's grip tightened around Julianna's wrist. "Let me walk you out," she said.

"So nice to meet you," Julianna told the women at the table.

In the lobby, a private corner tucked away from the elevators, Lacey wheeled on her. "What is your *problem*?" she said.

For an instant, Julianna felt like she was twelve years old again, with Lacey lounging lazily on Genevieve's bed and spitting venom at Julianna for sport. The flood of pure, sweet joy was so overwhelming that Julianna almost burst into tears.

She managed to hold herself together. "I need to know exactly what you saw that night."

Lacey didn't ask which night. Julianna would have slapped her if she had.

"I already told you," Lacey said. "I told the police. I told them like a million times. Why?"

"Just tell me," Julianna said. "Tell me everything, *exactly*. Lacey. The last time you saw Genni, on the midway, what was she wearing?"

"What was she wearing? You know what she was wearing. What is *wrong* with you?"

Lacey turned and started to walk away. Julianna grabbed her arm. Lacey's eyes bulged.

The last time Julianna had seen Genevieve, she'd been wearing jeans and her favorite BORN IN THE USA T-shirt. Julianna could *see* that T-shirt. She had described it in detail for the police. But while the days in September were hot, the nights could turn chilly. That particular Saturday night was chilly. When Julianna first saw the photo of the girl by the fountain, hugging herself, the girl she'd thought for an instant was Genevieve, Julianna had remembered sitting alone on the curb in front of the rodeo arena, the wind biting. Their mother had insisted she bring a sweater, but she didn't want to look dorky—the sweater tied around her waist all day—so she'd left it in Genevieve's Cutlass.

"Let go of me," Lacey hissed. She yanked her arm free and started to walk away again.

Julianna stepped in front of her. She kept her voice calm. "I will make your life a nightmare, you stupid bitch. Do you think I'm kidding? If you don't give me five minutes, right now, I'll make sure your husband and your daughter and every person you know finds out exactly what a coke-snorting slut you were in high school."

Lacey stared at her with a degree of loathing that Julianna wasn't sure she'd ever encountered before. "What do you want?" she said.

"When you saw Genni the last time," Julianna said, "did she have a sweater? I can't remember if she brought a sweater. I never told the police that maybe she'd brought a sweater with her that day."

"I guess so. Yeah."

"Did you tell the police that?"

"She wasn't wearing it. She just had it tied around her waist."

Because Genevieve never had to worry about looking like a dork. A sweater tied around her waist would only make her, magically, even more desirable.

She had two lightweight wool V-necks that she'd been wearing that autumn. One was navy, the other caramel-colored.

"You didn't tell the police she had a sweater?"

"Why would I?"

"You stupid bitch," Julianna said. But *she* was the stupid bitch here, not Lacey. Julianna was the one who'd described Genevieve's BORN IN THE USA T-shirt to the police with such precise detail. She was the one who'd told them Genevieve was wearing that T-shirt when she vanished.

But it was already chilly by the time Genevieve had left Crowley's trailer. Which meant she would have pulled her sweater on. That was why she'd brought it with her, after all. Her navy or brown sweater, pulled on *over* the white BORN IN THE USA T-shirt. Which meant there was no way Genevieve could have been the girl the rancher's wife from Okeene had seen on Food Alley.

Lacey stepped closer. "Now, listen to me," she said.

Julianna shoved her away. Lacey stumbled backward and almost fell. A security guard on the other side of the lobby glanced over. Julianna walked quickly toward the exit. When she got to her car, in the garage, her hands were shaking so badly she could barely dial her phone.

DeMars didn't answer. Julianna drove to his house. She'd been there two or three times over the years. DeMars lived in a beautiful old Tudor not far from the State Capitol, the nicest neighborhood in the part of the city—east of Lincoln, north of downtown—that Julianna's mother had always called "Colored Town." Everyone had, back then, unless they called it something even worse.

There were several cars in the driveway, including DeMars's forest green Subaru. Julianna relaxed, a little. He was home. She rang the bell. After a minute the door flew open. A dark-skinned teenage girl with elaborately coiled and plaited hair stood there, tugging on the hem of her shimmering gold dress. Mayla, DeMars's daughter. Her smile, when she saw Julianna, turned quizzical.

"Hi!" she said. "Are you here for the party?"

The party. Her fourteenth birthday. Julianna remembered now that DeMars had mentioned it. When had he mentioned it? That evening seemed like a hundred years ago.

"Can I talk to your dad?" she said.

"Sure. Come on in. He's around here somewhere."

Julianna moved through the living room, where the older partygoers were gathered. Aunts and uncles, friends of DeMars and his wife—chatting and drinking, dressed to the nines. Most of them were black, but not all. A few people glanced curiously at Julianna as she passed. She ignored them. In the family room, a group of teenage girls shared a karaoke microphone and belted out a Beyoncé song that Julianna recognized but didn't know the name of.

DeMars was in the kitchen, brushing barbecue sauce onto a platter of chicken breasts. He grooved his shoulders to the faint beat of the Beyoncé song from down the hallway. He did a snappy little half spin every time he reached over to dip the brush into the bowl.

He looked up and saw her. "Juli," he said. "You all right?"

"He doesn't have an alibi," she said.

"What?"

"Crowley. He doesn't have an alibi. Abigail Goad never saw Genevieve that night."

DeMars wiped his hands on a towel and came around to the other side of the butcher-block island. She could tell he was measuring twice. Trying to find the words with the right fit.

"This isn't a good time, Juli," he said. "Mayla's birthday party. You can see that."

"Listen to me, DeMars. The girl in the photo was wearing a white T-shirt. That's what the police thought Genni was wearing. That's who " Julianna stopped herself. She knew she wasn't making any sense. She had to be precise or she'd blow this. "DeMars. I told the detectives that Genni was wearing a white T-shirt. But she'd brought a sweater with her. I forgot about the sweater. It would have been navy or brown. That night when it turned chilly, Genni would have been wearing the sweater over her T-shirt. Do you see? She—"

"Juli," DeMars said. "Stop now."

"Abigail Goad never saw Genni," Julianna said. "So the last people who ever saw her alive—it was Lacey, and the kid who sold corn dogs on the midway. They saw her *before* she went to Crowley's trailer. No one ever saw her *after* he was arrested. He doesn't have an alibi."

"Have something to eat. Say hello to Angela. Sit down and have something to eat. We can talk about all this tomorrow."

He put a hand on her shoulder. The gentle father. She shrugged his hand off. She didn't need the gentle father right now. Or ever. She needed the focused fucking homicide detective.

"No! We can't. Crowley is leaving town tomorrow. You have to arrest him. Or at least hold him for questioning. I'm meeting him tonight. He admitted he was lying before, that Genni *did* come to his trailer."

"You got in touch with him?"

"Yes."

DeMars studied her. The warmth in his eyes was gone. "What do you think you doing, Juli?"

"Your job," she said. "The job you should be doing."

It was a weak shot. He didn't even flinch.

"You coming apart, Juli," he said. "Only so many times you can do that before you don't never come back together."

Mayla, the daughter, popped her head into the kitchen. "Daddy!" she said. "Mama says she wants to know where her about-to-be ex-husband's gone and got to. She said to say those words exactly. Hi again."

"Happy birthday," Julianna said.

"Thank you."

"I'll be there in two shakes, baby," DeMars said. "Ask your mama if she divorces me, then who gonna be her body-and-fender man?"

"Dad-*dy*!"

DeMars took the platter of chicken in one hand and Julianna's elbow in the other. He steered her out through the French doors, onto the big wooden deck in back. A trio of slinky teenage boys nosing around the smoky grill quickly slunk back inside.

"DeMars," Julianna said. "Listen to me. Crowley admitted he was lying. He admitted she came to his trailer. And he doesn't have an alibi. You have to question him."

She wished he understood that she'd come apart long ago. That this was her only chance to be made whole again.

He lifted the hood of the grill. He moved the sausage aside and loaded in the chicken breasts. He wouldn't look at her. She knew then it was hopeless.

"Where you meeting him?" DeMars said. Wanting to know so he could stop her. "What time?"

Julianna realized that this would probably be the last time she ever saw him, this man who'd been a part of her life for so long, who'd genuinely cared for her. That was his only mistake.

She started walking away, back toward the house.

"Juli!" he called.

"Thank you for everything," she said.

Wyatt

CHAPTER 20

That summer, that August, it stayed hot long after the sun went down—it stayed hot all night long. You stepped out of the air-conditioned mall, at midnight or one o'clock in the morning, and the heat fell on you like a fat drunk in a bar.

Nobody on the crew had access to a swimming pool. So after work on the hottest of the hot nights, everyone would drive out to one of the apartment complexes on Hefner, scale a fence, and splash around until the manager or a security guard ran them off. Some nights no one ran them off. They'd have chicken fights in the deep end and then sprawl on the pebbled concrete apron of the pool, exhausted, enjoying the chlorine tingle and the buzz of cheap whiskey.

There was something beautiful and mysterious about a pool at night—the only light in the darkness, a glowing green jewel.

Wyatt lay in his hotel bed, almost fully awake but not quite yet, and remembered the night after he and Theresa first had sex.

Everybody at the pool, the stars above. This was an apartment complex they'd been chased from before, so Grubb's boom box was turned low—Run–D.M.C.'s *Raising Hell,* which O'Malley had picked up at Rainbow Records in exchange for a movie pass.

Melody wanted to hear some Prince. Karlene complained that her skin always smelled like popcorn. She said that when she finally got to Hawaii, she was never going to go near popcorn again. Theresa did a handstand underwater. Her long hair billowed around her head like dark liquid. O'Malley suggested that they could torment Mr. Bingham by unscrewing the peephole in the office door and reversing it. They would be able, O'Malley said, to watch Mr. Bingham like he was a fish in an aquarium. An ugly fish, Karlene said. A stupid fish, Grubb said. Janella said Mr. Bingham might be stupid, but even he would eventually figure out that the peephole had been reversed. O'Malley agreed but said it would be fun while it lasted.

Wyatt didn't know which side of grief was worse. The feeling that these people had always been in his life and were now gone or the feeling that they'd never really been there at all.

Theresa had climbed out of the swimming pool, sleek and glittering. Janella handed her the bottle of whiskey. Theresa took a sip and carried the bottle over to Wyatt. When she sat down next to him, when she rested her head against his shoulder, everyone stared. Grubb almost fell off the diving board. Wyatt tried to be cool. He took a long drink and counted the stars.

He knew that O'Malley was watching him. Wyatt took another drink and glanced over. O'Malley arched an eyebrow and gave Wyatt a nod of approval.

"Well done, Heinz," O'Malley told Wyatt later, when the sky was turning gray in the east and they were all straggling back to the cars. "I can always say I knew you when."

That had been, possibly, the best moment of Wyatt's life. The best moment of the best night of the best year of his life. The only year, he sometimes felt, of his life.

Now his alarm went off. He knocked back a couple of painkillers—his knee looked like an exotic overripe fruit you'd buy at an Asian market—and called Dixon, Lyle Finn's manager.

"Oh, man," Dixon said when he answered, "you really scared the shit out of Lyle last night."

"I need the names of all the groupies who hang out at the warehouse."

"He won't tell me what happened. What happened? He said it was the worst Halloween since he was twelve and his mother told him he was too old to go trick-or-treating anymore. I'm not making that up."

"Can you get me their names?"

Silence. "I don't need to call a lawyer, do I?"

"No," Wyatt said. "I think you were right about Lyle. I don't think he's got anything to do with it. But I need the names. First and last. I need to run background checks on everyone."

"Okay. Sure. It could take me a day or two. They kind of come and go."

"That's fine. Thanks."

Wyatt hung up and dialed his contact at the *Daily Oklahoman*.

"What?" Bill Haskell said.

"Bill," Wyatt said, "this is your old friend Wyatt Rivers, the private investigator."

"What do you want now?"

"Nothing. I'm taking the morning off and want to pay my debts. How about I buy you breakfast?"

Haskell grunted skeptically, but he was a newspaperman—a free meal was a free meal.

"Cattlemen's," he said. "Twenty minutes. It's down in Stock-yards City. You need the address?"

"I'll find it," Wyatt said, and waited for Haskell to grunt skep-tically again. He did.

Wyatt got dressed and jumped on the Lake Hefner Parkway. He hadn't been down to the stockyards since he was nine or ten years old, a school field trip. Stockyards City drew a few tourists, but it was also a working livestock market, gritty and authentic in the way Bricktown, with all its frat-rat bars, wasn't. Down here you could buy a wide-brim straw Stetson at Shorty's Caboy Hat-tery or, on auction days, a few hundred head of Angus.

Cattlemen's was an old steak house on the main drag, a couple of blocks from the maze of holding pens. At eight in the morn-ing, only the diner side of the restaurant was open. Paneled walls, blood-colored leather booths, the rush of bacon grease and black coffee when you stepped inside—a time-traveling cattle buyer from 1950, from 1930, would feel right at home.

Wyatt had no trouble recognizing Bill Haskell. He was the heavyset guy at the counter, suspenders and a breast pocket full of pens, a tight, tiny mouth like the beak of a snapping turtle. Only the absence of an old-school felt fedora disappointed Wyatt.

Haskell glanced over when Wyatt sat down, an action that took more shifting and squinting and beak snapping than Wyatt would have thought possible. Haskell was a little younger than Wyatt had expected—mid-sixties.

"You're late," Haskell said.

The waitress filled Wyatt's coffee mug. He glanced at the plas-tic menu.

"Biscuits and gravy," he said. "Two eggs over easy and a side of bacon. No, make that sausage patties. No, make it bacon and sausage both. And a paramedic standing by."

Haskell gave a curt nod. Wyatt had passed the test.

"A place like this," Haskell said, "you don't order granola and yogurt."

Wyatt's phone rang. Chip. Wyatt put the phone back in his pocket. He took a sip of coffee and looked around. "So what's the story with this place?"

He knew the story but suspected that Haskell would relish the telling of it.

"Opened 1910, three years after statehood," Haskell said. "In 1945 the owner, Hank Frey, got in a dice game at the old Biltmore Hotel downtown with a rancher named Gene Wade. Frey bet his restaurant against Wade's life savings that Wade wouldn't roll a hard six. A pair of threes. Wade rolled them and won himself a restaurant."

"Now, that's a story," Wyatt said.

"Oklahoma has a fascinating history. Bloodthirsty Comanche war parties. Ruthless outlaws who fled to the Indian Territory to escape the long arm of the law. Wildcatters and gamblers, boomers and sooners. You might be surprised to learn that Oklahoma City is the final resting place of the man who killed the man who killed Jesse James."

Wyatt hadn't really been listening until then. He glanced up from his coffee.

"The man who killed the who?"

"That's exactly how the headstone reads. *Sic erat scriptum.* 'The man who killed the man who killed Jesse James.' Edward O'Kelley. He's buried in Fairlawn Cemetery on Western Avenue. *Jesse* is spelled incorrectly, with an 'i.'"

The waitress brought their food. Haskell had ordered a bowl of granola and yogurt.

"My daughter wants me to live long enough to play with

my grandchildren," he said. "So she claims. I come here for the memories."

"And the smell."

"And the smell."

Haskell measured out exactly half a teaspoon of sugar and tipped it into his coffee.

"Tell me something, Bill," Wyatt said. "Do you remember those killings that happened at the movie theater way back when?"

"Of course I do. The old Pheasant Run Twin in the old Pheasant Run Mall. My wife and I went on one of our very first dates at that theater, right after it first opened. *Logan's Run*. The theater closed immediately after the crime, the mall shortly thereafter."

"Were you on the story?"

"I wasn't one of the lead reporters. No. But it was all hands on deck. I covered the OSBI press conferences. I spent more time sleeping on the sofa at OSBI headquarters than I did in my own bed."

"The police, the OSBI, they decided the killers got into the theater because an employee neglected to lock one of the back exit doors. Correct?"

"One of the theater ushers. Correct. If memory serves, he left the door ajar when he took the garbage out."

Haskell had finished his granola and yogurt. He studied his empty bowl. He looked hungrier now than when he'd started eating.

"And the killers snuck in," Wyatt said. "That was the only possible explanation. There were no signs of forced entry. The front doors were locked."

"If memory serves. Yes. You know, one of the killers used a gun loaded with bullets called wadcutters. That's always stuck with me. It's odd, the details one remembers."

Wyatt took a couple of bites of his biscuits and gravy and then pushed the food around on his plate. He tried to look at the evidence with clear eyes, a skeptical head. There was the possibility that Grubb, when he came back inside after dumping the trash, had failed to pull the exit door all the way shut. But really that *wasn't* a possibility. The exit doors were designed to swing shut and lock on their own—that's why you had to prop them open. And anyway, the doormen always yanked the doors shut behind them, always, as hard as they could, because the boom annoyed the shit out of Mr. Bingham. It was a central pleasure of the job.

The only other entrance to the theater was the glass front doors that led from the theater to the rest of the mall. And Mr. Bingham was a fanatic about locking those as soon as the last customer was gone. Wyatt had watched him do it a million times. Two different keys on the ring, one for the top dead bolt, one for the bottom. *Snap. Snap.*

The locks were security double dead bolts. The front doors were *glass*. So even if the killers had tried to pick the locks, they would have been completely exposed the entire time. The only way the killers came through those doors was if they had their own set of keys. But if they had their own set of keys, how did they get them? Was it possible the killers had an accomplice the police knew nothing about, someone who worked at the movie theater but hadn't been there when the robbery went down?

An inside man.

Haskell eyed Wyatt's plate. Wyatt nudged it toward him. Haskell selected a strip of bacon.

"If you insist," Haskell said.

"I have a favor to ask, Bill," Wyatt said.

"Gambling in Casablanca? I'm shocked." But Haskell helped himself to another strip of Wyatt's bacon. He removed, from his back pocket, a spiral reporter's notebook almost identical to the one Wyatt carried. "What now?"

"Do you know any of the investigators who were on the movie-theater case?" Wyatt said. "OSBI or OCPD. Someone I could get more information from."

Haskell glanced up. Surprised. "What's this have to do with your Land Run case?"

"I'm just curious," Wyatt said. He had the lie all lined up and ready to go. "I think there might be a book in it."

Haskell grunted. "Just what the world needs."

"Another writer."

"If you have a day or two, I can share my own bitter experiences with the publishing industry."

"Don't make me beg, Bill."

Haskell helped himself to Wyatt's last strip of bacon.

"Carl Friendly was killed in the Murrah bombing," he said. "He was the lead investigator on the OSBI side. Jack Siddell with the OCPD died a few years ago. His heart. A surprise to all who knew him, that he had one. Randy Plunkett. No. Let me think."

Wyatt didn't remember Carl Friendly or Randy Plunkett. The only detective from that time he remembered with any clarity was Jack Siddell. The acne scars, the cold, hoarse voice. Jack Siddell, who'd demanded to know why Wyatt thought he was still there and all the others gone. But who also, once near the end of the investigation, after Wyatt had been unable to identify the three dead killers, hesitated at the door on his way out. Maybe Jack Siddell didn't have a heart, but he'd met Wyatt's father, he'd met Wyatt's mother. He'd been there to see Wyatt painted with the blood and brains of his friends.

"You can't think about it, son," he said. "It won't do you any good."

Why am I still here and all the others gone?

"Think hard, Bill," Wyatt said. "Who can give me the inside skinny on the investigation?"

How late was too late to move on with your life? What if, after all these years, there was someone—*an inside man*—who might be able to answer the question Wyatt had been buried beneath for the past twenty-six years?

"I suppose Brett Williams might be willing talk to you," Haskell said finally.

"Can you set it up for me? Pave the way?"

You would have thought, from how Haskell grunted and sighed and tightened the beak of his mouth, that Wyatt had asked him to hoist both Sisyphus and boulder upon his back and carry them up the hill.

"I suppose," he said.

WYATT PICKED THE public library on Villa—the Belle Isle branch, just a few miles from the Pheasant Run Mall, on the opposite side of the neighborhood where he had grown up.

A librarian showed him to the dusty old microfiche readers. Wyatt sat down and loaded the first reel of film. The librarian lingered.

"You know," she said, "the *Oklahoman* archives are all digital now. Most people do it that way."

"In this particular instance, Becky," Wyatt said, "I'm not most people."

He waited until she left and then spun through the first seven months of 1986. Yes, digital would have been more efficient, but he wanted as much of the full newspaper experience as possible— the original dot-screen photos and smudged ink, the widows and orphans, the crooked jump columns.

He reached the issue of Friday, August 15, 1986. The day of the robbery. The big front-page news that day was that the city council had annexed land for a new water-supply line.

At the back of the sports section—beneath the much larger schedules for the multiplexes, down next to tiny ads for the Blue Moon Saloon strip club and the Bombay Wig, Costume, and Lingerie Shoppe—were the show times for the Pheasant Run Twin theater.

One Crazy Summer, with John Cusack and Demi Moore. *The Fly,* with Jeff Goldblum. *"Bargain matinee half price every show 4–6 P.M."*

Wyatt had to spin two issues forward, to August 17, for the first article on the massacre—the pre-Internet world, when news wasn't news yet if it happened after the paper had been put to bed for the night. The initial coverage took up the entire front page of the *Daily Oklahoman.* A photo of the Pheasant Run mall ran above the fold, photos of the victims below it. Grainy high-school-yearbook shots of O'Malley, Theresa, Grubb, Melody, and Karlene.

The photos looked nothing like them. Grubb, his hair parted on the side, a grave expression, could have been the president of the chess club. Theresa, who never smiled, was smiling. O'Malley, who always smiled, wasn't. Melody, the photo taken before she'd discovered cornrows, looked like a young Donna Summer. Karlene wore glasses.

They all looked so unbelievably *young,* like children. Wyatt wondered why the newspaper hadn't been able to find more recent photos.

The photo of Mr. Bingham was the only one that truly captured its subject. A candid shot. He wore a short-sleeved dress shirt and looked only a little less sour and puckered than usual.

He held something in his arms—a bag of groceries, maybe—that had been cropped out of the picture.

Wyatt spun through issues of the *Oklahoman* until he found what he was looking for. In early October, a day after the killers had been gunned down in Arizona, the newspaper ran a double-truck spread that included a wide-angle photo of the theater's back parking lot. The auditorium exit doors were the focus of the shot, but you could see the Dumpster in the background—you could see, clearly, that the Dumpster was angled toward the building, no longer parallel, just the way Wyatt remembered. Grubb would have seen the killers approaching.

So. Say there was an inside man. Say someone gave the killers the keys to the theater, someone the police didn't know about.

Who? As far as Wyatt knew, only Mr. Bingham had keys to the glass front doors. The mall security guards didn't. Mall management didn't. The movie theater operated under a special lease—it was a sovereign tenant, the self-important term Mr. Bingham liked to use. The Vatican City of the Pheasant Run Mall.

The janitors didn't have keys either. They had to wait every morning until Mr. Bingham arrived to let them in.

The question, then, had to be this: Who had *access* to the keys? Who could have borrowed or stolen them and had copies made?

Mr. Bingham kept all his keys on a single ring—the key to his office, the cash box, the ticket boxes, the projection booth, the cabinet where he locked the movie poster one-sheets, the glass front doors. Those and a dozen others. The crew always joked about it, how the weight of the keys in Mr. Bingham's pocket dragged his pants down, how he was constantly pausing to hitch them back up.

Almost always, he kept the keys with him. *Almost* always. During an extra-hairy weekend rush, when Mr. Bingham had to work the box office so Karlene or Janella could help out in the concession stand, he'd stash his keys in the drawer beneath one of the cash registers. That way the girls wouldn't have to bug him every time they needed to make a run to storage for napkins or straws. Sometimes the keys stayed in the drawer for thirty or forty minutes at a time.

Was that long enough for someone to grab the ring of keys, make copies, return them? No. But you wouldn't have to take the entire ring—you could take only the keys to the front doors, which Mr. Bingham probably wouldn't notice missing until the very end of the night. You'd have to figure out a way to get the keys back *on* the ring. You'd have to plan for a particularly busy weekend, when there were three different rushes, at six, eight, and ten. Take the keys at six, make copies during your break, put the keys back on the ring at eight or ten.

Maybe. It wasn't implausible.

Wyatt took out his notebook. He wrote down the name of every theater employee who had not been working the night of the massacre.

The list wasn't long. The Pheasant Run Twin was small even by the standards of the day, with only two screens and auditoriums that held maybe two hundred people each. On a slow day or night, three employees could run the place—a cashier to sell and tear tickets, one person to work the concession stand, the projectionist.

On the day of the massacre, Tate and Janella had worked the matinee shift and clocked out at six. They were gone even before the old lady rammed the Dumpster with her Cadillac.

The matinee projectionist, Haygood, had also clocked out at six. Ingram, the night projectionist, never stayed a minute longer than he had to—you could hear him thudding down the stairs almost before the last reel of the night stopped spinning. Wyatt couldn't remember precisely, but he knew that Ingram was gone before Grubb even started the auditorium sweep—at least thirty minutes before the killers showed up.

Tate. Janella. Haygood. Ingram. At the time of the robbery, there had been ten employees of the Pheasant Twin: the five dead, the four living, and Wyatt.

He switched off the microfiche reader—the fan panting, the metal growing warm from the lamp inside. He tried to get his head around the possibility that someone he'd known, someone he'd seen every day for months, had been working with the killers.

Tate. Janella. Haygood. Ingram.

On the way to the library, Wyatt had driven up Northwest Expressway. On the north side of the curve, near Classen, was a development of big-box chain stores—Old Navy, Walmart, Babies "R" Us, a Nordstrom Rack. In the eighties, that had been the site of the abandoned Belle Isle power plant, its smokestack visible for miles around. Steel plates welded over the doors and lower windows had enticed local teenagers to break in. Rumor had it that the power plant was haunted by the ghosts of kids who'd plunged to their deaths in the darkness while exploring the massive, derelict building.

Wyatt himself had never been inside. One afternoon in May, though, after a late-spring thunderstorm, Tate bought a couple of forty-ounce Budweiser bottles from the Circle K on Western and took Wyatt four-wheeling on the muddy grounds of the power plant, in his old red Ford F-150. It was a blast. Wyatt didn't remember where O'Malley had been at the time. If O'Malley had been there, he would have insisted they explore the abandoned power plant. He would have figured out a way to get in.

Tate and Wyatt had gotten along well, but they weren't tight the way Wyatt was tight with O'Malley or the way Tate was tight with Grubb. Wyatt couldn't think of another time when it had been just him and Tate hanging out together, none of the others around.

Was it Tate who made copies of the front-door keys and gave them to the killers? But why would Tate have them murder Grubb, his best friend, and leave Wyatt alive?

Janella's attitude toward Wyatt, most of the time, was one of general annoyance. That was her attitude, most of the time, toward everyone. She was a tiny wisp of a girl, but she could drink anyone except O'Malley under the table. Her relationship with Melody, the other black girl at the theater, was prickly. Janella had much lighter skin than Melody, and straightened her hair. Melody had the cornrows and went to church every Sunday.

Janella liked Wyatt, she tolerated him. They'd even made out a few times on break, getting moderately hot and heavy, the winter after Wyatt started work at the theater. More from boredom, though, than anything else. If Janella was the one who gave the killers the keys to the theater, why would she tell them to spare Wyatt and not Melody? Janella's relationship with Melody was prickly, but they were like sisters.

After the murders Wyatt never saw or talked to Tate or Janella again. He didn't try to contact them, and they, as far as he knew, didn't try to contact him. Maybe they found the prospect of meeting again as unbearable as he did.

If you set aside Tate and Janella, that left only Haygood and Ingram, the projectionists. They were surly old union guys in their fifties, heavy smokers, limpers both. Haygood was white, Ingram black. When they arrived for a shift, they limped across

the lobby without making eye contact and headed straight upstairs to the booth. O'Malley called Haygood and Ingram the
phantoms of the opera. He claimed that he'd seen the inside lid of
Haygood's toolbox, and it was decorated with full-color close-up
beaver shots that Haygood had clipped from nudie magazines.

Ingram, the other projectionist, had a crush on Melody. He'd
come downstairs every now and then when she was working,
when he knew she was trapped behind the candy counter and
couldn't flee. He told stories about his time in the army, in Ger-
many. Best days of his life. The bane of his existence now was his
wife's enormous standard poodle, which would climb onto the
sofa and refuse to get off.

"If that damn dog *standard*," Wyatt remembered Ingram saying
once, "I never wanna see no *jumbo* size."

Haygood didn't know that Wyatt existed. Ingram only noticed
Wyatt when he needed someone to fill his thermos with Sprite.

Wyatt looked at the list. *Tate. Janella. Haygood. Ingram.* That
was everyone. And Steve Herpes. Wyatt had almost overlooked
the snotty rich kid Mr. Bingham had hired at the beginning of
the summer. His real last name was Hurley, but that had been
quickly modified when everyone realized how snotty he was.
Steve Herpes had quit around the middle of July, long before the
murders, but he would have had access to the keys before that.
He would have had even better access than the rest of them, since
he was always in Mr. Bingham's office, sucking up to the boss.
Everyone feared that Mr. Bingham was grooming Steve Herpes
to be assistant manager.

Wyatt hadn't given Steve Herpes much thought over the years.
He was tall and square-jawed and looked like a lifeguard. Karlene, Wyatt remembered, had been interested in him for about a
minute, until Steve Herpes casually mentioned three times in a

single conversation that he drove a Porsche that his parents had given him for his birthday. How it cost a fortune to insure, how it didn't handle well on ice, how the cops were always pulling him over for speeding, even when he wasn't.

Karlene twisted a strand of hair around her finger. She did her best dumb blonde.

"Is a Porsche one of those cute little cars from Yugoslavia?" she said. "I love those."

Really, though, everyone had tried at first to welcome Steve Herpes into the tribe. But whenever Tate or O'Malley asked him to come along to the park or the pool after work, he always had something better to do—a party to attend, friends to meet.

Friends to meet. Putting a point on it, that the people he had to work with were just the people he had to work with.

Steve Herpes refused to take his turn with the popcorn machine. Officially, the concession girls were supposed to clean the popcorn machine, but it was such hot, nasty work that the doormen always pitched in—Wyatt would clean the bin, for example, while Melody cleaned the kettle.

"Not my job," Steve Herpes would say if any of the girls asked him for help.

Most grievously, he would check out his own square-jawed reflection in the glass of the framed, outdated one-sheets in the lobby—*What's Up Doc?, Rocky, Chitty Chitty Bang Bang*—when he thought no one was watching.

So they called him Steve Herpes and parked too close to his Porsche and spent the long, empty hours in the lobby giving him shit.

Wyatt had given him as much shit as anyone else. Maybe more. And yet Wyatt had been spared. So again: *Why?*

He flipped his notebook shut. Too many questions. Too many

paths that looped around and left him back where he'd started. But still there remained the strong possibility that *someone* had given the killers the keys to the theater. With luck, Bill Haskell's contact at the OCPD would be able to point Wyatt in the right direction.

It was almost one. Haskell still hadn't called. Wyatt swung by Whole Foods for a rotisserie chicken and drove to his uncle's house. Once again his uncle was sitting on the porch, even though the temperature had dipped and there was a real nip to the wind. In another week or so, the leaves on the old trees along the street would burst into flame: scarlet, saffron, goldenrod. And then down they'd come.

"Mikey!"

Wyatt shook his uncle's hand. "How have you been, Uncle Pete?"

"As good as can be expected under the circumstances."

"What about some lunch?"

"What about it?" his uncle said, and they both laughed.

Wyatt was on his way to the kitchen with the chicken when his phone rang.

"Don't tell me you forgot," Candace said.

"Of course not." Wyatt tried to remember. Lunch? Yes. Candace had invited him to lunch. Shit. "I'm on my way now. I'm pulling in to your driveway as we speak."

"Ha."

"Do you mind if I bring a date for you? My elderly uncle. I think you two are a match made in heaven."

"Sure. You've got an uncle in Oklahoma City? And you never told me what you were doing at Burlington Coat Factory at one o'clock in the morning."

"We're on our way," Wyatt said.

CANDACE LIVED ONLY a few miles from Wyatt's uncle, in a neighborhood of small, tidy ranch houses built in the fifties. When she answered the door, she gave Wyatt a glare. She gave his uncle a big white flash of a smile.

"I'm Candace," she said.

Wyatt's uncle shook her hand, gravely. "I'm Pete," he said, "and I'm an alcoholic."

Candace laughed. "Hi, Pete!"

"Sixteen and a half years."

"Good for you! My dad just got his ten-year chip."

"I stopped drinking the day of the bombing. Tell her, Mikey. Not a drop since."

"It's true," Wyatt said.

"Good for you, Pete!" Candace said.

"I didn't do it alone, I'll tell you that."

Candace looked at Wyatt. "Mikey?"

"Middle name," Wyatt explained. "I switched over a long time ago. There were four other Michaels in my senior class."

He felt a small, warm hand work its way into his. He looked down. Lily, pale and solemn. Wyatt wasn't sure what to do with her hand, so he just held it.

"We're having a picnic, Wyatt," she said.

"It's pretty chilly out, Lily."

She looked up at him with the long-suffering patience of a medieval saint. "In the living room."

"Got it," Wyatt said.

"I don't know what she sees in you," Candace said. "It was her idea to invite you over."

Wyatt doubted that, but Lily nodded. She tugged at Wyatt's hand and led him into the house. Candace took Pete's hand and followed them.

A picnic blanket was spread in front of the sofa. Lily served everyone chicken-salad sandwiches that had been cut into triangles, with Cheetos and grapes. When she finished, she sat down next to Wyatt, so close he could feel her breathing. She watched him and waited until he took the first bite of his sandwich before she took the first bite of hers.

"There are three different kinds of grapes in the world," she said.

"No!" Pete said. "I don't believe it!"

"Grapes that make raisins," Lily said. "Grapes that you eat. Grapes that make grape juice."

"Very good," Pete said.

Wyatt picked up a grape and examined it. Lily watched him.

"This one might be the fourth kind of grape," Wyatt said.

Lily looked at her mother for a ruling. Wyatt tried to remember how to do the trick, the only one he knew. O'Malley had taught it to him one night after he'd gone up to the bar above the theater to swap movie passes for booze. O'Malley had used a cocktail olive and told Wyatt that the secret to magic was a full commitment to believing your own lie.

"You know, this might be the kind of grape, Lily," Wyatt said, "that is impossible to squash."

He set the grape on the coffee table. He covered it with a napkin.

"You're cleaning that up," Candace said.

Wyatt slapped his palm down hard on the coffee table. He felt Lily jump. He removed the napkin. The grape had vanished. Lily's eyes went wide.

"Take off your shoe, please," Wyatt told her. "Unsquashable grapes sometimes like cool, dark, stinky places."

Candace laughed. Lily pulled off her sneaker and handed it

to Wyatt. He reached deep inside the sneaker and produced the grape. He sniffed it, wrinkled his nose, and then popped it into his mouth.

A beat passed, and then Lily giggled. It was the first time, Wyatt realized, he'd seen her look her age, five, and not a century or so older. Candace, laughing harder now, poked her daughter in the ribs, and Lily kept giggling. Wyatt's uncle laughed, Wyatt laughed.

It was a nice moment, a moment of simple, stupid human happiness, the best kind. And yet even as Wyatt sat in the middle of the scene, he remained outside it, apart, as if partitioned off behind special glass that let in light but not heat. He'd experienced this sensation before. It was like looking at a photo of a family gathered around a roaring fire. The fire warmed the people in the photo but not the person holding the photo. You'd have to be crazy to think it ever would.

After lunch Wyatt settled his uncle in the rented Altima. Lily waved good-bye from the porch and went back inside to play.

"So everything's been quiet at the Land Run?" Wyatt asked Candace when they were alone.

"Yeah. Do you think it's over? Maybe he's mad it's over, so he beat you up."

Wyatt didn't think it was over. He doubted that Candace did either.

"I may have a real lead, finally," he said.

"It's about time."

Wyatt dropped his uncle off at home and drove back up Classen. He didn't want to run into Chip at the hotel, so he found a bar on Western that had strong and reasonably priced drinks, with a bonus view of the Baptist church across the street. The sign in front of the church said AUTUMN LEAVES, JESUS DOESN'T.

Wyatt had purchased a pack of three-by-five index cards. He wrote down the names, one per card—*"Tate," "Janella," "Haygood," "Ingram," "Steve Herpes"*—and lined the cards up on the bar in front of him. On the other cards, he wrote down everything he could remember about each person, every point of contact, one memory per card.

Haskell called around nine.

"Brett Williams will talk to you," he said. "Tomorrow morning at ten. La Oaxaqueña Bakery on Southwest Twenty-ninth."

"You're a prince, Bill," Wyatt said. "Don't ever let anyone say otherwise."

Julianna

CHAPTER 21

A little before seven, Julianna called and told the supervising nurse in the ER she had a family emergency and wouldn't be in for her shift that night. She said she was sorry for the last-minute notice.

Silence. Julianna waited. "Hello?" she said.

"Is there anything else?"

"Just that."

"Okay."

The supervising nurse hung up. Julianna went to the fireplace, opened the damper, and reached up into the chimney. She'd been too enthusiastic when she'd taped the packet of cash to the metal wall of the firebox. She had to yank and yank. Ash sifted down. The plastic Target bag, once it came free, now smelled like the ghost of fires past. So did she.

An hour before she was supposed to meet Crowley at the lake, Julianna drove to the Double R Ranch, the big barn of a bar where she'd watched him pick up the woman with the braid. She thought it had been around this time, eleven or eleven–thirty. She hoped so.

She didn't see Crowley's truck in the crowded parking lot. Either he'd switched vehicles, which was likely, or he continued to avoid places he knew Julianna could find him. Also likely. She left the cash in her car, tucked under the seat, and went inside.

Her first scan of the room came up empty. The man next to her, a biker standing alone at the bar, gave her a nudge with this elbow. His beard was gray and long, trembling and nebulous, like the stuffing a dog might tear from a plush toy.

"How 'bout a drink?"

"I'm meeting a friend," Julianna said.

"We can be friends."

She scanned the room again, losing hope. And then Julianna saw her, the hard-looking redhead, hitching her big turquoise purse onto her shoulder as she emerged from the ladies' room.

Julianna ignored the biker and followed the redhead to a booth in the back. The redhead slid in across from her drunk friend, who seemed even drunker tonight than before. She swayed back and forth to the song pounding from the speakers, so far out of rhythm she was almost about to be back in rhythm.

"Well, well," the redhead said when she saw Julianna. "Look who it is."

She patted the seat next to her. Julianna sat down.

"I need a favor," Julianna said.

"You find that man you was looking for?"

Julianna leaned close. She lowered her voice. "I'll give you three hundred dollars to borrow your gun."

The redhead lifted her drink, mahogany liquor on the rocks,

and took a dainty sip. "You don't have to whisper. Does she, Carla May?"

The friend swayed to the music, her eyes half closed. "Huh," she said.

"Three hundred dollars," Julianna said. "Just for a couple of hours."

The redhead turned to study Julianna. "You think I'm crazy?"

"It's just for protection. Just in case."

"Don't answer that." She laughed, turned away, took another dainty sip.

"I did find him," Julianna said. "The man I was looking for. But he's not who I thought he was. He *might* not be who I thought he was."

"Come on with us over to the Land Run. We'll find us a couple of college boys and dance all night."

"No. How much?"

"What if you go off and shoot somebody? And they find out I gave you my gun?"

"I'm not going to shoot anyone. It's just for protection."

"You can stop talking. 'Cause I stopped listening."

"Five hundred dollars. That's really all I have."

A new song began to play. Julianna recognized the simple, gritty guitar lick, as rough and elemental as a cave painting: Lou Reed's "Turn to Me." Genevieve had played it incessantly when the album the song was on first came out. The spring of 1984? Genevieve would have been fifteen years old, Julianna ten. Genevieve said the song cheered her up—the idea that there was one person out there in the world you could always turn to. If your car broke down, if your apartment had no heat, if your father was freebasing.

Julianna, age ten, had thought freebasing was some kind of sport. With Frisbees, maybe? She disliked the song. She thought the man singing sounded menacing, his voice sinuous and insinuating—he seemed like he *wanted* your car to break down so you would *have* to call him. Julianna had been grateful she already had someone she trusted, Genevieve, who for the rest of her life she could always turn to.

The redhead was studying Julianna again.

"Scootch on over," she said.

Julianna slid back out of the booth so the redhead could slide out, too.

"I need to use the ladies' room," the redhead said. "Wait here and we'll head on over to the Land Run."

Julianna knew it was hopeless. She'd never be able to talk the redhead into loaning her the gun. This woman wasn't crazy. Julianna's idea to borrow her gun *had* been, all along, crazy.

"We never had this conversation," the redhead said. "All right?"

Julianna nodded. She turned to leave.

The redhead caught her by a belt loop and reeled her back.

"Where you going?" she said.

"I have to go."

"I need to use the ladies' room," she said again, more slowly this time. "And you need to keep an eye on my purse, 'cause Carla May's too drunk to do it. All right?"

She waited until she saw that Julianna understood, then walked away. The drunk friend swayed to the music. Julianna sat back down. The big turquoise purse was on the seat next to her, unzipped. Keeping her eyes straight ahead, following the swaying beat of the drunk friend's head, Julianna reached into the redhead's purse. She felt a wallet, a cell phone, a tube of lipstick, a box of what were probably pads or tampons, and then she found the gun, small but heavy. The drunk friend watched Julianna through half-closed eyes as under the table Julianna moved the gun from the redhead's purse to her own.

Julianna wondered if the redhead would report the gun stolen right away or wait to see what Julianna did with it.

"Where'd that bitch go?" Carla May said, slurring her words. "She was just here."

"She'll be right back," Julianna said. She stood up and left.

Julianna had thought the entrance to Stars and Stripes Park would be gated after hours, but it wasn't. She turned off the lake road and drove a few hundred yards through the darkness, past stands of trees and a baseball field. At the playground area, the road branched. She couldn't tell in the darkness if the rocket-ship slide was still there or not. She steered right and made a long, slow loop around the flat brick pavilion that you could reserve for family reunions and T-ball team picnics. The parking lot in front of the pavilion was empty.

Julianna kept driving. She saw a solitary car, a small sedan, parked near the slender finger of land that poked out into the lake. Where the nail of the finger would be was a round plaza with a flagpole. No flag flew this late at night, but when Julianna parked next to the sedan and walked closer, she saw that the surface of the plaza was itself a flag—colored tile formed white stars on a blue background, red stripes on white.

Crowley was standing out past the plaza, at the very edge of the park, where the red-dirt bank crumbled into the water. It was dark and very quiet. No wind. In Oklahoma you never noticed the wind, did you? You only noticed that one day out of a hundred when it took a breather.

Julianna had removed the gun from its turquoise holster. It

rested naked now in her purse, a small snub-nosed revolver, next to the bundle of cash.

The ground was uneven. She stumbled and almost fell. Crowley glanced at her, then back at the water.

"You know what I heard?" he said. "Just the other day. I don't know it's true or not, but a lady I met told me. We was driving along, and she said when they built that highway over there, they drained part of the lake and found a '63 Cadillac with a skeleton behind the wheel."

The highway was less than half a mile away, but due to some trick of topography the sound from it didn't carry this far. Julianna watched headlights float silently along, the glowing bellies of fireflies that had paired off to mate.

"The old duck pond," she said. She knew the story.

"It was a lady been missing thirty years. All that time police thought her husband must have done it, made her disappear 'cause of an inheritance she came into. Turns out the road was icy and she just missed a curve in the dark. Went under and never came up."

He looked out at the water. Julianna knew why he was telling her the story. He was letting her know how easily she could disappear, too. He was playing his game, enjoying it.

"It was the woman and her daughter," Julianna said. "They disappeared the night before Kennedy was shot."

"So it's true, then?"

"You don't have an alibi."

He chuckled again. "You don't need an alibi, darlin', if you don't get caught. I'd be halfway to California by morning."

"No," Julianna said. "I mean the night my sister disappeared."

He turned to her. In the darkness his blue eyes were a pale gray. He reached up to hook a strand of his long, greasy hair behind his ear, and Julianna almost flinched. Crowley smiled, then lowered his hand, his big gut shifting beneath his plaid shirt.

Because the bank sloped a little, he stood a couple of inches below her. But he was still so much taller than Julianna that she had to look up to look him in the face.

"I was in jail that night. If that ain't an alibi, I don't know what is."

"The woman who said she saw my sister after she left your trailer never really saw her. She saw a girl who looked like my sister."

Crowley mused. He stroked his goatee.

"You bring my money?" he said.

Julianna reached into her purse and handed Crowley the packet of cash. He tore open the plastic Target bag, removed the three envelopes, then dropped the bag to the ground. He kicked the bag away.

"How much?"

"Twenty thousand."

He licked his thumb and counted the money in the first envelope. Julianna held her purse tight against her, a hand resting on top of it. Crowley counted the money in the second envelope.

"What did my sister say to you?" Julianna said.

He counted the money in the third envelope, taking great care to make sure no bills stuck together. When he finished, he put the three envelopes in the back pocket of his jeans.

"She turned up at my trailer, and we talked for a minute or two. Like I told you. I don't remember what all we talked about. I probably told her my name, she probably told me hers. I said I had a guitar and we could make some music together. She said— what was it?

"Let's not and say we did."

"Let's not and say we did."

Crowley had turned back to look out at the lake. The water, with no wind, was a flat, impeccable black. So, too, was the sky to the north. Julianna could barely make out the hinge between sky and water—a line of faint light running along the top of the dam.

"I was a young man," he said. "Shit."

"Keep going," Julianna said.

"So I said, 'Okay. Why don't you come on inside then and party with me.' Don't tell me your sister didn't like to party. I could tell. I didn't have no dope on me at the moment, but I knew where I could get some. There was so much dope in that camp people was giving it away."

He made Julianna wait.

"What did she say?" she finally had to ask.

"She just started walking off. Not the way she came, though. I remember that. Not back toward the rides, I mean more off toward the sideshows and such."

"What did she say to you?"

"'First things first.'"

"I gave you the money."

He laughed. "No. That's what she said. I told her, 'Hold on a minute now,' but she just kept on walking. She looked back over her shoulder and said, 'First things first.'"

Julianna waited. Crowley yawned.

"What does that mean?" Julianna said.

"You tell me."

"So was she planning to come back?"

"Struck me that way at the time, but she never did."

First things first?

"Where was she going? Why was she heading toward the race-track?"

"No idea."

"So that's all she said?"

"That's all. 'First things first.' So I ran out to buy some beer and find some dope. Glad I did it in that order, the beer first and not the dope. Glad that cop stopped at 7-Eleven for doughnuts. Hell. Otherwise I probably woulda ended up in the electric chair."

Julianna had her hand around the grip of the revolver before she was even aware of it. She had dropped her purse and was pointing the revolver at Crowley.

"You told me it was important," Julianna said. "What my sister said to you when she left."

Crowley regarded her. His eyes stayed on her eyes. The barrel of the revolver was a foot from his chest, but he ignored it.

"I never did," he said calmly.

Julianna's finger was tight on the trigger. She could feel the trigger begin to give. You were supposed to squeeze, she remembered hearing somewhere once, not pull. She'd never fired a gun in her life. She told herself she was too close to miss.

She tried to keep her voice calm, too. "You told me I'd want to know what she said."

Crowley gave Julianna his innocent look. "Didn't you?"

"What did you do to her?"

"I ain't giving you your money back, if that's what you want. We had a deal."

"What did you do to her?"

"I fucked her first," Crowley said. "Backwards and forwards. She couldn't get enough of it. She rode me so hard that I—"

And then out of nowhere his hand was on the revolver, wrenching hard, and Julianna's head exploded—a slap, or a punch, from his other hand. She stood frozen while the ground rushed up and slammed against her.

Crowley held her down, his knee on her chest. The weight crushed. Julianna fought to draw in a breath. Crowley used the torn plastic bag from Target to hold the gun while he wiped it clean with the tail of his plaid shirt. When he finished, he flung the gun into the lake. The splash sounded like a kiss.

He moved his knee off her chest. Julianna gulped air, but before she could move, Crowley straddled her and pinned her wrists above her head—both of her wrists locked in one of his big hands. She kicked and twisted. With his free hand, he slapped her. When she screamed for help, he clamped his hand over her mouth. She tried to bite his palm, and he slapped her again.

"Stop it," he said. "Look at me."

She wouldn't. She focused on his tattoo. The blurred blue snake that wound around his thick forearm. She focused on Genevieve, standing off to the side, bemused and bored.

Genevieve shook her head. *Is this what you wanted all along, you idiot?*

I don't know.

"Look at me," Crowley said.

Julianna wouldn't. He sighed.

"Everything I told you's the truth," he said. "I never touched your sister. I don't know what happened to her. I wish I did. She showed up, we had those few words, she turned around and left. That's all. She never even came inside. She didn't say where she was going, and she never came back. That's it. You understand?"

He's telling the truth, Juli. You idiot.

I know.

She knew. He had no reason to lie.

Crowley let go of her wrists and straightened up. He looked back out at the water.

"I wish she had come inside," he said. His voice was quieter now, with a touch of something—sadness, maybe, regret—that Julianna hadn't heard before. "You never know, do you? She comes inside and listens to me play my guitar, maybe it all ends up all right for everybody."

Life, Julianna thought he meant. She didn't know if he was still playing with her or not.

He climbed to his feet. Slowly, in stages, wincing at each stage.

"I'm keeping your damn money," he said. "We had a deal."

Julianna lay on her back, staring up into the darkness. She listened to Crowley start his car. She listened to the engine fade as he drove away.

How could it be so quiet in the middle of a city? Oklahoma City without the wind was not Oklahoma City at all. She lay on her back, eyes open, and now, finally, she could hear it—the cars on the highway a mile away. Just an occasional whisper, a soft hushing, *shhhhh, shhhhh.*

Wyatt

CHAPTER 22

Sunday morning, Wyatt's tour of Oklahoma City's authentic old-school breakfast joints continued. La Oaxaqueña Bakery was just off Olie, on a stretch of SW Twenty-ninth where the signs in Spanish far outnumbered those in English. The place was homey and unpretentious, with plastic tablecloths, ripped vinyl seats, and a tile mosaic on the wall of what appeared to be a Mayan god devouring a small human being. All that and a pastry case that boggled the mind.

Wyatt, running a few minutes late, looked around. Most of the tables were occupied by multigenerational Latino families and a few older couples. Only one person sat alone, a non-Latina woman in a wheelchair, early fifties or so. Wyatt checked his watch and then noticed that the woman in the wheelchair was eyeing him. He realized that Brett Williams was a woman, a fact Haskell had failed to mention. Wyatt supposed he'd failed to ask.

He walked over. "Detective Williams?"

The woman nodded and motioned for Wyatt to sit. "Pardon me if I don't get up," she said.

Wyatt smiled and sat. "Who says cops don't have a sense of humor?"

"I've been retired almost ten years. Call me Brett."

She studied Wyatt, so he felt free to study her back. She had strong, square features and dark, shoulder-length hair shot with gray. She was neither attractive nor unattractive. Wyatt wondered if she'd had to work at that balance the years she'd been on the force or if it was just her natural state. Her eyes were so pale they seemed empty.

"Thanks for meeting me," he said.

"How can I help?"

She put a hand over her coffee mug before Wyatt even saw the waitress approaching.

"Try the concha," Brett Williams told him. "Or the churro with caramel."

Wyatt shook his head. "I'm fine with coffee," he said. "So you remember the details of the movie-theater case?"

She laughed. "I'd made detective exactly four days earlier."

"Welcome to the big leagues."

"Something like that. So yes. I remember."

"The afternoon of the murders," Wyatt said, "an elderly woman accidentally rammed her car into the Dumpster behind the theater."

"Yes. The young man who survived the shooting told us about that."

"The collision left the Dumpster at a slightly different angle to the building," he said. "He didn't tell you that. So on that one night, Grubb wouldn't have had his back to the exit doors, not completely. Grubb, the doorman who took the trash out that night. He would have been turned a little to his right when he lifted the lid of the Dumpster. I think he would have had a clean view of the exit doors."

Brett Williams listened, neither frowning nor not frowning. A placid expression. That was the best way to describe it, Wyatt supposed—a surface unruffled by breeze above or by current below.

"The killers couldn't have snuck past him," Wyatt continued. "They had to come through the front doors of the theater. They had to have keys. There were no signs of forced entry. Correct?"

"Correct," Brett Williams said. Placidly.

Wyatt realized he was leaning forward across the table. He was coming off as the kind of crackpot who fluttered around the edges of every high-profile crime, a species dreaded by cops.

He sat back in his chair. He took a sip of his coffee.

"Was that avenue ever investigated?" he said. "The possibility that someone who worked at the theater gave the killers the keys?"

"Of course."

"How seriously, if you were certain the killers came in through the exit doors?"

She regarded Wyatt with what might have been amusement. Or contempt. Or boredom.

"Seriously," she said.

"I'm not talking about the kid who survived, I'm talking about the theater employees who weren't working that night." Wyatt realized he was leaning across the table again. "How did the killers know that the deposit didn't go to the bank until Monday morning? The entire weekend take, all cash, was in the safe that night. The timing was clockwork. It was perfect."

"We looked at everyone who wasn't working that night. We looked at them twice. Every possible connection. The theater employees, the mall security guards. The brass kept it out of the papers, for obvious reasons."

"But—"

"Janella Crawford, one of the girls who worked behind the candy counter. Seventeen years old. Her sister's boyfriend had been picked up a couple of times for possession with intent, so we brought him in. The poor guy. We scared the shit out of him. We kept at him in the box for eight, nine hours. I talked to Janella myself probably half a dozen times. I knew that girl's life inside and out. I knew what brand of shampoo she used. We knew everyone, all of us did, inside and out."

"Okay," Wyatt said.

"Toby Haygood, the daytime projectionist. He was a diabetic. Do you want me to tell you what his hobbies were? Who he played poker with every Saturday night?"

"I get it."

"We looked hard at everyone."

Not everyone. Not hard enough. *Someone* had to have given the killers the keys to the theater. Wyatt could feel the anger building, a hot blue bubble at the base of his throat. Why was he so pissed? He couldn't say for sure. Who was he pissed at? That one was easier. He took a breath.

"There was a kid," Wyatt said, "a doorman who only worked a couple of months that summer. He quit in July. He wasn't on the payroll at the time of the murders."

Brett Williams shifted in her wheelchair. Leather creaked. Her expression remained placid.

"Steven Hurley," she said. "His family owned one of the big furniture stores on Reno."

Steve Herpes. "You knew about him?" Wyatt said.

"We knew about everyone. We ran down every person who'd worked at the theater in the previous five years."

Wyatt, the way he was seated, could see one of her legs under the table. When Brett Williams shifted again in her wheelchair, the leg didn't move at all, the foot resting dead on the chrome footplate.

So that was that. Of course the police had investigated the possibility of an inside man. Wyatt should have known that. He *had* known it. The movie-theater massacre had been the most notorious crime in the history of Oklahoma City up till then. Every question had long ago been asked. If there was an answer, it had been found.

Grubb had been stoned the night of the murders. He was stoned every night. The Dumpster had been angled toward the building, and still he hadn't noticed the killers slip through the auditorium exit door. He probably wouldn't have noticed them riding horses across the parking lot.

"You don't remember me, do you?" Brett Williams said.

Wyatt looked up at her. "What?"

"That morning. The morning after."

For an instant Wyatt didn't understand what she was talking about. The morning after what? And then suddenly he could see her face again, those pale eyes searching his. Her hair back then was shorter, no gray in it. She'd patted his knee. His ears were still ringing.

Is there anything else you remember? Try hard, hon.

Brett Williams had been the female detective, the one who sat with Wyatt on the grassy median between the back lot of the movie theater and the street. Who'd assured him, just before the EMTs loaded him into an ambulance, that this was his lucky day.

"They sent you over because you were a girl," Wyatt said.

"I guess I was supposed to be comforting. Nurturing? I didn't have a clue what I was doing."

"What happened to you?"

She didn't have to ask. "A bullet. A ricochet. Quarter of an inch higher and the vest catches it. That's what the doctor told me anyway."

"That was an asshole thing for him to tell you."

"Maybe." She sipped her coffee. "I don't know how you did it. Sitting there, fifteen years old. I would have lost it. I did lose it. That night when I got home."

"They gave me a Valium."

"I'm serious."

"So am I," Wyatt said. "How did you recognize me after all these years?"

She shrugged. "How could I not?"

That sat in silence.

"I never remembered your face until just now," Wyatt said. "I remembered your shoes. You had ugly shoes."

"I did?" She seemed genuinely surprised.

Wyatt stood up. "Thanks for your time, Brett."

"I'd help you if I could," she said. "Do you understand that?"

"Sure," he said.

Driving back to his hotel, Wyatt saw a sign for the Oklahoma City National Memorial. On impulse he made the turn. He'd read about the memorial but had never been there. He parked and crossed Robinson to the massive bronze gate at one end of the reflecting pool. Cut into the panels above the entrance was the time that morning in April of 1995—9:01—when Oklahoma City had last been whole. At the opposite end of the reflecting pool, on the other side of the grounds, was an identical gate. The time cut into that gate was 9:03, one minute after the bomb in Timothy McVeigh's Ryder truck had detonated.

Wyatt walked through the 9:01 gate and took a seat on one of the sandstone benches. On the spot where the Murrah Federal Building once stood, there was now an open lawn, filled with row after row of empty chairs. One hundred and sixty-eight chairs, one for each person killed in the blast. Nineteen of the chairs were sized for children.

The empty chairs were powerful in a way Wyatt had not expected. They captured something essential about the dead—how they could be so far away and yet at the same time right here, right now, right next to you, close enough that you could still hear them breathing.

One evening, a week or so before the murders, Wyatt and Theresa had parked by the lake. They sat on the long hood of her old yellow Buick Skylark and watched the setting sun hit the water and shatter—a thousand fragments of unbelievable color.

Wyatt couldn't believe he was here with her. He still couldn't believe that she'd picked him.

"Why me?" he asked her.

Theresa had her slender arm looped around his neck. "Because why," she'd said.

Two benches down from Wyatt, an older woman sat gazing at the empty chairs of the memorial. One strand of white hair lifted in the wind and then settled. Who, Wyatt wondered, had she lost? What had she lost?

One hundred and sixty-eight chairs. Wyatt knew that the toll was much higher than that. Oklahoma City was a small town at heart, and everyone knew someone who had been killed or maimed in the blast or someone who'd descended into hell to help with the rescue.

And yet a minute after the explosion, at 9:03, the city had begun to pull itself back together, to become something new. The gate at the opposite end of the reflecting pool didn't mark the end of something. It marked a beginning.

There was a lesson here for Wyatt. Wasn't there? He could walk out the far gate and out of the past. All he had to do was leave behind the dead and stop asking questions.

Why am I still here and all the others gone?

He knew he couldn't do it. He knew he'd never be able to do it.

It was eleven o'clock in Vegas. On most Sunday mornings, Laurie went into the office for a couple of hours to catch up on e-mail. Wyatt took out his phone and called her.

"You're right," he said.

There was a long silence. "What does that mean, Wyatt?"

"It means you're right."

"Wyatt. Talk to me."

"I can't do this right now."

"Call me later, then."

"No," he said. "I can't do this. Us. You were right."

"Wyatt."

He could picture Laurie at her desk, her back turned to the doorway of her office in case someone walked past and saw the tears rolling down her cheeks. Wyatt wanted, so badly, to reach out and take her hand and never let go.

But he was cut off, shut out, partitioned behind glass. She was there, and he was here. She was real, and Wyatt was just a memory of a person, a ghost, a dead planet anchored to its orbit while the rest of the universe drifted farther and farther away.

He didn't understand why he was so fucked up. He was the one who had survived.

"I'm sorry," he told Laurie. "You were right."

WYATT'S PHONE RANG. Chip, yet again. Wyatt answered.

"Hello, Chip."

"Hi, Mr. Rivers. I'm really . . . I'm sorry to bother you. I know you're really busy with your other case, aren't you?"

"Yes, I am, Chip," Wyatt said.

He was driving north on Western, past Fairlawn Cemetery. *The man who killed the man who killed Jesse James.* Wyatt wondered if O'Malley had known about Edward O'Kelley when he picked Fairlawn for their game of graveyard Frisbee. It was the kind of shit O'Malley would have loved. If there was any justice in the universe, O'Malley was the boy buried next to the man who killed the man who killed Jesse James.

"I know, I'm really sorry. But I'm just wondering if . . . you know, if maybe you had a chance to look into it yet? My situation with my wife? How I think she might be having an affair?"

"I remember, Chip. Yes, I looked into it."

"And did you— What did you find out?"

This was truly the last thing in the world Wyatt wanted to deal with right now. Or ever again.

"Where are you, Chip?" he said.

"Where am I?"

"Are you at work?"

"No, Mr. Rivers. It's Sunday. I'm off on Sunday."

"Meet me in twenty minutes. The hotel lobby."

"Oh," Chip said.

Wyatt remembered. Employees weren't supposed to approach guests for personal reasons. An excellent rule. Wyatt wished it were better enforced.

"Across the street from the hotel to the west," he said. "What is that? It's a burrito place, I think."

"It's a Chipotle."

"Twenty minutes. Okay?"

"Okay, Mr. Rivers. Thank you, Mr. Rivers."

When Wyatt got to the Chipotle across from the hotel, Chip was already there, seated at a table, his broad shoulders bowed around a napkin he was carefully shredding into a thousand tiny pieces.

Wyatt sat down across from him. Chip looked up. His cheeks were even rosier than Wyatt remembered, as if someone had given them a few hard slaps. Wyatt couldn't tell if he'd been crying. Maybe he had.

"It's bad news," Chip said, "isn't it, Mr. Rivers?"

"It's no news."

Chip wasn't sure what to do with that. He swallowed. He picked up another napkin and began to shred it.

"No news at all?" he said.

"None worth reporting."

Wyatt knew that was probably a lie, but he saw no reason to tell Chip about the male barista at Starbucks or the hand squeeze that Wyatt had witnessed between the barista and Chip's wife. A little information could be a dangerous thing, and he didn't want Chip jumping to any conclusions based on partial, potentially misleading evidence. Maybe Chip's wife was banging the barista, but maybe she wasn't. Maybe she was banging someone else entirely.

"But you saw my wife?" Chip said.

"I did."

"So no news is maybe good news?"

"No news is no news," Wyatt said. "Here's the deal, Chip. Why I wanted to talk to you in person."

Chip scooped up pieces of shredded napkin and clenched his fist hard. "Are you married, Mr. Rivers?

"No."

"But . . . you've been in love? Really, really, really in love?"

"Chip—"

"Because when you lose that, when you think you might lose that—you just feel broken. It's the worst feeling in the world."

He loosened his fist and sprinkled bits of shredded napkin across the table. Wyatt was glad he hadn't said anything about the barista, the hand squeeze. Chip, with his bashful smile and rosy cheeks, the sweet-tempered demeanor, didn't seem like the kind of guy who would flip out and open fire on the man who might or might not be banging his wife. But there was something there, a dark nuclear throb far belowdecks. Wyatt realized he'd picked up on it in the elevator, the first time they met.

Who knew what a broken heart could drive a man to do? Well, Wyatt supposed, everyone knew.

"I know you want an answer, Chip," he said.

"I do, Mr. Rivers. I just want an answer."

"I get that. But I'm not your guy."

"If it's about the money, then—"

"It's not. You need an investigator who can give you his full attention, Chip. I told you when we met, I'm working another case."

"But maybe— What about when you solve that other case, Mr. Rivers? I mean, if you're close to solving that case? Then I can just wait and—"

Wyatt laughed. "Chip. You'd probably die waiting. That's how close I am."

Chip's eyes pleaded. Before he could say anything else, though, a woman came over to their table. She was smiling. She smiled at Chip and then smiled at Wyatt.

"Did you hurt your hand?" she asked Wyatt.

She'd seen the bandage on his hand. Wyatt was confused. Did he know her? He didn't recognize her.

"Just a few stitches," he said.

"Can we pray for your hand?" the woman said. She pointed to another woman, also smiling at Wyatt, a few tables over.

Wyatt thought he'd misheard. "Pardon me?"

"They want to pray for your hand," Chip said.

Wyatt searched for a response appropriate to the situation. "No, thank you," he said finally, giving up.

Her smile faltered. She walked back to her table and said something to her friend. Her friend's smile faltered.

"That was kind of weird," Chip said.

Wyatt held out his hand, his good hand, for Chip to shake. He wanted to get the hell out of there before Chip remembered that forty-five seconds ago he'd been in the process of falling apart. He wanted to get the hell out of there before Chip resumed doing so.

Chip shook Wyatt's hand.

"I wish you the best, Chip," Wyatt said. He meant it.

He walked back across the street to the hotel parking lot. As, wouldn't you know it, the stitches in his palm began to ache. And—this was clearly the vengeful God of the Old Testament at work here—the bar in the hotel lobby didn't open until five o'clock on Sundays.

Wyatt drove down to the Plaza District and found the tattoo shop, Ink & Roses. It was closed all day on Sunday, but the lights were on. Wyatt rapped on the shop's plate-glass window until a heavyset guy in a black T-shirt emerged from the back. The guy crossed his arms and stared at Wyatt.

"I'm looking for Dallas!" Wyatt yelled through the glass.

The guy gave Wyatt the finger and then a thumbs-up. A mixed message if ever there was one, but Wyatt managed to sort it out: *Fuck you, dickhead, for ignoring the Closed sign,* and *She's upstairs.*

Wyatt walked around to the side of the building. A flight of stairs led up to the apartment on the top floor. Wyatt knocked.

After a few seconds, Dallas opened the door. No makeup, her hair piled precariously on top of her head. She didn't seem surprised to see Wyatt.

"Hey there, you," she said.

"I was in the neighborhood."

"Were you, now?"

Her skin was pure cream, an immaculate canvas for all those colorful tattoos. The phoenix rising from the ashes, a woman's face painted to resemble a Día de los Muertos skull, a vine bristling with poisonous-looking flowers. Beneath the thin cotton fabric of Dallas's T-shirt, Wyatt could see the rumor of even more tattoos.

"I'd never lie to you, Dallas."

"You know that's my last name, don't you?" she said. "Dallas is?"

Wyatt hadn't known that. "What's your first name?"

"Tiffany."

"Tiffany. You don't look like a Tiffany."

"That's why everybody calls me Dallas."

She opened the door wide. Wyatt stepped inside. A one-bedroom flat, sunny and tidy. On the wall in the living room was a large oil painting, a version of the phoenix on Dallas's arm. Moon-faced dolls filled a bookshelf, along with framed photos and a vintage red Bakelite telephone.

"Beer or whiskey?" Dallas said.

"Sure."

She smiled and went into the kitchen. Wyatt picked up a framed photo. In it Dallas was maybe eight or nine years old, grinning cheek to cheek with a woman Wyatt supposed was her mother. The daughter, Wyatt saw, had inherited her mother's nose, her feline eyes.

Dallas returned and handed him a glass with two fingers of scotch.

"That's my mom," she said. "She used to work at the Land Run, too, way back when. She worked the door. How do you like that?"

What was it O'Malley used to say about the relationship between past and future? Wyatt couldn't remember. O'Malley's theories were endless and arcane.

"Where's your mom now?" Wyatt said.

"Florida."

Wyatt observed that every photo was just mother and daughter. He picked up one of the moon-faced dolls.

"I can't remember what they're called," he said. "I remember they were very popular. There were fistfights at Christmas."

"Cabbage Patch Kids."

"That's it."

She took the doll from him and pressed it to her nose, breathed in the scent.

"My father used to bring me those."

"Where's he?"

"Gone. He died when I was little. Killed."

"I'm sorry."

She shrugged. "I don't remember anything about him. He got my mom pregnant and ran out on her. I remember the way he smelled."

"Tell me about this old telephone."

Dallas took the glass of scotch from Wyatt's hand and set it on the shelf.

"You want to see the rest of my place or not?"

The bed, through another doorway, was unmade, the sheets invitingly rumpled.

Wyatt thought about how nice it would be to step into that

room, into this woman's life for a while. How nice she would feel pressed against him, his mouth on her neck and her ribs beneath his fingers. Wyatt would be able, for an hour or a week or a year, to stop asking *why*.

"I don't think so," he said.

Her feline eyes remained unperturbed. Or seemed to. "Okay."

"I'll see you around."

"I guess."

Wyatt went back to his car. He used his phone to search for nearby pizza places and picked the one that popped up first. Hideaway Pizza. He called in an order for a large cheese and a large pepperoni.

Candace had just pulled in to her driveway when Wyatt arrived. She glanced at him, at the pizza boxes, and then went around to the backseat to unbuckle Lily.

"I was going to call you," Candace said.

"Have you guys had lunch?"

Lily climbed out of the car. "Hi, Wyatt."

"Hi, Lily."

"We went to the Science Museum."

"Was it fun?"

Lily considered the question gravely. You could see her stacking the weights, lining up the measures, checking her math.

"Yes," she said finally.

Candace handed Lily a small pink backpack, decorated with the face of a Disney princess Wyatt couldn't place—one of the newer, multicultural ones. Candace handed Lily her keys.

"Go on inside, baby. I'll be there in a second, okay?"

"Okay."

Wyatt watched Lily climb the steps to the porch. She unlocked the front door and went inside. He gave it another try.

"Have you had lunch?" he said. "I thought Lily might like pizza. Kids like pizza. That's my understanding. That, actually, is the beginning and the end of my understanding."

Candace slammed the car door shut. And then she yanked it back open, just so she could slam it shut again, even harder.

"You!" she said. "Are! Un! Be! Lievable!"

Wyatt didn't know what she was talking about. He did know better than to ask. Any way he asked would make him sound like a smart-ass.

"I called Dallas a few minutes ago," Candace said. "To see if she could watch Lily today for an hour or so? And she said you just left."

"Candace—"

"I can't believe you're doing my bartender and not working on my case!"

"I'm not doing your bartender."

"Then why were you over at her place?"

That question was more complicated. "Candace—"

"I don't care!" she said. "I don't care who you're doing or if you're doing anybody! I don't care if you bring over stupid pizza at two o'clock when every normal person has already had lunch! Do you know what I care about?"

Wyatt kept his mouth shut. Candace was really pissed, more pissed than he'd ever seen her. He set the pizza boxes on the hood of his car and walked up the driveway to her.

"Do you?" she said.

She opened the car door and prepared to slam it again. Wyatt reached for her wrist to stop her but then—the look Candace gave him—thought better of it. She slammed the door so hard the car rocked.

"What *have* you been doing?" she said. "I mean, seriously? Besides my bartender. Ha. Have you been doing *anything* to help me? Gavin said you were like the best private detective he'd ever worked with."

Again Wyatt kept his mouth shut. This time because he couldn't argue Candace's point. What *had* he been doing? In the past twenty-four hours, he'd spent roughly five minutes thinking about Candace's case. Maybe less. He should have been pressing Finn's manager for the list of fans, he should have already started bracing them. And before that? Wyatt had been off his game the minute his plane touched down in Oklahoma City. He'd never, he knew, really been present.

"What happened?" he said. "Why were you going to call me?"

"Mr. Eddy's brother called me this morning. He said he was going to get the court to reopen the estate."

"He can't do that."

"He said his lawyer can. He said I better get a lawyer, too. The best one I can afford."

"He might be able to get probate opened again, but he won't win."

"Does he have to?" Candace said. "I'm not stupid. He said I can sell him the Land Run now or I can sell it to him later."

So that was Jeff Eddy's play, to make Candace spend so much money on lawyers she'd have to take a lowball offer.

Wyatt shook his head. "It's okay," he said. "You don't have to worry about any of that."

"Oh?" Candace said. "Really? I don't?"

"No." He smiled. "Trust me."

She looked like she was going for the car door again but then stopped. Lily had emerged from the house and was standing on the porch.

"Hi, baby," Candace said. "What's wrong?"

Wyatt felt it, too. A ripple of uneasiness moved through him, almost too faint to notice—a pebble dropped into a pond.

"Mama," Lily said. "I don't understand."

Another pebble dropped into the pond.

"Don't understand what, baby?" Candace said.

Without another word Lily went back inside. Candace followed her. Wyatt followed Candace. Everything in the living room looked normal, everything in the dining room. And then a gust of chilly air raised the hair on the back of Wyatt's neck, and he noticed the open window in the dining room, the splintered casement. Candace noticed it a second later. Wyatt felt her tense.

"Go outside with Lily," he told Candace. But Lily was already halfway down the hall leading to her bedroom. Candace caught up and stopped her before she could go in. Wyatt stepped in front of them both. He looked through the doorway.

The room had been stripped—posters removed from the walls, sheets and pillowcases pulled from the bed. The dresser drawers were open and empty. The closet was empty, just a few plastic hangers left crooked on the rod. In the center of the room sat three big cardboard moving boxes. The boxes were taped up and neatly labeled: CLOTHES. TOYS. MISCELLANEOUS. Next to the boxes was a child-size pink roller bag, packed so full that Wyatt could see the zipper straining.

Candace had stopped breathing. Lily looked up at her.

"Where am I going, Mama?" she said.

Wyatt

CHAPTER 23

The door on the opposite side of the hallway was open. Candace's bedroom. Wyatt saw that nothing in there had been touched—it was only Lily's room the intruder had boxed up. The significance of that wasn't lost on Wyatt. He could tell it wasn't lost on Candace.

I know where you live. I know what's important to you. I can take it away from you at any time.

Candace knelt next to Lily. She flicked a strand of blond hair from her daughter's face.

"Let's go over and see Aunt Dallas," Candace said. "What do you say about them apples?"

Wyatt didn't know how Candace was keeping it together. He himself was so furious he was about to put his fist through the wall. He wanted to find the person who'd broken into Candace's house and put a fist through his head. He wanted to put a fist through his own head.

"Wyatt brought pizza," Lily said.

"We can take the pizza with us."

"But we already ate lunch."

"Then we can have it for dinner."

"Or a snack," Wyatt said. "I always say that the midafternoon snack, not breakfast, is the most important meal of the day."

Lily considered. "Okay," she said.

Outside, Candace buckled Lily back into the car. Wyatt loaded in the pizzas. After he gave Lily a fist bump and shut her door, he took out his phone. Candace came around to his side of the car.

"What are you doing?" she said quietly.

"I'll stay here and handle the police."

"No."

"Yes. Take Lily to Dallas's place. The police will want to talk to you, but they can do that later."

"No. I mean don't call them."

Wyatt had set his phone on the roof of her car, the paint blistered from bird poop, so he could search his wallet. The cop who'd interviewed him in the ER three nights ago had given Wyatt his card, but he couldn't find it now. He told himself to slow down. Cool off.

He looked at Candace. "What?"

"I don't want you to call the police."

"What?"

"No. Not yet."

"Not yet?" He could see her mind working. "What is it?"

She shook her head. "Nothing. I don't know what to do. I need time to think about it."

"Candace," Wyatt said. "Candace. There's nothing to think about. What happened in there, do you understand what it means?"

She'd been about to move past him. Instead she stopped, waited for a second, and then looked up at him. Her eyes were stone. Wyatt felt like she'd just kneed him in the balls. He wished she had. He would have preferred that to this.

"I'm sorry," he said.

"You think I don't understand what it means?" Her voice was cool, quiet. "She's my daughter."

He stepped out of her way. Candace got into her car and started the engine.

"Are you coming with us?" she said.

"I'll be over in a little while. We have to talk about this, Candace."

"Promise me. You won't call."

"Won't call who, Mama?" Lily said from the back.

Wyatt bent down. "My buddy, Jimmy Stinken von Poot-burper. Your mom doesn't want to invite him over for pizza. I have no idea why."

"Promise," Candace said.

"For now," Wyatt said. He reached in and gave Lily another fist bump. "See you later, alligator."

After Candace and Lily drove off, Wyatt went back inside the house and used his phone to take photos of everything—the broken window, the stripped room, the moving boxes. He was careful not to touch anything, in case the intruder had left behind any kind of physical evidence. Fucking hell. Wyatt knew he needed to call the cops. He also knew, fucking hell, it wasn't his call to make.

Instead he called Finn's manager and left a message. "I need that list, Dixon. Now. Call me."

The anger he'd felt earlier had returned—a carrion bird drop-ping heavy from the sky, claws first, digging in, its cry a hoarse, giddy scream. Wyatt locked the house and walked to his car. He took his phone back out and called Jeff Eddy.

"Damn it," Jeff Eddy said. "I've been trying to get holda you. I must have called half a dozen times."

That sounded about right to Wyatt. He hadn't listened to any of the voice mails that Eddy had left him since the football game.

"I may have something for you."

"About time. Are you working for me or not? I talked to my lawyer about getting the probate back open, put a little extra squeeze on—"

"Are you home? I can come by."

Eddy huffed. "If you come right now. I'm leaving for the Thunder game in half an hour, rain or shine."

"Text me your address," Wyatt said.

It took Wyatt only ten minutes, light Sunday traffic, to drive out to the development north of the Kilpatrick Turnpike where Eddy lived. His house was brand new and big, but—Wyatt had to admit it—in surprisingly good taste. The architect had put in fat, Prairie-school porch columns and used Oklahoma limestone the color of buttered toast. Eddy's house looked like it might actually belong here on the southern plains, not in Santa Fe or on Martha's Vineyard.

Next to the front door was a carved pumpkin painted Sooner colors, crimson and cream. Wyatt picked up the pumpkin. It was big but not heavy. He could hold it with one hand.

Jeff Eddy opened the door. "Well?" he said. "What have you got for me?"

"Are we alone?" Wyatt said. "This is sensitive stuff."

Eddy huffed. "Yes. We're alone. Karen's with the kids at soccer."

Soccer. Eddy made a face when he said it, the way someone else might make a face when discussing intestinal parasites or drug-resistant oral gonorrhea.

"I'm not a huge fan of soccer either," Wyatt said. He lifted the pumpkin above his shoulder. "I think you probably have to grow up with it."

Eddy shook his head. The mere discussion of the sport was beneath him.

"What are you doing with that?" he said. "Are you coming inside?"

"Sure," Wyatt said.

He stepped inside and hit Eddy with the pumpkin—in the face, with so much force the pumpkin split apart into jagged chunks and Eddy staggered backward. He collided with a wooden coatrack and went down heavily, dragging the coat rack with him. When Eddy tried to get up, Wyatt kicked a chunk of broken pumpkin at him. It glanced off the side of Eddy's head.

"You piece of shit," Wyatt said. Eddy might not be the person who'd threatened to kidnap Lily—Wyatt, deep down, knew he probably wasn't—but at the very least Eddy was trying to extort Candace into selling him the Land Run. Wyatt wanted to break a branch off the coatrack and pound Eddy's head until it, too, split apart. "What did Candace ever do to deserve a piece of shit like you?"

Eddy's eyes roamed the foyer, wild with panic.

"I've got a gun," he said.

"Do you want me to wait while you go upstairs and unlock your safe?" Wyatt kicked another chunk of pumpkin at him.

Eddy started to get up again. "This is assault," he said.

"Shut up and listen to me," Wyatt said.

"This is assault and battery. You're going to jail."

Eddy was on his feet now—his jowly jaw slack, breathing hard. He was thinking about putting his shoulder down and taking a run at Wyatt. He had fifty or sixty pounds on Wyatt, maybe more. But he was cautious. Jeff Eddy liked to fight dirty. He didn't like when his opponent did.

"Tell me why you slept with Greg's wife," Wyatt said. "Were you genuinely attracted to her, or was it just about proving to yourself what a dumb-ass your brother was?"

Eddy's expression changed. And then changed again. Surprise, fury, fear, rapid calculation—all in the course of a single blink.

"Now, hold on," he said.

"I'm holding," Wyatt said.

"That was— Their marriage was already over, for all intents and purposes."

"So you won't mind if I tell your wife about it. I think she suspects. She suspects *something.* But suspecting and knowing are two different things. I hope you had a prenup."

"Now, hold on. *Damn it.*"

"Probably you didn't. Thirty-four years ago? And good luck with probate, when the judge finds out the exact circumstances of why Jeff didn't leave you the Land Run."

The foyer had begun to smell faintly like pumpkin pie. The bone that cupped Eddy's right eye was red and shiny, with a single pale pumpkin seed stuck to the skin like a perfectly placed teardrop. Wyatt wondered what lie Eddy would tell people when they asked how he got the bruise.

Wyatt bent down and started picking up pieces of the jack-o'-lantern.

"How much money do you want?" Eddy said.

"I don't want any money, you piece of shit. I want you to back off Candace and keep backing."

"You're the piece of shit."

Wyatt found a trash can and dropped the pumpkin inside. He wiped his hands on his socks, a trick O'Malley had taught him long ago, to keep your pants clean at work.

Eddy was still considering a charge. Wyatt wished he *would* charge, come what may.

"So we're good?" Wyatt said. "The terms of our gentleman's agreement are clear? You back off Candace and I keep my mouth shut."

"You sure as hell better."

"*You* sure as hell better." Wyatt peeked into what appeared to be a study or a library. "Do you have anything to drink? We can drink on it. Your finest scotch."

Eddy glared. He seemed to be under the impression that Wyatt was kidding. Wyatt walked into the study and snooped around until he found a liquor setup in the cabinet behind the desk. The scotch was eighteen-year-old Laphroaig. Not bad. The really good stuff was probably behind lock and key.

Wyatt poured two stiff ones, neat, and brought them back into the foyer. He offered one to Jeff Eddy. Eddy ignored it and continued to glare at him.

"Get out of my house," he said.

"Boomer!" Wyatt said, and knocked his drink back.

BY THE TIME Wyatt got to Dallas's apartment, it was almost five.

"Never thought I'd see you again," Dallas said when she opened the door.

"Life works in mysterious ways," Wyatt said.

She hesitated, then let him in. Candace was curled on the couch with Lily, reading a book. *Elmer and the Dragon.* Wyatt remembered it from his own childhood. Well, he remembered a dragon with stripes. And a little boy who wore a matching shirt. That had struck Wyatt, even at the age six or seven, as a little weird.

Lily looked up and regarded him. "We had pizza for a snack," she said.

"I approve."

She turned to Dallas. "Wyatt can push a grape through a table."

"I'll believe that when I see it," Dallas said.

"He can."

"Lily," Wyatt said, "can I borrow your mom for a minute? I promise to return her in original and pristine condition."

Candace got up. Wyatt followed her into Dallas's bedroom. He shut the door behind them.

"Is everything okay here?" he said.

"I want to say I'm sorry," Candace said.

"You're sorry?" Wyatt said, surprised. "For what?"

"For some of the things I said earlier."

"Stop it. You're weirding me out."

Candace sat down on the edge of Dallas's unmade bed.

"Jeff Eddy's not going to be a problem for you," Wyatt said. "The probate thing, it's taken care of."

"But he's not the one, is he?"

"I don't think so. No. But—"

"You did your best. You did a lot more than anyone else would have."

"I'm serious, Candace. Stop being weird."

Wyatt wanted her to yell at him, to demand results, to whack him on the sternum with her hard, brown knuckles.

Instead she sighed. "Lily's my life. The beginning and the middle and the end of it."

"That's why we need to call the police. Now."

"We're gonna move back to Vegas."

"Candace," Wyatt said, "just listen to me for a minute, okay?"

"Mr. Eddy's brother can buy the Land Run if he wants. I don't care. It's not worth it. It was never really mine, you know?" She leaned her head against Wyatt's shoulder. She closed her eyes. "I'm so tired. I can't wait to sleep for like a month."

Wyatt watched the last breath of afternoon sunlight slip away through the window. Shadows stretched.

"It was yours," he said. "It is yours. Mr. Eddy wanted you to have the Land Run. You."

"Mr. Eddy would understand," Candace said. "He was an understanding dude."

"An understanding old dude."

Her big white smile flashed, but she didn't open her eyes. "Yeah."

"Candace. I'm sorry I fucked this up for you. But you're just going to give up? Surrender?"

She didn't take the bait. Wyatt didn't think she would. She smiled again.

"Wyatt," she said. "I'm not five years old."

"I just want you to think about this decision."

"I have. And I give up. I surrender."

"Let me have another week. Go back to Vegas with Lily for a few days."

"No."

"I'll call the police, and then—"

"No."

The room had cooled quickly now that the sun was down. The only remaining source of warmth was Candace's head, resting against Wyatt's shoulder.

"You have a bony shoulder," she said after a minute.

"You have a bony head."

"Go home, Wyatt," she said.

Julianna

CHAPTER 24

The next evening, before work, Julianna returned to the Double R Ranch. The hard-looking redhead was nowhere to be found. Julianna went table to table, booth to booth, searching the faces, just to make sure. She checked the ladies' room.

Julianna asked one of the bartenders if he knew the woman. The bartender listened to Julianna's description of her and laughed.

"You're talking about just about every redhead ever came in here," he said.

"Do you know a customer named Carla May?"

The bartender was annoyed now. The place was packed.

"You want a drink or not?" he said.

Julianna walked back to her car. In her purse she had the five hundred dollars in cash she planned to give the redhead. She couldn't guess how much the gun Crowley had thrown in the lake was worth, and she hadn't bothered trying to find out the price online. Five hundred dollars was all she had, so five hundred dollars was all she could give. That and the turquoise leather holster that matched the redhead's purse. Julianna suspected that if she was never able to locate the redhead again, the woman would regret the loss of the holster, hand-tooled with rose blossoms, more than she would the gun.

A pickup truck behind Julianna honked, the driver wanting to know if she planned to surrender her parking space or not. Two bikers turned in to the lot, the sound of their motorcycles trailing behind them, a sound like the pavement was being jackhammered up. Julianna waved at the driver of the pickup to go on. A second later she realized he was already gone.

Julianna sat in her car. All day she'd felt that way—a beat behind the music, slightly stupefied. It was like being stoned, but with none of the pleasure. She'd slept seven or eight hours, so that wasn't the problem.

What *was* the problem? The problem was, Julianna had started with nothing and now she had even less. She'd given Crowley twenty thousand dollars and received in exchange no answers, only questions. Only more questions.

Why would Genevieve abandon her little sister on the curb outside the rodeo arena? Why would she journey to the midway and through the midway and all the long way to Crowley's trailer, dodging Lacey and leaping hydraulic cables, navigating the scary carny camp, only to leave again almost immediately?

Why?

Where was she headed when she told Crowley, "First things first"? Not back to Julianna. Crowley said Genevieve walked off a different way than the way she'd come.

Last night at the lake, Julianna had believed that Crowley was telling her the truth. Now, with distance and perspective, in the light of day and all that, she still believed him. He might lie like he breathed, but those lies served his own interest. Profit, pleasure, self-preservation. The tale he'd told Julianna about the last time he saw Genevieve—she didn't think Crowley had anything to gain from it.

Then *why* did Genevieve leave Crowley's trailer so soon? Where did she go? Who did she find there?

Another car honked at Julianna. She backed out and drove to the hospital. She was early for once, ten minutes, but both Ben and the supervising nurse were already waiting for her outside the on call room, where Julianna planned to change into her scrubs.

"Can we have a word, Julianna?" the supervising nurse said. She wrinkled her nose. "You smell like a bar."

"Do I?"

"Have you been in a bar?"

"I have," Julianna said. Mystery solved. "I need to change, please."

"You've been drinking?" Ben said.

"No."

"You don't need to change," the supervising nurse said. "Martina agreed to come in and cover your shift tonight."

"But I'm here. I'm early."

"Ben and I wanted to tell you in person. We've scheduled a meeting for tomorrow morning at nine, with HR. I hope the time is convenient for you."

She was frowning. Ben was trying not to smile, his lips pressed together.

"Am I being fired?" Julianna said.

I wish it were that easy, the supervising nurse's eyes seemed to say.

"We're starting a process," she said instead, carefully. "It's our hope, Ben's and mine, that we can find a satisfactory way to address issues that, I think for all of us, need to be satisfactorily addressed."

"Or else," Julianna said. "Right?"

A doctor passed them, his sneakers squeaking on the tile floor. Julianna truly despised that sound.

"So we'll all meet at nine tomorrow," the supervising nurse said.

"I know what!" Julianna said, as if she'd just been struck by the best idea ever.

They looked at her.

"What?" Ben said.

Julianna turned and walked away. "Let's not and say we did."

"Julianna!" Ben called after her.

SHE SLEPT TILL ten and might have slept even later. But the doorbell rang. It kept ringing. Julianna pulled on a pair of sweatpants. Friendly Christians often roamed her neighborhood, going door-to-door with pamphlets and invitations to pancake breakfasts. They had special powers and could sense when you were home and just hiding. So did the unshaven guys who wanted fifteen bucks to spray-paint your house number on the curb. Five dollars extra for the red and white of the Oklahoma Sooners, the orange and black of the OSU Cowboys.

Julianna wondered how much longer she would have a house. No job, no more emergency cash. Her interest in the matter was surprisingly mild. Maybe she could get a job spray-painting house numbers on curbs. Or holding a sign on the corner of May and Hefner.

By the time she reached the door, the bell had finally stopped ringing. She opened the door anyway.

A very thin woman in a tailored wool pea coat stood on the porch. She was using the surface of a porch column to write a note. When she heard the door open, she turned.

Genevieve's friend Lacey. *Lacey.* Ringing Julianna's doorbell. Julianna wondered for an instant if she was still asleep, still in bed and having a dream. A bad one.

Lacey saw the surprise in her face and smiled. That curl to her lip, such disdain, so familiar. Julianna braced herself. *Never piss off Lacey,* Genevieve had told her once. That was the first rule of being friends with Lacey.

Julianna had taken half a step backward, without even realizing it. Lacey smiled again.

"What do you think I'm going to do?" she said.

"I don't know."

"Do you think I'm going to attack you or something?"

"Why are you here?"

Lacey inspected the collar of her pea coat and found the one fleck of pine bark that had settled there. She flicked it off.

"To tell you I'm sorry," she said with her usual annoyed impatience. "That's why I'm here."

And then, before Julianna could absorb the full impact of that first surprise, Lacey threw her arms around Julianna and hugged her, tightly.

"I miss her so much," Lacey whispered. "Oh, my fucking God, Juli. I miss her so much."

Julianna knew now that this was a dream. It had to be. Lacey's cheek was wet against hers. Julianna stood with her arms at her sides. She lifted a hand and placed it on Lacey's back and pressed lightly. Lacey was made of featherweight balsa wood and rubber bands, like the toy airplanes Julianna and Genevieve had played with when they were little.

Lacey released Julianna and stepped away. She unsnapped her purse and removed a tissue. She dabbed the corner of one eye.

"You can see your nips, you know," she said.

Julianna looked down. She was wearing the sheer cotton undershirt she'd slept in, no bra. She looked back up at Lacey.

"Well, I was hoping you were one of those Christians that go door-to-door," Julianna said.

Lacey laughed, the wicked cackle that Julianna knew so well from her childhood, and then she started crying again. Julianna felt the tears rolling down her own cheeks now, too. Lacey plucked another tissue from her purse, handed it to Julianna.

"That's so Genni," Lacey said. "Oh, my God."

"Do you want to come inside?"

Lacey shook her head. "I'm sorry I didn't tell the police about the sweater. I didn't even think about it."

"I didn't either."

"I'm sorry I don't remember more. I was flying that night, Juli, I'm not lying. I don't even know how I got home. When I saw Genni on the midway, I should have followed her. I was so chapped at her, that she blew me off. She'd been blowing me off for weeks. I should at least have chased her and asked where she was going."

"She probably would have lied to you," Julianna said. If Genevieve didn't want you to know something, you didn't know it.

"She was the best liar," Lacey agreed. She blew her nose. "Do you remember her diary?"

Julianna did. When Genevieve was a sophomore in high school, she'd started keeping a "secret" diary that she hid in places where she knew their snooping mother would be sure to snoop. In the dresser drawer behind her panties, in the closet at the bottom of a shoe box filled with old birthday cards. The diary had a little lock, cheap copper starting to turn green, that you could pop open with your a fingernail.

"'Dear Diary,'" Julianna said, "'I find it very rewarding to volunteer at the old folks' home. I feel like the elderly have so much to teach us about life.'"

Lacey cackled. "'Brad in my algebra class is very handsome and such a gentleman,'" she said. "'Dear Diary, do you think he will ask me to the winter dance?'"

Their mother had not been fooled. She knew Genevieve too well. But eventually she gave up the snooping, which had probably been Genevieve's plan all along.

Genevieve continued to make regular entries in the diary, just as a goof. Sometimes she'd read the latest entry aloud to Julianna, or to Julianna and Lacey, cracking them up.

"Do you think it was my fault?" Lacey said. "Whatever happened to Genni?"

"I don't know," Julianna said.

"I know you miss her more than me, but I miss her, too, Juli. It almost killed me."

"Do you want to come inside?"

"I don't." Lacey remembered the piece of paper in her hand. "I was writing you a note. I didn't get very far. Just your name."

"I'm sorry, too, Lacey."

"Don't worry," Lacey said. "I won't hug you again."

"Good."

Lacey turned and walked to the car parked in the driveway. She didn't look back.

Julianna shut the front door. Her cell phone, in the bedroom, was ringing. When she reached the phone, she saw that the call, according to the ID, was coming from YOUR NEW BFF. Julianna was baffled. The redhead from the bar? But how had the woman found her number?

"Hello?" she said.

"I stopped by to see you this morning at the hospital, and you weren't there!" a girl's cheerful voice said. "I'm very disappointed in you, madam."

It took Julianna a second. And then she pictured an old canvas-winged biplane doing barrel rolls in the sky. Aerial. *Ariel*. Julianna remembered now, in the parking lot of the hospital—the blond girl taking her phone from her, punching keys.

"I wasn't there," Julianna said. "I'm not working today."

"Neither am I. What do you want to do? I'm so bored, Julianna. How about the zoo?"

"The zoo? No. I don't think so."

"When's the last time you've been to the zoo?"

"I have to go, Ariel," Julianna said.

"I'll bet you a kabillion dollars you've never been to the zoo on a weekday. When it's kind of chilly out and not crowded at all?"

Julianna could hear something ragged along the edges of the girl's voice. If Ariel had stopped by to see her earlier, at the hospital, that meant she'd had another round of chemo. Had she gone through it alone again?

"Ariel," she said, "do you have family here?"

"Here? Where? The Nordstrom Rack by Penn Square, where I am currently located? No, I do not have family at the Nordstrom Rack by Penn Square."

"In Oklahoma City."

"No. And this is starting to be a boring conversation, Julianna. I'm sorry, but it's true."

"Do you have family anywhere? Parents?"

"Not for— How do you say it? For all intents and purposes, no."

Julianna wondered about that for a moment, how a relationship could be so broken that not even a daughter's cancer couldn't
mend it.

"Now, pay attention, okay?" Ariel said. "Eyes on the prize.
The zoo on a weekday when it's chilly and empty is *awesome*. It's
like your own private zoo, Julianna. The giraffes will come to
the fence and lean over and try to bite your hair. It will take your
frown and turn that fucker upside down!"

Julianna almost smiled, despite herself. "I have to go now,
Ariel," she said.

"Okay. Call me, then. Call me later."

"Good-bye."

"I mean it."

"Good-bye, Ariel."

Julianna ended the call. She sat at the kitchen table for a few
minutes, then went out to the garage. A rope dangled from the
trapdoor in the ceiling. The previous owner of the house had used
a piece of string to attach a tennis ball to the rope. The string had
been carefully measured: the tennis ball hung four feet off the
floor, at the height of a car windshield. When the previous owner
pulled in to the garage, the tennis ball told him or her exactly
where to stop the car.

Told *her* where to stop. Julianna guessed that a wife had mentioned, one night at dinner, how tight the fit in the garage was.
The husband had come up with the tennis-ball solution.

Julianna couldn't grasp a life like that—people who actually
spent time thinking about those kinds of things, then actually
spent time doing them. She envied those people, she supposed.

She tugged on the rope. The trapdoor creaked open, and the
rickety wooden steps unfolded themselves, *thunk-thunk-thunk,*
dust puffing each time. She climbed up into the attic. The box

she wanted was at the far end, and heavy. She dragged it across the planks and then let it slide back down the steps above her. *Thunk-thunk-thunk.* Julianna could hear the old cassette tapes rattling in their plastic cases. There was nothing breakable inside the box—just the cassettes and some photo albums, some scrapbooks and yearbooks, letters, paperbacks, a braided leather belt that their mother thought made Genevieve look like a hippie.

The box was too heavy to lug all the way into the house and then back out again, so Julianna sat down right there, cross-legged on the cold cement floor of the garage. It had been a year or two since she'd looked through the box—all that remained of Genevieve—and the tape came off easily when she pulled. She folded the cardboard flaps back. At the top of the pile inside was a single tube of Bonne Bell Lip Smacker lip gloss, Dr Pepper flavor.

Julianna dug around until she found Genevieve's diaries. There were three of them, each with a floral-patterned fabric cover and a cheap metal lock. She selected the last one. Genevieve had written *"1986"* on the spine with purple Magic Marker ink that once upon a time had smelled like grape pop. No longer. Julianna sniffed to make sure.

She flipped at random to an entry near the middle of the book. July 19:

"I have decided to learn a foreign language, Dear Diary, so I may broaden my horizons. I know that the process will not be easy, but nothing worth doing ever was!"

Genevieve had wild, terrible handwriting, as if she wrote while slamming around in one of the bumper cars they used to have at Crossroads Mall. And all the coke she'd been doing didn't help either. Some words were in cursive, some not, with no rhyme or reason as far as Julianna could tell. When Genevieve wrote in her "secret" diary, she made a point to dot the occasional *i* with a fat cartoon heart.

February 4:

"My first kiss! It was as magical as I had hoped. Bertram's lips were like snowflakes falling on my lips. Afterward we held hands in the park and picked up litter."

April 12:

"Why am I so lucky, Dear Diary, to have the best *little sister in the world? She is my hero and my inspiration! And Martin Luther King, too."*

Genevieve's efforts to learn Chinese became the running theme in August and early September. In between building houses for Jimmy Carter and staying home on Saturday nights to brush her hair one hundred times, Genevieve took classes at the ("renowned") Francis Tuttle Vo-Tech School of Extremely Difficult Languages. She also met with a private tutor, an ancient and mysterious Chinese woman who told hopeful fortunes and tried to teach Genevieve how to roll her *r*'s.

The last entry in the last diary was dated September 16, 1986, four days before Genevieve disappeared.

"Dear Diary, fall is my favorite time of year."

That was true, actually. Julianna knew it for a fact.

She closed the diary and set it aside. The rest of the box awaited her. Was there something in there—a hint, a clue, a wink, a nudge that would guide her to an answer? Any answer?

No. Nope. Julianna had gone through the contents of the box a hundred times over the years. Nothing there had changed or ever would. She'd reread every line of every diary, she'd scrutinized every photo in every album and every yearbook, she'd memorized the photocopied flyers for frat parties and the smudged song titles handwritten on the liners of mix-tape cassettes. The contents of the box belonged more to Julianna at this point than to Genevieve.

Why did Genevieve do it? How could she do it? How could she leave Julianna alone on the curb outside the rodeo arena, dusk falling fast, and never come back?

Julianna would never know. She had nothing and understood that would never change. She understood, clearly and piercingly, *she* would never change.

Wyatt

CHAPTER 25

The first available flight back to Las Vegas didn't depart Oklahoma City until three o'clock on Monday. Wyatt slept in, stopped by the front desk to arrange for a late checkout, and then drove over to his uncle's house to say goodbye. His uncle was sitting on the porch, as usual.

"Mikey!" he called when he saw Wyatt.

Wyatt shook his uncle's hand. "How are you, Uncle Pete?"

"As good as can be expected under the circumstances."

Wyatt smiled and sat next to him on the porch slider. It was sunny but chilly, a brisk wind shaking the leaves up and down the block. Pete was wearing a short-sleeved plaid shirt.

"Aren't you cold?" Wyatt said. He wondered now if that was the same shirt his uncle had been wearing at Candace's house two days earlier and if his uncle had changed it since. "Do you want a jacket?"

"Do I?" Pete said, and chuckled.

They sat and watched the squirrels make daredevil leaps between branches. Wyatt didn't know how much longer his uncle would be able to live on his own. Probably he shouldn't be living on his own right now.

Pete and his wife had never had children. His only surviving relatives, other than Wyatt, were distant.

"Remember Old Man Mooney and his old dog?" his uncle said.

"Who?" Wyatt said.

"Old Man Mooney. You remember. He lived just up the block from us when we were boys."

"From you and my father," Wyatt said.

His uncle turned to look at him. His eyes floated and then steadied. "That's right."

"Tell me about him. This Old Man Mooney and his old dog."

"No." Wyatt's uncle lifted a hand and then dropped it back into his lap. "Who cares about that?"

"I care," Wyatt said. "And don't say I don't."

He thought that would get a chuckle out of his uncle, but it didn't.

"I remember that dog like it was yesterday," his uncle said. "I can smell him. How do you like that? But I can't remember the first time I saw your aunt. First time I kissed her. I can't hear her laugh or cry."

Wyatt didn't know what to say. What was there to say?

A squirrel leaped from a tree next to the house onto the roof above them, landing with a thud and the furious scrabble of claws. Wyatt and his uncle both looked up and waited. They heard the squirrel scramble up and away across the shingles, a close call.

"I'm heading out today," Wyatt said. "Heading back to Las Vegas."

"Las Vegas!" his uncle said. "How do you like that?"

Wyatt thought he could probably talk his uncle into moving to Las Vegas. Wyatt had plenty of room in his house, an extra bedroom. But he couldn't say for sure how much longer he'd be there. He could feel the familiar tightness in his chest, the screw turning. There was nothing to keep him in Vegas, not really. There was nothing to keep him anywhere.

He stood. He could get in touch with a local senior-care service and set up something for his uncle.

"I'm going to give you a call every week, Uncle Pete," he said. "I'm going to keep my eye on you."

"Very good," his uncle said. He stood, too, slowly, so he could give Wyatt one last handshake, grave and formal, as if they'd just concluded negotiations that would bring peace to the continent. "Take care of yourself, Mikey."

WYATT STILL HAD hours to kill before he needed to pack and head to the airport, so he cut over to Twenty-third Street and stopped by the place he'd discovered when he first got to town, the coffeehouse located in the old 1920s bungalow. The pretty baker in the flour-dusted apron greeted him as if she'd known him forever. Wyatt appreciated that.

She showed him a tray of cupcakes on the counter.

"Fresh from the oven," she said. "How can you resist?"

Wyatt decided not to even try and bought a salted caramel cupcake to go with his coffee. He made his way from the counter to what had once been the bungalow's living room. College students had staked out all the tables. Every student seemed to be studying either a medical textbook, sheet music, or a Bible. Wyatt supposed that covered most of the important bases.

He found a nook with a pair of empty easy chairs and sat. The tightness in his chest was like a finger plucking a guitar string. Wyatt wondered if he'd ever made a decision worse than the one that had brought him back to Oklahoma City. On the other hand, though, maybe he was confusing cause with correlation. Did he, right now, truly feel any shittier than he'd felt a week or a month or a year ago? Or was he just more aware of how shitty he felt? He couldn't say for sure.

He wished he'd been able to help Candace. He didn't think he'd ever forgive himself for blowing that.

A woman sat down in the other leather chair. She looked familiar, but Wyatt couldn't place her right away.

"How's the palm?" she said.

It clicked for him then—she was the emergency-room nurse who'd stitched him up.

"Is that all I am to you, Julianna?" he said. "A damaged extremity?"

She sipped her coffee and gazed out over the tables filled with college students. A long moment passed. The nurse appeared to be finished with the conversation. Wyatt felt relieved. Sometimes, like now, playing the role of a lifetime took too much effort. It drained your power cells bare.

"I wonder who used to live here," Julianna said finally. "When it was just somebody's house. What they'd think about all this now."

Wyatt took a bite of his cupcake, then set it aside. He hadn't wanted it, he realized, in the first place.

"I don't remember your name," Julianna said. "I'm sorry."

"How old are you?" Wyatt said.

"Thirty-eight."

"So you probably knew Rainbow Records. The record store that used to be just up the street, on the corner of Classen?"

"Yes." She tucked her legs up beneath her. "Do you remember a place on Classen called Moon Breeze? They sold New Age crap. The woman who owned it was a witch. A Wiccan? That's what everyone said."

Wyatt laughed. "She always wore black."

The woman in black had been a regular at the Pheasant Run's bargain matinees. Other times she brought her toy collie to be groomed at the pet shop on the second floor of the mall.

"Rings on every finger, even her thumbs," Julianna said. "She claimed she was psychic."

Another long moment passed.

"When I was in high school," Wyatt said, "none of us, none of my friends, had a swimming pool. So, late at night after we got off work, we'd find an apartment complex that had a pool and we'd hop the fence."

Julianna smiled and nodded. "Sure. Yeah. My older sister did that all the time. My older sister and her friends. She took me along a few times, when I begged. I was always scared to death."

"It was harder to pull off during the day," Wyatt said. "During the day the people who lived there used the pool. They'd ask you what apartment you lived in, what your father's name was. But late at night was usually okay."

"I remember one night. It was August and so, so hot. My sister and I were in the pool, some random apartment pool. A guard had come around earlier and tried to kick us out, but he didn't stand a chance against my sister. You should have seen her." She smiled. "Anyway, all the tornado sirens started going off. You know how they sound. Really loud, but like they have to take a big breath every now and then."

Growing up, there had been a siren on the corner of Wyatt's

block—a beehive of yellow horns at the top of a telephone pole. Every Saturday at noon in Oklahoma City, the tornado sirens sounded and all the neighborhood dogs would howl along.

"Yeah," he said.

"It had started to rain a little, big fat drops, but we didn't worry. It was August. Tornadoes happen in the spring, everyone knows that. My sister said something like, 'Oh, it's just a test or whatever.' So we kept swimming. The raindrops felt nice. It was really dark out. The pool didn't have any lights, and the moon must have been behind the clouds. And then there was this intense flash of lightning, and I saw it, the tornado. It was so close, almost on top of us. It was right there. It had been there all along, and we didn't know it."

Suddenly it was night, not day, August, not October, and Wyatt was outside, not in. He could feel the hum and electric bristle in the air, he could feel the raindrops whipping against his face, he could see—when for an instant the flash of lightning lit the whole world up—the elongated snout of the tornado, nosing across the lake.

"Holy shit," he said. "I remember that, too."

The clarity of detail was a shock, the richness of color and texture. Wyatt realized he hadn't thought of that moment since the day he lived it. The memory was original, fresh, intact—not a photocopy of a photocopy, the way most memories were.

Wyatt's shift had just ended. He'd just stepped outside. The sirens wailed. He'd taken off his orange blazer and slung it over his shoulder, one finger hooked through the label sewn inside the collar. He smelled the rain and his own sweat and the heat still baked into the asphalt of the back parking lot.

Where were the others? Scattered. The crew hung out together often that summer, but not always. One or two nights a week,

Wyatt clocked out and walked home alone, his blazer slung over his shoulder. Those were the nights, he realized, he didn't really remember.

That night, Wyatt was pretty sure, Theresa had clocked out around seven so she could attend a cousin's rehearsal dinner. Mr. Bingham had sent Wyatt home early, too, before the ten-o'clock shows ended, because he'd received a call that morning from corporate telling him to cut weekday hours. O'Malley had stayed behind to do the auditorium trash sweep. Melody had stayed behind to finish cleaning the concession stand.

"I screamed so loud," Julianna said. "My sister did, too. We ran back to the car in our swimsuits, screaming and laughing, soaking wet. When the lightning flashed again, the tornado was gone. It just . . . it must have just lifted away."

The wind shifted. The rain stopped. The sirens wailed for another few minutes, and then Wyatt started walking home. He thought about going back inside to tell O'Malley and Melody about the tornado he'd seen, but he didn't. He knew he could tell them later. Had he told them about the tornado the next day? Surely he had.

It was an unsettling sensation, a kind of vertigo, to suddenly remember a part of your past you never realized you'd forgotten. Wyatt closed his eyes and stood there on the steps outside the Pheasant Run Mall, smelling the rain, listening to the tornado sirens.

He opened his eyes. Julianna sipped her coffee. In profile she looked a little like Theresa. A little like Theresa might look now. Who could say?

Wyatt understood he'd been enslaved, his whole life, by a love that had never really existed. If Theresa hadn't been murdered, she and Wyatt would have stayed together a few months more, maybe less. He was fifteen years old, she was seventeen. It was a brief summer fling that would have burned brightly and faded almost instantly. It was a cool three-minute song you heard once on the radio. If Theresa hadn't been murdered, Wyatt couldn't say for sure he'd even still remember her. He was absolutely sure Theresa wouldn't still remember him.

But understanding that, understanding all that, didn't change anything.

"Did you ever go see movies at the Pheasant Run Twin?" Wyatt said.

"Where everyone was killed? No. I grew up on the Southside. We went to the Southpark. Or the Apollo Twin in Midwest City."

The Apollo had been in the Monarch chain of theaters, which meant you could use the movie passes there. Wyatt didn't remember how many Monarch theaters there had been in Oklahoma City. At least six or seven. That's what made the trafficking of the movie passes so lucrative.

"We left our clothes at the pool," Julianna said. "I don't know if we ever went back for them. But I remember the knob of the gearshift in my sister's car. Her old Cutlass. The knob was black leather with red stitching."

"It's funny, the things you remember."

"Yes."

"My uncle stopped drinking and joined AA the day after the bombing downtown," Wyatt said. "His wife was supposed to be at the Murrah Building that morning but wasn't. He remembers that. But I don't know if he remembers *her*. He remembers the neighborhood dog from seventy years ago. I don't know if he remembers anything that matters. Maybe he does."

"Our cousin was in AA. My sister used to make fun of it, all the slogans they had. Instead of 'Let go and let God,' she'd say, 'Let go, God! You're hurting me!'"

Wyatt finished his coffee and set the cup on the saucer. He still had a long time before his flight, and this was as agreeable a place to pass it as any. But he thought he might as well jack up one last shot at the buzzer. Maybe he could do at least a little good before he left town. Maybe he could get Chip an answer.

He stood. "Have a nice day," he told Julianna.

She looked up at him. A second later she saw him. "You, too," she said.

Wyatt drove up Western to Nichols Hills Plaza and parked across from A Snip in Time. He entered the salon. The receptionist was applying bloodred lipstick. She popped her lips and smiled at him.

"Help you?" she said.

"Do you have to ask that?" Wyatt said. "Look at my hair."

The receptionist smiled and reached for an iPad.

"What day were you thinking?" she said.

"Today," Wyatt said. "Now. It's an emergency situation, and I'm willing to pay a premium."

His hair wasn't bad at all, actually. He'd had it trimmed a few days before he left Vegas. But Wyatt wanted thirty minutes in the chair with Chip's wife. If she was the chatty sort, if Wyatt was at the top of his game, if the conversation broke just right, he might be able to find out if she was cheating on her husband or not. No, the chances for success were not good. Under normal circumstances he would never have tried this approach. Blow it and you're blown, you're off the case, and you've screwed up your client's life even more than it was already, presumably, screwed up. This approach, though, and the thirty minutes were all Wyatt had left if he wanted to put Chip's mind at ease, one way or another.

He glanced past the receptionist. Because of the shoji screen
behind her, he could see only half of the main salon area. Three
stations, all occupied. One of the stylists was male. Neither of the
two female stylists was a fresh-faced pixie with cubist hair.

"Well," the receptionist said, "April might be able to squeeze
you in."

Wyatt shook his head. "My friend at work says I must have
Megan. Megan or bust."

A customer, a greyhound of a woman in her fifties, sat on the
sofa in reception. She snapped to a new page in her *Vogue* with
great annoyance. Wyatt guessed what the receptionist was going
to say before she said it.

"Oh," she said, "I'm sorry. Megan is running late today."

"She was supposed to be here at *eleven,*" the woman on the
couch said. She snapped to a new page in the magazine.

Wyatt felt his grand plan go down like an old casino hotel
imploding—a shudder, a hesitation, the sigh of collapse.

"Oh, well," he said. He wasn't shocked, the way things had
been going for him. "Better luck next time."

He stepped out of the salon just as an old Jeep Cherokee
squealed into the parking lot and pulled in to the space right in
front of him. Megan, Chip's wife, popped out of the passenger
side. She started toward the salon but then stopped and came back
around to the driver's side of the Jeep. She leaned in the window
and gave the young black barista a long, lingering kiss on the lips.

"Bye, sweetie," she told him.

Wyatt held the door of the salon open for her.

"Thank you, kind sir," she said, and went inside.

The Jeep backed up and drove off. Wyatt walked over to his
car. He considered, not for the first time, how often his profession

involved the discovery of that truth which destroyed the lives of others.

He got out his phone to call Chip. He didn't know how Chip would take the news that his wife was in fact having an affair with another man. Not well, Wyatt supposed. People never took the news well, no matter how prepared they thought they were. Wyatt had an uneasy feeling that Chip might handle the truth even less well than most.

He scrolled through his contacts until he found Chip's number. But he didn't press the CALL button. Why did something feel wrong here? Why, buried within the swell of the orchestra, did a single woodwind sound flat?

Wyatt couldn't put his finger on it. Chip's wife had arrived with the barista. She'd kissed him on the lips. A kiss—emphatic, intimate, lingering for a beat—that in no known universe would ever pass for friendly or platonic. Wyatt had been standing ten feet away. He'd seen the barista put his hand on Megan's cheek, sliding his fingers up under the slanted chop of her hair.

Wyatt would have staked his career on the position that Chip's wife and the barista were sleeping together. It was obvious. So what was the problem, then?

Wyatt had spent hundreds of hours, no exaggeration, secretly observing the mating rituals of the North American adulterer. He'd found that every cheating couple, like Tolstoy's unhappy families, cheated in its own particular way. Some couples were fanatically cautious and discreet, with Cold War dead drops and car swaps. They wore wigs and paid for motel rooms with cash. Other couples seemed to thrive on the thrill of potential discovery. There was one guy, Wyatt remembered, who'd taken his girlfriend to Mon Ami Gabi, an outdoor café at the Paris. The

Paris was directly across the street from the Bellagio, where both their spouses worked. The guy had finger-banged his girlfriend under the table during dessert.

In Wyatt's experience, though, all cheating couples did have one thing in common: The married half of the couple (or both members of the couple, if both were married) always displayed a heightened self-awareness that he, or she, was cheating. For some people, such as the public finger-banger, that self-awareness was probably half the fun. For others a nerve-racking drag. The self-awareness could be subtle or not, but it always *was*. At least one member of a cheating couple was always glancing, if only figuratively, over his or her shoulder.

Married couples didn't do that. Who was watching *them*? Nobody.

Chip's wife had popped out of the Jeep without thinking about it. She'd gone around and kissed the barista without thinking about it. She'd barely glanced at Wyatt on her way into the salon. The barista had backed his Jeep out without even noticing Wyatt.

Maybe Chip's wife and the barista were the exception that proved the rule, but Wyatt still found it strange. They were acting like they were married to each other, not their respective spouses.

He put his phone away without calling Chip and walked back to the salon. The receptionist was applying a fresh coat of lipstick, a darker shade of red.

"Help you?" she said. And then, when she recognized him, "Oh, hey. You're back. Megan just got in, but she's crazy booked today."

Wyatt saw Chip's wife at one of the sinks, lathering up the annoyed woman who resembled a greyhound. He moved past the receptionist.

"Hey!" she said. "Wait!"

Next to Megan's sink was her station. A chair, a mirror, an antique oak cabinet. The top of the cabinet was crowded with various jars and tubes of hair-care products, combs and scissors, a blow dryer, a box of Kleenex, a pack of Nicorette gum, an iPhone.

No photos.

Megan looked at Wyatt, bemused, as she continued to knead the annoyed woman's soapy scalp. The annoyed woman's eyes were closed.

"Hi," she said.

"Excuse me, Megan," Wyatt said. "This is going to sound crazy."

He wore the suit for moments like these. People tended to give you the benefit of the doubt when you were nicely dressed.

"Okay," Megan said.

The annoyed woman opened her eyes. "Excuse *me*," she said.

Wyatt ignored her. "The guy who dropped you off," he said. "The guy driving the Jeep. Who was that?"

"*Excuse* me," the annoyed woman said.

Megan began to knead the woman's scalp more vigorously. The woman closed her eyes again. Megan gave Wyatt a look that said, *Welcome to my life.*

"Oh," she said. "That's Jake. That's my hubs."

The shampoo smelled like jasmine. The hot water Megan was using to rinse made the annoyed woman's head steam. Wyatt felt a little light-headed himself.

"The black guy," he said. "The guy driving the Jeep. He's your husband?"

She laughed, but Wyatt could see her wondering if maybe the guy in the suit was crazy after all.

"Last time I checked," she said.

Wyatt

CHAPTER 26

Wyatt walked back to his car, fast, and drove to the Marriott. He recognized the woman at the front desk. She was the one he'd asked about a late checkout.

"Hello, Mr. Rivers," she said. "Did you change your plans?"

"I'm looking for Chip," Wyatt said. "Is he working the front desk today?"

The woman cocked her head. "Chip?"

That was all Wyatt needed. He turned and strode back across the lobby.

"Mr. Rivers?" the desk clerk said. "Is everything okay?"

Wyatt sat in his car and worked his way through the facts, one at a time:

Chip said he worked at the Marriott. He did not.

Chip said Megan was his wife. She was not.

He'd even texted Wyatt a photo of her—a photo, Wyatt realized now, that Chip had probably harvested from Megan's Facebook profile. He'd probably lifted the Marriott name tag off some guy in maintenance or room service.

Chip had begged Wyatt to investigate the affair he suspected his "wife" was having.

Why?

The answer was there before Wyatt could even finish scribbling down the question.

Chip—bashful, broad-shouldered, aw-shucks "Chip"—had used the fake wife, the fake affair, the fake case, as a way to keep tabs on Wyatt, as a way to track the progress of the *real* investigation. *He* was the person, all along, who'd been harassing Candace.

Wyatt remembered the first telephone conversation he'd had with Chip. It was the morning after Wyatt had been attacked in the playground across the street from the Pheasant Run.

So you're still going to help me, Mr. Rivers?

Chip had attacked Wyatt in the playground. And then he'd called Wyatt to find out if the message had been received, if Wyatt had decided to bail on Candace and head back to Las Vegas.

You haven't changed your mind or anything?

And Wyatt remembered the conversation he'd had with Chip at the burrito place yesterday morning.

You need an investigator who can give you his full attention, Chip. I told you when we met, I'm working another case.

But maybe— What about when you solve that other case, Mr. Rivers? I mean, if you're close to solving that case?

Wyatt couldn't believe how stupid he'd been. But before he called the police, he needed confirmation. He needed more information.

He took the Broadway Extension south and then merged onto I-40, keeping his eye on the rearview mirror to make sure he wasn't being tailed. The first exit dropped him onto Robinson. Two minutes later he pulled up in front of Lyle Finn's warehouse.

Finn was in back, sitting on the loading dock, doing yoga again in nothing but his kilt. He'd twisted around in such a way that the top half of his body faced west, the bottom half east.

"Lyle," Wyatt said.

Finn turned his head. When he saw Wyatt, he looked the way Wyatt felt when a doctor grabbed his balls and told him to cough. Wyatt's doctor back in Vegas was a petite, soft-spoken woman with a surprisingly robust—and icy—grip.

Wyatt didn't give him a chance to freak out.

"The first time we met," Wyatt said, "you said a blogger had been there the day before me. That's why you thought I was a blogger, too. I need to know what he looked like, Lyle. The blogger."

Finn slowly brought the upper half of his body back into alignment with the lower. He brought his head back into alignment with his body and warily regarded Wyatt.

"The blogger?" he said.

Who, Wyatt guessed, had spent much of his time inside Finn's warehouse on the top floor, at the windows that looked down on the back of the Land Run, plotting the perfect way in and out.

"What did the guy look like, Lyle?" Wyatt said.

Finn sprang to his feet. Wyatt saw him glance at his escape route, the door on the far wall of the loading dock.

"This is a weird conversation," he said.

Wyatt took a deep breath. He needed it.

"Lyle," he said. "You can do some good here. Remember the Vedas? What did the guy look like?"

"I don't know, man. Youngish, I guess. Like in his early twenties?"

"Dark hair?" Wyatt said, testing him. "Glasses?"

Finn shook his head. "He had blond hair. I remember that. And no glasses. He was very polite. He reminded me, I remember now, of one of the von Trapp kids. You know? One of the von Trapp kids from *Sound of Music*. Like he could have been wearing lederhosen?"

That was Chip. On the nose. It had to be him.

But now Wyatt faced the bigger questions: Who *was* Chip, and why the hell was he harassing Candace?

Wyatt knew he had to go back to the beginning, the very beginning, and walk the entire path again. Somewhere along the way, he'd missed the importance of a detail, he'd stubbed a toe on it but kept right on walking.

He took his notebook out and flipped to the beginning, the notes he'd taken during his very first meeting with Candace. Halfway through the second page, he saw a phrase he'd scribbled down—*"sore loser"*—and stopped. Occam's razor, Wyatt realized. The correct explanation is often the simplest one.

Finn was still standing on the loading dock, watching him.

"Does that help?" Finn said. He seemed hopeful.

Wyatt nodded. "Thank you, Lyle."

He left his car parked out front and took the shortcut, squeezing through the fence between the warehouse and the Land Run. There was one car, not Candace's, in the employee lot. Wyatt pounded on the back door. A few seconds later, Jonathan, the sound engineer opened it. He looked worried.

"Have you talked to Candace?" he said. "Fudge says Dallas says we might not open tonight. He says she says we might not open at all."

Wyatt pushed past him and headed to the bar. Jonathan followed him.

"We've got two bands on the bill tonight," he said. "What am

I supposed to tell them? We haven't paid them yet. One band is driving like eight hours from Albuquerque."

"Don't worry about it," Wyatt said. He found the shoe box that Candace kept under the cash register. He dumped onto the bar the postcards Candace's ex-husband had sent from Hawaii.

"Whoa," Jonathan said. "Hey. I would *not* do that if I was you, dude. Candace is *not* going to be cool with that."

Wyatt picked up the most recent postcard and read it.

"Maui is better then ever," Candace's ex-husband had written. *"Its always nice weather. Sabrina and I have a house on the beach now. One wall is all glass. My new job pays two times what the old one did. Life is good!"*

Sore loser. That had been Wyatt's first thought when Candace explained the real purpose of her ex-husband's upbeat messages. Her ex-husband knew she'd inherited the Land Run. He knew she had a shot at a fresh start. He couldn't stand the thought that she might be happier than him.

Sore loser. It was right there, day one, in Wyatt's notes. He'd never given it much thought because most of the cards were postmarked—Paia, Maui—*after* the harassment had begun. The most recent one was postmarked only four days ago, *after* Wyatt had arrived in Oklahoma City. He had just assumed that Candace's ex couldn't be in two places at once.

Wyatt arranged several of the cards, overlapping, so he could compare the postmarks. He leaned close. *Fuck.*

"What's wrong?" Jonathan said.

In each postmark there was variation in the integrity and darkness of the ink. That made sense, since the postmarks were hand-stamped and it would have been impossible to apply uniform pressure, at a uniform angle, with a uniform amount of ink, every single time. But Wyatt could see that the variation *in* each of the postmarks was identical—the cancellation bars over the stamp faded at exactly the same point, the circle that enclosed the date and location had exactly the same slight, ragged blotch, the *P* in every "Paia" looked like more like an *F*. Only the date, in each postmark, was different.

He supposed that some sort of clip-art image had been used for the postmark and then the dates had been changed individually in Photoshop. The postcards, in other words, had never been mailed from Hawaii. They were designed to make Candace think her ex-husband was far away when the harassment started. Otherwise she would have suspected—instantly—who was behind it.

"It's her ex-husband," Wyatt said. "Chip is Candace's ex-husband."

Jonathan frowned. "No. I think his name is Brady. Or Brandon. Something like that."

Wyatt called Candace and got her voice mail. He sent her a text: CALL ME. IMPORTANT. He called Dallas.

"What?" she said. "She doesn't want to talk to you, Wyatt."

"Is Candace still at your place?"

"She doesn't want to talk to anyone. She turned her phone off."

"Dallas," Wyatt said. "Tiffany. Is she at your place right now? Give her the phone. I have to talk to her."

The tone in his voice got her attention.

"What's going on?" she said. "Yeah, she's there, but I'm down in Norman for a class. I'm taking her and Lily to the airport in a couple of hours."

"Don't. She doesn't have to leave now." Wyatt piled the postcards back into the shoe box. "Never mind. I'm heading over there now."

"What's going on?"

"I'll see you at your place."

Jonathan was shaking his head. He pointed to the shoe box full of postcards that Wyatt had tucked under his arm.

"Oh," Jonathan said. "Oh. You can't have those, dude. That is definitely not cool."

"It's okay," Wyatt said. "I'm bringing them to Candace."

He pushed past Jonathan again and exited through the front door, not the back. Wyatt was 95 percent certain he had not been tailed coming to the Land Run, but he wanted to be 100 percent certain he was not tailed leaving it. He cut through the parking lot of the abandoned body shop next to the Land Run and walked all the way up to the corner. Turning right, then right again, he landed at the top of the block that Lyle Finn's warehouse was on. He watched from a distance for a minute, to make sure his car was the only one around, then hurried down the block and got in.

He jumped back onto I-40, then jumped right back off at the first exit. No tail—Wyatt was 100 percent certain. He headed toward the Plaza District, where Dallas lived, using surface streets that took him past the old mansions of Heritage Hills and Mesta Park.

Wyatt didn't want to call the police yet, not until he could provide them with solid information on Chip's—Brandon's— location. He thought for a second and then dialed Chip's number.

"Mr. Rivers?" Chip said, surprised. "Hey!"

"Hey, Chip," Wyatt said. "I have an update for you. About your case."

"Really? But I thought— That's awesome, Mr. Rivers!"

The performance was sensational. Wyatt felt a chill—he couldn't help it. The guy was even better at this than Wyatt was. A sobering thought.

"It's an update," Wyatt said, "not an answer. Not yet."

"Okay, Mr. Rivers."

"I told you I couldn't work your case anymore, but I had some free time this morning. I felt bad about bailing on you. So I went by the salon where your wife works."

All that was true. Why take chances?

Chip let it hang there for a beat. An exquisitely timed beat.

"What did you see, Mr. Rivers?" he said.

"I can't talk right now. Can you meet me later this afternoon? I've got to wrap up the other case I was working. Well, shut it down is more like it. It's over."

"Sure, Mr. Rivers. Just say when. Just say where."

"I'll come to your place. Three o'clock. Text me the address."

Wyatt hung up without waiting for an answer. That was what Chip would expect him to do. He waited. A minute. Another minute. Finally Wyatt's phone chimed. A text from Chip—an address on Penn, an apartment number.

SEE YOU THEIR THANK YOU SO MUCH.

Wyatt was almost to Dallas's apartment. He tried Candace again. This time she answered, with a sigh.

"Please," she said. "Okay?"

"I know who it is," Wyatt said. "I know who's been doing this to you."

"Who?"

"Your ex-husband."

The silence lasted so long that Wyatt thought he'd lost her. "Candace?" he said.

"He's here?" she said. "Brandon is in Oklahoma City?"

"I'll explain. I'm almost there."

The Plaza District at lunchtime was buzzing. Wyatt didn't see anyplace to park on the street.

"We have to call the police," she said. There was something in

Candace's voice, a rawness, he'd never heard before. "He's a bad person, Wyatt."

"I know," Wyatt said. "And I know. Believe me."

A silver SUV pulled out of a space directly in front of the tattoo parlor Dallas lived above, but—as luck would have it—not until just after Wyatt had already passed by. He nosed slowly along for another block, then gave up trying to park on Sixteenth. He turned down the next side street.

"I've got his address," he told Candace. "And when he'll be there later. We'll give all that to the police."

"Wyatt."

He pulled to the curb. "I'll be right up."

He glanced at the rearview mirror to make sure he wasn't blocking a driveway. The silver SUV that had pulled out behind him turned onto the side street, too. Wyatt had a fraction of a second to register that, to put the pieces together, and then the silver SUV was accelerating, veering, smashing into the driver's door of his Altima. The impact of the crash slammed Wyatt sideways as the side air bag exploded. His shoulder strap snapped him back hard, and his head felt like it had come off his neck. He couldn't see—everything went black, then blazed white, then went black again.

He heard the passenger door of his car open. He didn't know how much time had passed. It could have been days, weeks. Chip leaned in. Smiling at Wyatt.

"Oh, my God, Mr. Rivers!" he said. "Are you okay? I'll call an ambulance."

Wyatt felt Chip's hand groping him, patting Wyatt's legs, his chest.

"What are you doing?" Wyatt said. He tried to say. "You fucker."

"I'm not stupid, you know. I could tell you were lying on the phone. Not right away, but pretty quick." Chip found the cell phone in the inside pocket of Wyatt's suit coat. "I'll take this, if you don't mind."

Wyatt's left arm was pinned between the crushed panel of the door and his seat. He reached across and tried to unclip his seat belt with his bandaged right hand. Chip grabbed his wrist and pounded Wyatt's hand against the steering wheel. Wyatt felt the stitches in his palm pop. His hand burned.

"And I thought you might be coming here," Chip said. "This was just bad timing for you, Mr. Rivers, wasn't it? Wrong place, wrong time. No hard feelings, okay? Even though you stabbed me with a pen."

"Brandon."

"Had to run to get to Chipotle before you did. So you wouldn't see me limp in."

"Brandon." Wyatt fought the dizziness. It felt like he was still moving, like he had never stopped, like he was trapped forever in the instant when Chip's SUV slammed into him. "You won't get away with this, Brandon. The police know about you."

Chip held up a knife so Wyatt could see it. A hunting knife with a five-inch blade, flared and beautifully faceted, the tip whipped like meringue into a cheerful point. The edge of the blade looked sharp enough to move through matter without touching it.

Chip angled the knife toward the light and admired the way the metal shimmered and turned liquid, colorless.

"It's okay," he said. "I only need to get away with it for like two more minutes. I don't care what happens after that."

"No," Wyatt said. "You don't want to hurt Candace. You don't want to hurt your daughter."

Chip nodded. "You're right. I really don't. That's what makes this so sad."

"Then why?" Wyatt said. He knew he had to keep Chip talking. "Why hurt them if you don't want to?"

"That's a great question. I wish I had time to explain."

"Talk all the time you need."

"You're trying to stall me, Mr. Rivers, aren't you? You're sneaky!"

"Why hurt them if you don't want to?"

"Because a family should be happy together, not apart."

"You mean you don't want them to be happy without you."

"This way we'll all be happy."

Chip backed out of Wyatt's car. Wyatt hit the center of the steering wheel with his bleeding hand and kept it pressed there. The horn blared. Chip leaned back in, half in the car and half out. Wyatt saw the knife flashing toward him and twisted hard to his left. The blade skipped off his collarbone and slid smoothly into the seam between Wyatt's sternum and shoulder. There was no pain at first and then what seemed like all the pain in the history of humankind, concentrated in that one spot. Wyatt felt like he was underwater. The whole world seemed to warp and ripple.

Before Chip could pull the knife out and strike again, Wyatt hooked his right arm around Chip's neck and yanked him close. He finally managed to free his pinned left arm. He hit the horn again, with his elbow.

Chip tried to jerk away, but Wyatt held tight. The horn blared and blared. All expression was gone from Chip's face. He was so close that Wyatt could smell the wintergreen on his breath.

Chip punched Wyatt in the head with his other hand. He punched him again. Wyatt was upside down now, tumbling through time and space. He felt Chip fling off his arm. He felt the blade slide from his flesh. Chip, still without expression, raised the knife again.

A shadow rippled across the dash. Wyatt caught a glimpse of Candace, behind Chip, as she used both hands to slam the passenger door shut on Chip's legs. He grunted, with pain and surprise. He turned. She slammed the door again.

"You bitch," he said.

The knife turned when Chip did, the blade melting as light from the windshield caught it. Wyatt grabbed Chip's hand and drove the knife forward, drove it down. Chip turned back toward Wyatt at the same instant, and the blade buried itself deep, almost to the hilt, in the hollow at the base of Chip's throat. Chip opened his mouth. His mouth was empty one moment, and then in the next moment it was full of blood, a cup about to spill. His expression, no expression, never changed.

Wyatt tried to let go of Chip's hand, but he couldn't. He didn't have the strength. The light began to fade. Wyatt was surprised to discover it really did that. He could feel the grudging pump of his heart. Like a cranky old man trudging up a flight of stairs. *I'm sick of this shit. This is the last time.* Wyatt thought he heard a voice, voices, but too faint to understand what they were saying. The light continued to fade. It was taking its sweet fucking time. The voices went silent. The pain eased. Finally all that was left was the darkness, the stillness, and the hot, coppery smell of everybody's blood.

Julianna

The guy she'd stitched up looked at his cupcake as if some-one had slipped it onto his plate while he wasn't paying attention.

"My uncle stopped drinking and joined AA the day after the bombing downtown," he said. "His wife was supposed to be at the Murrah Building that morning but wasn't."

Julianna thought of their cousin Mercy, who lived in Tulsa. Their father's sister's daughter, ten years older than Genevieve and fifteen years older than Julianna. They saw her only once a year, on Christmas Eve, when she would drive down to visit friends and family in Oklahoma City and parade before them another year of her sobriety. Genevieve said Mercy chose Christmas Eve in order to cast the maximum pall.

"Our cousin was in AA. My sister used to make fun of it, all the slogans they had." Julianna tried to remember. "Instead of 'Let go and let God,' she'd say, 'Let go, God! You're hurting me!'"

And whenever Mercy preached the necessity of living life one day at a time, Genevieve would break loudly into the dumb, cheerful theme song to the TV sitcom of the same name. It made Mercy furious.

"Have a nice day," the guy said.

When Julianna looked up, a beat late as usual, he was already standing, already moving away.

"You, too," she said.

Do you remember that security guard at the apartment complex, Genni? The one who tried to kick us out of the pool? He was so young. He probably wasn't much older than you, but he thought he was such hot stuff. Do you remember his T-shirt? Oh, my God. How did I forget that? A dark blue T-shirt with a gold badge that was just an iron-on decal. He called us 'Ladies.' He said, 'Ladies, the pool is closed. You are in violation of the rules.' Oh, Genni. You loved when guys thought they were hot stuff.

"Don't you want to violate the rules, too?" Genevieve had asked him. "You know you do."

Most pools had lights. A light. A glowing green porthole beneath the diving board. That pool didn't have a light, or the bulb had burned out. To the baby security guard with the iron-on badge, Genevieve and Julianna were just two heads floating on the dark water. He couldn't see that they were wearing swimsuits. For all the security guard knew, Genevieve and Julianna were as naked as the day they were born.

"Ladies, I will not warn you again," he warned them again.

And then he turned and fled. Genevieve smiled, sucked in a breath, and slid beneath the water. It started to rain.

On the way home, after the tornado passed and they did or didn't retrieve their wet clothes from the side of the pool, Genevieve told Julianna to shut the glove box and keep her grubby paws off her cassettes.

"I will *not* warn you again," she said.

Julianna left the coffeehouse. She paused to stroke the head of an affable old pit bull mix leashed to one of the iron patio railings. That dumb TV theme song was now stuck in her head. "One Day at a Time."

She tried to remember the other AA slogans Mercy had tormented Genevieve with. "Easy does it." "Gratitude is an attitude." But you had to give Mercy credit. AA had helped her get sober, stay sober, and turn her life around. "From darkness comes light." "First things first."

Julianna stood up so suddenly that the old pit bull yipped with surprise and scrambled to its feet.

First things first.

That's what Genevieve had told Crowley when he asked if she wanted to come inside and party. When she'd turned him down and walked away instead.

"First things first," Julianna said.

Julianna thought about Genevieve's diary. Why hadn't she stopped making entries once their mother stopped snooping? Why had she so thoroughly described the challenges of learning a foreign language and so dutifully noted every class she attended?

Without fanfare, without the low moan of a tornado siren or a flash of lightning, Julianna realized that Genevieve had been in AA. She'd joined AA. When Crowley asked if she wanted to party, Genevieve had turned him down. The first thing—*first things first*—was staying clean.

Genevieve in AA was such an unlikely possibility that Julianna had never even imagined it. But that explained the diary. That last summer and fall, the diary hadn't been a goof at all. Genevieve had been keeping track of the time she stayed clean. Staying clean, for Genevieve, *was* a foreign language.

The classes at the Francis Tuttle Vo-Tech School of Extremely Difficult Languages had been the AA meetings Genevieve attended. Two or three times a week, all through August and into September. And the old Chinese tutor, the private tutor Genevieve wrote about, must have been her— What did they call them in AA? Her sponsor. The person you could call, any hour of the day or night, if you thought you might be about to slip.

Julianna gave the affable pit bull one last pat and stepped slowly onto the sidewalk. She understood why Genevieve had kept her involvement in AA hidden from their mother. Their mother thought AA attracted weak, selfish people who blamed their problems on others and used the program as a way to clear their slates so they could behave badly all over again.

And Genevieve hid it from Julianna, too. Julianna, twelve years old, was too young to understand. Genevieve thought she was oblivious about the drinking and the drugs. She wanted to keep her that way.

The coded entries in the diary were not for their mother. They were for Julianna. Their mother had stopped snooping, but Julianna hadn't. She snuck peeks at Genevieve's diary whenever she could.

The police hadn't investigated the AA connection. They never knew about it.

Julianna's heart began to pound. Faster and faster, a prisoner of its own momentum. She ran toward the parking lot behind the coffeehouse. The guy whose palm she'd stitched up had said his uncle was in AA, a long-timer. Maybe the uncle would be able to put Julianna in touch with people who'd been in the program back in the eighties.

When she got to the parking lot, though, the guy had already driven off. Julianna didn't remember his name. The hospital would have his contact information, but she'd burned that bridge, unfortunately.

She took out her phone. Did she know anyone in AA? Did she even know if she knew anyone in AA? Julianna had never seen DeMars touch booze—he always asked for lemonade or Pepsi. That was another bridge burned, though: Julianna's gift. Their cousin Mercy had moved to Florida, or maybe it was to Arizona. Julianna had lost touch with her long ago.

She tried a Google search for *"Alcoholics Anonymous OKC."* It turned out to be that simple: A link sent her to a page where she could find a meeting, open or closed, by city and date. She selected *"Oklahoma City"* and *"Monday"* and clicked SUBMIT.

The screen filled with results. Julianna scrolled down. And down. And down. She was startled there were so many meetings, dozens and dozens of them. And that was just today, just in Oklahoma City.

"God, give me the courage to change the things I can," their cousin Mercy would say.

God, Genevieve would say, *I will accept the change you give me, but no pennies, please.*

Julianna counted eleven different locations where the various meetings—Big Book, Step Study, As Bill Sees It—were held over the course of the day. She ruled out all the locations in the south part of town: Genevieve would never have risked running into a friend of their mother's. That left six places north of downtown. One of them, something called the MacArthur Club, wasn't far from the Sonic on Meridian where Genevieve had worked in high school. Julianna decided to try there first. A Big Book meeting ended in fifteen minutes.

She drove across town. The Sonic had been replaced, probably years earlier, by an upscale Mediterranean restaurant. The MacArthur Club was a mile farther west on NW Sixty-third, between two strip malls, an unmarked, unremarkable building that, if you noticed it at all, you would think was a tag agency or a State Farm office. As Julianna pulled in to the parking lot, the doors opened and people began to exit the building. Men, women, young, old. They lit cigarettes and tilted their heads back. They breathed great gray sighs of relief into the sky above.

Clusters formed. Laughter rang out. Julianna got out of her car and approached a man who was standing off by himself, examining the tip of his cigarette before and after every drag he took. He was in his fifties, Julianna guessed, maybe older.

"Excuse me," she said.

He held out his pack of Camels. "Help yourself," he said.

"No. Thank you. I wondered if I could ask you a question."

"Ask away."

Julianna showed him the picture of Genevieve she had on her phone, a scan of a photo their mother had taken on her seventeenth birthday. Genevieve, about to blow out the candles on her cake, was cutting her eyes at Julianna, who sat outside the frame. She was starting to laugh at something Julianna had just said or done. Julianna didn't remember what.

"Do you happen to recognize this girl?" she said.

The guy took another drag off his Camel, examined the tip, then looked at Julianna instead of the photo.

"I see you inside just now?"

"No."

"I didn't think so."

"She's my sister."

"They call it Alcoholics *Anonymous*," he said, but with a smile. "That's the whole point."

"She disappeared twenty-six years ago, about two months after this was taken. She was in AA. She hadn't been in long. I'm trying to find someone who might have known her."

He glanced at the photo of Genevieve. He glanced again, and his eyes lingered this time. He shook his head.

"Before my time," he said. "I've only been sober seventeen years. Hold on."

He walked over to the nearest cluster of smokers. After a minute he brought back two elderly men, dapper in tweed blazers and windowpane-plaid slacks. The men could have been twins, with the same narrow, mournful faces, the same Clark Gable mustaches. They even held their cigarettes the same way, between the first and second knuckles of their fingers.

"This is Chester and Lawrence," the first man told Julianna. "I explained what you were looking for. They might be able to help."

He gave Julianna a nod and moved away. Julianna showed the photo of Genevieve to the two elderly men. Each man took out a pair of gold-rimmed reading glasses and put them on.

"Oh," one of the men said. Chester. "Sure."

"Sure," Lawrence agreed.

Julianna felt something inside her give way—a minute but resonant pop, like the lead point of a pencil snapping off when you pressed too hard.

"You remember her?" she said.

"I do," Chester said. "Sure. I don't think I ever knew her name. Did you?"

"I didn't," Lawrence said. "No. We exchanged the occasional cordial hello. At the coffeepot."

"That was all. Ships passing in the night. She came to meetings for a month or two."

"For no more than a month or two. She seemed lovely, though. Didn't she?"

"She did. Just lovely."

The two men huddled over the screen of Julianna's phone. They weren't smiling, but they seemed no longer quite so mournful.

"Her name was Genevieve," Julianna said. She supposed it should come as more of a surprise that two elderly men who'd known Genevieve twenty-six years ago, in passing, for only a month or two—two men who were probably gay!—would still remember her. But that was Genevieve for you. She made an impression.

"Genevieve," Lawrence said, giving it the French pronunciation—*Zhawn-uh-vyev*. Julianna would do that sometimes, when she wanted to tease Genevieve.

Chester looked up at Julianna. "You say your sister, she just . . . disappeared? Oh, that's just terrible."

"Is there anyone else here who might have known her?" Julianna said.

The two men removed their reading glasses and studied each other.

"Was it Howard B.?"

"I believe it was."

"Sure. I believe it was Howard B."

"Howard B. He was her sponsor."

Julianna's heart was pounding again. Chester—or maybe it was Lawrence, Julianna had lost track—took a puff of his Parliament and sighed. He turned to her, fully mournful again.

"Howard B. was your sister's sponsor in the program," he said.

The other man took a puff of his Parliament and sighed, too. "Howard B."

Julianna wanted to know what their sighs meant. "And?" she said.

Both men sighed again.

"Howard B. was something of a boor. A jerk. I'm sorry, but he was."

"No, it's true. He was. He was an attorney, though I don't mean to imply that all attorneys are boorish."

"Howard B. certainly was. Ever tedious, never brief."

"With a certain charm, though. To be fair. He was a partner in one of the big firms downtown, as I recall."

"A certain charm at times. Yes. Though I don't know why anyone would deliberately choose him to be their sponsor. I suppose Howard B. did the choosing, don't you?"

"I do. One bowed to Howard B.'s will. He was very pushy."

It wasn't difficult for Julianna to imagine why Howard B., why a man like Howard B., would have chosen Genevieve.

"Was," Julianna said. "You keep saying *was*."

The two elderly men seemed mildly, mournfully surprised to realize she was still there.

"Howard B. died a few years ago. Five or six years ago?"

"Five or six, I believe."

"You should talk to Pauline. His wife. I believe she's still alive. Isn't she?"

"Sure. I believe so. The last I heard."

CHESTER AND LAWRENCE had forgotten, or had never known, Howard B.'s last name. Julianna drove to the nearest branch of the public library, in Warr Acres, and told the librarian at the reference desk what she was trying to find. The librarian lit up: the highlight of her day. She started clicking the mouse before Julianna stopped talking. Five minutes later the librarian had located an obituary printed in the *Daily Oklahoman* on March 31, 2006.

"Howard Neil Bridwell, 65, prominent Oklahoma City attorney."

A graduate of the Northwest Classen Class of 1959. President of Pi Kappa Alpha fraternity at the University of Texas. A juris doctorate from UT in 1966, after which he moved back to Oklahoma City, passed the bar, and joined the firm of Kirkland and Nash. Senior partner of the firm from 1984 until his death.

Devoted father, loving husband. Survived by his wife of forty-one years, Pauline. Two daughters, one son, four grandchildren.

No photo of the deceased.

The librarian was beaming at Julianna, as if to say, *What else you got for me?*

"Can you find contact information for his widow?" Julianna said.

The librarian seemed disappointed, the task beneath her. But she turned back to her computer and quickly found a phone number for Pauline Bridwell, an address. Julianna entered both into her phone.

"Thank you," she told the librarian.

Pauline Bridwell lived just off Western, on one of the streets in Nichols Hills where the houses were expensive but older, smaller, less aggressively landscaped—homes, not compounds. She answered the door wearing jeans, an oversize wool cardigan, and a pair of garden gloves.

Julianna didn't know what she'd been expecting. Pearls? Howard B.'s widow was in her seventies and seemed appealingly unconcerned by that fact. Her face was lined the way a face should be lined, her hair a natural shade of silver-gray.

She smiled warmly at Julianna. "Sorry. I was out back with my pansies."

"Pauline Bridwell?"

"Yes." She took off her gardening gloves. "Can I help you?"

Julianna tried to detach herself from the moment, from herself. Pandora's biggest mistake wasn't opening the box, it was slamming the lid shut again before the last item could escape.

That was the curse Julianna wouldn't wish on her worst enemies: *May you always have hope.*

"You husband, Howard," she said, "was my sister's sponsor in AA."

"Oh?"

"A long time ago."

"Howard was very active in AA, until the day he died. I think he must have sponsored dozens of people. He wanted to give back. He always said his life began the day he joined AA. You know he passed on, don't you?" She reached out to touch Julianna's arm, as if Julianna were the one who might need consoling. "A few years ago."

Julianna nodded. "My sister's name was Genevieve. Genevieve Rosales. Your husband was her sponsor in the summer of 1986. The summer and fall of 1986. Did you know her? Did your husband ever mention her?"

"Genevieve?" Pauline Bridwell considered. "I don't think so. At least I don't recall the name. I was in Al-Anon in those days, but not as regularly as Howard went to his meetings. I really only got to know a few of the people he sponsored over the years."

"Can I show you a photo of my sister?"

"Of course."

Julianna took out her phone. Pauline Bridwell studied the photo taken of Genevieve on her seventeenth birthday.

"I'm sorry. I'm afraid I don't recognize her." She looked up at Julianna. "May I ask what this is about?"

That warm smile again. Her consoling hand again, on Julianna's arm.

Why? Could she see that Julianna was doomed? Was the pain in Julianna's eyes that obvious?

"It doesn't matter," Julianna said. "Thanks for your time."

She started walking back to her car. Halfway down the flagstone path, though, she stopped. She wasn't sure why. A sixth sense, a sudden chill in the wind. Or maybe it was the sound of Genevieve's voice.

Juli, wow, she's even a better liar than you.

She turned and saw Pauline Bridwell standing in the doorway of her house, watching her. The woman's smile was gone, and her face—in the one instant after Julianna turned and before Pauline Bridwell shut the door—looked a thousand years old.

Julianna walked back up the path. She rang the doorbell again. This time there was no answer, so she went around the side of the house. The gate to the backyard was unlocked.

Pauline Bridwell was on her knees, next to a flat of amber and auburn flowers, stabbing the soil with a garden spade. She didn't look up as Julianna approached.

"Did your husband kill her?" Julianna said.

The woman paused to dab sweat from her forehead with the back of her glove. She still wouldn't look at Julianna.

"It was an accident," she said.

"An accident."

"He said it was an accident."

Julianna felt light-headed but calm. There was an otherworldly glow to Pauline Bridwell's backyard—the sun low, the leaves changing, the grass fading to a pale gold.

"What did he say happened?"

Pauline Bridwell gently tucked a plant into the hole she'd dug for it.

"She phoned him that night. The people he sponsored would phone at all hours, day and night. And Howard would always go. He would drop everything and go." Her tone was matter-of-fact, but she stabbed so hard at the ground that the garden spade slipped from her hand. "Howard told her to meet him in the parking lot by the entrance to the fair. They sat in his car and talked. Howard liked to tell the people he sponsored about the dark before the dawn. How life is about progress, not perfection. Do you know how many people he helped over the years?"

Julianna understood now why Genevieve had left Crowley's trailer so soon after she arrived—why she hadn't stayed to get high with him. Temptation had drawn her there, but at the last moment she'd decided to turn away. She'd decided to find a pay phone and call the one person who could help keep her straight.

"He said she wanted him to drive her home," Pauline Bridwell said. "There was an accident, and she wasn't wearing her seat belt. She hit her head."

Here was the lie, finally, that Pauline Bridwell had chosen to believe twenty-six years ago.

"Why would she want him to drive her home?" Julianna said. "Her car was there. *I* was there."

Pauline Bridwell stabbed at the ground. She continued as if she hadn't heard Julianna.

"After she hit her head, Howard panicked. He didn't know what to do. He couldn't take her to the hospital, because she— It was already too late. Thirty or forty minutes after he left the house, he called me, crying. He said there'd been an accident."

What had really happened? Julianna could guess. Genevieve's

sponsor had coaxed her into his car. He'd made a pass, and she'd resisted. Maybe he struck her in anger. Maybe she'd banged her head hard against the glass of the car window during the struggle and an artery in her brain ruptured. Maybe, in that sense, her death *had* been an accident. Or maybe her sponsor had been planning to rape and kill her for weeks and had just been waiting for the exact right opportunity to strike, to look into her eyes as the life drained from them.

Julianna realized she didn't want or need to know what had really happened in those last few minutes. She didn't want or need to know what Genevieve's sponsor had done to hide her body. Or what, maybe, his wife had told him to do with it.

Pauline Bridwell set the spade down and turned, finally, to Julianna. Her eyes blazed.

"We couldn't call the police," she said. "Howard had a career, a reputation. A family. To throw all that away, what good would it have done? Would that bring her back?"

Julianna wondered if the woman kneeling before her really believed what she was saying, if the line of Pauline Bridwell's jaw was trembling with defiance or with shame.

Julianna didn't want or need to know that either.

All these years she'd hated Genevieve so much, for abandoning her at the state fair. Now, though, she pictured Genevieve standing on the dark side of the midway that night, outside Crowley's trailer, feeling a pull that must have been almost impossible to resist.

But she *had* resisted, Julianna knew now. Genevieve had turned and walked away and called her AA sponsor.

Why? What opposing force at that moment was even more powerful than the temptation that had drawn Genevieve there? Was it maybe the thought of Julianna, alone and afraid on the curb outside the rodeo arena, waiting for her sister to come back for her?

Julianna heard Genevieve's voice again, laughing.

Of course it was you, you dumb-ass. What else would it be?

Pauline Bridwell had bowed her head. Julianna couldn't hear what she said.

"What?"

"He was a weak man."

"Okay," Julianna said, and walked out to her car.

Wyatt

CHAPTER 28

Wyatt dreamed he was in an old house, the light dim and the air thick with dust. He was going through cabinets and dressers and closets, sorting through what seemed like a century's worth of worthless old junk. Broken alarm clocks, yellowed table doilies, chipped glass paperweights. He suspected he was dreaming, but he couldn't quite convince himself of it. *This is a dream,* he would think, but then he would shake his head and think, *No, this is real.*

Back and forth like that, over and over, Wyatt arguing with himself and breathing dust and opening yet another drawer full of half-melted candles, of frames without photos. It was the world's least enjoyable dream.

When Wyatt woke up, a big black guy was sitting in the chair next to his bed, leafing through a Disney Princesses coloring book.

This is still a dream, Wyatt told himself.

Definitely, he agreed.

"Mr. PI!" the big black guy said when he noticed that Wyatt was awake. "Mr. VIPI!"

Dark and sweet. What was dark and sweet? What could the girls never get enough of? Wyatt almost fell back to sleep.

"Fudge," Wyatt said. His mouth was dry. His mouth was the charred remains of a terrible fire. "Hello, Fudge."

"You in the hospital," Fudge said. "You been on some *legit* drugs."

Wyatt nodded. The effort made him swoon. "I know."

"You *know* it."

He offered Wyatt a fist to bump. Wyatt felt a spike of panic. He couldn't remember what had happened after he'd stabbed Chip. Chip had been alive. Chip's expression had never changed. Had Chip pulled the knife from his throat? Had Chip managed to turn and grab Candace's arm, to finish what he'd meant to start?

"Candace," Wyatt said.

"She been up here most the time. Lily, too." Fudge held up the coloring book as proof. "Candace back at the Land Run now, now the doctor say you be all right. She say to tell you she got a damn *business* to run."

Wyatt, smiling, was drifting off again. A nurse entered the room, a guy. He checked Wyatt's IV. He checked the dressing on Wyatt's hand, the dressing on his upper chest, the dressing on his collarbone, then handed Wyatt a Styrofoam cup full of ice chips. Wyatt shook an ice chip into his mouth and let it melt.

"How long have I been in here?" he said.

"You ask that every time you wake up," the nurse said.

The nurse had a big handlebar mustache. He looked more like a gunslinging sheriff, more like a Wyatt, than Wyatt did.

"I do?"

"You do," Fudge said. "Been almost two days now."

The doctor came in. A woman.

"Hello, Mr. Rivers," she said. "How are you feeling?"

"As good as can be expected," Wyatt said. "Under the circumstances."

She smiled and looked over his chart. "Here's where we're at, Mr. Rivers."

She went on for a while. About blood loss and the subclavian artery, about the subclavian vein and the very narrow space between it and the subclavian artery, about the difference between a grade-one concussion and a grade-two concussion. The gist, Wyatt gathered, was that he'd been lucky. For a guy who'd been rammed by a CRV and stabbed in the upper chest, he'd been lucky.

Wyatt remembered now waking up and asking the male nurse how long he'd been there. He remembered Candace sitting next to his bed. In the sunlight, in the moonlight. He remembered Lily gazing gravely at him, her small hand on his. And . . . Gavin. Gavin? Yes, Gavin, too. Sitting in the chair, shifting uncomfortably. Unless that had been a dream.

The doctor was saying now something about the probability, on all counts, of a full and successful recovery. And then she was saying something about a credit card.

"It's in my wallet," Wyatt said.

The doctor looked up from Wyatt's chart. She glanced at the male nurse.

"I don't think you understand, Mr. Rivers," the doctor said. She explained that a Good Samaritan with military training had known to seal the knife wound in Wyatt's chest with the edge of a credit card. He'd probably saved Wyatt's life.

A credit card, Wyatt thought. Crazy. But that was life for you, full of surprises. It never got old.

"So that's where we're at. We should be able to get you out of here tomorrow."

"A farm boy from Oklahoma gets a scholarship to Harvard," Wyatt said.

The doctor and the nurse, on their way out of the room, paused.

"First day on campus," Wyatt said, "the Oklahoma farm boy goes up to a fellow student, an older student. And the farm boy says, 'Excuse me, can you tell me where the library's at?' The other student, he turns up his nose, and he says, 'Here at Harvard, sir, we do not end our sentences with prepositions.'"

The doctor and the nurse waited. Fudge waited. Wyatt shook another ice chip into his mouth.

"So the Oklahoma farm boy says, 'Okay. Where's the library at, asshole?'"

The next time Wyatt woke up, a guy was sitting in the chair that Fudge had occupied. He wore a corduroy jacket and cowboy boots, a weary expression. It didn't take a detective to know the guy was a detective.

Wyatt started at the beginning and walked the detective through everything. *Almost* everything. He left out the part about bashing Jeff Eddy in the face with a pumpkin. He left out the part about Jeff Eddy's affair and how Wyatt was using it to keep him off Candace's back. The detective didn't want to know any of that. Wyatt was doing him a favor.

The detective nodded along, taking notes. He only asked a couple of questions, getting the timeline straight. Wyatt had a feeling the detective already knew from Candace most of what Wyatt was telling him.

Wyatt didn't play it down, how dumb he'd been not to figure

out sooner that Chip was the person harassing Candace and that Chip was her ex-husband. The detective declined to weigh in on the matter one way or the other.

"Why were you honking the car horn?" he said. "Get attention?"

"I wanted her to run," Wyatt said. "Candace. I hoped she'd hear it and take Lily and run."

The detective wrote that down. "That little lady is something," he said, admiringly.

"What about him?" Wyatt said. "The ex-husband?"

He didn't want to hear the answer. He already knew the answer. Wyatt had killed a man, a human being. The worst kind of human being, and Wyatt hadn't had much choice in the matter. But the truth was the truth. He would have to live with it for the rest of his life.

"Deceased," the detective said.

"Am I going to be charged?"

The detective closed his notebook and stood up. "With what?" he said.

He gave Wyatt a nod—of respect? of pity?—and left.

Wyatt slept. He dreamed about the old house full of worthless junk. When he woke, it was dark outside. Candace sat in the chair next to his bed.

"About time," she said.

"Better late than never."

She yawned. "I guess."

"Go home."

"That goof in the kilt brought me a clay dildo he made."

"He finds it deeply offensive when people call them that."

"He said it was an apology. A peace offering."

"Go home. What time is it? How's Lily?"

"I told her you had a car accident. I didn't tell her the rest."

Wyatt nodded. "Sometimes partial honesty is the best policy."

"She was worried you would die and turn into a ghost."

"You'd never get rid of me."

"Ha."

Wyatt slept again. He woke, morning now, with a clearer head. The male nurse with the handlebar mustache unplugged him from the IV and heart monitor while Gavin sat in the chair.

"I'm gonna be paying for this until the end of time," Gavin said, "aren't I?"

"Now that you mention it," Wyatt said.

A nurse's aide gave him his phone, wallet, and watch. She offered him a plastic bag stuffed with the blood-soaked clothes and shoes he'd been wearing when they brought him in. He declined politely.

"We have to ask," she said. "It's a rule."

Gavin had brought Wyatt a new set of clothes, a long-sleeved shirt with some kind of Navajo print and a pair of pleated Dockers, the Dillard's tag still attached to both. White New Balance sneakers. Wyatt knew that beggars couldn't be choosers.

He had to take his time getting dressed. A clearer head had its price, and he felt like a cork bobbing in a sea of pain. His chest, his head, his hand, his ribs. He felt slightly nauseated, too, as a bonus.

The pharmacy in the lobby of the hospital filled Wyatt's prescriptions for various anti-inflammatories, antibiotics, and painkillers. Gavin was waiting for him out front. He helped Wyatt ease into the passenger seat of the Town Car he'd rented.

"I had a steak last night," Gavin said as they merged onto the Lake Hefner Parkway.

"Tell me more," Wyatt said. "I beg you."

Gave shot him an irritated glance. "The joke," he said. "Your dumb joke about the two guys eating steaks in Oklahoma."

"New York. They were eating steaks in New York. That was the point of the joke."

They pulled in to the Marriott parking lot. Home, sweet home.

"I got you a flight out tomorrow morning," Gavin said. "I figured you could use a good night's sleep."

"Thanks."

"Call me if you need anything."

"A hug?"

"Smart-ass."

Wyatt took the elevator up to his room. He ordered eggs from room service and ate a few bites so he'd feel less guilty about cracking open the first miniature bottle of Jack Daniel's from the minibar. The first bottle made him less guilty about cracking open the second one.

He took off the clothes that didn't fit and climbed into bed. Now that he wanted to sleep, though, he couldn't. He could feel the blade of the hunting knife slide into him. And then slide in again. And then again. Each time the sensation was a surprise.

To distract himself Wyatt thought about the night of that long-ago tornado, August of '86, the small forgotten memory he'd stumbled upon at the coffeehouse. He'd been saving the memory for a special occasion. This qualified, didn't it? The details were so vivid, so fresh. It was his one memory of that summer that was not yet a memory. Wyatt was *there*, his finger hooked through the label of his blazer, the raindrops blowing against his face.

He tried to grope his way back in time, back inside the mall and the movie theater. Just a few minutes before he stepped outside into the wind and rain, just a few minutes before lightning lit up the sky and he watched the funnel of the tornado twisting like a snake on the road, Wyatt knew he would have told O'Malley good-bye. He would have told Melody good-bye. Theresa was already gone, but maybe a faint trace of her scent had lingered in the lobby. *That* was a moment Wyatt would love to live again.

This new memory, though, like all memories, was just a broken fragment of the whole—the edge crumbled when he stepped there, fell away beneath his feet. Wyatt stood outside the mall, the raindrops blowing against his face, but he couldn't get back to the good stuff.

The tornado sirens died. The raindrops blew against his face. Already they were becoming photocopies of raindrops. So he tried walking forward, not back. And what do you know? That edge of memory supported his weight. Wyatt was still *there* as he headed home across the wet, black street, as he cut through the park behind the movie theater. He smelled fresh-mowed grass and heard the deafening chirr of cicadas in the trees. The clouds broke open, and the stars spilled across the sky like confetti. Wyatt recognized the car parked up the street, an old black VW Bug that belonged to Bingham's nutty friend Donald.

If you had an existential bent, if you believed in a cold and indifferent universe, here was the proof. Instead of a rediscovered memory that gave him five more precious minutes with O'Malley or Theresa, with Melody or Grubb or Karlene—Wyatt had been given the gift of Pet Shop Boy instead.

"Hey," Donald said as Wyatt approached.

"Hey," Wyatt said.

He didn't slow down. He was tired. He had blocks to go before he slept. He didn't want to hear about yet another of Donald's dumb, can't-miss moneymaking ideas.

"Mr. Bingham's going to be in there another hour at least," Wyatt said.

"Okay," Donald said. He stood up as Wyatt passed and walked

alongside him. "Hey, do you want to hear about this idea I have? Get ready. Swedish porn films."

Wyatt didn't feel bad for Mr. Bingham that his only friend in the world was Pet Shop Boy. You got the friends you deserved.

"I have to go home," Wyatt said.

"Okay."

Donald stopped. Wyatt kept walking.

"Later, Donald," he said, without looking back.

And then that was it. Wyatt, in his hotel bed, had reached the far boundary of the rediscovered memory. He didn't remember walking the rest of the way home. Or, more accurately, he remembered walking home a hundred different times, no one particular time more distinct than any of the others.

The last place Wyatt was really *there* was in the playground, hurrying away from Pet Shop Boy. The chirr of the cicadas, the stars like confetti, the street wet and black from the rain. Wyatt hadn't wondered what Donald was doing alone in the park across from the theater at eleven o'clock at night. He was waiting for Mr. Bingham to get off work. Why else would he be there?

Why else, on that night in August, a week before the murders, would Donald be alone in the park across from the movie theater?

Wyatt saw Donald sitting on the end of the teeter-totter— perched there, tall and skinny, like some awkward flightless bird— just outside the reach of the weak light cast by the streetlamp.

Hey.

Hey.

Mr. Bingham's going to be in there another hour at least.

Okay.

Wyatt's hotel room was too hot. Every breath he took was an effort. He kicked off the sheet and swung his legs off the bed. He stood up, too quickly. The room grew hotter. The drapes were pulled wide, and the sky outside his window was blue and bright and empty. He made it to the thermostat on the wall and punched it down to sixty degrees.

Donald, Wyatt realized, wasn't waiting for Mr. Bingham to get off work—he'd been casing the theater. He'd been sitting on the teeter-totter and clocking the routines of the doormen, of the mall security guards.

And Donald had access to Mr. Bingham's keys. He was Mr. Bingham's one and only friend. He had better access to the keys than anyone else.

Mr. Bingham had sent Wyatt home early. It was the first time he'd ever sent the second doorman home early. Corporate had told him, only that morning, to cut back on weekday hours. So Donald hadn't expected to see Wyatt come walking across the park toward him.

Pet Shop Boy. He was the inside man. He'd given copies of Mr. Bingham's keys to the killers. He'd cased the theater for them.

Wyatt felt like he'd crashed through a glass door he hadn't realized was there, the world around him shattering into fragments of bright, winking light.

What was Donald's last name? Wyatt tried to remember. He knew he knew it. At one point in his life, he'd known it. What was it?

Wyatt rested his forehead against the wall next to the thermostat and let his mind float. He pictured the pet shop on the second floor of the mall. The lamps that kept the reptile tanks heated. Donald, when he was at work, wore a white smock that made him look like a pharmacist. The sleeves were too short for his long arms. Next door was a shop that sold pipes and fancy pipe tobaccos. Next to that were two vacant stores and then the bar directly above the movie theater.

Wyatt floated. A name bumped up against him. *Furst.* That was it. *Donald Furst.* Pet Shop Boy's father was a Donald, too. Donald had liked to introduce himself as "Furst the second."

O'Malley had thought Donald's chances of finding a woman willing to procreate with him were slim. So sometimes O'Malley had called him "Furst the last."

Wyatt moved to the desk and opened his laptop. A Donald David Furst Jr. lived on Penn, just past NW 122nd, barely five miles from the hotel room Wyatt was sitting in.

He got dressed again. His own clothes this time, a pale blue shirt and dark gray suit, leather oxfords. He wasn't thinking about the pain anymore. The front-desk clerk sent the bellhop to whistle up one of the cabs lurking along the side of the hotel.

The apartment complex on Penn was a shabby, anonymous cluster of two story boxes painted a chalky shade of green, with rusting gutters and dead leaves trapped in the ivy. Wyatt had lived in places like this before, his first month or two in a new city, before he found a house he wanted to buy. An apartment complex like this was just nice enough—an ornamental wrought-iron fence around the perimeter, a perfunctory stab at landscaping— that you could talk yourself into believing it was nice enough. Most of Wyatt's neighbors had been single, middle-aged men who looked like they'd lost everything in the divorce. They came and went quietly, at odd hours of the day and night.

Wyatt told the cabdriver to wait for him, however long he took. There was a small swimming pool between two of the buildings, but this wasn't one of the complexes Wyatt and the others had snuck into after work. This one was too far north, too depressing.

He found number 219, a second-floor unit, and rang the bell. He didn't have a plan if Donald Furst Jr. no longer lived here or wasn't home or wasn't the one Wyatt was looking for. Wyatt was just concentrating on each breath he took, in and out, nice and easy.

Donald opened the door. *Pet Shop Boy.* Twenty-six years later, Wyatt recognized him immediately. The awkward tall kid's stoop, the teeth too big for his mouth, the heavy freckles. Wyatt had forgotten about the freckles until he saw them now.

Donald had aged badly. He was even skinnier than he'd been before, cadaverous, with sunken cheekbones and, beneath all the freckles, skin the unhealthy color of dirty dishwater. An incisor was missing. He reminded Wyatt of one of the elongated, decomposing zombies in Lyle Finn's Halloween army.

He was wearing slacks and a dress shirt, untucked. No shoes or socks.

"Can I help you?" he said.

"I'm Michael Oliver," Wyatt said. "From the Pheasant Run."

The sound of the TV from the apartment next door came through the thin walls. Judge Judy. She was haranguing some poor bastard. Donald nodded. He didn't seem surprised to see him.

"Oh, sure," he said. "I didn't recognize you. Heinz."

"Yes."

"Come on in."

He shuffled back inside. He had to duck his head beneath the hanging pendant light in the foyer, the frosted glass speckled with dead bugs. Wyatt followed him. In the living room of the apartment, there was what looked like a brand-new sofa and nothing else—no other furniture, no TV, nothing on the walls. Against the wall leaned a black-and-yellow foam-board sign that said OIL CHANGE $22.90!

Donald lowered himself to the couch. Wyatt kept standing.

"Did you just move in?" he said.

Donald gave him a blank look. "No."

Wyatt walked over to the wall and pounded on it. "Turn the fucking TV down!" he yelled.

Judge Judy continued to harangue away.

"He's not home," Donald said. "He's never home."

Wyatt had brought his new painkillers with him, in the pocket of his suit, as well as three miniature bottles of booze from his hotel room. Gin. He swallowed a couple of painkillers and washed them down

"Why do you have an oil-change sign?"

"I work there. Sort of. It's where I work."

"Do you know why I'm here?"

"No."

"You look like shit, Donald. Are you sick?"

Donald laughed, a sound like bare winter tree branches scraping against a roof. Wyatt offered him the second bottle of gin. Donald shook his head. His laughing had turned into crying. The sound was basically the same, just different branches on a different roof.

"Tell me what happened," Wyatt said.

"Nobody was supposed to get hurt."

"Tell me what happened."

"It was just supposed to be me and the one guy. Dale. He seemed like an okay guy. But the night everything went down, he showed up out of nowhere with his two friends. He said his friends wanted in on the score. It was just supposed to be me and Dale that night. That was the plan. We were just going to scare Tim and make some serious money. It was supposed to be quick and easy. Nobody was supposed to get hurt."

Who was Tim? Wyatt realized that was Mr. Bingham's first name. And *Dale*. Dale Earl Barrett was the killer who'd worn the pantyhose over his head.

Wyatt didn't feel anything yet. It was like he was standing in the desert, dispassionately watching the flash of a distant explosion, waiting for the shock wave to trundle across the flats and reach him, to sweep him off his feet and carry him away.

He walked into the dining room. There was no furniture there either. In the kitchen he found a single metal folding chair. He carried it back into the living room and sat down across from Donald.

"Start from the beginning," Wyatt said. "How did you know Dale?"

"At the bar. He used to come in and drink there. That little bar upstairs at the mall?"

Wyatt nodded. The bar directly above the movie theater, where ten movie passes were worth a bottle of bottom-shelf booze, if a bartender was inclined to cut a deal with O'Malley.

"Dale was a tough guy," Donald said. "You could tell. But he seemed like an okay guy."

"Was it your idea to rob the theater?" Wyatt said.

"Was it my idea?" Donald said. "No. No! It was a lot of money, though. It was a lot of money because it was the end of the weekend. The money from both nights, Friday and Saturday? It was supposed to be quick and easy."

"You said that."

"But right beforehand, when we met to drive over, Dale shows up with his two friends. They were psycho. They were high on some crazy shit. Angel dust or something. I had a really bad feeling about it. So I bailed. I just . . . I bailed."

Wyatt, from habit, had taken out his reporter's notebook. He flipped it closed and put his pen away. "That's why there were only two rubber masks," he said. "That's why the third guy had to use pantyhose to cover his face."

Donald nodded. "I only had two masks. One for me and one for Dale. But then his psycho friends showed up, and I bailed. I wanted to bail even earlier than that. I'd been having a bad feeling about Dale, too. Everything was getting out of hand."

"What do you mean?"

"First we weren't going to have a gun, and then yes we were. Then we were going to have two guns. And then Dale showed up with his psycho friends, and I bailed. Dale said it didn't matter. He said I was part of it now. He said I was in the mix now, whether I liked it or not."

Donald was crying again.

"The next day I saw what happened on the news," he said. "What happened. You don't know how crappy my life has been since then. Every single day I wake up."

Wyatt waited for the rest of the sentence, but there was no "and" or "but." That was it: *Every single day I wake up.*

Wyatt still didn't feel anything. He didn't hate Donald. He didn't pity him. Wyatt just wanted to know, now, after all these years, why he alone had been left alive in the projection booth that night.

"Donald," he said. "Why did they kill everyone but me?"

Donald just keep crying. Wyatt scooted the folding chair a couple of inches closer. The shock wave from the explosion still hadn't reached him yet. He didn't know what would happen—or what he might do when it did.

"Donald."

"What?"

"Look at me. Why did they kill everyone but me?"

Finally Donald looked up. He wiped his nose with the cuff of his shirt. The cuff was already filthy. He shook his head. "I don't know."

"You have to know."

"I don't, Heinz. I swear. They weren't supposed to hurt anyone! Dale said that! He swore! Nobody gets hurt."

He shook his head again. His big head, his skinny neck. Donald's neck was so skinny that Wyatt thought he could grab it with one hand, he could squeeze slowly, he could squeeze until there was nothing there.

Wyatt scooted the chair another inch closer. "Think," he said. "What did they say? Did one of them know me?"

"No. I don't know. I know that Dale never went down to the theater. Before that night, I mean. He said . . . he said it was safer that way. He said he was being careful!"

Wyatt had been too young to pass for eighteen, so he'd never set foot in the bar upstairs. But had he crossed paths with Dale on the mall escalator? In the parking lot?

Had they exchanged a few words? What words?

"Did you hear them say anything, Donald?" Wyatt said. "Can you remember any detail? The smallest thing might matter. Why would they kill everyone but me?"

Donald wiped his nose again. He bit his bottom lip. His effort to remember seemed genuine.

Wyatt waited. Donald started crying again.

"I don't know, Heinz," he said. "I really don't."

Wyatt stood. He carried the metal folding chair back to the kitchen and opened the refrigerator. Inside were a few cans of Coors Light and a half-empty package of cotto salami. He went back to the living room. Donald was watching him.

"Are you going to turn me in?" he said.

Wyatt couldn't tell if he looked hopeful or hopeless.

"Shut up," Wyatt said.

"I should have turned myself in. But I didn't know— After the police killed Dale and his psycho friends, I didn't think that—"

"Shut up."

Wyatt knew he could turn Donald in, but what was the point? *Every single day I wake up.* Wyatt didn't find it hard to believe Donald when he said how crappy his life had been for the past twenty-six years.

It was an odd sort of numbness that Wyatt felt. He still didn't hate Donald. He didn't pity him. He just felt a profound, empty indifference.

"I'm so sorry, Heinz," Donald said. "I'm so sorry. I swear. After they drove off, Dale and his psycho friends, I tried to stop it. You remember! I tried to warn him."

"I remember?" Wyatt said. He didn't know what Donald was talking about. "I remember what?"

"You answered the phone when I called! I was calling to warn him! But I couldn't do it. Dale said I was in the mix now, whether I liked it or not. One of Dale's friends, the really psycho one, said I was a dead man if I said anything to anyone. They knew where I lived. When I bailed, when I was walking back to my car, I thought they were going to shoot me."

Wyatt thought back. The night of the murders, the pay phone in the lobby rang just after the ten o'clock show started to roll. Wyatt had answered.

"Pheasant Twin," he'd said.

"Who is this?"

Wyatt had recognized the voice. He'd wondered why Donald was calling Mr. Bingham in the lobby and not in the office like he usually did.

"Heinz speaking," Wyatt had said, just before Mr. Bingham pounced and grabbed the receiver. Mr. Bingham was always trying to catch them in the act of using the lobby pay phone for personal calls, but tonight the tables were turned—the personal call was for him.

"It's your friend," Wyatt had told Mr. Bingham pointedly. "Pet Shop Boy."

"I was going to warn him, but I couldn't," Donald said now. "I'm so sorry. Nobody was supposed to get hurt."

Nobody was supposed to get hurt.

Wyatt tried to guess how many times over the years Donald had told himself that. Not enough times, apparently.

"Why didn't you call the office phone?" Wyatt said.

Donald lifted his face out of his hands. Confused. "What?"

Wyatt didn't really care why Donald had called the lobby pay phone instead of the office phone. But it was one answer at least that he knew Donald could give him.

"When you called Mr. Bingham to warn him. Why didn't you call the office?"

Donald seemed even more confused now. "I wasn't calling Tim," he said. "I was calling O'Malley."

Wyatt didn't understand. "O'Malley? Why were you calling O'Malley?"

"To warn him! To tell him it was getting out of hand! I'd told him that before, a couple of times, but he always said don't worry, he had it under control. He said we could trust Dale. But he didn't know about Dale's psycho friends! Don't you see? O'Malley only knew Dale. He didn't know that Dale's friends were going to show up until that night."

Wyatt felt his brain suddenly cut out—the machinery seized up, all the spinning flywheels and humming belts froze in place.

For a second, Wyatt was just gliding, silently coasting off the edge of a cliff into the bright blue nothing.

"You're saying— What the fuck are you saying?" Wyatt said.

"O'Malley wanted there to be two robbers, me and Dale," Donald said. "With the rubber masks? He said if it was just me, just one person, it wouldn't be badass enough."

Wyatt remembered what Donald had said earlier: *We were just going to scare Tim and make some serious money.* Wyatt had assumed that "We" meant Donald and Dale Earl Barrett.

Wyatt was still gliding, soaring—nothing above or below him.

"You're telling me O'Malley was part of it?" he said. "You're lying."

"I'm not! I swear! It was O'Malley's idea."

Donald shrank back. Wyatt realized he was standing over him, fists clenched so tightly they throbbed.

"You're lying," he said. "That's ridiculous. Why would O'Malley do something like that?"

"I don't know. I really don't. All he ever said to me— He said it would be a hoot. He said we'd scare Tim and make some money."

"No. O'Malley wouldn't do something like that."

"I know he was in kind of a bad mood that summer. The end of that summer."

"What?" Now Wyatt knew for sure that Donald was lying. O'Malley was never in a bad mood. "Why was he in a bad mood?"

Donald shrugged. "He didn't talk to me about things like that. I just know he said we'd scare Tim and make some serious money."

"No. There's no way O'Malley would ever— They *murdered* him. They put a gun to his head and blew his brains out. If he was part of it, then why—"

"I don't know. Nobody was supposed to—"

Wyatt grabbed the collar of Donald's dress shirt and heaved

him to his feet. Donald weighed nothing. When Wyatt shoved him against the wall, though, the wall shook, the foam-core Midas sign flopped to the carpet.

"Okay, listen to me," Wyatt said. "I know you're lying, Donald. You're trying to make yourself feel better about what happened. You trying to save whatever fraction of your sorry soul is still left. I understand that, but if you don't stop lying, right now—"

"Okay!" Donald said. "I am. I'm sorry. I am lying. It was me. It was my idea all along."

His eyes were wide, searching Wyatt's face. He tried to smile.

Wyatt held his collar tight. The fabric cut into Donald's neck, lifting his chin high.

"It was all you, wasn't it? Not O'Malley."

"No. I mean yes."

Wyatt knew O'Malley. He knew him like a brother. There was no possible way O'Malley could have conceived a plan so crazy, so reckless, so dangerous.

But Donald, Wyatt realized, could not have conceived it either. Idiot Pet Shop Boy? No. The mastermind behind the robbery had to be Dale Earl Barrett. It was his plan, and he'd recruited Donald to help him carry it out.

Why, though, would he do that? Dale Earl Barrett was a hardened ex-con. Why would he recruit someone like Donald to help him rob the movie theater? Donald was the last person on earth he'd recruit.

Did Dale Earl Barrett know that Donald was friends with Mr. Bingham? Did he know that Donald had easy access to Mr. Bingham's keys? Did he know that that Donald was not too bright and easily manipulated, always trying to raise capital for his next big loony, can't-miss venture?

O'Malley knew all that.

"I can't breathe very well," Donald said.

Wyatt released his collar. Donald sank back to the sofa.

We were just going to scare Tim and make some serious money.

Donald had no reason to scare his only friend in the world. It was O'Malley who thought Mr. Bingham was a pompous prick, who was always looking for ways to— How did O'Malley put it? *Dupe and bamboozle the Little Cheese.*

"You're lying, Donald," Wyatt said.

"Yes. I swear."

Wyatt thought about that night at the pool, a couple of weeks before the murders, when Theresa did a handstand underwater and O'Malley suggested they reverse the peephole in Mr. Bingham's office door.

When a man in a mask knocked on the office door the night of the murders, Mr. Bingham had not been able to see out. He would have assumed that the knocker was Grubb or Melody or Karlene. He would have unbolted the office door and opened it.

"I wish they'd killed me," Donald said. "I wish they'd shot me in the back when I bailed. I'm so sorry."

Wyatt didn't answer. He picked up the Midas sign and propped it back against the wall.

"Later, Donald," he said, and headed to the door.

WYATT HAD THE cabdriver drive west on Memorial Road until the city fell away behind them. Then back east, past Frontier City amusement park. From there southwest to the First Christian Church on the edge of Crown Heights, a giant white spaceship egg that had been built in the 1950s and known at one time as the "Church of Tomorrow."

The cabdriver didn't complain. The meter ran. He was making a killing.

Just a few blocks from the Church of Tomorrow, on Western, was Fairlawn Cemetery. Wyatt found a groundskeeper with a long beard the color of old charcoal. Denim overalls, a stoop, a squint.

"How do," the groundskeeper said.

"I'm looking for the man who killed the man who killed Jesse James," Wyatt said.

The groundskeeper used the handle of his rake to point Wyatt in the general direction. After ten minutes of searching, Wyatt located the simple stone that marked the grave. Sure enough:

EDWARD O'KELLEY
1858–1904
THE MAN WHO KILLED
THE MAN WHO KILLED JESSIE JAMES

Wyatt looked up. Yes, he was pretty sure of it. They had played midnight Frisbee right around here.

O'Malley's grave was on the other side of the cemetery. Wyatt walked halfway over and then decided that was far enough. He found himself out of breath, light-headed. He sat on a bench beneath a redbud tree and swallowed another pair of painkillers.

He tried to imagine how it might have happened. O'Malley going upstairs to barter movie passes for booze, striking up a conversation with the guy at the end of the bar. O'Malley wouldn't have been intimidated by someone like Dale Earl Barrett. O'Malley was never intimidated. He would have been intrigued.

O'Malley already had the idea for the robbery. But he was unsatisfied. A single robber, Pet Shop Boy, wasn't badass enough, wasn't dramatic enough, wasn't *loud* enough. When O'Malley met Dale Earl Barrett, he'd spotted an opportunity to crank up the volume.

That was O'Malley for you. That was why everyone loved him. He always cranked up the volume.

The cemetery groundskeeper moseyed past.

"Find it?" he said.

"Yes."

The groundskeeper nodded and moseyed on.

Wyatt took off his suit jacket. The sun felt good. The sun and the painkillers.

He thought he understood why O'Malley had not played the role of the second robber himself. Because, of course, he was too smart for that. O'Malley, who'd figured out countless ways to pilfer concession-stand candy and movie passes without getting caught. Who'd devised an elaborate scheme to palm tickets and hand back previously torn stubs, so he could resell the intact tickets and pocket the cash.

If anything went wrong during the robbery, O'Malley would have a bulletproof alibi. Donald would take the fall and O'Malley would deny everything.

Wyatt thought about the day they'd all gone skiing on Lake Dirtybird, O'Malley gunning the boat so close to the shoreline that Wyatt could feel the scrape beneath the hull, could see the horizon line start to tilt.

Afterward no one could figure out how to get the trailer hitch locked again, so they drove all the way back from Norman with the coupler resting precariously on the ball. That worked fine on the highway, but once they hit surface streets, every big bump or pothole would bounce the trailer. The boat would veer off onto the shoulder, a few times barely missing an oncoming car. O'Malley, laughing, started to steer *toward* the bumps and potholes.

O'Malley.

Wyatt had survived a knife to the chest. He'd survived a mass murder. He didn't know if he'd be able to survive this. He didn't know if he wanted to.

O'Malley had been surprised when the storeroom door banged open, when the killers herded them all upstairs to the projection booth. None of that was part of the plan. Wyatt realized that O'Malley had started the new tradition, gathering in the store-room to toast the end of a shift, so he and the rest of the crew would be out of the way when the robbers robbed Bingham.

O'Malley must have wondered why there were three robbers, not two, and why one of them was not tall, skinny Pet Shop Boy. But O'Malley played along anyway. He didn't understand what was about to happen until it was too late, everyone lined up on the floor of the booth, their hands tied behind their backs. That's when he'd tried to turn over and sit up.

"Wait a second," he'd said. O'Malley had great faith in his abil-ity to talk his way out of anything. It had never let him down. "Just listen."

Earlier that night O'Malley had been standing next to Wyatt when Donald called the lobby pay phone.

What if Mr. Bingham hadn't snatched the phone away? What if Wyatt had handed the phone to O'Malley and Donald had been able to warn him about Dale's psycho friends? Would the night have ended differently?

Wyatt doubted it. If he knew O'Malley—and who knew O'Malley like Wyatt did?—O'Malley would have told Donald to chill out, everything would be cool. Never fear! Because weren't three robbers even better than two? O'Malley could just imagine the look on Mr. Bingham's face.

Who knew O'Malley like Wyatt did? Wyatt supposed he didn't know him at all.

The cemetery groundskeeper moseyed past again.

"All right?" he said.

"Just fine, thanks."

Was *that* why Wyatt was still alive? Did the killers confuse Wyatt with O'Malley? Was it O'Malley who was supposed to survive, and not Wyatt?

That couldn't be right, though. Dale Earl Barrett knew O'Malley well. They'd planned the robbery together. In the projection booth, Dale Earl Barrett was the one who told O'Malley to shut up. He was the one who brought the shotgun down on O'Malley's head.

The sun and the gin and the painkillers Wyatt felt weightless, transparent. The next time the groundskeeper moseyed past, maybe he'd notice an odd shadow on the cemetery bench, nothing more.

There was no answer, Wyatt realized. There were answers, but no good ones. And there never would be. He could choose to accept that or not.

"Why me?" he'd asked Theresa that day they sat on the hood of her old yellow Skylark watching the sun set, watching the colors eddy and roll among the clouds.

Because why.

Julianna

CHAPTER 29

The sun was out, a beautiful November afternoon. But chillier than it looked, especially when you weren't moving, when you stood still on a low rise with only a few trees to block the wind. Julianna had left her leather jacket at home. She regretted it.

Ariel hadn't worn a jacket either, or even a sweater. She was in a shimmering red top with a keyhole back. She looked like she'd just stopped by Forever 21 before a night out in Vegas.

"I don't know where the giraffes are," Ariel said. "Fickle fuckers. Cross my heart, sometimes they really do come right up to the fence, close enough that you can smell their breath. It's so sweet."

"Aren't you freezing?" Julianna asked.

"You're standing in the shade. You picked like the one tree for miles around to stand under."

Julianna realized it was true. She stepped into the sunshine.

"Come on," Ariel said. "I know where we can go."

She led Julianna down the hill, across the tracks for the kiddie train. They turned onto a wide walkway that curved past the rhino paddock.

Julianna hadn't been to the Oklahoma City Zoo since she was a child, a school trip. She was old enough to remember the concrete pit that used to be just past the main entrance. Inside the pit was a replica of a sunken pirate ship, teeming with small monkeys. The monkeys climbed the mast and swung from the rigging. They took public poops that made the kids laugh.

"Here," Ariel said. "We can get warm in here."

They entered a building that was humid and pungent. On the other side of floor-to-ceiling Plexiglas windows, a gorilla family loafed outside in the sunshine.

Julianna took a seat on the low ledge that ran beneath the windows. She watched a gorilla mother groom her baby. Farther down an enormous silverback sat with his back to the window, ignoring a kid who was hammering on the glass and trying to get the silverback's attention.

"I love their eyes, don't you?" Ariel said. "They're so beautiful. But it does kind of freak me out, too, how human their eyes are. I love that the scientific name for gorillas is *Gorilla gorilla*."

"Is that really true?"

With the tip of her finger, Ariel drew a heart on the glass between them and the gorilla.

"Julianna," she said. "Why did you call me?"

"What?"

"Today. I thought you were just gonna keep dodging me forever. You are a skillful dodger, Julianna."

"Yes."

"So why did you finally call me?"

Julianna considered the question. She didn't know how to answer it. For so many years, she'd cared only about a life that was already gone. Here, now, she'd decided to try caring about the here and now.

"Because I knew you'd never leave me alone until I did," she told Ariel. "I knew I was doomed."

"Exactly!" Ariel said.

"Hey! Hey! Hey!" the kid hammering on the glass said. He was too old to be doing that, six or seven years old. His mother stood behind him and beamed.

"What's the latest?" Julianna said. "Have you had a new PET?"

Ariel nodded. "Allegedly I was hot. Isn't that a funny way to say it? 'Hot on the new PET'? My dumb ovaries this time."

Julianna looked at her. "A scan's not conclusive."

"It still sucks."

"Yes."

The enormous silverback suddenly rose to his feet. It was impressive, like watching a mountain break through the crust of the earth.

"Hey! Hey! Hey! Hey!"

The silverback shot a dismissive glance at the kid hammering on the glass and moved toward Julianna. He sat back down directly in front of her, facing the window. He was so close that she could see the fine grain in the leather of his forehead.

The silverback leaned forward, gazed into Julianna's eyes, and grunted.

That fucking kid, he seemed to be saying.

Julianna and Ariel burst out laughing.

"He's in love!" Ariel said.

The silverback's eyes, it was true, were beautiful and human.

Though Julianna didn't know if what made them beautiful was necessarily the same thing that made them seem human.

"So am I," Julianna said.

"He must like brunettes better than blondes."

"Don't be jealous. You're cuter than me."

"Am not."

"No," Julianna admitted.

Ariel giggled. "Bitch."

The kid and his mother, the only other people in the building, left. The baby gorilla lay cradled in its mother's lap, blissed out. An adolescent male decided to do a somersault, apparently just for the hell of it.

"I told you it would be awesome," Ariel said. "Did I not?"

"You did," Julianna admitted.

The sunlight banked off the rose-rock walls of the gorilla enclosure and spread over her. The temperature was just about perfect. Julianna could see the silverback's nostrils expand, ever so slightly, every time he inhaled.

"Do you want to talk about it?" Julianna said.

"My dumb ovaries? Not really."

"Because we can."

"I just want to sit here for a while. You know?"

"Okay."

"And then maybe go get some hot chocolate or something." She glanced over at Julianna.

"Let's do that," Julianna said.

Wyatt

CHAPTER 30

The TSA agent at the airport was thorough but apologetic.

"Sorry, sir," he said every time Wyatt winced.

"I mentioned, didn't I," Wyatt said, "that I was in a car wreck less than a week ago?"

"Yes, sir."

"Did I mention that I was clinically dead at one point?"

"Is that right?" But the TSA agent's look said, *Bullshit.*

"Are you going to buy me dinner at least?" Wyatt said.

The TSA agent had probably heard that line a few hundred times. He peeled off the latex gloves he'd used to pat Wyatt down.

"All done, sir," he said. "Have a nice flight."

Wyatt retrieved his personal effects and laptop bag. His uncle, who'd passed through security without setting off any alarms, stood beneath the giant overhead monitor that listed all the flights departing Oklahoma City in the next few hours. Wyatt liked the monitor, a new feature of the new airport. It made him think of a train-station destination board in an old black-and-white movie.

"I'm going to tell you again," his uncle told Wyatt again.

"You're just coming out for a visit," Wyatt said.

"I'm not moving out there."

"It's just a visit. See if Las Vegas agrees with you, and we'll go from there."

"I like it right here, Mikey. I've lived my whole life right here in Oklahoma City."

Wyatt supposed he could say the same thing about himself.

"That's why you need a change of scenery, Uncle Pete," he said. "Showgirls. Velvet-voiced crooners. And that's just where I get my teeth cleaned."

His uncle chuckled.

After they landed at McCarran, down in baggage claim, Wyatt recognized a guy waiting for his bags at the next carousel over. Bledsoe, his old buddy, whose promising future as the Mirage's senior VP of sales and marketing had been nipped in the bud. Bledsoe was out of his usual expensive suit and in cargo shorts, a Hawaiian shirt. He looked rested, relaxed. On his arm, laughing, was a petite blonde with bangs.

How about that? Wyatt thought. Maybe the loss of Bledsoe's dream job had turned out to be the best thing that ever happened to him. Maybe his life had been shaken to pieces at exactly the right time, in exactly the right way. Maybe he'd kicked his meth habit and rediscovered his passion for . . . whatever Bledsoe might have forgotten he had a passion for.

Maybe? Why not?

It *had* been bullshit, what Wyatt told the TSA agent. Wyatt had not been clinically dead, not even for a second. But he liked to think so. He liked to think that sometimes an ending cleared the way for a beginning.

Sure, that might be bullshit, too. But it was a philosophy Wyatt thought he could get behind. He was prepared to give it a try.

His uncle watched a team of uniformed flight attendants march past in lockstep. The tinted doors of the terminal slid open, and the flight attendants disappeared into the hard, bright light of the desert.

His uncle looked at him. He seemed resigned but resolute.

"What happens now?" he said.

Wyatt couldn't say for sure. Nothing. Something. Anything. Who knew?

He grabbed his uncle's roller bag. "Only one way to find out," he said.

O'Malley

Time, if O'Malley had his way, would turn the corner and make its way back to the beginning. A fresh lap, like horses pounding around a track. Time would run rings around you. What a beautiful world that would be.

Instead, though, here O'Malley stood, left behind, enveloped by the dust of his own life. Almost nineteen years old. Nearing the end of another summer.

What cruel fate was this?

Indeed.

There was nothing dreamt of in his philosophy that had prepared O'Malley for the possibility he might spend the rest of his life at the Pheasant Run Twin Theater in Oklahoma City. Neither Rousseau nor Hobbes had sounded the alarm. The Clash had remained silent on the matter.

He'd only skimmed Rousseau and Hobbes, to be honest. Maybe he should have read more closely.

Karlene was leaving in a few weeks. Tate was leaving. Everyone was leaving. Do you know who was staying? Bing-ham. Bingham and O'Malley, together till the bitter end.

Theresa was already gone.

Even Grubb was going to college. Grubb! O'Malley hadn't bothered to apply anywhere. His grades were very, very bad. He'd skipped class for four years, he'd blown off tests. It was a principled stance against the narrow-minded hegemony of the public-education system. So he'd told himself at the time. Now he wished he'd listened less attentively.

He had no money anyway. No money saved. Nothing. His step-aunt said he had to start paying rent or get his own place.

His step-aunt was getting crazier and crazier every day. A few weeks earlier, O'Malley had woken up in the morning soaked from the waist down with lighter fluid. His aunt had boiled him an egg and asked why he smelled funny.

Today, eleven o'clock, O'Malley still had an hour until work. He stopped by Rainbow to swap for the new Nick Cave album. He shared his musings on the nature of time with the friendly, long-haired freak who occasionally manned the counter. The friendly freak wore a Cramps T-shirt and a plaid skirt. It was not for O'Malley to ask why.

"Do you get where I'm going with this labored anal-ogy?" O'Malley said.

"Like horses on a track?" The friendly freak nodded and used a ballpoint pen to write something on the ball of his thumb. "The hooves of time. I'm gonna use that, man."

The friendly freak had started a rock band. So he claimed. He was on the prowl for lyrics.

"No charge," O'Malley said. "Remember me in your memoirs." He handed over the movie pass. The friendly freak accepted the pass, but with a mournful shake of his head.

"Has to be the last time, man. Sorry."

"What do you mean?" O'Malley said.

"Has to be cash from here on out. My boss, man."

"No fucking way."

"Yeah. Fucking way."

The friendly freak felt bad, so he threw in, gratis, a MARS NEEDS GUITARS! promo card. O'Malley drove to the Sonic on May. He'd left home at ten-thirty. It was almost noon. He was now that much closer to age nineteen, to the end of another summer.

He was happy that Theresa and Heinz were together now. He loved them both. He wanted them to be happy.

Yesterday Bingham had invited O'Malley into his office. O'Malley sat down and crossed his legs. He straightened the lapels of his blazer.

"How my I help you, Mr. Bingham?" he said.

O'Malley could think of three reasons, maybe four, that he might be in trouble at the moment. A part of him hoped Bingham had finally mustered the courage to fire his ass. A large part of him.

"I need an assistant manager," Bingham said.

He had to repeat it.

The hooves of time.

"Think it over."

Never, O'Malley wanted to say. But he didn't.

"I was just like you once, you know," Bingham said.

Fuck you, O'Malley wanted to say. That isn't true.

At Sonic his foul mood lifted a bit when O'Malley got a gander at his carhop. He'd never seen her before. She was incandescent, with two feathered wings of dark hair that framed her face like parentheses.

"You're new here," he said.

"How astute of you."

His foul mood lifted. O'Malley's heart lifted. He couldn't explain why, exactly, but this girl gave him hope for his future.

"I've been sent here," he said, "to observe the indigenous inhabitants."

"I'm not one of them."

"No. I know. I can tell you're not long for this world."

She understood what he meant and laughed.

"God," she said. "I hope not."

"In Thailand there's a festival I read about. Once a year in November, during the full moon. The people make paper lanterns and then light them. The lanterns rise gently into the night sky. The effect, I'm assured, is transcendent."

"Get me to the airport," she said. "Put me on a plane."

O'Malley's second favorite Ramones song, "I Wanna Be Sedated."

"Hurry, hurry, hurry," he said, "before I go insane."

When he returned for the lunch the next day, though, the girl was gone. O'Malley's regular carhop didn't know her name. He told O'Malley the girl yesterday had just been filling in. Usually she worked at a different Sonic. There were lots of Sonic drive-ins in Oklahoma City, spread all over the metro. The regular carhop didn't know which one the girl worked.

That, O'Malley supposed, was just his luck.

Genevieve

September 1986

Maybe saying no to drugs did get easier with practice, Genevieve considered as she turned her back on the sexy carny and walked away. At least it couldn't get any harder. That thought cheered her up, believe it or not.

She found the pay phone she knew was over by the south gate and dropped in a sticky coin.

"I can be there in five minutes," Howard said.

"No," Genevieve said. "You don't need to come. I just wanted to call and, you know, check in."

"That's what a sponsor is for, Genevieve."

"I've got to get home, Howard."

"Stay right there. I'll be there in five minutes."

Ugh. Genevieve knew well the futility of arguing with Howard. He was a dog with a bone. Howard said so himself.

"I'll meet you in the parking lot," she said.

She didn't want Julianna to see them and start asking questions. If their mother ever found out that Genevieve had joined AA, it would just confirm once and for all how fucked up her fucked-up daughter really was.

"I'm on my way," he said.

Genevieve hung up. Howard lived ten minutes away, in one of the big houses over by Mesta Park. Genevieve would spend five minutes in his car so he could do his sponsor thing. But that was fine, that was only fifteen minutes total. She had only been gone for ten so far. It still wasn't even *dark* dark yet.

While she was waiting for Howard, Genevieve walked up to the rodeo arena so she could peek around the corner and keep an eye on Julianna.

Genevieve watched her eating cotton candy and had to smile. Genevieve needed AA. She needed the meetings and the slogans and the sponsor, the stair steps to reinvention. She really did. But she knew what she needed most of all, what she couldn't live without, was the little dork sitting on the curb, meticulously stripping the last pale wisps from the paper cone.

The cotton candy was pink. Genevieve guessed that Julianna had picked the color because it matched her new Pink Panther. Genevieve planned to give her such shit about that, all the way home.

Acknowledgments

I had a lot of help writing this novel, starting with my terrific agent, Richard Parks, and my terrific editor at William Morrow, Trish Daly. My cousin Steve Harrigan read an early draft of the first several chapters and provided an essential boost of encouragement right when I needed it. Sarah Klingenberg was willing and able to answer research questions at any time of the day or night.

I'm also enormously grateful to Liate Stehlik, Carla Parker, Danielle Bartlett, Joanne Minutillo, Maureen Sugden, and everyone else at William Morrow and HarperCollins for their expertise and hard work on my behalf.

The best thing about being a mystery-crime writer is that you become part of the wonderful and amazing mystery-crime community. I want to thank all the writers, readers, reviewers, bloggers, marketers, and booksellers who have been such an invaluable source of support and advice. In particular, I'm indebted to Jon and Ruth Jordan, Jen Forbus, Sean Chercover, Marcus Sakey, Timothy Hallinan, Bud Elder, and Dana Kaye.

There are so many other people who've also been incredibly generous with their time and friendship. Thanks in particular to the Sanchez-Westenberg family, the Shuford family, Thomas Cooney, Rosemary Graham, Julie Chappell, Hank Jones, Lisa Lawrence, Mary Stroemel Hauk, Christine Hieger Carter, Becky Westerlund, Chris Borders, Bob Bledsoe, Adam Klingenberg, Jake Klingenberg, Sam Klingenberg, Lauren Klingenberg, Squire and Hannah Babcock, Roxanne and Matt Robertson, Rosa Standiford, and Elva Aldaz.

My colleagues and students at the University of Oklahoma and in the Red Earth MFA program at Oklahoma City have been a constant source of joy and inspiration. They're the best, truly, and I'm lucky I've had the opportunity to work with them.

And I can't say it enough, how incredibly grateful I am that I ended up with two sisters like Ellen Berney and Kate Klingenberg.

Finally, and most important, I want to thank my wife, Christine. She's the reader I write for, and always will be.

About the Author

LOU BERNEY is the author of the novels *Gutshot Straight*, named one of the best debut crime novels of the year by *Booklist*, and *Whiplash River*, nominated for the Edgar and Anthony awards. His short fiction has appeared in publications such as the *New Yorker*, *Ploughshares*, and the Pushcart Prize anthology, and was collected in *The Road to Bobby Joe and Other Stories*. He's written feature screenplays and created television pilots for, among others, Warner Brothers, Paramount, Focus Features, ABC, and Fox. Currently he teaches in the graduate creative writing program at Oklahoma City University.

BOOKS BY LOU BERNEY

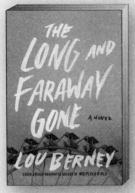

THE LONG AND FARAWAY GONE
A Novel

Available in Paperback and eBook

In the summer of 1986, two tragedies rocked Oklahoma City. Six movie-theater employees were killed in an armed robbery. Then, a teenage girl vanished from the State Fair. Neither crime was ever solved. Twenty-five years later, private investigator Wyatt, the sole survivor of the movie-theater massacre, finds himself pulled back to the hometown he's tried to escape. Julianna too was marked by that summer; when she discovers that one of the suspects in her sister's disappearance has resurfaced, she'll stop at nothing to find answers. As they each dredge up the past, can the truth heal—or ultimately destroy them?

WHIPLASH RIVER
A Novel

Available in Paperback and eBook
Edgar Award Nominee

In this sequel to *Gutshot Straight*, Charles "Shake" Bouchon has finally realized the dream of owning a restaurant in a Caribbean paradise. He's left his life of crime behind for good—but business is slow, and to stay afloat he's borrowed money from local thugs. Things suddenly go from bad to worse when a masked gunman shows up, and before Shake knows what he's gotten himself into, his restaurant explodes in flames. Now he has no choice but to skip town with an eccentric old hustler, whose help comes at a price—Shake's assistance with a half-baked, risky score. And Shake only knows one person who could pull it off: his fearless ex-lover Gina. If she doesn't kill him first.

GUTSHOT STRAIGHT
A Novel

Available in Paperback and eBook
Barry Award Nominee for Best First Novel

Professional wheel man Charles "Shake" Bouchon, fresh out of prison, is supposed to deliver a package to Vegas strip-club owner Dick "the Whale" Moby and pick up a briefcase for Shake's former boss, head of L.A.'s Armenian mob. When the "package" turns out to be Gina, a wholesome young housewife, Shake nobly decides to set her free. But Gina has other ideas. Soon Shake and Gina are on the run in Panama, looking to unload the briefcase's unusual contents while outmaneuvering two angry crime bosses…and Shake's learning that Gina is a lot more complicated than he imagined.

Available wherever books are sold.